WE'RE NOT
SOLDIERS

**Robert Nelson
and Ronald Nelson**

ISBN 978-1-63874-969-1 (paperback)
ISBN 978-1-63874-970-7 (digital)

Christian Faith Publishing, Inc.
832 Park Avenue
Meadville, PA 16335
www.christianfaithpublishing.com

Printed in the United States of America

Contents

1

Endings and Beginnings

When he opened the fourth seal, I heard the voice of the fourth living creature say, "Come!" And I saw, and behold, a pale horse, and its rider's name was Death, and Hades followed him; and they were given power over a fourth of the earth, to kill with sword and with famine and with pestilence and by wild beasts of the earth.

—The Book of Revelation 6:7–8

"Wake up! John! Wake up!" Laura yelled. I opened my eyes and sat up. I could see my wife Laura leaning over me, her face framed in her curly reddish-brown hair and her blue eyes wide with fear. I tried to wipe the sleep out of my eyes as I said, "What is it?!"

Laura, in a panicked voice, said, "There's something wrong with the neighbor. He's lying in the street. I...I...I think he's dead." She was shaking and pointing toward the stairs. I could see the fear in her eyes. *This was serious.* Tears were forming, and she motioned for me to hurry. Any lingering drowsiness that I had felt was gone and replaced by a rush of adrenaline.

"Okay, okay, I'll check it out," I said. I quickly put on a pair of pants and pulled on a shirt. I still felt tired because I had gone to bed after 3:00 AM. I had worked the swing shift as usual at the truck rental outfit where I am employed as a mechanic. I was still trying to orient myself as I stumbled around trying to find my other shoe. As I went down the stairs, I tripped over the Rollerblade of one of my seven kids and then jammed my toe into the doorjamb trying to catch my balance. "Ouch!" I exclaimed. Grumbling under my breath and cradling my bleeding foot, I hopped over to the window. When I peered into the street, I saw something—somebody lying in the street. *What is going on?*

I limped to the door, having forgotten about the bleeding toe. *There was definitely something wrong*, I thought. *That is the understatement of the year.* I crossed the porch and descended the stairs onto the driveway.

I paused, listening, wondering if there was danger that I needed to be aware of. My senses were heightened. Something was out of place even more than the man lying in the street. Something just felt off, wrong. By all accounts, it was a nice, warm July morning.

However, the birds were not chirping, and no dogs were barking. No, they were replaced by more disturbing sounds. I could hear sirens in the distance, I could hear the volunteer fire fighter alarm wailing, and I thought that I could hear distant popping sounds. *Were those gun shots?* As I looked down at the man in the street, any sounds that I had noticed were forced out of my consciousness. *Was that man on the ground my neighbor Charles? Was he hurt? Dead?*

It was Charles. He was lying face up with one of his legs bent underneath him at an awkward angle. I ran toward him, yelling, "Charles, are you okay?" There was no response or movement. I looked at his now ashen face, and there was red foam oozing out of his mouth. His eyes were open, vacant. It was obvious that he was dead. *What could cause this? He didn't deserve this. Our daughters are good friends. He's a nice guy who loves his family.* Suddenly, I heard movement and looked up. A little girl no more than six years old was stumbling toward me. *That is Charles's daughter!* Her face was turning blue, and the same bubbling foam was spilling out of her mouth. It oozed slowly down her chin and on to her dress. I could see terror in her eyes, and she was clawing at her throat. The whole front of her dress was covered with the red foam. I didn't know what to do. The only thing I could think of was that she needed to breathe. I ran to her and flipped her upside down and gently shook her up and down, hoping to clear her airway. The foam just kept coming out of her mouth in an oozing pile on the road, and then all of her muscles tensed up and with a final spasm, she went limp. I laid her down on the street and knelt next to her. I started chest compressions, but all I could hear was a gurgling sound deep in her lungs. I frantically tried to use my finger to get the red foam out her mouth, but it just kept bubbling.

I yelled, "Lizzy! Stay with me!" There was no response. Then I switched back and forth between chest compressions and trying to clear her mouth with my finger. I don't know how long I worked on her, but finally with arms sore and a sheen of sweat on my face, I stopped. I could tell from her blank stare into the sky that she was gone. I felt a pang of guilt. I wanted to give her mouth-to-mouth

7

resuscitation, but God forgive me, I was afraid to try. *I don't want that red foam in my mouth.*

My knees were throbbing because of kneeling so long on the asphalt. I sat back on my feet. For a minute, nothing seemed real. *This must be dream...a nightmare*, I thought. It was one thing to find a dead man, but quite another to have child die in your arms. I looked at her face, and as strange as it sounds, I thought, *She looks peaceful now. She's not scared anymore.*

I was startled out of my morbid thoughts by the sound of weeping. I looked up, and Laura was sobbing. Her hands were over her mouth, and she was shaking her head back and forth. Coming back to myself, I yelled, "Call 911! Lizzy is dead too, and I can't clear her airway."

Laura said, in a hurried blast of words, "I've been trying this whole time, but the phones are not working. I even tried both our cell phones. It just rings and rings with no answer. Nothing is working!" Tears were streaming down her face. "What's happening?"

I don't know! I looked at her. *How do I comfort her?* I tried to keep the waver out of my voice as I answered her question, "I wish I knew."

Laura glanced at the neighbor's house. "Try their phone!" I looked up at the neighbor's manufactured double wide. It was neat with painted white trim, which seemed incongruous with the horror on the street. I jumped up. I could feel a thousand needles in my legs as blood rushed back into my limbs. Despite the pain, I ran to the neighbor's, leaped over their small white fence, and stopped at their open door. I paused for a second to brace myself for what I might see. I took a deep breath. As I entered, I could smell something akin to a mixture of vomit and blood wafting out of the house. I could see that the rest of Charles's family was dead too; they were sprawled out across the floor. Their little brown Chihuahua, Tito, was licking up a pile of red foam in the middle of the carpet. Tito looked up at me questioningly, gave an obligatory bark, and went out of the room into the kitchen, making a little growling sound, nails clicking on the linoleum. Charles's wife Susan was face-down on the floor; she was clutching the telephone in her pale hand. She wasn't moving.

There was a trail of red foam on the floor ending at her mouth. Her daughter was limply draped over the side of the couch, a trail of red foam streaming out of her mouth onto the floor. Her eyes stared into eternity.

I went in. Tito had returned to licking up the red foam, so I yelled, "Get away from that!" He scurried down the hall. I tentatively took the phone from the woman's already cold hand, and in the process, I almost slipped on the red foam on the kitchen floor. *Of course, it was my bare foot!* I wiped my foot on the carpet, trying not to think about where the red foam had come from. I raised the receiver to my ear. *No dial tone.* It made a rapping noise as I let it drop to the floor. I heard something in the bedroom and stepped over Susan's body and peered into doorway. Karl, Charles's son, was sitting in a recliner facing a television, which seemed strange because Karl is blind. I think he liked listening to the news, but at this moment, there was merely static. The room was dark, and the television illuminated the walls with ghostly flickering. The back of the chair was angled toward me. I walked in and peeked around the chair. His eyes were dim, all life gone. There was red foam oozing out of his mouth down the front of his shirt. He was dead. *They're all dead! His family is all dead! What's going on?*

I looked down in disgust as I noticed the foam smeared on my jeans and feet from trying to save little Lizzy. My shirt was covered as well. All I could think was, *I have to get this stuff off me!* I ran directly to the neighbor's garden hose, pulled off my jeans and my shirt, and rinsed off. Shivering, I walked over to Laura. She seemed to have snapped out of her initial shock, perhaps confused that I was now walking around in my underwear.

I said, "Keep trying 911! His whole family is dead. The same foam stuff is coming out of their mouths. I need to get this stuff off me, it might be contagious." I must have been quite the sight, a grown man in his underwear, shivering, and limping around with only one shoe on. I kicked off the shoe before I entered the house.

I went straight to the shower. I turned the faucet all the way to hot and ignored the pain as the streaming hot water poured over me. I furiously scrubbed my skin with a washcloth and soap. A few

9

minutes later, Laura came in the bathroom. Before she could say anything, I asked, "Did you get through?"

"No," she said quietly, with an unnerving quiver in her voice.

As I toweled off and put on the underwear that Laura had brought down for me, she said, "You need to look at something." She started crying and said, "It's happening all over the world. Everyone is dying!"

Everyone is dying! All over the world! Her words seemed to echo in my head. Time seemed to slow down. Laura was talking, but what she said didn't even register. She might as well have been talking to a statue. I was deep in my own thoughts, trying to make sense of what was happening. I didn't feel the chill from getting out of the hot shower; I didn't hear the children crying. I only heard the beating of my own heart as I tried to comprehend what this all meant. Then Isaiah, my oldest, knocked on the door, and I was shaken out of my shock.

He said, "Faith has a dirty diaper, and the girls won't change her." He looked at me, perhaps wondering why I was half-naked.

Laura wiped away her tears, pointed to our homeschooling room, and said, "Go look at the computer!" Then, as she walked out of the room, she said over her shoulder, "I'll change Faith and meet you in there."

I quickly finished dressing into the clothes Laura brought me. I opened the bathroom door and noticed Laura had closed the curtains facing toward the neighbor's house. My twins, Eve and Eden, were standing in front of the curtains, trying to get enough courage to peek out at the bodies. I spoke softly to them, "You don't want those images stuck in your brain." They flinched upon hearing my voice and quickly moved away from the window. *What images would be stuck in their brains in the future? What will the future bring?*

I walked into our home schoolroom and sat down at the computer. Laura already had a news website on the screen. There was report after report of a catastrophic infection or virus killing people all over the world.

A couple days ago, we had begun to hear about some deadly flu outbreaks in parts of Europe, but it had seemed so distant. We didn't think it was anything to worry about. But now it has come to our own home, and now it is everywhere. Some of the first reports were from Asia. The virus had spread rapidly, and the disease centers were trying to quarantine the smaller infected countries. Whatever they were doing, it wasn't working. It just kept spreading. England was a dead zone. No one was allowed in or out. There were no more communications coming out of England and other parts of Europe. No one seemed to have any idea how this virus, or whatever it was, had spread so quickly and effectively.

One news service said that China, Russia, the US, and the Middle East started having massive amounts of cases late last night. China already had over two million dead. The US also had well over ten million dead and was rising quickly. Russia had deaths in the millions. The Middle Eastern countries had an estimated half million dead also. Several terrorist groups were claiming responsibility. The news anchor said, "The only way this virus could be spread worldwide so quickly is if it is man-made and distributed around the world. It would need to have been a coordinated effort to release it all at once in different locations." Then he added, "We have no proof of this yet, but it is a likely scenario."

The news reporters interviewed several people, and a large bald white man said, "I think God got tired of us playing God and gave us this virus to kill us off."

A little old black woman said, "I sure hope mankind survives this."

There was another report about groups of protesters and rioters, who had marched along the streets in Washington, DC, causing trouble by breaking windows and spray-painting graffiti along the walls of the buildings that they passed. The news anchor said, "That was the scene just two hours ago. This is the scene now." The camera panned along a street filled with bodies of the same protesters with red foam trailing out of their mouths on to their clothes and on to the street and sidewalks. There were puddles of red foam everywhere, and there was one woman crawling along the sidewalk, clutching her throat as red foam spewed from her mouth. The view suddenly lurched sideways as the camera fell over and hit hard on the concrete.

A crack had formed in the lens, and the camera skidded sideways and then rolled over facing the camera man himself. Even in the tilted view, one could see that his eyes were wide and panicked; he turned to run away from the scene that he had been filming.

The scene switched back to the news anchor who was saying, "Doug…Doug, are you there? Can you hea—"

He was cut off by a view of the presidential seal of the United States. I leaned back in my chair trying to process what I had just seen. The view of the presidential seal quickly switched to a view of the vice president. An announcer's voice broke in: "We interrupt this broadcast for a special message from the acting president, Madam Wilson. The former vice president had her swearing-in ceremony only moments ago as commander in chief. Madam President, you are live."

I watched in confusion as Madam Wilson, the now acting president stepped up to the microphone. *What is going on? What happened to the president?* She gave a short speech explaining that the president and his family had been killed by the plague that was sweeping the nation. She said that America would survive this. She prayed we would all remain strong. Then she declared a state of martial law, telling people to stay in their homes.

Although she tried to hide it, I could see that she was not feeling well. I could see sweat on her forehead, and her armpits were soaked. She was clearly trying to stifle a cough as she spoke. She ended by saying, "God bless you all." And she signed off for the last time. The presidential seal remained on the screen for a long time.

"Are we going to die, Daddy?" I heard behind me. I hadn't even noticed that my kids had come into the room. I looked back. Isaiah, my eleven-year-old, was standing with my ten-year-old twins, Eve and Eden, and Abigail, my eight-year-old. They all had their eyes glued to the computer screen, and then they all looked at me with their puppy-dog eyes. I wanted to promise them that I could protect them, but I thought, *No, that might be a lie.*

I said, "I hope not." I grabbed Isaiah's chin and lifted it toward me. I looked him in the eye and then made sure the rest of the kids were looking at me, and I said, "I hope not, but if God wants us in heaven, then that's where we'll go. You kids need to go out of the room now, okay?"

They filed out, and I heard a cough from one of the news anchors on the computer. I turned, and they showed footage of one of the anchor women who had contracted the virus. A commentator was saying that the symptoms began like that of a common cold. Within forty-five minutes, the "cold" moved down into her lungs, and the coughing started. Then the scene cut to some video footage of the woman coughing spasmodically.

"The coughing got progressively worse within another hour," continued the commentator, "and thirty minutes later, she passed out because she couldn't breathe." Then the footage showed disturbing images of the anchor waking up and gagging on red foam. There was a horrible gurgling noise. Her eyes were wide with terror as she clutched at her throat. *How can they be showing this!* The commentator said, "And then, she basically drowned in that red foam. The total time lapsed two hours and fifteen minutes before she succumbed to the disease." Then he solemnly looked into the camera and said, "I have the symptoms as well." Then he coughed.

I turned off the computer.

I sat in shock. I know it sounds like a cliché, but I pinched myself to make sure I was really awake. Sadly, I was. *What should we do? Where should we go?* After a few minutes, I called all the kids and Laura to the dining room. I looked at my seven beautiful children and wife and said, "Kids, go upstairs and pack your clothes! You need a week's worth. You older kids help the younger ones." Strangely, none of the kids complained. They all went upstairs and started to pack.

Laura said, "I'll pack food and get our clothes."

I said, "I'll get the camping stuff and pack the van." Laura eyed me questioningly. I said in response, "I don't know what to do here. I think we need to be prepared to go at a moment's notice." She nodded.

I grabbed an old tarp out of the basement and covered the bodies of the neighbors in the street. I wasn't sure what else to do. Then I began loading up the van.

Thankfully, we had a Ford van with the capacity for fifteen passengers to accommodate our large family. We were short a couple of seats in back because we typically kept them out for groceries and other storage. I loaded the bags of clothing, camping stuff, and food. When the kids were done, I told them to get into the van, and then I went to my gun safe. I knew that when things get crazy, people tend to get crazy too. I got out my Glock 9mm pistol, .44 Magnum six-shooter pistol, and my hunting rifle, the Mosin-Nagant 7.62 rifle. I put my holster on and slid the 9mm in place. The other two guns, I placed in a case and grabbed a bag for the ammo. When I slid into the driver's seat and everyone was in the van, Laura looked at me. She asked, "Where are we going?"

I put the van in reverse and said, "To the church. If we're going to die, then we are going to visit God's house first. Maybe we can go to confession and get our last rites."

2

Family

"Is any among you sick? Let him call for the priests of the church, and let them pray over him, anointing him with oil in the name of the Lord; and the prayer of faith will save the sick man, and the Lord will raise him up; and if he has committed sins, he will be forgiven."

—The Letter of St. James 5:14–15

The church was only a few blocks away. Sacred Heart Church is in the same small town of Gervais, so it takes only a minute to get there by car. It just so happens that my brother, Father James Fide, is the pastor there; the last name is pronounced "*Fee-day*." Too often people mispronounce our last name: "*Fai-duh*." It is pronounced *Fee-day* like in the Latin word *fidelis*.

As I backed out of the driveway, I made sure to avoid the tarp covered bodies in the street, and then I took another look at our house. It was a large brick home constructed in the 1920s with a half wrap around porch. We had been working on it since we moved in three years ago. I didn't know if we would be coming back, so one last look seemed appropriate.

I realized that my family is much more important than any material object. It was time to go. On the way to the church, we saw corpses on the ground by their houses; there were more in or near their cars as if they had made one last effort to seek help. I started thinking to myself. *I'm not sure why we're not infected yet. Death may still be coming, and I need to make the best of the time I have and get right with God. Am I scared of death? I don't think so, but I'm not inviting him over to hang out.*

My eye caught some movement. There was an elderly man wearing blue jeans and a red flannel shirt barely crawling on the sidewalk. Red foam streamed from his mouth. He turned toward our van when he heard the motor. He reached out a hand as though trying to grasp us.

"Mommy, Daddy, we should help him," Eden said through her tears.

I was scared; honestly, I didn't want to stop. I glanced at Eden in the rearview mirror and knew what I had to do. I put the van into park, and I got out. The man convulsed and made a gurgling scream. It was a sickening scream of terror and desperation squeezed into one sound. As I approached him, he slumped down on his face with his arm extended before him, deathly still. A puddle of chunky red foam slowly oozed out of his mouth. Holes had been worn into the knees of his jeans and the sleeves of his shirt as he had crawled along seeking help.

I poked his side with the toe of my shoe to see if he would stir. I backed away slowly and turned. Suddenly, he grabbed my ankle with force. Laura and the kids echoed my scream. The man lifted his head slightly and tried to say something before he really did succumb to death. I quickly pulled my leg free, and I shuddered as I got back into the van. Laura and the kids were crying. I tried to reassure them, but there were no words. "I'm sorry I can't…he's…" I put the van in drive and drove another block to the church.

Sacred Heart Catholic Church and grade school were now in front of us. There were bodies everywhere. It was as though they had gathered hoping that somehow death wouldn't find them there at the house of God. *It seems we all had the same idea.* I was very thankful that it was summer, and the school was closed for the season. I'm not sure that I could have handled seeing the bodies of a bunch of grade school kids; nonetheless, there were a few children scattered among the dead.

Cars were parked every which way. The owners were obviously panicked as they got here. Some of the bodies were in the grass; some were near the entrance of the church, but it appears that most had made it into the church before they had died. It was too much to take in. Words cannot describe the emotional impact of it all. We all just stared for a while.

I wanted to check if my brother was still alive. With all the bodies scattered around, the chances didn't seem good. I said to Laura, "I'm not sure that I can do this."

Laura said, "I can go if you like."

I looked at her and said, "Really?"

She tried to smile and said "No, I can't either."

I looked at her. "I have to know if my brother is alive." I willed myself to get out of the van. It seemed like I had to command my hand to open the door. I had to command my leg to slide off the seat, but once I got moving, it was easier.

I had to walk around the bodies of friends and people that I knew, and I stepped over puddles of red foam. As I worked my way to the entrance of the church, I could tell that I was still shaken from the dead man on the sidewalk a block away. My heart was beating furiously in my chest. I had the irrational feeling that the bodies were poised to reach out and grab me. Images of zombie horror films came to my mind. Only one of the doors to the right did not have a body leaning against it. I closed my eyes as I opened the door. *Thank God it isn't locked.*

Immediately, the smell of vomit overcame me. It was potent in the enclosed space. Pushing my way back out the door, I ran to the grass near the door of the church, and I threw up. Thankfully, what came out wasn't red or foamy.

I looked over at my family in the van, embarrassed. Their faces were composed into a mixture of disgust and concern. I held my hand up signaling that I was okay. I braced myself and went back through the front door of the church, searching for Father Jay. I yelled, "Father Jay!"

I saw him bent over a body making the sign of the cross on the man's forehead. I presumed that he had been praying the last rites over the many dying and praying the prayers of the dead over the rest. He was wearing full vestments and his five-foot-six frame straightened up when he heard my voice. He'd obviously recently finished celebrating a mass. I could see sweat pouring down his forehead out of his brown mess of hair. I wasn't sure if it was because of the temperature or the stress, but I hoped the sweat didn't mean he had a fever.

Father Jay is my older brother, my only sibling. As the firstborn, he was named after my dad, so he is named James Jr. He was fairly recently ordained as a Roman Catholic priest after years of required education and preparation. I could see that the purple vestments that he was wearing were rumpled and had red foam splattered on them…red foam from other people. I felt the remnants of my last meal trying to force their way up my esophagus, but I suppressed the nausea.

Father yelled, "I'm over here by the altar." He closed his eyes and moved his head side to side and arched his stiff back. Then he breathed out a sigh of relief. He looked up through his sweat-stained glasses, *or were they tears?* He whispered under his breath, "Thank you, God." He pulled off his chasuble. We walked toward each other, and we would have hugged each other, but I held up my hand and pointed to his red foam-stained vestment. "Right, right," he said as he shook his head. He went to the sacristy and washed his hands and took off his vestment. He returned a short while later, and with a look of concern in his eyes, he asked, "Are Laura and the kids okay?"

I smiled tightly. "Yes, they are in the van outside. We wanted to see if you were okay. The phones are not working, so we drove over."

Father Jay stared at me over the glasses on his nose and said, "John, do you or your family need to go to confession or anything? You know, just in case."

I said, "Yes, we would like that very much. We would also like the sacrament of anointing of the sick, if that is okay?"

Father said, as he looked around, "Of course. Under these circumstances—of course."

I followed his gaze and looked around at all the bodies in the church, slumped over the pews. Several people died in a kneeling position. Others were prostrated in front of the altar and tabernacle. It was the last expression of their incredible faith.

In one pew, I saw an entire family hunched over leaning against the pew in front of them. *Was that the Vanderheim family? Yes, even in death they sat in their usual pew.* I couldn't remember their names. *Why can't I remember their names?* Behind them was another man I recognized.

It was so quiet in the church. Too quiet. I was snapped out my introspection by muffled cheering and crying. I turned toward the outer doors. My family was cheering from the van at seeing Father Jay as he stepped out of the church. He waved, and I hurried out after him.

19

Tears streamed down his face as he hugged all the kids. After everyone calmed down, I asked, "Have you heard from Mom and Dad?"

Father Jay said, "No, but I'm not sure that I would have answered my phone even if it had rung, with all that's happening." He shrugged and reached into his pants pocket, taking out his phone. The screen showed "Emergency Calls Only."

I looked at him and said, "I'm going to check on them. I'll call you if I can get through."

Father said, "Okay, but let me say a prayer over your family."

After we prayed, each of us went to confession. I went last wanting to ensure that my children and wife had received the sacrament first. I had a little trouble thinking of my sins; I just kept replaying the morning events over in my head.

As I entered the confessional and knelt down for my turn, I broke into tears. I sobbed almost uncontrollably. I could barely get my usual sins out of my mouth, and I couldn't get the image of the little girl on the street out of my mind. *Her eyes! Her unblinking eyes!*

I confessed, "Why didn't I give her mouth to mouth? Maybe, I could have saved her? I was afraid. I didn't want to get that red foam in my mouth. I couldn't…" I felt Father Jay put his arm over my shoulder. He had knelt beside me.

He said, "John, you couldn't have saved her. It wasn't your fault. What you did was right. Paramedics and medical personnel"—he paused for emphasis—"even medical professionals do not do mouth-to-mouth without some kind of one-way barrier between them." He hugged me tighter, and then he pulled back. "Look at me," he said more firmly.

I turned to look at him. He had tears in his eyes, but a stern look in his eyes. He said, "I'm getting off point. That is not a sin! That is not your fault! The blame is on the disease." His eyes softened. "You, my dear brother, are in shock. You have experienced a very traumatic event. I can't take away the trauma of it, but at least I can help you to understand and help you not to blame yourself for something outside of your control."

I breathed a little more easily, understanding. Smiling slightly, I said, "So you are saying that I'm not the savior and to leave the saving to the savior."

He grinned. "I couldn't have said it better myself." He gave me a penance and absolution, and I felt as if a great weight was lifted off my shoulders. It was a peace that was beyond understanding in a world filled with death. Father Jay put his hand on my shoulder and added, "Remember, John, that your family is probably in shock too."

I reached for the door and then turned back. "What about you?"

"Me?" He shrugged. "I'm not immune to shock and trauma. I'll probably be crying on your shoulder later on." He smiled tightly. Then he looked up at me questioningly. "I lost count. Are you the last one?"

I chided, "Come on? I don't have that many kids!" Feigning impatience, I added, "Yes, I'm the last one."

Father then gave each of us the sacrament of healing, the anointing of the sick, or as it used to be called, last rites. It didn't take too long because we received the sacrament as a group. It gave me great peace of mind as a father and husband to know that my family had received that grace.

When we were done, I said to Father Jay, "We'll come back from Mom and Dad's place as soon as we can. You look like you need some help. Are you feeling okay?"

Father said, "Yeah, I'm just tired, not sick. It started very early this morning—people knocking on the rectory door, wanting last rites. I opened the church, and people just kept coming." He closed his eyes and shook his head slightly. Then he looked up. "Yes, I would appreciate your help. You know, you all could come back and stay here. We've got the school, the church, and the food bank. It would be a good place to meet and figure some things out." He gestured with his arm indicating the church. "Besides, as we have already seen, people are drawn to the church to seek help."

I looked around and said, "I don't know. It looks like half the town is gathered here, and I don't know if this is contagious or what."

Father looked around thoughtfully and said, "Well, yes, we'll have to do something with the dead, but we could meet in the gym or the school. Those areas are clear. Besides, I've been dealing with dying people all morning, and I'm not sick—yet. And you aren't sick either. Maybe it's a genetic thing. I don't know."

I looked back toward the van. "I don't know what's going on either. I'll see if some of the other family members, that is, if they are alive, want to come back here. It would be good to be together."

We loaded my family in the van, and I started it up. I thought about checking on the rest of the family by myself, but leaving my wife and kids alone was out of the question now. *Can I keep them from seeing bodies of loved ones?*

Father Jay would not leave the church now. He had the dead to attend to—a lot of dead. I had mixed feelings about him touching and being around all those infected corpses, but I knew he wouldn't be dissuaded. He wanted to be there if any more sick people showed up. Father sent us off with the words, "God bless, and I love you, guys."

Everyone returned the blessings and love. We decided to swing back home, and Laura made a couple of signs out of plywood and spray-painted letters. They read "AT SACRED HEART CHURCH ON SEVENTH STREET AND DOUGLAS." Then, for good measure, she added her cell phone number on them. She said, "You never know." She had hung one sign on the front fence and the other on the side fence. We got in the van. Before we started driving toward Salem, I took one last look at the house. I wondered, *Will we be back? Will anything ever be the same again?*

We drove in silence as we passed wrecked or abandoned cars or bodies along the way. Among the abandoned cars, I saw a police cruiser and a fire truck, and unfortunately the bodies of those emergency personnel assigned to them. Fortunately for us, most people seemed to have had the presence of mind to pull over to the side of the road when they were too sick to continue driving. I looked up at the sky and thought, *How can the sky be clear? How can the sun be shining?* I wanted the world to reflect the darkness and uncertainty that I felt inside.

Laura's cell phone rang. We all jumped at the sound. She looked at the caller ID.

"It's my mom and dad," she said, and with tears of joy, she greeted them. After a short time of listening to Laura speak to them, it became clearer that they hadn't caught the virus.

I said to her, "Tell Phil and Karen hi for us."

Phillip and Karen McHale live about thirty minutes away from us, which has always been a blessing. They come from good Irish stock, which perhaps explains the reddish tint to Laura's hair. The McHales have always been willing to take their grandchildren for a sleepover and to help out in any way they can. There is that cultural stereotype of the in-laws disapproving of the man who married their daughter, but it has never been that way with us. I have always felt welcome in their family. I was glad that they were alive.

Laura told them about our plan to meet up at the church in Gervais. They agreed and said that they would bring their large recreational vehicle. Laura's mom told her that they wanted to stop at the house of their son, Eli, and check on him and his family. I handed my cell phone to Isaiah, my oldest, and told him to keep trying to call Grandma Victoria and Grandpa Jay, my parents, until he got through. Isaiah started dialing.

I was happy that at least one branch of the family tree seemed to have survived. It was time to check on the other branch. My family is from good German stock, near as we can figure. This is, perhaps, surprising with a surname like Fide. There must have been an Italian in our ancestry somewhere. Anyway, no one has really done much work to trace the family history back more than a few generations. I wondered if our family tree would survive.

"We're almost at Mom and Dad's place," I said. It was a fifteen-minute ride from our house in Gervais to theirs in Keizer when there wasn't much traffic. There wasn't much traffic.

Laura had finished talking to her parents and tried several times to get hold of one of her sisters. "The lines are still busy," she said with frustration.

I said under my breath, "With the number of people dying, the lines will free up shortly." We finally turned the corner street to my parents' house. We pulled in front of the driveway.

"No!" I shouted. There was a dead man lying at the front door of the house. Laura looked over and started to cry. I was sure the body was my dad's. I jumped out of the van and ran over to the body. I slowly rolled the body on its side and, with relief, realized that it was not my father. Then I heard a gun cocking and a voice on the other side of the door.

My dad yelled, "Get away from the door! I will kill you." I backed away and said, "Dad, it's me, John."

I heard my mom say, "It's Johnny! Put down the gun, Jay!"

Then I heard an electric drill pulling out screws from the make-shift boards on the inside of the door. I heard my mom's voice on the other side of the door, "Hurry! We need to see if they are okay."

"Victoria, I'm going as fast as I can!" Then with the cracking sound of splintering wood, the door opened. I rolled the body onto the grass. Then I looked up. It was a comforting sight to see my dad there, imposing with his blue sleeves rolled up over his large forearms holding the drill in his right hand. His unkempt silver hair hung down just over his kind brown eyes, and a ready smile was surrounded by gray facial stubble. My mom was just behind him, holding his arm. She was a jumble of colors compared to my dad, wearing her favorite dark blue pants with some kind of flower stitching on them, and she was wrapped up in a warm, multicolored sweater. I could tell that she wanted to push her petite frame past my dad to run out to embrace the grandkids. It was perhaps only the body on the ground that stopped her. I marveled that somehow her hair remained dark brown with only a few stray gray hairs, a stark contrast to my dad's unruly mop of gray. She finally did get the courage to slip past him, as a multicolored flash zipped by me.

Laura and the kids got out of the van, and my children ran to embrace their beloved grandparents. Meanwhile, I went into the house to thoroughly wash my hands. On the way out, I grabbed a bedsheet to cover the body. Thankfully, Mom didn't object, although I saw her raise an eyebrow in a disapproving way. For a few minutes, there were tears and cries of "Grandpa! Grandma!" When all the kisses and hugs were exchanged, we sat down in their living room. The kids surrounded my mom and dad on the couches. They all wanted to keep snuggling their grandparents. Mom and Dad didn't mind at all.

I said, "Father Jay suggested that we all stay at the school and church. It has food, shelter, and we would all be together."

Mom and Dad both said, "Oh, thank God that he is okay too."

Dad said, "So you saw Jamie, I mean, Father Jay?"

Laura said, "Yes, we were just over there. He's okay but a little overwhelmed with so much death. There are bodies everywhere—in the church, on the grass outside the buildings, and in the parking lot. He needs help, and he recommends that we gather there."

Mom looked at Dad and said, "Sounds good to me. Just as long as we're together." She paused a moment and said, "The news reports said it, this plague, is worldwide. The news reports are conflicting. Some think it started over in China or Russia. Then it seemed to spread to Europe a few hours later. Others say that it started here in the US."

Dad grabbed Abigail and set her on his lap and said, "You're the only family or people we've seen that are healthy besides me and Victoria." Abigail just smiled and hugged her grandpa with all her strength.

Then Dad told us about the body by the door. The man was their neighbor Ralph. He and Mom had been watching the news all night and had heard someone at the front door. They were already scared from watching the news; going to the door at three in the morning was not something they wanted to do. Dad had yelled, "Who is it?" But the knocking became hard and intense. Someone was making some kind of screaming noise, but they couldn't make out what he was saying. The pounding on the door became so intense that the door started to crack. So Dad had run to the door to brace it with his body. He had looked out the peephole and saw that it was his neighbor Ralph. He'd told Ralph to stop, but Ralph kept pushing and beating on the door. Mom got a chair and propped it under the knob. Dad had yelled for Mom to get his gun. Mom ran into the closet and grabbed the 30.06. With his back against the door, he loaded the rifle and then fired a warning shot at the edge of the door.

"In hindsight," he said, "that might not have been my brightest idea. I looked over at Victoria, and she had her hands over her ears." Then suddenly, all the sound had stopped except the ringing in their ears. Dad had looked out the peephole again, and Ralph was lying motionless in front of the door, so Dad had cautiously opened the door. Ralph had the same signs as the others on the news. There were no bullet holes in him, but he was dead just the same, with red foam pouring from his mouth.

They had decided to fortify the house. Dad had gone out to the shed while Mom kept guard, and he'd brought some plywood and two-by-fours to secure their now cracked door and door frame. They had decided to leave the body there. Neither had wanted to touch him for fear of contagion. Ever since, they'd been trying to figure out what they were going to do next while Dad boarded up the windows. It wasn't long after that when we had arrived at the house.

After Dad finished telling his account of what had happened, we all sat in a kind of stunned silence, reliving and reflecting on our own experiences, still so fresh in our minds. Then Laura and I filled my parents in on what had taken place in Gervais.

In the middle of telling them our adventures, my mom gestured toward the landline and said, "I tried calling my mom, and my sisters, and brother, but there was no answer. And now there is no dial tone. I couldn't get through to you guys or Father Jay."

Laura said, "Yeah, the phone service has been sporadic at best. For some reason, our family has not been affected by this sickness. I've talked to my parents, and they are okay so far. That means John, me, our seven kids, you guys, Father Jay, and my mom and dad are all okay."

I said, "If we're okay, then there will be others. It's just a matter of finding them."

We all worked together to load up Grandma and Grandpa's stuff into each of their cars. I called Father Jay, and thankfully the call went through. I told him about our parents being okay. Mom and Dad both got to talk to their son, the priest, for a while; they looked relieved. As we were getting into our vehicles, my mom asked, "Shouldn't we bury Ralph?"

I looked over at the sheet-draped body, and I said, "Look, Mom, I want to show the proper respect to the dead, I really do, but if we stop to bury every corpse that we see, we won't be doing anything else. I want to spend my time with living." She nodded. "But," I added, "we can probably at least put him back in his own home."

Dad and I covered our mouths with some makeshift masks, put on some disposable nitrile gloves that Mom had under the kitchen sink and moved Ralph's corpse back into his own house.

After we deposited the gloves in the trash and washed our hands, we got into our vehicles and began the trip back to Gervais.

On the way, we saw a pickup truck speed down a side street and a couple people on foot who ducked behind a house when we drove by. The survivors were scared. I was wondering how we would survive, if indeed we would survive.

It was hard to believe all of this was happening. Just yesterday, the kids were playing outside in the sunshine. They had a great time running through the sprinkler and jumping on the trampoline. We had lunch together, and I went off to work. *Work? Will I ever be back to work?*

I caught some movement in my peripheral vision, and I slammed my foot on the brake pedal. The van skidded at an angle. I saw a dog run from the side of the freeway in front of the van. As we skidded, the view of the dog disappeared under the front end of the van. Then I caught a glimpse of the dog shoot across to the other side of the freeway. *I missed it—barely.* The kids were a little startled, but they were okay. I heard Abigail say, "It's a puppy!"

I said with frustration, "Yes, a very lucky puppy!" I straightened us out, hit the gas pedal, and we continued down Interstate 5. Thankfully, my parents were not driving directly behind me.

As we drove down the highway, Laura's phone rang. Laura's dad told her that he had made contact with the rest of her siblings. They told her tales of similar things taking place where they are: Dead people everywhere. Red foam. They were okay but just as freaked out as the rest of us.

Her brother Eli, his wife Leah, and their young son Conrad were going to a meeting at the state capitol in Salem. It was going to happen in an hour, and they were hoping to find out more information. Apparently, Laura's youngest sister, Hannah, and her family were already there.

Laura's father, Phil, said that they were going to help her other sister, Chloe, and Chloe's husband, Jared, to pack. They would all meet us at the church. I was happy to hear that so many of Laura's extended family were okay. It was a great relief and boon to my sinking spirits.

I called my dad on his cell phone and told him about the meeting at the capitol building. Dad said that he wanted to hear the plans that the government had come up with. Then he slowed down and did a U-turn. Mom pulled her car to the side, and I followed. Dad pulled up next to me. Over the top of his car, I could see a motorcycle on its side near the center divider. The unmoving driver was slumped down next to it with his back against the guard rail. I couldn't see his face because the inside of his visor was covered with red foam. I got out of the van to talk with my parents. My parents joined me in front of the van. Dad said that he would try to find other members of the family or friends at the meeting. Mom started to object, but Dad put his arms around her and said that he would be careful and that he had his rifle if things got ugly.

Then he looked at me and Laura and said, "You two need to protect my grandbabies. I'll be back in a few hours." Dad kissed everyone goodbye, and then he made his way to the capitol. We watched as he drove out of sight on the wrong side of the freeway against traffic, if there had been traffic. I guess he figured in light of the current circumstances, there was no need to worry about oncoming cars. I couldn't help but feel a sense of dread at the separation.

My mom got back into her car, and Elijah, my six-year-old, asked, "Can I ride with Grandma?"

I began with my usual line, "Honey, Grandma doesn't have a car seat..." Then I looked around at everything that had taken place, and I realized that car seats were the least of our problems. "Sure, Elijah, you can ride with Grandma."

With a big grin, he ran to the passenger side of my mom's car and got in. Then, Laura and I and the rest of the kids got in the van, and we continued back to Gervais. I drove the speed limit out of habit while Laura tended to our youngest. I could see my kids in the rearview mirror. I wondered, *What is going to happen to them? What would happen to us all?* But I couldn't dwell on that right now.

All of a sudden, I noticed in the rearview mirror a couple of growing dots on the freeway behind us. They materialized into cars...cars driving very fast. I veered to the right lanes of the freeway. Thankfully, my mom had the presence of mind to do the same, and a blue minivan flew by us, followed by a red Honda Civic. They seemed to be going at least a hundred miles per hour. The back windows of the minivan were broken out, and I could see that someone in the rear had a rifle pointed out the back window, presumably toward the car that was chasing them, but when I saw the rifle, I turned my head and yelled to my family, "All of you get your heads down, now!" I ducked down but kept my eye on the cars. I could only see the silhouette of the driver through the side window of the car, but more noticeable was the fact that his left hand was sticking out the window holding a pistol aimed at the minivan. I could hear the reports of his pistol as he fired at the minivan. I think the driver of the car looked over at us as he passed, because then, the little Honda swerved in a quick zigzag, and one of the tires blew out. The little car careened off into the guardrail, and with the sound of scraping metal, I watched in horror as pieces of debris flew off the car. Metal and plastic crunched as the little car flipped and then rolled several times. It then slid several yards on its top before it came to rest in the fast lane.

The blue minivan had never slowed down and was out of sight in a few seconds. I was shaking a little, perhaps from adrenaline, or perhaps from shock. I drove toward the flipped car. A couple of my kids were crying, probably because I had yelled, but Laura was quieting them down. As we slowly drove, I could hear the tires of our van crunching the small fragments of bumper, glass, and other bits of the car. I slowed down some more as we passed the car, but there was nothing left that was recognizable of the car or the person driving it. I could smell burning plastic, steaming radiator fluid, and raw gasoline. Fluids were dripping on the ground from the smashed front end. There was no point in stopping now. The mangled remains of the person who had been driving were hanging halfway out of the car. He was dead. I wanted to say a prayer or something for the person in the car, but I had no words. I just stared as I drove by and mentally entrusted him to the hands of God.

Laura gently put her hand on my arm. "We need to go," she said. I sped up and kept checking the mirrors every couple of seconds.

Mom and Elijah led the way as we drove another fifteen minutes. The blue minivan was stopped at the top of the next exit. The engine compartment was smoking, but I saw no flames. We could see and smell acrid smoke, and it was a good guess that the engine had seized up. *Apparently, its little engine wasn't built for extreme speed.* The people were no longer in the vehicle. We quickly passed it. Laura comforted the kids along the way, and finally, we arrived at our new home base, Sacred Heart Church.

As I looked at the front of the church, it was clear of bodies. Apparently, Father Jay had been busy moving the bodies. From the trails of red foam, I could see that he had dragged the bodies around the side of the church to the grassy area between the church and school. There was a single dress shoe lying on its side where the concrete transitioned to the grassy lawn.

Father Jay came around the corner wearing his alb. He looked tired. I wondered, *Should he be wearing gloves? A mask? Well, it's probably too late now if there was any danger.*

Laura and I got our kids out of the van and brought our food and gear over to the school. The kids were playing a game of tag, their voices echoing in the big gymnasium. I marveled. *Kids are amazing. They can find time to play anywhere.* They did not play with the usual intensity, but at least, they were playing. My mom kept watch over them. Laura started to make food for our family; she wanted to keep busy. Thankfully, the gas ovens still worked. We had electricity as well. She began to make food for the extended family that would be coming later.

My adrenaline levels finally dropped, and I went into the church to see what I could do to help. Father Jay looked over at me as I walked in and said, "We are going to have to find a way to bury them properly…or maybe it would be better to burn the bodies? I'm not sure."

I put my mask over my mouth and nose, donned some disposable gloves, and offered to help my brother carry corpses out of the church. My brother looked at my gloves and mask. Then he looked down at his vestment stained by red foam. Looking up he said, "That's probably not a bad idea, but I've already had this much contact…" He shrugged his shoulders. "Well, I'll clean it off later."

I helped him carry more of the bodies that were in the church out the side door to the Rosary garden that is tucked back between the church and the school. We made use of it because it was closer than the grassy area with the other bodies. Father had made four neat rows of bodies. I'm not sure how many bodies we moved, but they seemed to get heavier and heavier. Father Jay was stumbling and breathing hard; I could see he needed to rest.

"Look, Jay, this can wait a little while. You need a break," I said as we set down the body of a woman whom I recognized, but I couldn't remember her name.

My brother said, "You're right. I'm tired. You know what? She was the last one to go. I thought maybe she would pull through. I anointed her, and I thought maybe God would perform a miracle and let her live, but it wasn't his will." He rubbed his head absentmindedly and looked around at all the bodies scattered throughout the garden. "I don't know what is happening."

I didn't know what to say.

Father Jay walked back into the church and plopped down in the front pew and let his hands drop to his sides. He closed his eyes and said, "I'm just going to sit here and rest for a little bit."

I nodded and turned my head to listen; I heard the sound of motors from some kind of vehicles in front of the church. I went outside. Phil and Karen, Laura's parents, had arrived in their motor home. I could see Jared and Chloe Percy following in their little red Toyota. Chloe is Laura's sister and Jared is her brother-in-law.

Phil stepped out of the motor home and grinned at the grandkids. He towered over them with his six-foot-five frame. He was wearing his tan golf shirt and golf pants. Karen came around the other side with her arms out toward Laura. She was wearing light blue pants and a checkered shirt. We all greeted one another.

Laura walked toward the school with her sister, Chloe, and her mother, Karen. The three women chatted as they walked. Somehow, because of the mysteries of genetics, Chloe ended up with black curly hair and was about three inches taller than her reddish-brown-haired sister. Jared Percy, who was Chloe's husband and Laura's brother-in-law, walked with me over to the church, asking if he could help.

I looked up at him, thinking, *Why is everybody in Laura's family so tall?* Jared was built like a basketball player—well, anyway a short one by today's standards. I said, "I hope those are your work clothes because we need to bury all these people."

I watched Jared as he stood in the middle of the church. He turned around 360 degrees; the only sound heard for a moment was the legs of his blue jeans rubbing together as he spun. He said, "There's got to be close to thirty bodies—uh, people."

I said, "Yep, and there are more in the Rosary garden. I think we should clear these people out, and then let's go down the street to the city's maintenance yard to see if we can find some machinery to help bury them."

Jared saw my brother slumped in the front pew, hands limp at his sides, with his eyes closed, and the red foam that had stained his alb. Jared looked at me with true concern in his eyes and said, "John, I'm sorry...I didn't..."

I laughed; I couldn't help it. "No, it isn't that. He's just tired." Father Jay twitched a little bit as if to confirm that he was indeed alive.

Jared looked relieved. Then Jared turned toward the tabernacle and genuflected, made the sign of the cross, and said, "Well, that's something good in the midst of all this...this..." He shrugged his shoulders, unable to think of an appropriate word. Then he rolled up his sleeves, and I pointed him to a box of disposable gloves at the entrance of the church. When he was ready, we carried the rest of the bodies out of the church. It was back breaking work, made more difficult by the need to navigate the pews in the church, and dead weight is tough to move around, but with Jared's help we finished up the work. He rolled his shoulders back a couple of time and said, "Let's go to the maintenance yard."

Father Jay got up with a groan and said, "I'm going to take a shower, and then I'll continue disinfecting the church."

"I'll see if I can get Chloe and Karen to help you," I said. After throwing his gloves in the trash, Jared pushed his way through the front doors of the church and headed for his car. I thought, *This is good. We're together. We're forming a plan.* I felt hope start to rise in my heart.

3

Living among the Dead

And another angel came out of the temple in heaven, and he too
had a sharp sickle. Then another angel came out from the altar,
the angel who has power over fire, and he called with a loud voice
to him who had the sharp sickle, "Put in your sickle, and gather
the clusters of the vine of the earth, for its grapes are ripe."

—The Book of Revelation 14:17–18

As Jared and I drove to the city's maintenance yard, I couldn't help but ponder how everything had changed. Suddenly, within a few hours, things that had so much importance to me before now meant nothing. *My credit cards were useless. Money had no meaning.* It seemed that human life had little value anymore, or perhaps, on the contrary, it now had more value than it had ever had. For some reason, the hymn that is sung during Easter came to mind: "Life and death have contended in that combat stupendous." I prayed, "Lord, don't let death have the last word."

As we stopped in front of the maintenance yard, I could see that the gate was locked. Jared and I scaled the gate and looked around the building. There was one window that looked promising, so I grabbed a softball-sized rock. I smiled and said, "I guess I won't get in trouble for this."

Jared took it from my hand and said, "No, you won't." With a grin, he smashed in the window.

Jared found an old crate for me to stand on. I reached in through the hole to unlock and open the window. A high-pitched alarm bell sounded. I managed to climb in without too much trouble, and I let Jared in the front door. We tried smashing the little alarm keypad, but the alarm kept blaring. As we looked around inside, we managed to find a police car and a backhoe tractor.

"Perfect," I said.

Jared said, "Dibs on the cop car." He broke into the office, found the keys to the gate, and opened it.

I yelled, "Hey, Jared! You ever drive a tractor before?"

"Nope! But how hard could it be? I've never driven a police car before." He smiled as he got into the police car.

I replied, "It's not the same..." He ignored me, enjoying my discomfort immensely.

With a little trial and error, I managed to drive the tractor over to the church and park it. Jared was waiting for me in the cop car; tractors are not known for their speed.

He drove me back to pick up his car, and then driving his car, I followed him back to the church. Jared, of course, hit the lights and siren and the kids came out of the gym and ran around the car. I saw Father Jay poke his head out of the church to see what all the noise was. He smiled, shook his head, and went back into the church. Jared and the kids played in the car for half an hour. Then we all went into the gym and pulled Father away from his cleaning so that he would eat some food and keep up his strength. We had set up tables on one end of the gym and laid out mats that we could sleep on at the other end. We all wanted to stay together.

We set up our blankets and sleeping bags for the night, and my dad pulled up in his car. I heard him yell, "Johnny? Victoria?"

There were several shouts. "We're over here!"

We all gathered around him, wanting to know the news. He stopped for a second, looked over at Father Jay, and put his arm around him, clearly relieved that he was alive and well. Then he turned toward everyone and said, "There's not much news. There were people gathered around in groups, speculating on what had happened. Everyone that I talked to had a similar story to ours...finding dead people everywhere that had choked on red foam." Dad shook his head. "There were a few men who were dragging the bodies of the dead out of sight. I didn't recognize the people leading the meeting. I guess they figured that someone needed to take charge, but they were arguing the whole time. People were scared. Some people were just walking around aimlessly with blank stares on their faces, obviously in shock." He paused thoughtfully. "At this point, it was just a lot of sharing of stories, trying to understand what was going on. I might go back tomorrow, but I couldn't stomach any more today. It was clear to me that they had about as much of a clue as to what to do as we have, maybe less. A lot of people are camping right there on the grass, like some of your family," as he gestured to Phil and Karen.

Dad said, "Can someone turn off that blasted alarm? What is that?"

Jared and I looked at each other. I said, "We needed a tractor, and we couldn't figure out how to turn off the alarm."

Dad nodded. "I'll see what I can do." He started to walk that direction, and then he turned back to reassure Phil and Karen that their kids there were okay.

Some minutes later, we heard the alarm stop blaring, and my dad returned. Then we were all overcome by the smell of some home-cooked food. Laura had been busy. We all were drawn to the gym by the rich aroma of Laura's signature spaghetti with meatballs and Karen's chicken alfredo. The table was set with a variety of other dishes as well. My mom said, "I hope you don't mind, Father Jay... we raided your refrigerator." He just rubbed his belly in approval.

After we prayed and thanked God for bringing us together, we ate our meal and then tried to sleep. The kids were out like a light; I could hear their soft snoring in the background, but the adults slept fitfully.

Around 5:00 AM, just as it was getting light, I asked Father Jay, "Did you get any sleep?"

Father said, "No, not really. I'm too tired not to sleep, but here we are."

"Yeah, me neither," I groaned, "I was hoping that I'd wake up and find this was all a bad dream."

"Well, I'm not going to get any sleep, so I might as well get up," he said. "Besides, we've got to fulfill our corporal work of mercy of burying the dead now." With a groan, he sat up.

I said, "Yeah, and I've got a big grave to dig. Unfortunately, I think this is a corporal work that we will be dealing with on a regular basis."

Later, Father Jay invited the family to join him as he celebrated a funeral mass for all the dead. After the mass, I drove the backhoe to the cemetery and started to dig a very long trench. I had always wanted to operate a tractor and dig a trench or something, but not under these circumstances. It was challenging for the first hour, but then it became fun when the kids took turns sitting with me as I explained how the machine worked. Soon, they got bored and left. Then it became tedious and boring for me too. Still I was getting pretty good at it. Once the hole was done at the cemetery, I left the backhoe at the cemetery and walked back to the church. It was a beautiful summer day. The sun was shining, and there was a nice cool breeze blowing from the west. It was good to walk the stiffness out of my tensed muscles after getting jerked this way and that on the backhoe. I could almost believe that it was a normal summer day until I'd see the occasional body in a car or on the lawn as I walked through the neighborhood. *We'll have to bury those too*, I thought. *There are so many!* I was starting to feel overwhelmed. *Just stick to the task at hand*, I reminded myself.

When I arrived at the church, I could see a large flatbed truck in the parking lot. Jared and Phil had begun the grim work of loading the bodies on to it. I entered the church and found Father Jay sitting in the front pew of the church facing the altar. The church looked immaculate, and there was no longer any lingering odor of death or vomit. All that I could smell was Pine-Sol and carpet cleaner. I genuflected toward the tabernacle and sat down next to Father Jay. I could see tears on his cheeks. He looked over at me and wiped his eyes.

"Hey, John," he said. "This has been hard."

I nodded solemnly. "Yeah, I know. I've been staying busy to try to avoid thinking about it."

Father Jay shook his head. "Ah, so you do that too." He turned to look at me through his spectacles and smiled. "It's like were related or something."

"Yeah," I replied, "I wonder where we get it? Mom is probably scrubbing some pots and pans in the kitchen, and Dad is probably watering the lawn or fixing a car."

Father Jay laughed. "Close. Last I saw, Mom was mopping the floor in the kitchen. Dad went back to Salem to find out if there is any plan from the government."

I clapped him on the back and said, "Well, I've finished digging the trench at the cemetery. We are ready to start burying our dead."

It took all day, but we managed to bury 155 bodies in the cemetery.

Father did the Rite of Committal for all the dead. I was brought to tears at the beautiful prayer, "Lord Jesus Christ, by your own three days in the tomb, you hallowed the graves of all who believe in you and so made the grave a sign of hope that promises resurrection even as it claims our mortal bodies." After Father Jay sprinkled the large grave with holy water and did the final blessing, we went back to the school and washed up, rested, and ate. It was starting to get dark.

My dad made it back from the second day of the meeting in Salem. He said, "They think the cause of all the deaths is a mutated strain of the influenza virus. They think that it was man-made. There doesn't seem to be a cure yet, but there do not seem to be any new cases today. There were probably two hundred people at the meeting."

"Is that all?" my mom interrupted. "Only two hundred?"

My dad nodded with a grim expression on his face. "Yeah, I know. I would have expected thousands."

Father Jay added, "If the number of dead people at the church are any indication, I think we have lost over 90 percent of the population in this town. It sounds like it is the same all over."

Dad nodded, and he spoke about how he saw some other members of our extended family at the meeting.

"Laura, I saw your little sister there, Hannah, and her husband…uh…" He paused and scratched his head.

"His name is Connor," I supplied for him. Connor is Laura's brother-in-law who married her sister, Hannah.

Dad nodded his thanks and continued, "Yeah, so Conner and Hannah were there, and I also saw Connor's dad at the meeting."

"Seamus was there?" Laura asked, trying to save my dad the embarrassment of having to ask for his name.

Dad said, "Yeah, I saw Seamus there. He was trying to calm and organize everyone, but there was a group of guys who were intimidating people and trying to take control of the meeting. But Seamus did a good job of keeping his cool and trying to maintain control. I was about ready to get my rifle and chase those idiots away. Anyway, there is no real progress yet. Seamus is trying, but it is such a struggle with all the scared people and those jerks there. The frustrating thing is that the people don't want to do anything. They just want to sit there and discuss what the government can do for them."

The nine adults stayed up for a while discussing the future, while my seven children were sent to bed. As I watched them lie down for the night, I thought, *I hope you have sweet dreams little ones because reality seems especially harsh these days.*

4

Gathering

"Let us hold fast the confession of our hope without wavering, for he who promised is faithful; and let us consider how to stir up one another to love and good works, not neglecting to meet together, as is the habit of some, but encouraging one another, and all the more as you see the Day drawing near."

—Letter to the Hebrews 10:23–24

Early the next morning we heard a car pull up. Eli McHale, Laura's brother, and Leah, his wife, had just arrived with their baby named Conrad. I watched as Eli extracted his large frame from the car. He was just as tall as his dad, Phil.

Then, another couple of vehicles arrived. Connor Drennan and his wife, Hannah, and their kids pulled up in front of the church in their old Subaru hatchback. Hannah was Laura's youngest sister. I'd say that of all Laura's sisters, Hannah looks the most like their mother.

I turned to see another car coming down the road. It was Seamus Drennan with his wife Judy and his daughter Sally. When Seamus got out of the car, he walked over to his son Connor and embraced him, picking him up off the ground, probably just to prove he could still do it. Connor looked very much like a younger version of his dad, except Connor wore glasses and was even more pale than his father if that was possible. He laughed good-naturedly. They were both about six-foot-two and big-boned. I thought, *All of Laura's sisters married big men like her dad. How'd she get stuck with little five-foot-seven me?* Laura ran over and embraced her little sister, Hannah. Everyone greeted each other and settled in at the school. We all exchanged stories of what had happened in the last few days.

In his slight Irish brogue, Seamus told everyone about the morning meeting in Salem. He said, "Those same fellows that were pushing people around yesterday showed up with guns and said they were taking over. I think they broke into the National Guard armory. They all had machine guns, pistols, and camouflage. They are an intimidating lot. They rounded up some of the women there and took them into one of the buildings, where I think they raped them. We were powerless to do anything, and they looked as though they were going to get more violent." Seamus clenched his jaw and shook his head, regretting not being able to do something. "We all just ran for it and stuck together." He paused and looked around at the group before he added, "So I don't think there is a government anymore—well, at least not in Salem."

We were all silent for a few moments trying to process that bombshell.

Phil asked, "Are those guys still a threat?"

Seamus said, "Right now they are just bold thugs with guns. If they get organized, we're in trouble." Seamus hunched his shoulders, and his eyebrows furrowed together in thought. "I think a bunch of them were from the prison up on Highway 22. I heard one of them saying something about 'escaping.' One of the guys was wearing an orange jumpsuit with a number on it, but he had the arms tied at his waist."

With my fists clenched at my sides, I said, "So I guess to sum up the situation...most everyone is dead throughout the world, except for a few, and we don't really know why. There are some escaped prisoners who have machine guns, and we no longer have a government. Does that about sum it up? What else can go wrong?"

Father Jay said, "Well...we're still alive."

I looked at him and said, "Yeah, but for how long...? Sorry, I'm a little on edge."

Seamus straightened his shoulders and looked around. "Well, *we* should at least get organized. We need to have the attitude that we are on our own."

My dad piped in, "Everything has changed. Fuel is going to be a precious commodity. Our money isn't good for anything but starting a fire. People are going to be desperate."

Seamus nodded. "First things first: we need food, both short term and sustaining. Then, water: we have running water now, but with no one maintaining it, it will fail."

Father Jay said, "I'll gather up the kids and tell them to grab all the containers they can find in the cafeteria and fill them up with water. It will give them something to do, and it will help us for the time being."

Father Jay went off to get the kids together; we could hear them giggling as they ran in to do their part. They put the full containers in one of the schoolrooms.

Seamus looked at the rest of us. "Electricity! It will not last. Like the water, no one is maintaining it. Heat is the next thing. It's summer now, but we need to figure this out before it gets cold. We'll probably need to think about clothing too. Let's pool all our resources and see what we have and what we need."

My dad said, "You know, I think we are in a good place here. It's a farming community, and we are away from the cities. Plus, there will be wells nearby."

Everyone started to murmur about what resources we had on hand.

I held up my hand and said in a loud voice, "The WinCo grocery warehouse is just six miles away. It has food, and it probably has backup generators to keep things cold. Dad and I can drive truck and trailers. We could load up some trailers and bring them back with us. Walmart is there in Woodburn too, along with all the outlet stores. That will take care of a lot of our needs for now."

Seamus smiled and said, "That's the shot! I like your thinking. I'm not one for stealing, but I don't think there are any owners alive to care."

My dad said, "We'll need fuel too…gasoline and diesel. John and I could fuel up some tanker trucks and drive them here to Gervais before we do lose power."

"All these things are really just short-term solutions," Seamus said. "We will need to put our heads together at a later time to look at long-term survival: livestock, farming, etc."

I replied, "Well, let's just worry about surviving the short term for now."

Most of the adults loaded up in vehicles, minus a few to care for the kids, and drove to the WinCo warehouse. I figured we might have some problems getting into the warehouse, so I brought my sledgehammer and crowbar. I also brought my Glock 9mm in case we ran into trouble.

When we all arrived, the group split up. Half of us went to the outlet stores, and the other half went to the grocery warehouse.

The group that went to the warehouse consisted of me, Dad, Chloe, Jared, Laura, and Sally. The other group headed to the outlet stores consisted of Hannah, Connor, Eli, and Leah. When we arrived at the warehouse, Sally waited in one vehicle, and Chloe waited in the other. Both of them watched for trouble.

It was a strange sensation as we got out of the cars. There were no cars in the parking lot. We listened for any signs of life in the immediate area. The only thing we heard was a faint breeze and distant explosions. *I wonder what is causing that?*

We made our way to the entrance of the warehouse. Jared knocked loudly on the entrance. We waited. No one answered. Dad looked into one of the windows. No one stirred. I tried to kick at the door, but it didn't budge. So with a little good old American ingenuity consisting of a few swings from the sledgehammer, we got into the warehouse.

Jared yelled through the door, "Anybody home?" No one answered. It was dark. Finally, Jared walked in, and we followed. Jared found a light switch, which illuminated a typical warehouse office. There was a desk with a computer and some paperwork on it, and several filing cabinets lined the walls. Another door led into the warehouse.

As we entered, Jared found an electrical panel and turned on the lights. They made a humming noise and flickered as they slowly came to life, illuminating the very large space inside. There were rows and rows of shelves extending almost to the top of the twenty-five-foot ceiling. We could hear a radio playing distantly in the back of the warehouse. *I guess that Jared turned on more than the lights.*

Dad and I made our way to the loading docks. We decided that we would use the trailers that were already staged at the docks ready to be loaded or unloaded. We passed rows and rows of palleted boxes of food: huge boxes of still fresh vegetables and fruits, large containers of dried foodstuffs, and canned food wrapped in plastic.

I found another little office and the master key box in a back room marked "Employees Only!" There was a little window in the door where I could see two WinCo trucks hooked to the trailers that were backed up to the loading dock. I grabbed the whole box of keys, hoping that I'd be able to find those that would open the trailers and trucks.

I heard the sound of the motors of the large roll-up doors grinding open. *Good, Dad had unlocked those and found the switch to open them.* I walked over to him as he held the switch that opened one as it cranked open. He yelled over the sound, "Did you find the keys?" I nodded.

It took several hours, but we managed to pick out the types of food that we wanted and loaded them on the trailers with the electric forklifts. We decided to forgo the perishables and, instead, choose food that could be stored for longer periods of time. With seven kids, I was used to buying in bulk, but this was a whole new level of bulk. Once we had the trailers loaded, everyone got back into their cars except Dad and me, and they headed out. Dad and I debated as to whether we should leave the doors open for other people to get in. We decided that we would close everything back up, if for no other reason than to keep animals out. Dad and I ensured that the two tractors were properly hooked to the loaded trailers and started them up.

Everyone else in our group drove over to Walmart. I followed my dad's truck and trailer back to Sacred Heart.

After we parked the trucks and trailers in the church parking lot, we checked on the kids to make sure everything was okay. Then Dad and I got into one of the other cars and drove to meet the group at the Walmart. On the way, I dropped Dad off at WinCo to get another truck and trailer that we could bring to the Walmart. I waited as he started the truck and built-up air pressure in the brake system. He then followed me to Walmart.

Leah told me later about her adventure. She said that after they arrived at the little strip mall, they found that the buildings were mostly all locked up. Hannah, being the practical lady that she is, just backed the car up through the display windows to gain access. Their main job was to get clothing for everyone. They filled their cars with different sizes of clothing for both summer and winter. They made several trips. They got boots, shoes, and kitchen products. For each trip, they stuffed their cars full.

On the third trip, Connor saw two people in the store further down, grabbing clothing like the rest of us. It was two women. Connor laughed as he told the story. One woman was Hispanic, around forty years old. The other woman was black and in her thirties. They both grabbed the same outfit, and it turned into a tug of war. They started yelling and hitting each other. Eli had yelled at them, and they snapped out of it. Both women dropped the outfit and went for different clothing. Connor and his companions didn't see the women again after that.

Once Connor's crew had their final loads in the vehicles, they returned to camp. Thankfully, they encountered no problems.

The first group had made it to Walmart, but things didn't look right, so they decided shop somewhere else and then returned and decided to wait for us. Dad and I arrived a little while later. They had tried calling, but the cell phone service was hit-or-miss.

On the way, I reflected upon how eerie it was being all alone on the roads with no traffic. I was following the truck and trailer my dad was driving. On the overpass above the I-5 freeway, I stopped for a moment. I looked both directions, and for miles in either direction, there were no moving cars. There were no living souls to be seen.

After Dad had pulled into Walmart parking lot, I sped ahead of him to get to the loading docks. It was clear with no signs of danger. Dad was ready to pull in or drive off. I'm not sure why we were being so cautious, but it seemed the prudent thing to do. I signaled to him to back in. Dad backed the truck and trailer into the loading dock, and then with a rumbling bump against the dock, he shut down the truck. After he hopped out of the cab, he got into the car with me. We drove to the front of the store. The rest of our group was outside the store waiting for us. We got out and saw the concerned looks on their faces. We hurried over to Jared who was by the corner of the entrance.

There were two cars that had been in a head-on collision. There was coolant on the ground where the two cars were practically fused together by twisted metal and plastic. One headlight was still dimly lit on the white Chevy Impala. The blue Mazda was just a dead heap. The engines on both cars were still smoking a little. It was like walking toward a Halloween haunted house. It seemed like someone or something was going jump out at the opportune moment.

Jared said, "I peeked in the door, and I think I saw a body. We decided to wait for you—and your pistol."

We could see that the doors had been smashed open somehow, probably with a vehicle. It was a big open hole in the storefront. We slowly went inside; I had my Glock 9mm ready. The lights were on in the store.

Near the front door, or what was left of the doorway, was a dead man. He was obviously dead, but not from the virus. He had been shot in the chest; gauging by the amount of damage, it was most likely a shotgun. A bloody baseball bat was lying next to his body. A little further, another dead man was sprawled on the ground. The man's head was smashed in. Neither the sight nor the smell was pleasant.

I could feel my previous meal rising up in my throat; I wanted to vomit, but I forced it down with a swallow. It was one thing to see bodies killed by a disease, but it was quite another to see bodies that had been murdered. There is a different feel to it, as if the violence of it has somehow infected the air.

Next to the man was a spilled bag with some prescription drugs sprawled on the floor. All the cash registers were smashed open as well. Everyone instinctively looked around for some object that might be used as a makeshift weapon if the need arose. We all passed the dead men and looked around, wide-eyed. From the smell of decomposing flesh, it was obvious that at least one of the men had been killed more than a day ago.

Some sort of emergency lights were flashing. There was stuff scattered all over the floor. It was impressive how many flies and other insects were already in the store. A couple of people in the group saw a cat and a dog eating spilled food. I could hear some crows calling to each other and even saw some birds flying from aisle to aisle. The food was scattered and easy pickings for whoever or whatever came along.

Obviously, people had looted this store. Now it was our turn. Dad and I covered the bodies with grocery bags to get them out of immediate sight. We walked around the store to make sure it was clear of danger. We checked the store's back areas, freezers, and bathrooms. At the men's bathroom, I had trouble opening the door. As Dad helped me force it open, we discovered that it had been blocked by a body. He had the familiar red ooze all over his face and obviously had been killed by the infection. The man's body was bloated from the summer heat. His Walmart uniform seemed barely able to contain his bloated flesh. While getting into the bathroom, we had forced his body between the door and the wall. Some of the trapped decomposing gasses made a hissing sound as they escaped from his body. It was then that I did vomit. Luckily, I happened to be in a bathroom. Dad ran out, barely able to choke it back.

After I finished emptying the contents of my stomach, I met Dad out front. He said, "Should we say a prayer or something?"

"Yeah, I suppose we should," I said. We all made the sign of the cross, and I said, "Eternal rest grant unto them, O Lord."

Everyone else, in a jumbled rush of words said, "May they rest in peace, and may their souls and the souls of all the faithful departed rest in peace. Amen."

After our awkward prayer, and we were satisfied that no one else was in the building, each member of our group was assigned certain things to get. Sally's job was to go to the pharmacy and get all kinds of medicines, including specific prescriptions for those who needed them, along with vitamins and hygiene products. Jared was assigned to get all the hunting, camping gear, and ammo he could find. Chloe's job was to get fresh produce and bottled water. Laura's job was to get baby products, juices, and soups. My job was to get good meats, fish, and dairy products. Dad's job was to get as much ice as possible and then clear a path in the back of the store so we could load up the trailer.

We all grabbed carts, filled them, and rolled them on to the trailer. The first cart I grabbed had a screwed-up wheel. I already had it loaded with meat before I noticed it. It was hard to push straight. Several of the others laughed when it squeaked and shuddered past them. It took several hours, but we managed to just about fill the trailer. Then, just before we were ready to go, we all went to the toy section and filled a couple of carts with toys for the kids. It was very discomforting to see the store so empty. Although there was no need, we all spoke in hushed tones. It felt like someone was watching us, waiting to jump out at us.

We drove back to the church. My dad followed us in the truck and trailer. After we exited the freeway and Dad was crossing the overpass, out of nowhere, he heard the sound of shots being fired. He immediately ducked down and tried to keep the truck steady on the road. He looked down onto the freeway below. The only moving thing he saw was a dark-green, small-sized car. The driver had fired some shots from the freeway below the overpass. My dad just kept on driving with his head down, and the shooter kept driving down the freeway.

When we all arrived back to the school, my dad told us what happened. In surveying the damage, we found two bullet holes in the side of the trailer; they were high enough that they probably hadn't hit any cargo, but we planned to inspect the cargo to make sure our food was lead-free. There was one other bullet hole located in the passenger-side window. We were thankful the bullet hadn't hit my dad. Understandably, he was shaken up.

With clenched fists, he said, "What is wrong with these people? Who knows what percentage of people are even left on the planet? And we still have people who are trying to kill one another!"

We all said a prayer of thanksgiving that no one was hurt in the random shooting. Then we took a look at all the supplies we had acquired. All of us were ready for a break, but we wanted to unload everything before nightfall.

Phil and Karen took charge and set up an assembly line as we emptied the trailer. They organized the things as they came in. It took about five hours to unload the trailers. Meanwhile, Laura and my mom worked on cooking dinner for everybody. We filled half the gym with food, some in boxes and some still in the many shopping carts from Walmart. Some of the cold food would not fit into the refrigerators, so we placed the food in the reefer trailer and turned it on. Dad and I parked the trailers in the field across the street from the school.

When we walked back into the gym, it was satisfying to see the neatly stacked piles of goods that would help us survive. There was a mouthwatering smell coming from the kitchen. We all gathered in the gym. Laura invited everyone to line up and grab a plate, as she raised the serving window that connected gym to the kitchen. After a hard, stressful day of gathering supplies, the fried chicken, corn, and the various other delicious side dishes were truly a feast. It was so very good; there is nothing that advertises delicious food better than silence while eating it. About halfway into the meal, Seamus stood up and said, "Let's start putting together a plan on what to do next."

Conversation started up as everyone started kicking around ideas with the person next to them. Father Jay got up and walked over to the school and a little while later we all heard a strange rumbling sound. I thought maybe one of the kids was riding a skateboard, but Father Jay propped the door open and rolled in a chalkboard.

Wiping his mouth, Seamus stood up and said, "That's grand! Okay, let's write down your ideas." Seamus grabbed a piece of chalk and stood poised to write down the ideas as they came.

Some people wanted to go back to their homes. Others thought that our group should search for and join another surviving group. A good portion of us decided we wanted to stay put and start over.

After several minutes of heated discussion, Seamus said, "Thanks to you all, we now have food, water, clothing, and more outdoor gear. That is a big accomplishment and relief."

Father Jay said, "The majority of us, it seems, would like to stay here, and I think it is our best option. You are all welcome to stay here. We have farming land all around us. We have a church. Eventually, we will need to be self-sustaining. We will need to farm and raise animals. I'm sure that some of the farmers around here get their water from wells." He paused a moment. "Oh, yeah, I almost forgot. I wanted to let all of you know that my mom heard new news on the radio while you were out collecting supplies." Father Jay interrupted himself and looked at our mother. "Or did you want to recount what you heard?"

She waved him on, so Father continued, "Well, they—I mean the people on the radio—think this plague affecting the world is a man-made, mutated flu virus. Some group called the 'Prophets of Revelation' is claiming responsibility for the virus. They claim to have developed this strain and released it in the air in each country. All the major cities were the main targets. Then it spread to the smaller cities and towns. These so-called prophets claim that it was a coordinated effort, and they released the virus worldwide within minutes of each other. Apparently, they put the virus inside portable air compressors so that they could drive around and slowly release the virus in the major cities. These terrorists, apparently, were like suicide bombers who were ready to die for their cause."

Father scratched his head and said, "I suppose the idea is not too far-fetched. I have heard of such dangerous microbes being referred to as the poor man's nuclear bomb. Now, I am not a scientist, but I have my doubts about the description of how the virus was spread."

Father Jay continued, "Now there was a really weird story that we heard on the radio." He paused for emphasis. "It stated that around this time of year we have meteor showers and that some crazy population control scientists had created a virus that had been spread months before, and this virus was activated by the increased percentage of a particular compound found in meteors. This is the reason that people became sick all at once around the world at the same time because of this increase of meteor activity."

At this point, Seamus stood up and said, "That is about the most ridiculous thing I have ever heard. Can't they just stop the wild speculation and report the news?"

Father Jay looked around at all the glum faces and continued, "There is a bright side, however. The newspeople believe that the virus should have died off with all the infected. There have been no new outbreaks of the virus. Apparently, they have been testing the air and no more signs of the virus were found. According to those announcements, we shouldn't have to worry about it any longer."

Laura held up her hand, interrupting, "They tested the air?"

Father Jay shrugged. "I also have doubts about the scientists being able to check the air for more the virus. But there doesn't seem to be any more outbreaks." Father Jay looked at our mother. "Did I miss anything?"

She added, "The news station said that scientists in Omaha, Nebraska, claimed to have a cure after the first day, but they were overrun with people. They rioted. The scientists were killed, but apparently, there is a vaccine out there." She paused, then said, "Admittedly, the people reporting didn't sound very professional, but there isn't much to choose from."

Phil interjected, "I don't buy it. I don't see how they could have a cure in the first day. Besides, they don't even have a cure for the common flu."

Father Jay held up his hand. "I'm not arguing with you. I am just relaying what the radio station said."

Seamus grunted in disgust. "We don't know what's going on at all. They are just making stuff up."

After this, the conversations really started to heat up. I was afraid that we were going nowhere fast, so I raised my voice and said, "Let's just stick with what we know! Okay? We know that, for whatever reason, we have survived, and we need to make the best of it. I mean, at this point, does it really matter how it started?"

Laura spoke up and said, "Well, how come we didn't catch it? Why are we all still alive?"

My mom interjected, "Wait! Didn't we all have the flu three or four weeks ago? It just spread through the family after our big breakfast together, and I think all of us got it at some point."

Father Jay raised his hand. "I think that was my fault. I had visited someone at the jail who was dying and wanted his last rites. His lungs were filled with fluid, and he was coughing up a storm. I could hear other prisoners up and down the jail cells coughing as well. I got the cough a day later, and I think I got you all sick during that Sunday breakfast."

Mom said, "Well, if that is the reason, I'm glad you did because we might all be dead otherwise."

Connor said, "You know, that makes a lot of sense. I remember hearing that during the times of the smallpox plague, there were some people who survived because they had caught a similar disease called cowpox and were immune to smallpox. I mean, I'm no doctor, but it's the only thing that makes sense."

This brought up another lively round of discussion. The question on everyone's mind seemed to be do we trust what the radio says? Or are they just trying to avoid further panic? For the next hour, we discussed the various possible causes of the virus and whether we needed to worry about it or not. I tuned them out as I thought about plans for the future. I figured at this point it didn't matter what the cause was. We just needed to do our best to survive. *I'm worried that rule of law has not survived.*

As I was wondering about these things, I couldn't help but look around at my family. I hoped we would all be okay. My eldest, Isaiah, was speaking to his uncle, Father Jay. He was talking to him about everything he knew about viruses and bacteria. His blue eyes were animated. His uncle was smiling at him as he listened. Isaiah always had an interest in science-related things; it is for this reason that some of the family members call him "The Little Professor." He always pauses before he speaks, as if he tests the words in his mind first.

Eden and Eve, our ten-year-old twins, were talking to each other about ponies. They were very interested in having a farm with animals. Eve had her rainbow-colored hat on. I could see her long-curled hair sticking out the back. Eden's head was bobbing up and down as she explained the perfect pony that she wanted. Abigail was latched on to Grandpa Phil. Phil was telling her a story about his childhood. I looked over at my other two sons, Davey and Elijah. They were sitting on the floor with Mom, "Grandma Victoria," playing with Legos.

My beautiful wife was holding my youngest daughter, Faith, in her arms as she spoke with her mom, Karen. I was so grateful that my family was alive. I was grateful that I was alive. I wiped my eyes because I was starting to tear up. I looked around self-consciously to see if anyone had noticed.

My thoughts were interrupted when Seamus spoke up, "Let's figure out if we are going to stay here or go."

The consensus was that we should stay put for the time being. It seemed more important to everyone to stay together. Eli spoke up, "If we are going to remain here, then Leah and I should go back to our place and get our animals." Eli and Leah had a small farm in Silverton. "I've got a horse trailer," Eli continued, "that I can hook up to the truck. It's too late tonight, but we can start first thing in the morning." Seamus, Judy, and Sally all volunteered to help with the animals.

"Speaking of animals," Eli added, "I think that we ought to go to the neighboring dairy farms and such and let any penned-up animals loose. They will serve us well later as food."

We all nodded in agreement.

By this time, it was getting very late. The skylights in the gym were fading to black because of the gathering darkness outside. I couldn't help wondering whether the darkness was protecting us or was closing in on us. This evening, the adults at least were going to sleep better because we had acquired some camping cots from the stores we had looted. As we lay down to sleep, we could hear crickets chirping outside. *Ah, yes, crickets! That is something normal.* As sleep overtook me, I could almost imagine that everything was fine, that we were camping, and that the past few days were just a bad dream.

5

Assessments

Look at the birds of the air: they neither sow nor reap
nor gather into barns, and yet your heavenly Father
feeds them. Are you not of more value than they?

—The Gospel of Matthew 6:26

I was running. I was being pursued by a nameless, faceless monster. I could hear him breathing and grunting as he came after me. He growled, a deep raspy growl, and I could feel a shiver along my spine. I was in a forest. It was dark. I was making my way by the light of the moon. I couldn't keep the branches from breaking and snapping under my feet. Every step I took seemed to be a resounding gong announcing my presence. No matter how quietly I stepped, "Snap!" My legs felt like they were pushing through molasses.

I stopped and put my back against a tree. I listened. All that I could hear now was my own breathing. Had I lost the monstrous pursuer? Was he still there? I tried to quiet my breathing. I strained to listen. I heard nothing, only silence. My heart was beating loudly in my chest. I could feel my temples pulsing to the beating of my heart.

Then I could hear "it" growling. But it was growling words that I could just barely make out. In that low rumble, it said, "I'm coming for you. I'm coming for your family. I'm going to take your children."

I couldn't tell where it was. I was afraid to turn my head to look around the side of the tree. Its voice seemed to come from everywhere and nowhere at once. I ran, but it felt like I was running in slow motion. I stopped, I hid again, and I listened. I could feel the bark of the tree as I pressed my back against it.

A shooting pain stabbed my shoulder. I looked down. Wicked and twisted claws were pressed into my shoulder. I was pinned against the tree. I couldn't move. The pain was excruciating. I screamed, "Nooooo!"

*****

I woke up in a cold sweat. All was quiet. I was lying on my arm. It had fallen asleep, and it was tingling from the loss of blood supply.

I sat up and looked around. *Had I screamed in my sleep?* I could hear the snoring and heavy breathing of everyone around me. No one stirred. It felt like someone or something was watching me, and the hairs on the back of my neck were standing up. I had the feeling that something invisible, but evil was watching me. The sensation was so strong, I could even sense which direction it was in the room. It reminded me of my childhood, being scared of an imaginary monster under the bed and wanting to put the sleeping bag over my head to hide. I looked over toward the corner of the room, but I didn't see anything. I prayed for protection from my guardian angel. Gradually the sensation faded.

As I moved my arm around and massaged it to restore the flow of blood, I lay down again to try to get some more rest. I had a feeling that I would need it.

The following morning, after a light breakfast, the members of the crew who were going to Eli's place climbed into their vehicles and left.

Meanwhile, the rest of us gathered in the gym where we broke into smaller groups. One group climbed into vehicles and drove around to explore the neighboring farms with the goal, first of all, of looking for survivors there, and secondly, scouting out areas to farm and raise animals. This would include releasing any animals that were penned up in the surrounding farms. Another group scouted around for wells for drinking water. Phil and Karen stayed with the younger kids.

Father Jay took our mom and dad with him to drive to the churches in the surrounding areas to see if any priests or other of the faithful were alive. Also, if necessary, he would remove the Blessed Sacrament from the churches and leave a note that Father could be found in Gervais.

Laura and I were part of the group to check the neighboring farms; we decided to head west just past the church. We took the main thoroughfare to the first farm. We pulled into the long gravel driveway hearing the gravel crunch under the tires. We drove past a rusty metal gate, which let us make our way to the farmhouse. There were long, faded white fences on either side of us. We passed a couple of cows lazily munching away on grass in the field. We passed an old, rusty, yellow tractor as we pulled up to the garage door of the faded yellow house.

I looked over at Laura. "Ready?"

She nodded and reached for the handle to open the car door but stopped when we heard barking. A black lab padded up to my side of the car, barking dutifully. His tail was wagging excitedly. He didn't seem to be too much of a threat, so I opened my door and let him smell my hand. I got out and petted him around his ears. He whimpered happily and then padded toward the front door of the house.

Laura walked up beside me as we followed the lab to the door. He wagged and looked over at us expectantly and then looked at the door and huffed softly. I strode up and petted the dog on the head and tried the doorbell. I didn't hear anything, so I knocked loudly. I waited and listened. There was no answer. The dog began whining. I reached and turned the knob on the door and cracked it open slightly and yelled, "Is anybody home?" Again, no answer.

The lab pushed his nose into the crack I had made, widening it, and wiggled himself through into the house. He made a little huffing sound as if telling me to follow. I obeyed. Laura grabbed my hand and followed. We were startled as an orange cat scuttled out from behind the couch and ran outside through the door. I could tell from the smell that we were not going to like what we found. We made our way through a rustic but lovely little home filled with strong-looking, dark, wooden furniture. The walls were covered with family photos surrounded by dark frames hung lovingly with wires from the dark wood that trimmed the ceiling.

We followed the lab around the corner to a hallway that led to the bathroom. The dog stopped at a doorway halfway down the hallway and turned to look in. He whimpered and then turned to look at us as if we should do something. We caught up and looked in. It was what I expected. An elderly woman was hunched over the toilet with dried red foam crusted to her face, and a man was slumped over the bathtub. The stench of death was much stronger now that we were in the same room. I closed the door. I could hear Laura gagging a little bit behind me.

We walked out, but the lab didn't follow; he just lay down in front of the door, watching us go. I was glad to taste the fresh air when we got outside. I left the front door open so the dog could get out. Laura was holding her hand over her mouth. She looked at me, obviously reading the concern in my eyes. She said, "I'm all right."

I nodded and turned to survey the rest of the property. There was a large red barn tucked behind the house. We walked over to make sure that there were no animals in the barn. The door was unlocked. I slid it open and looked in. It seemed to be used more for storage than anything else. There were several bales of hay stacked in the back, and along the side, there were some stalls, but no animals in them. There was an old, rusted truck parked near the wall.

I turned around to look at Laura, but she was gone; apparently, she went around the other side of the barn. I came out and peeked around the corner. She had found another little shed. I was wondering if it was an outhouse. She opened the door and closed it. She turned around and yelled, "I think it is a well."

I yelled back, "That could be useful." Then I waved her back. I watched her as she walked back toward me. *How did I get so blessed to have a woman like this? I don't know what I would do without her.* She smiled as she came up beside me, seeing that I was watching her.

"What?" She said with a grin on her face.

"I was just thinking how lucky I am," I replied.

She hit me in the shoulder and said, "You're darn right you are."

I nodded toward the house. "You know that could be us someday."

"You mean dead in the bathroom and foaming at the mouth," she replied.

I laughed. "No, you know what I mean," I said, "having lived our lives, growing old together with pictures of our kids and grandkids on the wall."

She hugged my arm and set her head on my shoulder. "I hope that we can. I pray to God that we can."

We walked to the car, and then I stopped. "Oh, wait a second," I said to Laura. I ran back into the barn and stopped at a large gas can that I had seen in there earlier. I pulled open the cap and smelled it.

Yep, it is gasoline. With effort, I grabbed the handle with two hands and hoisted it a little above the ground and waddled it over to the car. I asked Laura to open the gas tank latch. She and I managed to pour the gas into the tank without spilling too much of it on the ground. I returned it to the barn, and then Laura and I went on to check more of the farms.

Each farm we went to was pretty much the same story. There were no survivors, except the animals. Laura and I managed to free three horses, two sheep, and surprisingly, an alpaca. Thankfully, it seemed the cows were out to pasture.

Our mini-expeditions trickled back to home base a few hours later to report back what we had found. Unfortunately, our worst fears were confirmed, no living souls were found. There were several little farms around, but more importantly, there were a couple of large, well-stocked farms not too far from the school. They had equipment and some seed for planting. The occupants were dead in or around their houses and would need to be buried. The first farm was on the north edge of town. It had a faded yellow, ranch-style one-level house with four bedrooms. In addition, there were two large pole barns with tractors and harvesters in them. We found pumphouses on some of the properties, but many hadn't been used in years.

The second farm had a living space, which was a two-story farmhouse with a wraparound porch. Its tan exterior was accented by chocolate brown trim. Near the house was a large barn with equipment and seed in it. With all the pastureland, it seemed perfect for raising livestock, which it already had in abundance.

Eli's group had to make a couple of trips to bring his animals, feed, and equipment. By the end of the day, they had brought over both of their cows, ten chickens, two goats, one horse, and everything to care for them.

The school had a fenced-in yard where we could keep the larger animals for the time being. We all got together and made a makeshift pen for the chickens at the rectory because it was fenced in. By the end of the day, we were tired but satisfied. We were making progress. Our scouting showed that there were many resources available to us, and we were beginning to fend for ourselves. It was also clear to us that the estimates of 95 percent of the population being killed off was too low of an estimate, at least in our part of the world. It seemed like more than 99 percent of us had died here.

Father Jay and my parents returned later, looking glum. They had visited the churches in Salem, Keizer, Woodburn, and the other smaller surrounding towns. It was the same story everywhere; bodies of the faithful were gathered in and around the churches. Sometimes, the body of a priest would be found having ministered to the dead and dying until he had succumbed to the disease, or no priest would be found, presumably having died at home. Father Jay had blessed countless bodies at each of the churches but felt guilty for not burying them, but they did at least bury the priests that they found. I could tell that it was weighing heavily on Father Jay. Importantly, they had been able to recover from the tabernacles in each of the churches the Blessed Sacrament—the former bread wafers now consecrated into the true presence of Jesus for consumption by the faithful—and safely brought them to the tabernacle here at Sacred Heart in Gervais.

Evening approached fast. I noticed that it was difficult to sleep. Some still had to sleep on the hard floors, and the air mattresses or cots were not a long-term solution. Besides, we just weren't used to sleeping in the same room with so many other people. So we addressed the problem the following morning.

We agreed to have two families go to the farms and get moved in. Father Jay decided that he would continue to stay at the rectory. He invited our mom and dad to stay with him there in the extra rooms. Then he went with my dad to collect and bury the bodies that were left behind in the farmhouses in the surrounding areas.

Eli, Leah, and their toddler, Conrad, took one of the houses. It had one hundred acres of farmland and about two acres of fenced pastureland that conveniently already had sheep and cattle. Connor and Hannah, and their two kids, Andrew and Margie, occupied the other house with fifty acres of farmland and a small creek. Seamus and Judy decided to live with Connor and Hannah. The rest of us took possession of some of the houses next to the church. Even though

Laura and I already lived in the town, we took the house kitty-corner to the church, in order to be close to everyone. Thankfully, we didn't find dead bodies there or in any of the houses near the church. Many, I suppose, had sought refuge in the church itself. We did find a few emaciated cats or dogs that scurried off as we searched the houses.

We did what we could in our new homes to make the places a little more comfortable. We took only the houses that we could heat with a woodstove. Over the next few days, we got together and decided that we needed to get more livestock for food.

Unfortunately, none of us knew much about farming on a bigger scale, so we researched what we could. Thankfully, we still had electricity, but we didn't know how long it would last. The Internet, by some miracle, seemed to be at least partially working. Eli, Jared, Laura, and Hannah got on their computers and retrieved all the info they could on farming and survival in the area. Although it was clear that the news sites were slightly outdated, the news didn't look good. This virus, or whatever it was, had spread worldwide. Estimates were that less that 5 percent of the global population had survived. Unfortunately, the devastation was as bad and worldwide as we expected. We were all stunned.

I said, "I hope those terrorists died a slow and horrible death."

Father Jay gave me one of his stern looks, which seemed to say, "Careful!" I didn't much care for the minor scolding that he gave me with his eyes, but I knew he was right. *Who would have thought someone could say so much with eyebrows? He must have got that from Mom.*

After we downloaded all the farming information that we thought we could use, we had lunch. Phil, Sally, my dad, Chloe, and I decided to drive to the Woodburn library. We carpooled in two vehicles because we were starting to get concerned about the availability of gasoline. We did stop by a gas station along the way. Thankfully we didn't have any trouble filling up. The pumps were working, but I wondered, *What would happen when the electricity went out?* As we drove to the library, we discussed which books we would need. We decided on books that dealt with farming, butchering animals, electricity, and any other books related to survival. It seemed a reasonable precaution. We figured that the computers would be fine for now, but soon the electricity would be no more, and there was a very good possibility that we wouldn't be able to access information on the computers when that happened. Thankfully, the drive to the library was uneventful. The doors to the library were locked. Apparently, looters weren't too interested in expanding their classic poetry collections right now. We broke one window to enter, trying to keep the damage to a minimum. *I guess we were a different breed of looter.*

We didn't see any bodies, thankfully. We had to work by the light that came in through the windows. We found the light switches, but they didn't work. We thought, perhaps, that it was the truck that had knocked down the power pole up the street. In any case, we weren't going to be able to access the library catalogue on the computers. Nonetheless, Sally found books on animal heath, first aid, and home remedies; and the rest of us sought out our assigned books. Chloe grabbed books on solar energy, water purification, and hunting. The rest of us grabbed all the books we could find on farming and survival and anything else that seemed relevant. As we loaded up carts and made several trips to the car, I couldn't help feeling a little bit guilty for taking the books out of the library. However, I felt a little less guilty with each trip to the car. We made one last trip to get some fiction and children's books for fun.

On the way back to the school, we stopped at the discount ammo and gun store. From the smashed-in windows, it was obvious that people had looted the shop when the plague first hit. As a precaution, my dad circled around the back, and Phil and I entered very cautiously from the front. Thankfully, no one was there. We were pleased to see that there were still many guns and much ammo to be found. It was obvious that someone had cleaned out a large section where the shotguns were kept.

As we were looking around, the power went out. The vacant gun store had just become a lot scarier. Instinctively, we all crouched down behind a cabinet and waited. We thought at first that someone had turned out the lights, but no one came out to attack us, and there was not a sound to be heard.

Phil had taken a look at the buildings nearby and didn't see any lights, so he deduced that the entire local power grid had gone down.

Well, we knew it was coming. Laughing lightheartedly at our reaction, we resumed our activities, but we still felt the need to whisper to each other. We loaded the two cars with guns, ammo, targets, holsters, hunting gear, and camo gear. It was a somewhat uncomfortable drive with books and guns and ammo packed in the cars with us. I think we significantly exceeded the weight limit for the vehicles, so we took it slow.

It seemed that dusk was trying to beat us home as we made our way to Gervais. Instinctively, we approached the overpass along Butteville Road with caution. As we looked north and south, there was no traffic, but we could see that there was smoke rising up out of the city of Salem to the south. It seemed that to the north toward Portland, there was also smoke. There were probably fires. I figured that with no living firefighters, the fires would have to burn themselves out.

When we got back, the others told us that the power had gone out a little earlier. Phil told the others about the gun store, and everyone got a chuckle. We had known that the power would not last, but when it finally did go, the reality of our situation sank in. The infrastructure that we had relied on for so long was gone. We were on our own.

Sally said, "What are we going to do without electricity?"

I said, "Maybe we don't have to go without electricity. That WinCo warehouse has generators, but they are huge. We would need a crane and a flatbed trailer to remove them. If we could do it, it should be enough for the school and a few houses."

Phil shook his head and said, "There is probably a lot of frozen and cold food there that we will need later. I think we should leave the generators there for now. We should probably check on them once a week or so and figure out how long their fuel will last. Maybe for now, we can concentrate on some smaller generators for each house."

Dad said, "That brings up another point. We need to think about fuel. I know we can siphon fuel from all these cars and tractors in the area, but it is going to run out eventually. I work—well worked—on fuel tankers in Portland, and I know we can get some trucks and trailers full of fuel and bring them back here. John and I can drive them back here."

Phil raised his head, "That is a great idea. It is going to get really dark here at night, but our future looks bright." We all groaned at the bad pun, which gave him just as much pleasure as if we had laughed.

Jared said, "At some point, I would like to drive around the area to look for survivors."

"Well, all of that will have to wait until after dinner," we heard behind us as Karen waved us toward the gym. "One can't solve all the problems of the world on an empty stomach." We all agreed whole-heartedly as we made our way to a candlelight dinner with family.

6

Trip to Portland

The Lord is near to the brokenhearted
and saves the crushed in spirit.

—Psalm 34:18

The following day, Dad, Mom, and I decided to drive to Portland. Father Jay wanted to go with us to see if the Archdiocese even existed anymore. He had told us more than once recently that the Church was more important now than ever.

We did not see any other people on the way there, at least not any living people. There were cars strewn along the side of the highway, but nothing blocking all of the lanes. I was thankful that people had the presence of mind to pull their cars off to the side of highway in their final moments. On the way, we stopped at Camping World, a large recreational vehicle and supply retailer, in Wilsonville. A manager had put a sign on the window: "Sorry, we're closed. Everyone called in sick." After knocking on the front doors for about five minutes, no one came, so we broke through one of the front glass doors. After looking around for about thirty minutes, we found five portable generators. Everything in the store seemed it would be useful and necessary. I must admit that I was tempted to take just about one of everything. But we had to show restraint.

In addition to the generators, we found a cargo trailer and hooked it to the back of the van and loaded the portable generators into it along with camping gear. We found a gas can in the service area and filled two of the generators with gasoline and got back into the van. We heard a ping and a gunshot. Obviously, someone had shot at us as we were leaving. I hit the gas and screeched out of the parking lot. The trailer made quite a racket as it went over the curb.

I called back to see if anyone was shot as I kept an eye on the side mirrors for trouble, but I couldn't see the shooter. No one was hit, but Father Jay said the trailer tire looked like it was flat. Once we made it to the highway with plenty of distance between us and the shooter, I stopped, and we checked out the damage. The tire was shredded on the right side of the trailer. True to Murphy's law, there was no spare in the trailer.

I said, "Should we go back and ask the nice shooter-man if he has a spare tire?" Mom punched me in the shoulder. We hoisted the generators into the back of the van and dropped the trailer there. Sadly, we had to leave most of the other things in the trailer. Father Jay and Dad moved the rifles into the van.

There were a lot of places that we wanted to check out while we were in Portland. We decided to check on family first. My grandmother's house seemed to be a good place to start. Chances are that she would know what was happening with the rest of the family. She lived near Mt. Tabor with my Uncle Ben. We had tried calling, but there was no answer.

As we approached Portland, we could see smoke looming over the city. There were obviously fires burning in different parts of the city. There were signs all over that the disease had ravaged the city of Portland as well. The smell of death was everywhere, and there were few signs of life other than the occasional stray dog or cat. The traffic lights weren't working, so it was clear that the city's power was out. There were decomposing bodies in front of houses and along the streets. With a greater concentration of people in the city, it wasn't surprising that the streets smelled of rotting flesh. We kept an eye out for survivors, but we saw none. *There had to have been more survivors here*, I thought. *It is a big city. Maybe they are in a different area, or maybe they are hiding.*

We pulled into my grandmother's driveway. I shut off the engine, and we waited and listened. Everything was quiet. My mom knocked tentatively on the door. There was no answer. With tears in her eyes, she knocked more loudly. She was afraid; so was I. None of us had a key to the house. Father Jay went around the back of the house. He checked the back door. It was locked. He broke into a basement window and managed to climb down. We all waited at the front door for him to let us in.

My dad had his arm around Mom. She leaned against his shoulder, trying to hold back her tears. "Jay," she said as she shook her head side to side, "I don't think I can go in there."

I pulled open the screen door. I didn't know what to say, but I wanted to say something. "It will be okay, Mom."

We heard the lock turn on the front door. The door opened, and I could see tears in Father Jay's eyes. He was holding his nose, and he had his hand over his mouth. When the door opened, a horrible stench wafted out the door. Father Jay looked at Mom and said, "Mom, you don't want to go in there." He then quickly pushed past us and threw up in the driveway. He took a couple minutes to regain his composure. He said, "I don't know what is wrong with me. I've been dealing with dead people all week."

I shrugged my shoulders. "I guess it is different with family."

Mom and Dad sat down on the swinging chair in front of the house. Father Jay said, "Wait here." A minute later, he came out with the bulletin board that Grandma had used to keep track of all the family members. Next to each picture, she had written a date for that family member's birthday so that she wouldn't forget the dates. We could see that recently she had added a date of their death next to almost all of them. Picture after picture we saw written, "RIP, July 14 or 15" as we scrolled down the list of family members. Next to our pictures there was a question mark.

Father Jay told us that it was obvious that Ben, my mom's brother, had cared for Grandma until the end before he himself had succumbed to the disease. "Ben was kneeling at her side. He had his rosary." Father broke into tears himself and couldn't talk any more.

I put my arm around him, and he cried into my shoulder. I cried too. I could feel him shaking with his sobs. He was always very close to our grandmother and Uncle Ben. It is a quirk of mine, but I've always been one who deals with my discomfort with humor, so after a while, I said, "You're getting snot all over my jacket."

Father Jay laughed. Mom and Dad hugged us. Then Dad grabbed us each behind our necks and gently massaged them and said, "I need to check on my brother." We buried Grandma and Ben in the side yard. They were quick and shallow graves, but this was the best we could do at the time. Father Jay led us in prayers, and then we stood there quietly for a few moments. *I had hoped that maybe all of our extended family had somehow survived, but I guess God had other plans.*

We climbed into the van and made our way east toward my Uncle Ted's house. It was a twenty-minute drive to Troutdale. Thankfully, it was uneventful. How strange it was to see cars stopped on the highways, dead bodies scattered all over the roadways and sidewalks. A section of barrier was missing where a truck and trailer broke through on an overpass. We slowed down; we could tell it was an old crash from the first signs of the virus. The truck was a mangled heap of metal. By the looks of the wreckage, it didn't look like the driver suffered. The most troubling sight was the crows and other animals feeding off the bodies. At least we knew now about our other relatives on my mom's side of the family. My grandmother had provided one last and very important service for our family. We drove in silence for a while. Then Father Jay said, "Let's say a prayer for our lost family members." He led us in a rosary as we drove through the remnants of civilization.

We arrived in Troutdale a short time later. It was eerie. As we pulled into the trailer park, the only movement that we saw was cats scurrying away or watching us with their unblinking eyes. When we pulled up, we could hear Uncle Ted's pit bull, Mascara, barking in the house. We walked by the sliding glass door, and Mascara was viciously barking on the other side of it. Her snout was covered, not in mascara, but blood. As she barked with her snout pressed up against the glass, she was smearing the glass with blood. We could see a few flies on the window and circling her snout.

Dad shouted, "Mascara! Quiet!" But the dog didn't listen. It seemed to have gone feral. Dad put his hand up above his eyes to shield them from the glare of the sun. Ignoring the dog, he pressed his face up against the glass and peered inside. Mascara was baring her teeth and trying to bite him through the glass.

"I can see him," he said in a low voice, "he is on the floor. He's dead." Dad smacked the glass with the back of his hand. Mascara was startled for a second but began her attack of the glass with renewed vigor. He started toward the front gate that led to the porch.

Mom, Father Jay, and I said, almost in unison, "Stop!" But Dad didn't seem to even hear us or even slow down. A pit bull is not a dog to mess with. We saw her disappear from the window. A second later, she popped out of the dog door and began her furious barking at the gate. Dad opened the gate latch and kicked the gate into the dog. Then he pinned the dog between the gate and the side of the house. Mascara yelped then tried to wiggle free. Then, to our great shock, Dad grabbed the dog by the scruff of the neck and slammed her head-first into the house. With a yelp, she went limp. Dad pounded her head a couple more times into the side of house until it was clear she was dead. *Crack! Crack! Crack!* He let her body slump to the ground with a thud. He walked to the door, slowly bent down, reached up through the dog door, unlocked the door, and went in. I just stood there with my mouth open, watching this crazed man kill a dog with his bare hands. I shook myself out of it, and Father and I looked at one another. I joked, "Remind me never to get on his bad side!"

Dad was pretty shook up. He, as well as the rest of us, had really hoped that Uncle Ted would somehow be alive. As we followed my dad into the house, we could tell by the smell that Ted had been dead for a while. Judging by the dried remains of red foam, trailing from the bathroom to where he lay, it was clear that Ted had died of the sickness. Sadly, it looked like his dog had grown hungry and began eating the only "meat" that was available. We dug a shallow pit and buried Ted. We buried him with his dog, Mascara, because we knew that he loved that dog, and he would have forgiven the fact that she had been using his body to stay alive. Ted had also had a parrot and a cat. All that was left of the parrot were some feathers, and the cat was nowhere to be seen.

Father Jay led us in prayer over the shallow grave. As we shoveled the earth over Ted with his beloved dog, Dad broke down into quiet sobs, and he and Mom just hugged and cried for a while. It felt like my tear ducts were all dried up. I could tell Father Jay was tired too, but there was no time to rest; we knew that we had more work to do.

Before we left, Dad had the presence of mind to grab Ted's guns and a couple of fishing poles and a box of tackle, things that we hadn't thought of at my grandmother's place.

We drove west back into Portland and stopped first at the pastoral center for the Portland Archdiocese on the east side of downtown Portland. This office is the business end of the Catholic Church, from the crest of the Cascade Mountain Range west to the Pacific Ocean.

We had tried to take the freeway, but it was jammed with cars with dead bodies in them, so we switched to the lanes for oncoming traffic hoping to make better progress. Unfortunately, we didn't get too far before we found those lanes clogged with stationary vehicles that had been trying to get off the exit toward the hospital. The cars were backed up for miles, so we turned around, left the freeway, and began taking various city streets. We didn't need to stop and look to know that all these vehicles had dead bodies in them. We could smell death in the air. It was the stench one experiences when a possum or deer has been left too long along the side of the road.

When we finally arrived at the pastoral center, it looked very quiet. There were no cars parked in the lot. Father Jay knew well the people who had worked here. There was a sign on the front door that read, "Sorry, Closed Due to Sickness." After breaking in through the front glass doors, Father Jay and I looked around but could find no one living or any instructions for surviving clergy. When we came out of the building, Father Jay shook his head dejectedly. He looked down at the sidewalk and with a haunted look in his eyes, asked of no one in particular, "Am I all that is left of the clergy in western Oregon?"

I looked at Mom. I didn't know what to say. Father Jay looked scared too. His expression mirrored the feelings in my own heart. Mom put her arm around Father Jay and led him to the van. Father Jay stopped and said, "Wait a minute! I've got to grab a few things." He left a note on the counter of the reception area for any clergy that might show up, instructing them how to contact him. Minutes later, he came back out with some books and a few other things.

Then he said, "I really need to go the archbishop's home at the cathedral. I need to know if he has survived."

My dad looked at my mom and said, "I understand. I think while you are doing that, Victoria and I will take that motorcycle over there and see if anything is happening at the hospital." He pointed at a motorcycle parked out front of an apartment building. "We should be able to maneuver between the cars easier than with a car. Maybe we can find someone living who has some answers." He looked at me and said, "John, why don't you go with Father to help him."

I nodded. Father Jay and I waited to make sure that Dad was able to get the bike started. He did and gave the helmet to my mom, and she hopped on back. They waved to us, and my dad put the bike in gear, and off they headed to the hospital.

Father Jay drove along Burnside Street, a major arterial that split Portland into its northern and southern halves. Along the way, I looked for any signs of human activity. I didn't see any. As we approached the Burnside Bridge to cross over the Willamette River, we could see that the lanes headed west were jammed with cars. There were bodies lying between the cars and hanging out of the cars. Fortunately, we were able to cross the bridge using the oncoming traffic lanes. The magnitude of the devastation was so much more apparent in the city than in the small towns and rural areas. The streets were lined with mile after mile of haphazardly stopped cars and garish bodies, exaggerated by dried, blood-red foam around each head.

We finally arrived at the cathedral in downtown Northwest Portland. We had to drive on the sidewalk to get close to the entrance because cars were blocking the nearby streets, parked crazily in all directions. St. Mary's Cathedral of the Immaculate Conception is a large brick building with large white pillars standing sentinel at its main entrance. What we saw mirrored our experience in Gervais but on a larger scale. The bodies of faithful were scattered along the sidewalk and steps as though they were hoping to find salvation from the virus at the house of God; they all had the familiar trails of red foam that trailed out of their mouths. The red foam had now dried and was crusted to their clothes, their faces, and the sidewalk.

Father Jay and I stepped over bodies to get into the church. It was both a morbid and inspiring sight to see. The pews were packed with the faithful slumped over or on their knees, a final prayer in death. We made our way to the front of the church, toward the sanctuary with the large marble altar in the center. The only illumination came from the beautiful stained-glass windows. The only sound to be heard was the gurgling of gases escaping from decomposing bodies. Even though I was in a church, it was creeping me out.

As we approached the altar, we could now see the body of the archbishop dressed in purple vestments sprawled out on the white marble floor. He had lain down prostrate on the ground with his arms out in the shape of a cross. His head was to the side where now a dried puddle of red foam had come out of his mouth. We paused silently to look upon the body of our lost shepherd.

We buried the archbishop in a shallow grave in the courtyard next to the church. We went back into the church and Father Jay, with deep sobs, blessed the bodies of all the dead sprinkling them with holy water. He retrieved the Blessed Sacrament from the tabernacle, and we returned to the van. As we walked, Father Jay looked around and said, "I wish we could bury them."

"Look, Jay," I said, "I know that it is part of your job to bury the dead, but you have done what you could. This is too much for us to take on. Every church that you have visited has been the same." I paused. "You've done enough. In fact, you have probably done more than anyone should have to. I'm sure that our Lord is pleased with you for the care and reverence you've shown him in your determination to care for the Blessed Sacrament."

"Thanks, John. I just need to process this. I need to bring it to prayer." Father Jay asked me to drive. We drove in silence, heading east over the river and back to the pastoral center to meet up with Mom and Dad.

As we drove, I reflected on what this all meant for Father Jay. It was more than just the death of his friends and colleagues, but it must have felt like the death of the Church itself. I didn't know what to say.

Our parents were already waiting for us at the pastoral center when we arrived. It was getting pretty late in the day. I recommended that we get over to the industrial tank farm and finish up our tasks for the day. None of us wanted to stay the night away from our surviving family members.

On the way to the industrial tank farm, someone came out of a house waving his arms. We stopped. He was a big, burly black man in blue jeans and a sleeveless T-shirt. I rolled down the window, and he walked up to the window, breathless. "Thank God! Someone else is alive! I've been wandering around for days looking for another living soul."

I said, "Are you okay? Do you need some help?"

"Look, man! Everybody is dead. I don't know what to do."

My dad leaned over my shoulder. "We've come up from the south, from the Salem area. You are welcome to come with us if you want. Right now, we are going to get some fuel, and then we'll be returning there."

"No, man. Thanks. I'm just glad to see that someone else is alive. Me and my wife and my kid live a few blocks down, and we are just trying to figure out what to do."

Dad said, "Well, if you want to find other people, I'd recommend going to the big stores with lots of supplies. Most people will probably be drawn there. But I'd arm myself if I were you. Desperate times call for desperate measures."

"Hey, man, thanks!" He reached up and shook my hand. "You guys be safe." Then he started to back up in order to head to where he had come from.

I called out after him, "Hey…um…mister. If you change your mind and want to find us, just head down south on I-5 and take the Woodburn exit and then take 99E south to Gervais."

"All right, thanks, man. I'll remember that—south on I-5 to Woodburn to Gerbils." He waved and turned to leave.

"Gervais!" I corrected as we watched him go out of sight. "Gerv…okay, close enough." We all got a laugh from the mispronunciation, and then we continued on our journey. I was glad to see someone else alive.

Along the way, our parents filled us in on what they found at the hospital. My dad said, "Every road to the hospital was clogged with traffic...well, dead traffic...well, you know what I mean."

Mom added, "We didn't find a single living soul. The hospital was absolutely overwhelmed with people. It didn't matter whether they were doctors, nurses, or patients. Everyone had died."

Dad shook his head as he drove. "The front glass doors were smashed open. People were so desperate to get in. There were signs of violence. Some people weren't willing to wait their turn."

"We walked all through the hospital," my mom added. "We looked in offices, patient rooms, bathrooms, and closets. No one survived."

I summarized our experience at the cathedral. I looked over at my brother and asked, "Is there anything you would add?" He held in his arms the large ciborium that contained the Blessed Sacrament that we had retrieved from the cathedral; he was looking out the window of the van. He merely shook his head absentmindedly. We were all in a subdued mood after the day's discoveries.

We headed north on I-5 and, after half an hour, arrived at the industrial area near the Columbia River where the fuel distributors and tank farms were located in North Portland. It was good to have a job to figure out and do to get our minds off of the somber events earlier in the day. We had decided that we were going to get fuel, and a lot of it. Dad and I got out of the van, and I grabbed a large sledgehammer out of the back. We walked up to the gate. Dad yelled, "Hello? Is anybody around?"

We didn't hear a sound. There were no motors, no voices, no birds. Even the wind was silent. I swung the sledgehammer and broke the lock on the rolling chain link fences. In the silence, it sounded very loud. The lock skidded across the pavement and then everything was silent again. Dad and I each grabbed a gate and slid them out of the way. Then we drove the van up to the pump platform where the tanker trucks come to be filled up with fuel.

Dad and I exited the vehicle and checked the electrical panels at the pump platform. Father Jay had followed us to the electrical panels. Dad and I looked at each other wondering what we should do next, and then we both looked at Father Jay. He said, "Don't look at me! You guys are the mechanics."

I had never seen how they filled the tanks of the trucks. We could see that the trucks and trailers would drive along either side of this platform and filling tubes could swing over the dome lids on top of the tanks' compartments to fill them.

My mom drove us over to some tanker trucks that were parked in the lot. There were no keys in them, and they were locked. We memorized the unit numbers on the sides of the cabs, and then Mom drove us over to the offices. It had two large glass doors in front. Father grabbed the sledgehammer with a grin and did his best Thor impersonation. The glass made a satisfying crash as the hammer flew threw it. Father asked us to wait a minute because he wanted to smash the other glass door. It was worth it to see the cheesy grin on his face; it was preferable to the haunted look that I had seen in his eyes earlier.

We found the locked key box on the wall. Father Jay greedily smashed it open. He wiped his face and said with a mischievous grin. "Man, it's hard work being truck and gas thieves! Okay, I've done the hard part. Now all you guys have to do is get the pumps running and fill the trucks without any electricity."

We laughed, but we knew he was right. We really had our work cut out for us. We grabbed the keys, and Mom drove us back to the trucks and trailers. Dad and I each parked a truck on either side of the filling platform. We climbed up on the platform and swung a tube over the dome lid. Dad showed me that there was a ground strap that you needed to run from the platform to the tank in case of static electricity. *I guess you would only need a little spark to light up your life, or should I say to end it.*

Unfortunately, Father Jay was right; there was no power, so we had to supply our own power to the pumps to fill the tankers. Dad removed the covers of the electrical panels and was trying to isolate the circuit for the pumps.

Dad yelled, "Found it!" It was marked, "Main Pump #1" and another circuit was called, not surprisingly, "Main Pump #2." He had wires hanging out of the two circuits that he wanted. Father Jay and I went to the van to retrieve our toolboxes and one of the generators. Mom carried a toolbox while Father Jay and I muscled the generator near the shed.

I sacrificed my set of jumper cables by cutting the clamps off of them. I stripped the wires and hooked them to the generator. Then I hooked the other side of the wires to the circuit breakers. I wiped my hands on my pants and looked over to my dad. "We're almost there. How are we going to get around the card lock system?"

Dad said, "Well, I think if we take the card lock box apart and find the wires directly to the pump, and then we'll get fuel." Dad got started taking the card lock box apart while I climbed up to the top of the tanks and opened up the dome lids and lined up the filling hoses.

As I got things set up on the tanks, I heard the pounding of a sledgehammer as Dad tried to apply some "American ingenuity" to the card lock system. There was a clang of metal as he tossed the covers on the ground to get access to the wiring.

"I think...I got it," I heard him say. "No, wait! I'll need the other bigger generator to make 220 volts."

With Mom's help, Father Jay wheeled the generator over and then ran over to one of the trucks and grabbed another set of jumper cables out of the cab. In a few moments, they had it hooked up.

"I'm ready up here," I yelled.

I heard the generators start up, and then, with a steady rumbling, the pumps turned on. It took forty-five minutes to fuel both the trucks and trailers. It was getting dark by the time we finished. My mom and Father Jay held flashlights for us as we worked while the sun slowly dipped over the horizon. With flashlights in hand, we loaded up our generators and prepared to leave. With a mischievous smile, Dad put the proper signage on the trucks indicating the type of fuel each carried, as if there were any chance of getting a citation.

"Oh, wait a minute," my dad said. "I need to get something out of the building over there." He looked over at Mom. "Victoria, can you drive me over there then come back here?" She nodded, and they hopped into the van and made their way to the building.

Father Jay and I looked at each other questioningly. A couple of minutes later, my mom returned. Then we saw my dad driving a forklift with a pallet stacked with red jugs back to our location. The large plastic jugs had "Sta-bil" printed on them.

"Hold the flashlight for me," he said. I held it while he read the back of the jug. "Yeah, that'll work," he mumbled to himself. He looked up. "Okay, John, climb to the top of the tank and pour this half of the pallet into the diesel." He handed me the jug. "And I'll put this half of the pallet into the gasoline."

He must have noticed the questioning look on my face. "Okay," he explained, "these fossil fuels degrade over time." He pointed over at the tanker that he would be driving. "Especially if it has any ethanol in it. These will help to stabilize the fuel for storage." He scratched his head. "We might be able to get these to last for two years if we are lucky."

I dutifully climbed up to the top of the tanker that I would be hauling, opened the top latch, and poured the contents of the fuel stabilizer. Mom handed the red jugs up to me, and I poured them into the tank. Father Jay handed the other jugs to my dad. As I poured jug after jug into the tank, I reflected upon what my dad had said: *No one is processing fuel. If what my dad said is true, in about two years' time, we may not be able to drive any vehicles that run on fossil fuel.* A felt a knot well up in my stomach at the uncertainty of our future.

The truck and trailer Dad was driving was filled with gasoline. The set I was driving was filled with diesel. Father Jay and my mom took the van. *That is just like my dad to take the tanker with the more flammable liquid in it, in case anything was to happen.*

I led the way, and my dad followed while my brother and Mom took up the rear in the van. It was very dark. There were no streetlights lighting our way. However, there did seem to be a slight glow coming from the city—probably from the fires. It was a surreal feeling. It seemed like we were driving down a deserted freeway in the open plains, but we were in the middle of the city. There were no house lights, streetlamps, or anything—only the light from our headlights and the light of the half moon. We felt like we were all alone in the world. *Maybe we were.* Perhaps that is why Dad and I kept talking with each other over the CBs. We had to be watchful because we could very easily find a rogue car in the middle of the highway from someone who didn't have the presence of mind to pull to the side of the road as they choked to death on red foam.

Once on the freeway, however, we saw a few signs of life in Portland. We saw a couple of men and a woman with flashlights on the other side of the freeway. They seemed to be searching the cars parked on the other side. Then they turned their lights toward us, and then, strangely, they turned them off. We couldn't clearly see anything. We wanted to stop, but we had a very uneasy feeling about them. I said over the CB, "Just go, Dad, I don't like it. We can't tell if they have guns or even who they are. Mom and Father Jay will follow us."

That was all the urging that my dad needed to hear; he felt the same way as I did. We just kept driving. I am sure that everybody else felt as guilty as I did about not stopping, but it seemed like the only safe thing to do.

After another twenty minutes of driving, we saw the lights of several vehicles coming toward us from the opposite direction on the freeway. As they got closer, I could see they were military Hummers and SUVs. When they saw us, a couple of the vehicles slowed down and climbed the grass median that separated the north and south-bound lanes. One of them even ran into the median cable fence that separated the two lanes as though he was going to turn around and chase us. The other stopped short of the cable fence. I could see silhouettes of men standing in front of the headlights. It looked like they were holding rifles. I was sure they were going to start taking shots at us as we passed by. I can't be sure, but it seemed like one of the men grabbed a hold of their rifles and pushed them up away from us. Perhaps he thought it was best not to shoot at something that might be carrying thousands of pounds of flammable liquid.

I yelled into the CB, "Don't stop! Don't stop! Keep going!" And I saw Father Jay drive the van on the other side of our tankers to keep the tanker between the van and the men with guns. Thankfully, none of the men took any shots. We could see in the side mirrors that the men had reversed their vehicles back on to the freeway, and judging from the taillights, they kept heading toward Portland.

I thanked God that they kept on going because I had no idea of their intentions. We continued on our way. We didn't see any more life along the highway, but as always, there were stopped and crashed cars everywhere along the highway. One car had smashed into the median safety fence and was somehow standing vertically, balanced on its front end; I thought that it was strange that I hadn't noticed it when we were coming the other direction. As we drove, our headlights would catch a glimpse of things spray-painted on the overpasses. Some of the writing was about the apocalypse being here; others had an artistic rendering of a red anvil. We could see that the body of one man was hanging by his neck with the other end of the rope tied to the fencing of the overpass. It was the perfect embodiment of the sin of despair. I guess that everything that had happened was too much for the poor man—at least I hoped some-one else hadn't done it to him. Now I am not saying that I think it is better if he hung himself; I just don't like the idea of someone else messing with peoples' necks.

When we reached the Woodburn exit, I thought I saw a couple of shining lights around where the Walmart was, but I couldn't be sure where the light had come from. Nonetheless, it was a clear sign that there was at least some human life around, but there was no way that we could know if it was human life that was respectful of humanity itself.

We were relieved to have finally made it back into our little town, Gervais. We parked the trucks, unloaded the generators from the van, and put them in the gym at the school.

Dad said, "We'll hook these up in the morning."

Father Jay took the Blessed Sacrament into the church to place into the tabernacle. He noticed the tabernacle candle was burning low and replaced it. I wondered, *What will we do when those run out?*

It had been a productive yet depressing day. We were tired both physically and emotionally, maybe more so emotionally. It was good to be back with our surviving family and our new home.

As we walked back toward the school, Chloe and Jared came out of the school and met us. I could see their silhouettes backlit from propane lanterns shining through the gym doors. Chloe said, "Hi, guys. We're glad you made it back. While you were gone, we found more survivors."

Dad said, "That's good. We were wondering how many people were really left. We met one in Portland, and we saw some kind of military convoy on the way back."

"And they didn't look friendly," my mom added.

We all followed Jared and Chloe into the school and along the checkerboard tile floor. With only the flashlight to show the way, the school felt like a haunted place with shadowy phantoms playing along the walls like mischievous children. We made our way to the combined fifth- and sixth-grade classroom. I could hear the steady hiss of the propane lantern as we entered the room. There were four newcomers inside sitting around the lantern: two men, a woman, and young girl about thirteen years old. Their shadows loomed large on the classroom walls. As we shared introductions, we discovered that the first man's name was Mario. Perhaps in his midfifties, he was a Hispanic man with salt-and-pepper hair and lean build which suited his five-foot-two frame. He wore a well-used gray sweatshirt and blue jeans. As I shook his hand, I could feel that it was thick and leathery. He had obviously done physical work most of his life. I briefly thought of the video game hero of the same name and wondered if this Mario had any Italian blood.

The second man, Ray, was probably in his midsixties; he was about six feet tall, thick with muscle, and looked like a biker. He smelled of leather, which was confirmed by his jacket and boots. He wore a red bandana on his head, which probably concealed a bald scalp, which he made up for by a long white beard and mustache, which was split by a ready smile. He had a rugged look about him, like he was ready for anything, which seemed incongruous to his fair freckled skin.

The woman, Gina, was in her early thirties; her dirty blue jeans and ripped red T-shirt covered her slim and perhaps emaciated build. Slightly taller than Mario, she looked to be about five-foot-four. She seemed to have a nervous habit of playing with her red ponytail. From her swollen left eye, it was obvious that she'd had a rough time of it lately. I immediately wondered if either of these men had done that to her. She was very quiet and was intently looking everyone over.

The young girl, Susan, was probably about five feet tall. She, too, was a skinny little thing wearing baggie green pants that were at least two sizes too large for her. She wore a large sweatshirt. She was standing close to Gina who was obviously her mother because she was the spitting image of her. She seemed to be favoring her right wrist, which was bruised. It was hard to be sure in the dim lighting, but she also seemed to have a bruise on her left cheek. Her unblinking gaze was fixed on the hissing light in the center of the room. Silent and tense, she reminded me of a startled deer—ready to bolt at a moment's notice.

Shortly after we met the newcomers, Chloe brought them into the gym and made introductions with the rest of the group. It felt like a camping trip with people gathered around gas-fed lights and sitting on folding chairs. I almost expected to see tents set up.

Karen came out of the kitchen and asked the newcomers, "Have you eaten yet?"

Our guests smiled, and Ray said in his big burly voice with a slight southern drawl, "No, but we would like to."

During the meal, I took Laura and Chloe aside and asked them to talk to Susan and Gina to find out if they needed first aid and how they got injured. I wanted to know if these men that were with them were dangerous. They said they would ask tactfully.

After dinner, Seamus and Phil took the opportunity to talk to the new people and see if they had any news. Ray said, "I heard that they were having another meeting at the capitol in two weeks." Then his smile faded as he continued, "There's this group of about fifteen men from North Salem who you've got to watch out for. They don't prepare like you all do. They just like to take from other people." He looked around the room at everybody gathered. "They've got guns and ammo and clubs, and they think that they can do whatever they want. I'll tell you what, keep your women and children away from the likes of them."

I looked over at the two ladies. They had their heads down and were looking at the table. They were definitely scared. Even hearing Ray tell the story seemed to put them into a melancholic mood.

Eli asked, "What kind of weapons do they have?"

Ray looked up as he tried to remember everything. "Yeah, they've got clubs, bats, and a few handguns. And they ain't afraid to use them."

Eli asked, "How did you come across them?"

Ray wiped his face with his hands. "I was riding my Harley away from the last meeting up in Salem there, and I ran out of gas. Gas ain't easy to come by these days. You can't just pull into a station anymore." He shrugged his shoulders. "So I was syphoning fuel out of this pickup truck and these guys came out of the neighboring houses. I figured, you know, they didn't need the gas anymore. It seemed everybody was dead. Well, at first I was happy to see other survivors, but then, they surrounded me, and they didn't look none too happy that I was there."

He shifted the bandana on his head and continued, "I apologized if I was taking their gas, but they didn't want to hear none of it. Then they took my bike and destroyed it with their pipes and clubs. Now I ain't a very fast man unless I am on a motorcycle, but I gave one of the guys a less-than-friendly shove, and I ran out there like bat outta…" He looked around and saw the kids listening to him, and he modified how he was going to end his statement. "Well, let's just say I didn't stick around. I took off and never looked back. I figure they got what they wanted. They scared an old man and took his stuff. So I just kept walking north away from Salem and eventually came to the town of Brooks."

He rubbed his leg a bit and continued his story, "So I walked to Highway 99 and stayed at the bar on the corner for a while. There was still some stuff in the fridge, so I've been eating okay. Well, so I met up with Mario the next day. I heard this strange noise, some kind of banging. I was half asleep. Mario was across the street trying to hot-wire a car in the parking lot. Then the car alarm was going off and woke me up. I was lying on the bar. I darn near fell off that thing. I'm too old to be sleeping in bars, let alone on bars. So I peeked out the window and took a chance. I yelled from a distance. We determined that we didn't mean each other no harm. So I tried to help him with the car. Between the two of us, it took like an hour to get the car running. We're terrible thieves."

Everyone laughed, and Mario added with his slight Spanish accent, "That's okay. It means we were honest before all this happened."

I was beginning to like these guys. I could tell that Ray liked to talk, and he could tell a good story. I knew that we needed to be cautious with strangers, though.

Ray said, "Funny thing is, they probably had all the car keys in the office on the lot. But neither of us thought of it."

Father Jay thought this was hilarious and was wiping tears of laughter out of his eyes as he tried to contain his laughter. I figured he was releasing some of the tension of the day.

Ray looked over, amused. "Well, anyway, we drove north on Highway 99 for a little while, probably only about four miles or so, and we came upon these two lovely ladies." He gestured over to Gina and Susan. "I saw one of them duck down behind a car. The other one was already hiding behind the car. I tried to convince them that we didn't mean them no harm, but...well...as you can see, I ain't the prettiest man in the world. And I look kinda rough, I suppose. But eventually, they came out to us. I think it was probably because Mario stepped out of the car. It ain't every day you see a biker and Mexican driving around together."

Father Jay snorted, "I'm sorry...I can't help it." He held his hand over his mouth, trying to hold it together. "Biker...and Mexican." Another little snort of laughter escaped his hand.

Pretty soon, Susan was smiling and sheepishly looking over at Father Jay while he was trying to keep his composure.

Ray looked over with a grin. "Hey, Padre, you are kinda takin' the solemnity out of my story here."

Then Susan snorted, allowing a little laugh to escape her mouth. She put her hand over her mouth. Her shoulders shook.

Ray lifted his eyebrow, and his eyes smiled. "Anyways, they were both kinda scared of us and didn't want our help until we all heard a few other motors coming down the road toward us. Well, the ladies quickly got into the car and told us to get off the road to hide. The ladies were obviously terrified. I could see they were a little beat up and had a right to be scared, so we drove up a driveway and parked near a house. I watched in the side mirror as four military Hummers drove by. From what I could see, there were several people in each of the Hummers, and they were probably armed."

Ray continued his story. "Well, after those guys had driven by, the ladies got out of the car. I could see that the least of their problems was that they had been smacked around. Now it ain't those bruises that I can see that I'm worried about for these ladies. It's the ones I can't see."

There was a period of uncomfortable silence. All we could hear was the steady hiss of the propane lanterns. Gina and Susan seemed to want to hide in the shadows. Laura broke the silence. "You are safe here and welcome to stay." Laura looked at Susan and asked, "Are you still hungry? We have plenty of food." The ladies nodded to her, and Laura motioned for them to follow her into the kitchen.

Phil stood up and stretched his legs a bit. He looked at the two men and said, "Well, you guys are welcome to stay in one of the rooms in the school or find one of the empty houses near the church and school. Now, we all pitch in around here, so if you do want to stay for any extended time, we'll need you to help out wherever you can."

Ray said, "I'm a retired army vet, and I worked on motorcycles for the past fifteen years. I'm not afraid of a little work."

Mario said, "I was a plumber. I've done it for fifteen years. I've also done a little bit of farming. But since I buried *mi familia…*" His voice trailed off as he hid his face in his hand.

Phil smiled and broke the awkward silence. "Well, if you guys are willing, we could use your skills, and we'd enjoy the company."

Gina and Susan had come out of the kitchen. Gina seemed to be munching on something. Gina said loudly, "You all seem like nice people. Maybe Susan and I should go. You see, it is my ex-husband that is the one that is after us, and you might be in danger if we stay."

I looked at her and asked, "What do you mean, Gina?"

Her voice broke, and she started to cry as she said, "He beat me and…and…our daughter!" Her voice went up an octave. "He's a monster, and I put him in prison. Now, somehow, he got out, and somehow, he survived this virus along with a bunch of his buddies. He's gotten out and is coming back for us! I know he's coming for us." Her voice dropped down to almost a whisper. "One of his men chased us in our minivan from Salem. He would have caught us, but his tire blew out, and he crashed. We would have kept going, but the motor died in the van near the Brooks exit.

I looked over at my mom. She was looking me. We remembered seeing that car chase.

Gina paused and took a breath and then continued in a more normal tone, "I think he's part of that terrible group of men at the capitol. They're most likely all from the prison. Some of his group came to a house where we were staying at in the Brooks area. I don't know how they found us, but they did. They broke in and beat us up. I screamed at the top of my lungs. They were dragging us out of the house! They were going to bring us back to him in those army trucks. Two strangers—I don't know who they were—saw them forcing us into the trucks, and they yelled, but my ex-husband and his gang started to shoot at them. While my ex's buddies were distracted by that, Susan and I ran for our lives. We were ducking and hiding for hours. Then Mario and Ray found us."

My brother-in-law, Eli, stood up, and in a deadly serious tone, said, "Like we said, you are safe here and can stay as long as you like. We protect our own." We all nodded in agreement.

Gina nodded and grabbed Susan and held her close to her side. They both sobbed in their embrace for half a minute. Then Laura guided them back into the kitchen.

Shortly after dinner, we all went to bed. We set up a temporary space for our new friends. We didn't even need to discuss it. We all knew that it was the right thing to do, and we were happy to help them out, but it seemed to me that our lives may have just gotten a lot more complicated.

*****

On Sunday, Father Jay celebrated Mass for all of us. Everyone was present, all twenty-eight of us. My oldest, Isaiah, assisted Father as a server. It was nice to have all the family gathered together. It was obvious that not all of our new guests were Catholic, but I think they joined us for some sense of normalcy.

After the Gospel was read, Father Jay spoke to us. It was the first homily that I had heard since the plague had come.

Father Jay stepped down in front of the altar. He looked around at each of us, and he began to speak: "My friends, we have gone through a lot in a very short period of time. These days have stretched us to the limit. We have seen too much death. I am sure that you have asked, like I have, 'Why is God allowing this to happen? Have we been abandoned?'

"In the mornings as I wake up, I hope that it all has been a nightmare, but it isn't a dream. It is real. One might be tempted to lose hope. I don't know why the Lord has allowed these things to happen, but what I do know is this: That our hope is in the Lord. He is Immanuel. God is with us.

"We look to the cross to teach us. As our Lord hung upon the cross, it seemed that all was lost. The One that was the hope of the Apostles, the promised Messiah, had been killed. But death and sin did not have the final word. Our Lord rose from the dead. So, my brothers and sisters, if you are tempted to lose hope, look to the cross. We are not abandoned. All is not lost. God is with us."

As the mass continued, we were heartened by Father Jay's words, and most of us received Holy Communion. As I knelt down to pray, I had a brief moment of peace. I knew that we had not been abandoned by God. I didn't know what was to come, but I knew that the Lord would give us the strength to continue.

7

Rebuilding

I will restore the fortunes of my people Israel, and they shall rebuild
the ruined cities and inhabit them; they shall plant vineyards and
drink their wine, and they shall make gardens and eat their fruit.

—The Book of the Prophet Amos 9:14

Our ragtag band of survivors spent much of the following day finding and cleaning up a few more houses for our new people. We set the two girls, Gina and Susan, up in a house of their choice; and Ray and Mario got along well so they took another house together. That night, we all gathered together in the gym like we had every other night since the virus, and we talked about our plans and needs.

Hannah spoke up, "We need to figure out how to get hot water and electricity, at least in the kitchen."

Dad put forth an idea: "I have a couple of ideas about the water supply. We know that there are some wells nearby. We could find a working pump and well and connect a transmission pipe into it. Maybe we could locate nearby wells at city hall if they kept paper records. If not, we could just look house to house. It would probably be a good idea to at least see what is available in the neighboring houses anyway."

I added, "Okay, that is good. We'll also want hot water…something beyond boiling it on the stove. So far, the natural gas keeps flowing, but for how long?"

"I've been thinking about that too," my dad said. "Of course, we can heat water on the woodstoves in the houses, but I was thinking something on a larger scale. The simplest way would be to get a large generator for power to the occupied houses. Then the electric water heaters already in the homes can heat the water. I mean, as long as the faucets keep flowing." He scratched his head. "I just realized that I have no idea where we get our water from and all the steps of how it gets to the faucet."

Mario smiled and said, "Yeah, we have taken a lot of things for granted, but I think that I can be of help there."

Unexpectedly, my oldest, Isaiah, piped up: "We could use solar panels."

We all looked over at him. Connor, with an amazed look on his face, said, "That…that is actually a really good idea, little professor." He ruffled Isaiah's hair. Then he looked up at the rest of the group. "I mean…we live in Oregon and have a lot of cloud cover, but if we had enough of them, it could be a great help." He sat up a little straighter. "In fact, I think we've all seen those solar panels at the I-5, I-205 junction just past Wilsonville."

Phil, who was a retired engineer, said, "Great idea!" He gave Isaiah a quick smile. Isaiah beamed a smile back at his grandpa and his uncle. Phil continued, "Let's check out city hall and see if we can come up with some information on water wells and water mains."

Phil looked over at Connor and added, "Before you go running off to collect solar panels, especially ones that are currently being used, let's do some research. I don't know much about them, and I'd hate for you to get electrocuted trying to disconnect them."

Without missing a beat, Connor replied in mock exasperation, "Well, I am just totally *shocked* that you would even think that you would need to mention that!"

Everyone groaned at the bad pun, so I added, "Well, as *electrifying* as this conversation is…"

Eli slugged me in the arm. He smiled mischievously.

"Ouch!" I said as I rubbed my arm.

Eli stood up and said, "Speaking of electricity, if we hook a generator up to the city hall electrical system, I might be able to get into their computer's system. I work on computers for a living, you know…well, at least I did before all this happened." He shrugged.

Ray, who had been uncharacteristically quiet, spoke up. "I've been thinking things over while you all were talking. I'm very glad to be with you all. I don't know if it is my place to say so, being so new to this community and all…" He paused and rubbed his chin. "Well, in light of the problems in Salem and the scary folks we saw…" He gestured toward Mario and Susan and Gina. "I think we really need to be thinking about security. You have such easy access to the town here." He looked around. "I mean, look, we just walked right into town and knocked on the door."

Seamus nodded and grunted. "Sure, I agree. Thanks for bringing it up, Ray. I've been wondering about this too." He looked around the room. "We have to decide. Do we want to advertise that we are here, or do we try to live under the radar?"

I sighed. They were right. This is a whole new world, a dangerous world. We were on our own.

Karen spoke up. "I think we need to welcome people. We need to start over, rebuild society."

This brought up a heated discussion in the group. It seemed that about half the group wanted to advertise that we were here, even placing signs on the freeway advertising our presence. The other half of the group wanted to do just the opposite. They wanted to remove any signs along the roads or highways that mentioned our little town of Gervais.

It was Phil who proposed a kind of middle ground. "Okay, everybody, how about we do this…" He held up his hand, and everyone quieted down. "Okay, I agree that we are going to be rebuilding society, but we need to be cautious, so let's start out that way. Let's get settled ourselves and then look at the question again in the future. There are a lot of unknowns. I say we take the most prudent and cautious course first. Then we can slowly allow ourselves to be known."

I thought, *What he says makes sense. We don't need to have everything figured out yet, but being cautious in the beginning is a sound idea.*

Almost everyone nodded in agreement. I think this moment strengthened the impression that Phil was the default leader of our little community, at least when consensus was difficult.

It was settled then. Eli, Phil, and Mario would go to city hall in the morning, and then they would swing by the library to see if there was information on solar panels. We decided that Dad, Chloe, Laura, and Judy would continue to explore the houses in the neighborhood near the school and church. They would look for candidate wells and anything else of use. Seamus, Connor, Jared, Ray, and I decided that we would split into two scouting parties to see how we could make a safer perimeter around our entire community. Father

Jay and the remaining crew decided that they would stay behind to take care of some things around church, tend to the animals, and keep an eye on the kids.

As I walked back to the house with the family, I had a renewed sense of hope. We had a plan. We were working together.

The following morning, we all went to our assigned duties. My group did its best to secure the roads into town. We spent most of the day finding keys or hot-wiring cars and making roadblocks with them. Then we disabled the cars to make them harder to remove, everything from pulling the batteries and spark plugs to flattening the tires and syphoning the gas.

There are only four main roads into town, so we blocked two of them completely. For the other two, one north and one south, we made makeshift rolling roadblocks. We moved a large broken-down farm truck to block one lane and a drivable car to block the other. We then made a couple of makeshift bunkers out of dirt and rocks with the backhoe. We put these bunkers off to the side about two hundred yards back with a good vantage point.

The biggest and most obvious security problem was the east entrance into town. It connected to the highway, and we had to block many of the side streets. By the time we were finished, we were satisfied that if anyone drove down any of the main roads, they would eventually see a roadblock and be discouraged. The plan was to give us a chance to arm ourselves quickly if needed. We knew that there were already two aggressive groups not too far away—one was in north Salem and the other at the capitol. We hoped that we would stay off their radar. We also hoped all these precautions would be unnecessary. But I had a feeling of foreboding that it was only a matter of time before our fortifications would be tested.

We all met at the school gym later that evening. Each of us had things to share with the entire group.

Unfortunately, the group at City Hall was not able hack into the computers, but they did find printed drawings of the town's water and sewer systems. They also located records of wells that had been drilled within the town in the form of well drilling permits. Eli discovered the location of the police chief's house from mail on his desk. He sent Mario to fetch his keys from the house and, if necessary, off his corpse. They stopped by the police station and took the firearms and ammunition that were stored there. They were thankful no one was in the jail cell.

Phil's group also had been able to find some information on solar panels at the library. They weren't sure yet what it would take to produce and store solar power, but they were excited about the prospect.

Later, the house-to-house reconnaissance group relayed their findings to the rest of us and presented the lists they had made. They found several more houses with fireplaces; some even had gas stoves. They also collected all the firearms and ammunition they found during their search. They also grabbed canned foods and other supplies for canning. They proudly pointed to the stack of weapons and food that they brought back.

They also told us the stench in some of the houses was so unbearable no one could live in those places. There was evidence that animals trapped inside the houses had been eating of some of the bodies. The group kept a list of these homes so we could later bury or burn those bodies. It was intimidating because we knew that there was no way we could bury all of them.

Father Jay interrupted at this point. "I know that the idea is that we bury the bodies, but under the circumstances, it might be better if we incinerated them instead. Although we all seem to be immune to the virus, burying hundreds of dead bodies could contaminate the ground water. I don't know, I'm no expert on these things. There is not a moral problem with this given our circumstances, even though the Church prefers burial. We could, perhaps, put all of the bodies in a house or a barn and burn everything at once…well, after we do a kind of group funeral for them." He paused. "Still, it's definitely not an ideal scenario."

Everyone agreed this was our best option, so we decided where best to put all of the bodies and how we might mark the site as a grave. One concern we had, however, was whether a burning house might draw attention to us, but we decided we would need to take that chance.

It was agreed that Mario, because of his experience, would be heading up the water project, working with Phil and my dad. While my dad wasn't a registered engineer like Phil, he had a lot of experience and skill with welding and metal fabrication that would be invaluable; plus, he was just a good problem solver. They figured they would need the backhoe and the portable generators. The plan was to hook the generators up to the houses to give them enough power to pump the water from the wells. It would probably take a couple weeks or so to get it all working.

We decided that for the next couple of days we would focus on the grim work of clearing bodies out of the houses. We gathered respiratory protection masks, paint suits, and safety glasses and rubber gloves collected during one of our "shopping sprees" in Woodburn. We went from house to house and loaded bodies that were in various stages of decomposition on the large flatbed. We found a suitable house on the outskirts of town, which didn't have any trees, vegetation, or buildings around it; and we put all the bodies into the house. Each house we entered that contained corpses was a kind of horror show, and even with the respiratory masks, the stench was gut-wrenching. We did our best to space the bodies around the house chosen for cremating the bodies, but in the end, we needed to stack bodies on top of each other.

After all the bodies were placed in the house, Father Jay celebrated a funeral mass outside the house on a makeshift altar. We all gathered with great solemnity. At some point during the mass, he walked around the outside of the house and sprinkled it with holy water, blessing it to make it holy ground. At the end, he lit incense and swung the thurible as he walked around the house singing, "In Paradisum." I caught a whiff of the incense as he loaded it into the thurible; it smelled sweet. It occurred to me that, before the days of embalming, incense would be useful in covering over the stench of dead bodies, or body odor of the living, for that matter. When Father finished incensing, he said the final prayers and gave us the final blessing. Father nodded his head to the men of our group holding the gasoline cans. Jared donned his respiratory mask and went inside the house to douse it and its deceased occupants with the flammable liquid. When he exited, the rest of men splashed gasoline and other flammable liquids on the side of the house. My dad poured a trail of gasoline to where the rest of us stood. Father Jay took one of the candles from the altar and lit the trail of gasoline. The line of liquid quickly ignited and rushed forward to the house.

Everyone backed up and took a position behind the vehicles parked along the side of the road, unsure how the fumes trapped inside the house might ignite. The house was quickly engulfed in flames. The front door had been left open, and we saw the darkness within illuminated. There did seem to be one quick puff out of the door which shook the windows when the fumes ignited, but the windows did not break. We watched as the house was soon engulfed entirely in flames. Soon the heat became too intense, even from the distance to where we had retreated. We all got into our cars and pulled away as Father Jay quickly threw the makeshift altar into the back of a truck.

The house burned for several hours and was still smoldering the next day. We were thankful the wind, for the most part, was blowing away from our homes. Nonetheless, occasionally we still caught the changing odors of toxic fumes that were reminiscent of burning plastic, campfire, and, more disturbingly, a barbecue. I was grateful when it started to rain which helped clean the air and extinguished the lingering embers.

8

Peaceful or Hostile

We cannot be ruled by fear! We have to be better than that!

—Leah McHale

Time passed. Hours turned into days, and days turned into weeks, and weeks into months. Summer had become fall. The leaves on the trees turned various shades of red and yellow. Our days blended together; one day seemed indistinguishable from the next. We worked, ate, slept, and prayed. And sometimes played. But along the way, our ties to one another grew stronger, and communal memories were formed and recounted.

I've often thought that if extraterrestrial beings existed, and if they were watching humanity from afar, they would probably notice that we are quite adaptable. Humans are able to live in some of the most inhospitable climates, from the heat of harsh deserts to the cold of the arctic. Thankfully, our part of the world was mild in comparison to those extremes. We adapted.

No longer were there movies, television, sports, or other such diversions to occupy our time. We worked the fields and took turns hunting for supplies. We became more attuned to our surroundings, to the silence, and to nature. We were more attuned to our thoughts and our feelings. Often, it was the children that were the evening entertainment. They would put on plays and reenact movies they had seen. Father Jay would bring out his guitar, and we would sing songs of praise. Our schedule seemed to be more in tune with nature since artificial light was more difficult to maintain in the evenings. Work ceased when night came.

That isn't to say that we gave up on technology completely. We now had our new water system operating because the town's external water supply had failed long ago. We had generators set up to use electricity when necessary. We had scavenged the freeway solar cells and were able to run various electronic appliances that didn't always require the generators to run.

Often, we listened to the radio. The FM stations were dead, but we did find limited programming on the AM stations. There seemed to be only a couple of stations broadcasting anything. In fact, there seemed to be only one station transmitting anything intelligible. Most were static or nothing at all, and others seemed to be transmitting sporadic bursts of Morse code or an apparent list of random numbers.

My oldest son, Isaiah, was fascinated by these transmissions and actually began to teach himself Morse code, trying to understand what was being transmitted. It turned out that many of the messages in Morse code were a series of numbers for some unknown purpose. The one station that was intelligible had a recording that was repeated over and over again; it was some kind of public service message. It told us that the death toll was estimated to be 95 percent of the world's population; although it seemed higher in our part of the world. It gave public service warning of the many diseases associated with coming into contact with dead bodies. The information also confirmed what Father Jay had proposed, recommending that we burn the corpses instead of burying them.

The recording was updated from time to time, and it spoke of a few known surviving groups in the United States and what were called "free zones." These free zones were bases run by the military that would protect and help any survivors that came along. They made it clear, however, that no freeloading would be tolerated; people living there had to earn their keep.

These recordings also listed off groups and free zones state by state. Within each state, the announcer listed surviving groups town by town. Unfortunately, even these free zones were not immune to conflict. The recording told about cities with different groups fighting and warned its listeners to stay away. It was nice to hear that others had survived, but we couldn't understand why everyone was fighting.

For some reason, terrorist groups seemed to be targeting these free zones. *Why? What more do they want? Aren't they satisfied that 95 percent of the world's population is dead?* I was anxious to hear if there was now a free zone in Oregon, but there wasn't one mentioned. Apparently, there were no free zones in Washington, Idaho, or Montana either. The closest one was in Los Angeles.

The broadcast spoke of several small groups that had formed in central eastern Oregon around Bend. Also, Portland had four main groups, but all of these groups were reported as hostile. The announcement continued and said that Salem has two main groups and one smaller group.

Then the announcement said Woodburn and Gervais each had a smaller group. We were speechless for a few moments. We all had the same question in our minds: *How did they know about our group in Gervais?*

I was unnerved. *Didn't they know that by broadcasting our where-abouts, they were putting us in danger? They must have been tracking all of this by satellite because I hadn't seen a single plane flying since the virus.*

When the announcement got to the end of the list a few minutes later, it recommended that all should travel to a free zone for safety. It recommended staying in groups for safety. The recording would then repeat the same thing day and night. It did, however, change slightly every few days. We decided at least one person would listen each day for updates. We had a meeting that night and talked about the information heard on the radio.

Phil said, "Well, if anyone else heard this, then they know for sure that we're here. We also know there is another possible friendly group in Woodburn. Should we contact them?" He looked around. "If you have suggestions, please speak up."

Connor stood up and said, "I think it's worthwhile to contact the group in Woodburn." Most everyone murmured agreement.

Then Father Jay spoke up. "But what if they are not the nice group of people we hope they are? Then they'll know for sure that we are here."

Then Phil said, "Well, if they've been listening to the recording, they probably already know that we are here. Besides, it is hard to imagine that we haven't been seen at some point during our trips into Woodburn."

Father Jay nodded, and Phil continued, "I'll go with a couple of volunteers once we decide what we are going to say to them. There could be an advantage to increasing our numbers."

Dad stood up and said, "There may be other people that will make their way here who want join the group. How do we deal with that?" He looked around at everybody. "I need to know what our consensus is because my first inclination will be to scare them off."

Karen said, "I think we should let anyone in who seems genuinely kind as long as they are willing help out and do their part. Maybe we could put them on a probationary period and keep an eye on them." Everyone agreed that was a good approach for now.

Time was now passing quickly, and it seemed that everything was coming together for our little community. I reflected how fortunate we were that we hadn't yet encountered any major problems, but the radio broadcasts made it clear that we needed to be thinking hard about security.

One afternoon, Gina addressed us all directly: "We need guards. There are bad people out there." She turned to hug Susan. I noticed that everywhere Gina went Susan followed. They were inseparable. The poor things were more screwed up than most of the people we met from outside our family. They had seen and experienced some terrible things. I hoped that in time they might be able to live normal lives—well, as normal as possible under the circumstances—but all this death and the threat of imminent violence were not helping us feel secure.

In any case, I had the sense that Gina was holding back important information; I could feel it. I figured, however, that everyone is entitled to their secrets as long as those secrets didn't compromise our safety.

After some discussion, we agreed to post regular guards. I spoke up and said, "I'll take the night watch. I'm used to staying up anyway."

Jared said, "And I'll join you. I think we need at least two people on watch at all times."

"It would be nice to have more, but our group is small," I said.

When the meeting was over, Jared and I loaded our rifles and handguns. We grabbed our two-way radios and tested them. Then we put some spare batteries in our pockets.

Karen said that she would stay up and listen for the radio. My two boys, Isaiah and Elijah, came with me to guard for a while. Jared went with his wife, Chloe, to the other side of town to keep watch. After a couple hours, my boys got bored and tired, so I sent them back to bed. Thankfully, the night was uneventful; Jared and I got relief from Connor and Seamus in the morning.

Security was now a priority. Soon, we had regular shifts assigned for guard duty. We felt we had done all that we could do. The roads were blocked, and we had good firing positions and even backup firing positions in case we were overwhelmed. I suppose it wasn't a good sign that I *already* felt overwhelmed, but we adapt as best we can.

One morning, a moving truck stopped in front of the north rolling roadblock, and Connor radioed in for help. Within moments, we had seven rifles pointed at the moving truck. I yelled to the driver to get out. The driver was a female who looked to be around thirty years old with darker skin, maybe Hispanic or Asian. She looked familiar, and she recognized me.

She said, "John, it's me Gabriella Stetson, Carter's wife."

I hadn't expected to see her here. I hadn't even thought about Carter or Gabriella in a long time. Gabriella had moved here from the Philippines to marry Carter, a guy I worked with at the rental yard.

I said to the rest of the group, "It's okay, I work...I mean...I used to work with her husband Carter." We all lowered our weapons. I looked at Gabriella and asked, "Did Carter make it?"

Then I heard a loud "Yes, I did" behind us. When we turned around, we found that Carter had sneaked up behind us. He was holding some kind of military-style shotgun. He smiled. "You might want to keep an eye on the railroad tracks too." I greeted him and his wife with a welcoming hug. He looked at me and said, "Somehow I knew you would make it. You are too stubborn to die."

"It must have been the flu we got a while back. It's the only thing that makes sense," I said.

He looked down at the rifle in his hand. "I don't know, but I'm just glad that I'm still upright." He looked me in the eye and asked, "Is your family…ahh…okay?"

I smiled. "Yes, we're all okay." I looked at him and his truck. "We've got plenty of room, if you want to stay with us."

Flashing his teeth in a grin, he said, "I was hoping you would say that. My son and daughter are here too." Cassie, his eighteen-year-old daughter, moved out from behind a car. She was five-foot-ten and wearing a full camo suit. She had dark hair that was tied back, presumably to keep it out of her eyes if she had to do some shooting. Her eyes seemed to smile behind her black-rimmed eyeglasses. She had been covering Carter and Gabriella with the Winchester .30-30 she was cradling. I heard someone coming up from behind us. It was Carter Jr.—we called him CJ at work—his fifteen-year-old son. He was about six-feet tall and skinny as a rail. His face was painted in camo green, black, and brown. His hair was the same dark brown as his father's, but without the gray highlights. I immediately noticed the AR-15 he was holding. He also had on full camo gear. He had a big grin on his face probably because he knew they would have had the drop on us in a fight.

I was glad that I hadn't seen them. I'm not sure how I would have reacted if I had noticed them sneaking up on us. I looked around and said, "We could sure use your help."

Carter rubbed his head and looked at our fortifications. "Great! I like the roadblocks, but we have a few holes to plug."

We all jumped as Connor started up the car that was blocking the road. He was moving it so that Gabriella could drive the truck in. Connor looked up and saw that we were all staring at him. "What?" he said. We all just laughed.

Carter started walking and waved for me to follow. "I have a surprise for you all." He led us around the back of his vehicle. He then opened up the back of his moving truck, and it was filled with guns, ammo, a little food, and camping supplies. "Help yourself," he said as he pulled out an AR-15 and handed it to me. I couldn't help but smile.

He said, "Here's the one you've been drooling over for years, and here are three magazines. Merry Christmas!"

I said, "God bless the gun collectors."

A short time later, we showed them a house they could stay in, and they immediately fit right into our little community. Carter took charge of our security and defenses. He had been a sniper in the Marine Corps at the tail end of the Vietnam War. I was so glad that he was here with us. I had known him now for a few years, and he was a good friend. It was nice to have another familiar and trusted face to whom I could entrust the lives of my family.

9

An Interlude of Fun

A glad heart makes a cheerful countenance, but
by sorrow of heart the spirit is broken.

—Proverbs: 15:13

I used to dream of winning a shopping spree on a game show. Our time after the virus could have been exciting like that, but the problem was that society's infrastructure didn't exist anymore. There was no electricity coming to the houses without starting a generator first. Mobile phones were useless. There was no Internet. Food spoiled and water stored in containers didn't stay fresh.

I was reminded of an old *Twilight Zone* episode where a bookworm of a man finds that all the people in the world are gone, and he has a library to himself. It is like heaven to him until he breaks his glasses and cannot read any of the books that he desires.

But if there is at least one advantage to having most of the population dead, it is that you can have just about any new or classic car that you want. For a brief time, we did drive the cars of our dreams. It was a fun moment in otherwise dismal circumstances.

It was merely a matter of going to the right dealership or going to the right showroom, and whatever car you desired was there for the taking.

My dad and I had decided that it was time to have a little bit of fun. It had been our turn for garbage duty, and we were just returning from the garbage dump in the outskirts of Woodburn. The old moving truck that we were driving had been loaded down with a month's worth of garbage, and we had just finished unloading the garbage and then squeegeed the brown and green sludge out of the back. Needless to say, the galoshes we wore stayed in the back of the truck and were used for nothing else.

It is easy to take for granted, I suppose, the ability to merely take garbage out to the curb and have somebody else take it away for you. We didn't have that luxury anymore. We had to take care of it on our own. Our group tried to minimize the garbage. We burned what paper and cardboard we could, and we composted what we could, but there was still a lot of garbage to be disposed of. We had decided that it was best to use the dumps that had existed before the virus, hoping that we would not attract dangerous animals looking for an easy meal. We had noticed during our trips to the dump that bear populations had grown, and there were a lot of stray dogs and cats; we even saw a cougar.

We decided that after having cleaned out the back of the old moving truck, it was time for a little fun. We pulled into one of the car dealerships in Woodburn. We could see the golden Chevrolet logo above the showroom doors.

We got out of our old, smelly truck and walked to the front glass doors of the building. There was a handwritten sign taped to the inside of door that read, "Closed due to illness." The once-manicured lawn was now tall brown grass, except for a few green weeds. The new cars in the lot had a light covering of dust on them. It was clear that no one had been around for a while. Nevertheless, I knocked loudly on the door and waited. To no one's surprise, no one came.

My dad picked up one of the decorative bricks that lined the lawn; he hefted it up and down, testing the weight of it. I stepped back. He threw it at the glass door. The silence was broken with the sound of glass shattering into a thousand little pieces. A startled pheasant flew out of the tall grass, which startled us. The door had obviously been constructed out of safety glass, which meant there was less of a chance of us getting cut as we entered through the door. With the sound of glass crunching under our feet, we climbed through the door, ducking under the push bar. We made our way through the showroom past a Camaro painted metallic green as we moved toward the back offices. With a little searching in the offices, we found the right one—the one with the key box. The only illumination in the office was the light bleeding through hanging blinds. I pulled the string that turned the louvers to let in some light. The key box was locked, of course, but it looked like it was made with flimsy enough metal that we could get into it easily enough.

Dad said, "I'll get the sledgehammer." He turned and left. I could hear his footstep crunch the broken glass as he went out the front door.

I took the opportunity to look around the office. On the walls were various images of classic Chevys. There was a desk in the center of the room with a rolling chair tucked under it. On the other side of the desk were a couple of plush chairs where prospective customers could sit and be convinced how much they needed a new vehicle.

The desk had a sleek looking computer on it and a pen. A picture of a smiling woman holding a freckled little boy with a big grin was sitting on the corner of the desk, obviously the family of the man who had worked here. I tried not to think about their fate.

On a whim, I looked in the top drawer of the desk and found the key that opened the key box. I had it open before my dad returned with the sledgehammer.

When he returned and saw the open box, he sighed. "Well, I guess that I got a little extra exercise for the day anyway." He set the sledgehammer on the desk.

I said, "The box is attached firmly to the wall, so I think we'll need to find the cars we like and come back to get the keys." I looked over at him.

He put on his reading glasses and began fingering through the keys and reading the tags. "I wish we had more light." He grunted. "I should have thought to bring a flashlight."

With a flourish, I held up a little pen light and said, "Ta-da!" I flicked on the light.

He gave me a nod of gratitude. "I'll bet," he said, "this is the key to that metallic green Camaro in the showroom, but I don't really feel like trying to get it out of the building." He squinted. "It looks like there's another one on the lot—a black one!" He smiled and grabbed the key.

But I had my eye on another key. The tag read, "Corvette ZR1." I grabbed the key and followed my dad out of the offices and into the showroom.

My dad found a beautiful new Camaro out in the lot. Despite the dust, it was a nice shiny black. It had the look of real muscle car; plus, it was a convertible.

My choice looked like a sleek race car. It was firetruck red, and it looked fast. It even had a spoiler on the back.

I opened the door and got in. I started it up and revved the engine; it sounded like a banshee screaming. It was glorious.

As I let the Corvette warm up, I walked over to the black Camaro. My dad had started it up and had just hit the button for the convertible top to start folding itself into the back. He had a big grin on his face as he revved up the engine. His engine had a deeper growl to it. "You wanna race?" he said with a mischievous glint in his eye. He revved the motor, punctuating the challenge.

I looked back at the sleek red Corvette. I smiled. "Are you sure that you want to race against *that* red beast over there?"

He nodded, put the car in reverse, and backed out of the parking spot; then he drove over to the ZR1. I followed him over on foot. He put the car in park and got out to look at the interior of the ZR1. As I walked up to him, he whistled, "That is an awfully fast-looking car." He turned to look at me. "Let's see what they can do!"

We pulled out of the lot and found a nice stretch of freeway that was clear of any cars, and we lined up next to each other. He revved his engine, and I revved mine. The engines roared at each other a couple more times. We made sure that we were strapped in tight. Then with a smile on his face, my dad counted down with his fingers. When he had counted down to one, we hit the gas.

My engine roared, but my tires broke loose and spun ineffectively as my dad shot forward like a rocket, his silver hair flapping in the wind. After I let up on the gas, I followed behind him. About a mile down the road he stopped, and I pulled up beside him. I could see him looking over at me and laughing. He got out of the car with his shoulders shaking with laughter as he walked over to me. His hair was a mess. I rolled down the window. He said, "Oh boy, Johnny, that is a fast car!" He pointed with his thumb behind himself and chuckled. "Somehow, I knew that you would spin the tires on the takeoff, so I took it easy. Oh, that was so funny!" He wiped his forehead and smoothed his hair back. "Okay, let's do it again!"

I couldn't help but smile at how much he was enjoying this. This had been a challenging time for all of us. It was nice to let off a little steam. I watched as my dad walked around the front his car, got in, and started buckling himself in again.

This time, I was ready. My dad held up his hand. Three...two... one! Our engines roared, and we were off. This time, I got traction. I was thrown back into the seat from the force of the acceleration, but I was ready for it. *Clutch, shift, gas...clutch, shift, gas.* I think I must have hit 60 mph in under four seconds, and I was increasing speed by the second. When I hit 100 mph, I let off the gas and slowed down. Then my dad shot past me. As much as I would have liked to have taken the car to its limit, prudence and maybe a little fear prevented me from doing so.

He slowed down, and I pulled up beside him again. This time I was laughing. I slapped the steering wheel and smiled at him. He had a wide grin on his face.

We raced back and forth a couple more times. We swapped cars and did it again. Then we got into the ZR1 together, and we pushed it to the limit—not the limit of what the car could do, but the limit to how fast we were willing to go.

But all good things must to come to an end. It was a good day. It would not be the last time that some of us would take advantage of the opportunity to drive some fast cars. With the fun concluded, we made our way back to the dealership and grudgingly climbed back into our stinky old garbage truck. If ever we did return to find a new car, we would probably have to find something a little more economical because fuel was hard to come by these days, and we needed to conserve it. So we dutifully left the cars parked in their spots and returned the keys to their box. We knew that we could find them again if ever we had a need for speed. Although we drove the truck at our usual speed returning home, it felt a lot slower than normal.

From time to time, someone in our group would mention that they had "a need for speed," and then we'd enjoy a little quality time on our stretch of highway that we nicknamed the raceway.

10

Problems

I like quick and easy solutions. I like to solve problems,
but people are complicated and not easily solved.

—Carter Stetson

I've often wondered what forces bring people together and what splits them apart. Is it chance? Is it God's providence? I have discovered that they show up at precisely the right or wrong time, whether for good or for bad. I don't know the reason, but they always bring change.

During the next week, several more people joined our group. As we had feared, word had gotten around that we were in Gervais. They had heard about us on the radio. The first to arrive was an older couple, Henry and Mabel Collins. They looked to be in their midsixties; both had hair that had silvered with age, which was in stark contrast to their black skin. Both seemed healthy and physically able to help out. Henry was a retired railroad engineer. His wife Mabel had been a receptionist, retired from the same railroad company. They seemed a nice couple, and it wasn't long before we discovered that they loved to play cribbage. I thought Henry could be of great use if we ever needed to use the locomotive parked nearby.

Not everyone, however, fit into our group as easily as the Collinses.

A few days later, another man walked up to the roadblock and was greeted by Carter's son, CJ (short for Carter Junior) who was holding a rifle while on guard duty. This newcomer was a scruffy-looking fellow. He looked as though he had been wearing the same jeans for months. He hadn't shaved in some time, and he smelled terrible. That was bad enough, but his attitude stunk as well. He was indignant toward CJ.

Carter and I walked up to join his son. The man asked, "Who is this snot-nosed kid with a gun?" He didn't want to let us frisk him, but Carter made the choice clear. "Be frisked, or be gone!" The man reluctantly allowed us to frisk him. I must admit that I was reluctant to even touch him; the smell was potent. He had a rather large knife along with a small .22 pistol. We put his weapons on the hood of the car. In addition, Carter found a syringe and some drug paraphernalia. I suppose I shouldn't have been surprised to see a drug addict among the survivors. *These are depressing times, and many people are looking for an escape.*

However, I didn't like the idea of a drug addict in our community. Besides, after Carter and I questioned the man separately, neither of us had a very good feeling about the guy. There was just something off about him. He had a kind of crazy glint in his eye. CJ watched him while Carter and I compared notes. We decided that the stories that he had given each of us didn't quite match up. Carter and I decided to send CJ back to the camp to get some food and water for the man.

When he saw the food, he knew we weren't going to let him in. Carter emptied the bullets out of the man's .22 pistol and handed the bullets to him. He stuffed his pockets and grabbed his knife and pistol. His demeanor escalated from a guy with an attitude to furious instantly, and he began yelling and cussing us out. Carter took a step forward and pulled his rifle off his shoulder and cocked it. An unused bullet was ejected as another one slammed into the chamber. The man stopped talking, grabbed his food, pocketed his knife and pistol, and turned to walk away.

I said, "What a waste." Carter looked at me like I was nuts.

I said, "No, you dropped a perfectly good unused bullet."

Carter started laughing. "Yeah, that was for effect," he said as he reached down to pick up the ejected round.

"Hey, it was a good effect," I said. Then I looked over at Carter's son. "You did well too. Don't sweat what that jerk said. We wouldn't have you doing guard duty if we didn't trust you."

He just smiled and said, "Thanks."

Later that night, someone sneaked past one of our guards. Karen was in the gym taking inventory of our stored food when she heard something outside and looked up. She saw a strange man looking in one of the windows. She screamed and then radioed the guards. The guards on duty stayed in their positions, like we practiced. But I got out of bed along with the other men, and we grabbed our rifles. The man sprinted behind the school into the ball field, scaring the horses. I just caught sight of him as he climbed the fence and ran through the fields. He was heading toward Eli's house. Jared took off after the man. Jared hopped over the six-foot fence like it was nothing. He could have caught the man in no time, but he was being cautious. The problem was, we didn't know whether the man was armed or not. I called to Eli on the radio to let him know the man was coming toward his house, and Jared was hot on his heels. The rest of us stayed at the school and checked the surrounding area for any other unwanted visitors.

A short time later in the distance, we heard someone yell, "Stop or I'll…" The words were interrupted by a gun shot. Dad, Phil, and Connor jumped into Connor's car and sped off to Eli's place. I called on the radio, but no one answered.

Many possible scenarios went through my head, few of them pleasant. I feared that Eli or Jared had been shot. The sound of the shot seemed to just echo in my head. Another frightful image going through my imagination was of Leah or their child, Conrad, being hurt or killed. I prayed that they would be fine as I searched around the school and neighboring houses. Once our area was determined to be secure, I called on the radio to say we were clear. Now we all waited with great anticipation to find out what happened at Eli's place.

By this time, we were all gathered around the two-way radio, our eyes trying to pierce the darkness looking out toward Eli's place. We were praying that everyone was okay. Common sense told us that we wouldn't be able to see anything in the darkness, but we couldn't help but direct our eyes toward Eli's house. It was probably only about ten minutes, but it felt like hours as we waited for some news as to what had happened. *Is he holding them hostage?*

We are all jumped when the radio beeped. Then I heard Phil's voice. "Everybody is okay." We breathed a collective sigh of relief.

As Phil relayed to me later, they had found Eli standing over the man's body. As Jared bent down to check for a pulse, Phil had asked, "Is anyone hurt?" Eli had responded that they were all okay, and when they had tried to confront the man, the guy had gone for a gun. It was then that Leah had to shoot him. Eli confirmed that it was the same man that had visited us earlier in the day. We were all sorry it turned out that way, but we were happy that Eli and his family were safe.

We now had our first encounter with violence and having to use deadly force, and unfortunately, it had to be sweet, mild-mannered Leah who had to kill to protect her family. *What kind of omen is this for the future?*

The men stayed up a few hours in order to bury the body.

Gina and Susan were huddled in their house scared half to death. They had heard the gun shot, and Gina thought that her ex-husband was here to take them back. My wife explained the situation to them and calmed them down.

I don't think that I slept a wink that night. I laid in my bed and stared at the ceiling. Every creak, scrape, or any other sound seemed to me to be an intruder. My imagination was playing tricks on me. My eyes were drawn to all the dark places, searching, until finally the sun came up and proved all my visions to be only phantoms.

The next morning, another man walked up to our guard position. My dad was on guard duty. He radioed back to camp. Phil and Connor came out and questioned the man. The man's name was Frank Tam, and he looked to be of Korean descent. Frank was thirty-nine years old, five-foot-seven, and in average shape. He had a 7mm rifle, which he surrendered to my dad on his arrival without protest. He was wearing hiking boots and blue jeans with a camouflage jacket. He told us he was a farmer and wished to join the group and said he would be happy to help out in any way needed. Phil and Connor took an immediately liking to him. He was introduced to the rest of the group and seemed to be a nice guy. He immediately understood our policy of the probationary period and that he wouldn't be allowed to be armed while in camp until the period was over.

"A reasonable precaution," he said. He informed us that he'd lost his family to the plague and had been wandering around, trying to figure out what to do next. It was another reminder of just how fortunate I was to still have my family. I lost much of my extended family, but I still had my immediate family and many others. With Frank's arrival, the population of Gervais rose to thirty-five.

When Frank heard that we were having Mass later that morning, he was overjoyed and attended with tears in his eyes. He made his responses in Korean, but I knew that he was going to fit in well with our group.

While I was on guard duty the following evening, a woman in her late twenties showed up at our blockade. She was a beauty, a fact not hidden by the camo pants and a thick black coat she wore. She had straight black hair and was petite. I was surprised because I didn't see or hear her until she was only thirty feet away. Luckily, she was not hostile because she could have easily had the drop on me. *Yikes! I'll have to be more aware of my surroundings.* She cleared her throat, and then I did see her; she raised her arms above her head and held the compound bow and quiver she was carrying in the air. Then she slowly set down her weapons and stepped away from them.

I told her that she needed to wait there until I could have another woman search her, and she appreciated that. I radioed to home base and had my wife and Chloe come to question her. My wife searched her while I held my weapon at the ready. After a long chat, we discovered that her name was Tina, and she was making her way to California to search for family. She just wanted to stay a couple of days before she moved on. Chloe and Laura decided to let her stay.

It is amazing how God's providence brings people together. After only a couple of days, Tina and the other new person, Frank, had hit it off well. They decided to head out together for California to search for living members of their families, as Frank had some extended family in California as well. They seemed to be good people and would have been great additions to our group, but they were in a hurry to find family. They decided to leave a week later and to head toward the LA free zone; Frank insisted that he wanted to leave after Sunday mass because he wasn't sure when he'd get another opportunity. It was sad for our group because they were so likable, and we would miss them.

It was kind of nice to see new romance budding in our community. However, it made me wonder, *Will my kids ever have that opportunity? What do their futures hold?*

It just so happened that in addition to joining us for mass on Sunday, Frank and Tina wound up staying longer to enjoy our celebration of Halloween—the eve of All Saints' Day—and then All Souls' Day the day after. The children were going to dress up in costumes and Father Jay recommended that they dress up as saints. Then the children went around the houses in our community and proudly showed off their costumes as the occupants gave them a piece of fruit or candy.

The following morning on Saturday, we celebrated a mass for All Souls'. Father Jay was always the most in tune with the calendar because he needed to keep track of the liturgical year. If it hadn't been for him, I don't think I would have even remembered what day of the week it was. This feast was especially poignant because we had lost many people who were close to us. It gave us the opportunity to mourn the loss of our loved ones and to offer prayers for the repose of their souls.

Although Frank and Tina had stayed with us for such a short time, Frank had been able to teach us a little bit about farming, and Tina had taught a couple of new recipes to the cooks. In addition, Tina had been an archery instructor. She taught anyone who was interested the basics in shooting a bow.

Since they were set on leaving, we warned them about the hostile groups in Salem. It turns out that Frank had been in the navy and figured that he could navigate his way south by boat up the Willamette River to try to sneak past the Salem group. That Sunday, we all went to the Willamette River to see them off.

On the way, Frank scanned the area and picked out an aluminum flat-bottom boat from a shed at a nearby farm. It had a Yamaha outboard with a jet drive—a good choice because of the debris in the river. It came complete with the additional gear needed to get them up the river. We topped off the fuel supply and gave them all the supplies the boat would safely carry.

We noticed that the water was a lot higher than normal. It had a stinking smell of death and feces. Actually, there was a time that this river had always smelled that way before it had been cleaned up; I suspected that the group to our south had been dumping the dead and sewage into the river, not caring about the contamination down river. There were more sticks and trees in it than normal too. *Probably all the rain we've had lately.* I warned Frank and Tina that the dams would not have had anyone maintaining them and that we had had heavy rainfall in the last few weeks. Frank was not worried about the water, just getting past Salem.

We said our goodbyes, and they sped off up the river toward Salem. They were waving goodbye and so were we. After they rounded the river bend, they were out of our sight. I could barely hear the motor. *Good*, I thought, *the motor is not too loud.* Their plan was to take it up to the Corvallis area and find a good vehicle to travel the rest of the way by land. "I hope they make it," I said under my breath and then turned it into a prayer.

A couple of days later, another young man wanted to join our group. His name was Jack Long. He was about twenty-five years old, white, and very skinny. He was about six-foot-two. He seemed harmless enough, even if he did have a cocky attitude, so we decided to allow him to stay with us, but letting him know it was on a probationary basis. For the time being, he would sleep in the common area at the school.

Seamus asked him what his abilities were, and Jack said he could do anything. We soon found out just the opposite was true. We tried to have him help with laying water lines, but he just got in the way. He tried helping with the animals, but Connor got tired of his negative and know-it-all attitude and ran him off. He tried to farm, but he said that it was too boring. Then I tried to put him out on the south line as a guard, but I caught him sleeping.

Besides all this, the whole time that he was with us, he kept trying to hit on Carter's daughter and then on Gina's daughter. Neither of them wanted anything to do with him. At that point, I met with Seamus and Phil. We knew that we were going to have to come up with some new rules for our little community.

I said to Seamus and Phil, "This guy is a disaster. He is not helping out. What do you want to do with him?"

Seamus said, "It's dangerous out there, and I really don't want to send him away."

Phil scratched his head. "I don't want to do that either, but we do need to have everybody contribute. Maybe we should implement a kind of three strikes and you're out policy."

I nodded. "Okay, I think that is a good idea. Although, I think Jack is on his third strike right now. I think that I have good job for him to do. It will keep him busy and keep him out of our hair for a little bit." I smiled.

The three of us sat down with Jack and explained the policy to him. He grumbled, as was to be expected, but nodded his assent when we made it clear to him that this wasn't a request or up for discussion. It is the way it has to be.

The job I assigned him was to go scouting from house to house (in a broader swath than we had covered earlier). I sent him out on a small motorcycle in order to conserve fuel. He was to make more lists of possible supplies in the houses and grab items like canned and dry foods and set them on the porches outside the houses for us to collect later. We gave him a respiratory mask and some Vicks VapoRub to smear under his nostrils. It would make the stench he might encounter more bearable. It wasn't as if we were giving him something to do that we hadn't done ourselves. We had all taken turns in the surrounding houses and knew what was involved. We did not need the supplies at the moment, but we needed to know what we had available to us and where.

Unfortunately, a short time later, he returned. He'd made it through only two houses and refused to do anymore. Phil came and got me and Carter. Some of the others had already packed him a bag with his personal items and some food. *Maybe if he was out there on his own for a while, he would see what a good thing he had here and come crawling back, ready to shape up.*

He was sitting on the front steps of the school complaining about the "grunt work" we gave him. Phil, Carter, and I walked up to him and told him it was time for him to go his own way. He seemed hurt at first as we explained it to him. Then he got mad. He pouted almost like little kid. It's an understatement to say he did not take it well. He grabbed his backpack and started to walk back into the school. We walked with him. As he started to walk toward the gym of the school, we told him that he was not going anywhere in the school but to the roadblock and that all his stuff was already packed. Carter's daughter, Cassie, was standing in front of the school. Jack saw her and said, "Come on, baby, it's your last chance." She turned red and walked away from the school.

I said, "No, Jack, you are coming now! We're taking you out of here."

He just ignored me and yelled after Cassie, "I didn't want you anyway, you stuck-up bi—" He didn't finish what he was going to say because Carter slapped him really hard in the back of the head. Jack fell down forward and barely caught himself.

Carter said, "I know you're a punk, but if you say a word to or even look at my daughter again, I will beat you down and leave your quivering body to die right here on the ground!"

Jack got to his feet and rubbed the back of his head. He gave Carter a dirty look and then to my horror, Jack reached for his pistol. In one fluid motion, Carter grabbed the gun with his left hand, pulled Jack toward himself, and brought his right elbow around in a kind of roundhouse, which connected with Jack's face. I thought I saw one of his teeth fly out of his mouth. Jack collapsed on the ground. Perhaps if it was anyone but Jack, I might have caught his unconscious body before it hit ground. Phil gave me a questioning look that seemed to ask why I didn't catch him. I just said in reply, "It's Jack, he earned it."

We checked to make sure he wasn't too badly hurt. He wasn't, so we shoved a little cotton up Jack's nose and taped the bridge of it to stop any bleeding, and then we loaded him, semiconscious, into the little Honda Accord. Carter took the bullets out of Jack's pistol and put the bullets and the gun into Jack's backpack. It wasn't right to send him out into the cruel world unarmed, but we didn't want him to have immediate access to his weapon. We drove him down to Brooks. As he started to wake up, he was groaning and crying.

We pulled into a small store and gas station and then pulled him out of the car and made sure he was well enough to walk and look around. Then we drove back to camp without him. True to character, as we drove off, he demonstrated his grasp of slang vocabulary with many rude comments accompanied by inappropriate gestures. We breathed a sigh of relief that he was gone. Unfortunately, that would not be the last that we would see Jack.

A few days later, while trying to fish the Willamette River, two of my kids, Abigail and Davey, spotted a boat in the distance drifting down the river toward us. We hid behind some trees and watched it slowly drift past us. It did slow lumbering circles. It was riddled with bullet holes and was partially sunken. It looked like the same boat Frank and Tina had taken. There was dried blood on the side of the boat just above the water. We could see a bloated arm hanging over the side; we could only assume that it was Tina's. What appeared to be Frank's leg was hooked to something in the boat, and his body was trailing the boat face down in the water. There was a seagull standing on his bloated body. It was bending down and pecking and pulling at a hole through his shirt. We had no way to retrieve the boat, so in stunned silence, we just watched it float by. I hugged Abigail and Davey tightly with their faces pressed into my chest.

I was overcome with a mix of emotions. I was angry, sad, revolted, and numb. It must have been the Salem group. It was clear that getting past them by water was out of the question. We had all prayed that Frank and Tina would make it; it would have given us all hope. If I had any doubts about how ruthless and aggressive the Salem groups were, those doubts were now dispelled. *What were the chances that we would have even seen the boat float by us? Would it have been better to have not seen it at all and gone about our lives in blissful ignorance? We would have been more hopeful. No, it is better to know what we are up against.*

I gathered my kids and the other adults who were fishing with us, and we headed back to the camp.

I told Phil and the others the bad news. Everyone was sad for the couple. The following day, Father Jay celebrated a tearful memorial mass for them. Those of us who were able to attend did. Afterward, we gathered outside the church.

I said, "It's only a matter of time before they come to check our group out—or worse. What preparations do you think we should make?"

Carter said, "I have lots of ideas about that, but it will take some hard work to tighten our security."

I looked Carter in the eye. "That's good. But I think we need some intelligence on just what we are up against."

11

Preparing for Trouble

Anything that can go wrong, will.

—Murphy's Law

I've come to understand about myself that I don't like surprises, especially the bad ones. I know that trouble in life is inevitable, but I want to at least know what direction it is coming from.

After some time, I decided to talk to Gina alone. Although the night of the shooting at Eli's house was intense, the fear that she and her daughter had shown seemed excessive. I decided that I needed to find out if Gina was holding anything back that could jeopardize our group. Specifically, I needed to know more about the Salem group. We sat down in one of the corners of the gym.

"Gina," I said, "after the night of the shooting at Eli's house, you mentioned that you were afraid that it was your ex-husband coming after you." I saw fear immediately enter into her eyes. *I need to be direct; I can't sugarcoat this.* "You need to tell me everything that you know for the safety of our community."

She obviously found my direct approach startling, and she started weeping; and through her tears, she said, "I don't even know where to start." She put her hands over her face.

I said, "Well, just start at the beginning, and I'm sure it will come to you."

She wiped her eyes with the back of her hand and looked at a spot on the floor and started talking: "We got married sixteen years ago. Ken was his name. I was only seventeen. I was just a lovestruck teenager. He was a few years older than me, and he encouraged me to drop out of high school and to get a job at the cannery in Salem where he worked." She paused to collect her thoughts. "Okay, you don't need the whole history. Well, it turns out there were some strange people that worked there at the cannery. They were involved in some dark stuff. Ken got sucked right into it. Soon, he had me involved. I realize now that I did it out of fear, but Ken did it because he liked it.

I just kind of watched, but soon, I became afraid. I wanted to leave, but Ken always convinced…well, forced me to stay. They performed pagan rituals and some kind of blood sacrifices. After a while, Ken told me he started to hear voices, telling him to do stuff. That was when he really started to get weird, well—weirder.

"He started his own cult and called it *The Anarchists' Anvil*. He started to do animal sacrifices and get into some really dark stuff. You've got to understand, Ken is very charismatic. He is persuasive, and he always gets his way. The strange people at the cannery quickly became his followers, because he was willing to do things that even they were hesitant to do. Some of them believed the voices he heard were prophetic.

"Then one day, his new followers brought a homeless man to him. They promised that they would get him some food and housing, but then they tied him down to the ground. They started chanting in some strange language and the poor man was so scared. I was just as scared as the man, but I had to put on a good face." She hung her head in shame.

"They tortured him and made him say stuff. When they were done, they beat him almost to death, and well, they may have after…" She trailed off, eyes wide, as if seeing the events again. "They smeared his blood on the floor in strange symbols. It scared me! *He* scared me, but he was my husband. He was all I had, so I excused myself and ran back to my room, and a threw up in the toilet.

"I wanted to run away from him, but I didn't have anywhere to go. Ken made sure of that! My parents didn't talk to me anymore after the cult stuff. They hated him, and they were ashamed of me. My dad was a preacher, so as you can imagine, me being in a cult destroyed our relationship. I was all alone, and I was scared.

"Then a few years later…" She looked up at me. "Yes, I didn't have the courage to run." She shivered. "Later, I got pregnant with Susan. It changes things when there's a baby, a new innocent life. I was going to be a mom." She smiled and looked down at Susan who was hugging her mom. "Having this new life inside me that I was responsible for gave me the courage I needed. I left him.

"But by then, Ken had some new disciples who were hardcore—the I'll-do-anything-you-ask kind of followers. They found me and dragged me back. That's when he started to beat me, and while he beat me, he would quote these strange phrases that sounded kind of like scripture—things like, 'The all-seeing one sayeth she who disobeys her master must pay in blood...' and other strange things like that. Ken was always careful that he didn't hit me near my pregnant belly, but everywhere else was fair game. I did eventually give birth to Susan, and he seemed happy with that as long as I did exactly what he wanted. It was that way for five long years. Then, Ken was sent to jail for a couple of months. I had a brief reprieve from the abuse, but when he got out, he was worse—much worse.

"Something changed. I'd overhear him tell his followers that he had seen an angel of light. He started calling himself the Obedient Servant, and he spoke of the Great Unicity. It all sounded like nonsense to me, but he wanted nothing less than perfect obedience to his will—and his voice changed. I mean, he used to be as American as apple pie." She laughed sarcastically. "Now he started speaking in some kind of British accent, and he just seemed so evil."

As I listened to her, her face seemed to lose all emotion, like there was no feeling left in her. She was relaying the story as if it had happened to someone else. To deal with all the abuse, perhaps she shut down emotionally. I was tempted to stop her because I didn't want her to have to relive all her pain, but I needed to know.

She continued, "Then one day, I caught him molesting our daughter." She paused. I could see a flash of emotion in her face then. She was clearly fighting back both tears and rage.

Her voice wavered as she continued, "Before I caught him, I had suspected something wasn't right, but I always assumed it was my own paranoia. I mean it was his own daughter! But now I knew.

"That day I walked in on him with her...well, the day he realized that I had seen him, he sent his goons in. They beat me and raped me, and he just watched. I remember him smiling at me and asking, 'How do you like being watched?'

"Then he said that I had interrupted his 'ritual' and that I had to be punished and that I would pay in blood. When they were finished with my 'punishment,' they locked us in the house. The windows had bars on them, and the doors only unlocked from the outside with a key. I rammed my shoulder into every door, but it was no use. Susan and I were stuck there for another two weeks. At random times, they would leave us a little food and water just inside the door. We remained there until I found an unlocked window on the second floor. With a board that I found from the frame of our bed, I was able to force the bars free of the window frame. We escaped into the night and went to the police.

"It took every ounce of courage that I had to involve the law. Fortunately, I still had bruises and cuts from the beating to make my story convincing—and Susan showed signs of abuse too. The police investigated and found bodies buried in our backyard. Ken was prosecuted and sentenced to prison for a minimum of twenty years. His closest followers had each gotten sentences of ten years minimum.

At the sentencing, he said that he would never stop trying to get his women back, and I believed him. That's why we are so scared. Somehow, no matter where I tried to go, it seemed that his letters would find their way to me. It was clear from his letters that new inmates were falling under his spell too. He had also found my e-mail address and kept sending updates on his new cult. I don't know why I chose to read them. I don't know why I kept the email account. I suppose one wants to know what her enemy is up to. His group still calls itself *The Anarchists' Anvil*, but some of the members also call it *The True Revelation*."

She turned to look me in the eyes. "You've got to understand! He survived the plague, and he is a monster on the loose, and now he's got more followers."

"This isn't just any group looking for an easy score," she said. "It's a violent cult, and they won't stop until they catch us or kill us, or they're killed first. He is obsessed, and he has passed his obsession on to his followers."

Her eyes were pleading, and her face was streaked with tears. I sat back and let out a breath. I said, "I'm almost sorry I asked. I never dreamed it was going to be that bad. I'm so sorry for everything he's put you through."

Susan and Gina looked at me with trepidation, probably expecting me to tell them to leave. I contemplated their fearful, tearful eyes for a moment and said, "I need to tell the others." I turned to leave, and then I stopped. I looked back at her and said in a calm voice, "Gina, you and Susan are welcome here. We will protect you with our lives if need be. But I need to give the others this information so we can plan our safety. Okay?"

Gina let out the breath that she had been holding, and I saw a much different kind of flood of tears fall from her eyes. "Yes, that's fine. I'm sorry for not telling you sooner, but it's not an easy thing to talk about—and I was afraid that if you all knew that you wouldn't let us stay." She hugged her daughter tightly.

I thanked her for her courage and told her that she did well putting her ex-husband in prison. I would have been hesitant to share that information too, and I couldn't fault her for that.

Later, I gathered most of the adults in a corner of the gym and told them Gina's story. At first, a couple of the women were mad at me for prying into her past, but I could see their anger turn to shock then sadness as I recounted Gina's story.

From what I gathered from Gina's account, her ex-husband, Ken, was a charismatic guy. But I wondered, *How many depraved people could he really have as followers?*

Guard duty seemed even more critical with this new information. Knowing the threat was serious and imminent, we made a map of the town and discussed where to locate snipers, including several back up positions. Once again, we started up the old backhoe and built more firing positions. I had forgotten how high the water table was in the area, and it had been raining a lot lately; we didn't have to dig very deep before the dirt turned to mud. Nonetheless, we tapered the back sides of each bunker in case we got overrun. They might not be comfortable, but we would have cover in a forward firing position. And if they overtook the forward positions and we had to retreat to positions further back, they wouldn't be able to use the same bunker that we had just left because there would be no real cover.

As a further precaution, we double-stacked disabled cars along problem areas along the roadways using a large forklift supplied by a local metal fabrication business. We also set up key rooftop locations as sniper posts. With Carter's coaching, we practiced test firing from these posts and even made quick-sight adjustment cards.

We created action plans that even addressed what-if situations. We had several scenarios in mind, addressing if enemy forces came down one or more of the roads leading into town. There was a southbound train parked just outside of town that was probably two hundred cars long. We devised a plan to use the train to split the town in two, blocking enemy vehicles. It would take a lot of time for an enemy to drive around the blockade, which could make those tracks vital to our survival. However, they also could provide possible access to the town from an enemy, so we created defensible positions surrounding the tracks as well.

The hardest thing to plan for was the evacuation of everyone if it became necessary. We had put a lot of thought into the plan, but if we were overrun, it would be difficult to leave safely. The main challenge would be keeping the children out of harm's way. This had to be factored into each strategic plan. We drilled each other on them daily until we all had them committed to memory. We toyed with the idea of naming each plan something edgy like "Plan Alpha" or "Crack Back 9." But we quickly realized that would be too confusing. We decided just to use our own English alphabet. So we numbered (or lettered, actually) our defense and attack plans accordingly: Plans "A" though "E." Plan "A" meant "All-out war." Plan "B" signified "Barricade defense." Plan "C" was "Circle up the wagons." Plan "D" meant "Divide and conquer." Plan "E" was designed for a small force attacking, which signified "Elevated defense." Finally, there was the escape plan. This we referred to as plan "F." We hoped it would never come to that. The "F" stood for "Failure" or "Flee." Of course, some of the men joked about other words that "F" could stand for. All in all, for a small group with limited training and resources, we felt as ready as we could be. We figured that we would eventually be faced with some sort of violence. It was only a matter of time.

12

A Dog-Eat-Dog World

I've seen many types of evil in the world. There is natural evil like diseases and disasters, and then there is the evil of men. I think the natural evil is easier to forgive.

—Phil McHale

After the celebration of Christmas, we started to put together hunting parties to go out at least once a week looking for deer, elk, or geese. We knew that we had supplies for a good long time, but they wouldn't last forever. Besides, it was a good way to hone our skills, and although none of us wanted to admit it, hunting skills would be essential if we were ever attacked by outsiders. As we looked around for game, we were also on the lookout for wild dogs, not that we developed a taste for dog meat, but some of our livestock were being attacked by dogs in the evenings.

Another disturbing discovery was that we were finding both animal and human body parts scattered around town. Worse, these were relatively recent kills and not from the outbreak of the virus. It made sense at the beginning of the plague that the dogs would get into houses with corpses in them to get an easy meal, but the problem was that any fresh meat would have been gone long ago. It sure made all of us uneasy knowing living humans were on their menu too. We were used to being on the top of the food chain.

One morning, as I was scouting east of town, I saw a medium-sized gray and brown dog tugging on something long and hose-like. The dog was pulling at it from the front steps of a house. The hose thing was caught on something inside the house. The dog was persistent and had its own tug-of-war going on. Though the door to the house was open, I could not see inside from my position down the road. The hose, or whatever it was, just kept stretching longer and longer.

I chased the dog off. The dog had dropped his hose with a yelp and a growl. I followed the hose into the house, but it didn't look like any hose I had ever seen before. It ended up being the small intestine of a dead man. He was an overweight bald man, and his stomach was ripped open. He must have been recently killed because the stench wasn't too overpowering. It appeared that he had been killed by wild dogs judging from the bite marks left on his throat, legs, and arms. Already there were flies all over the body along with busy maggots around his eyes. A couple rats scurried off when I entered the room. The smell of death was much stronger inside the house. I decided that I had seen enough. I turned around and left the house in a hurry, slamming the door and cutting the intestine in two. I stepped over it and swatted away a couple yellow jackets or hornets that had been attracted by the odor.

I walked away barely able to keep myself from vomiting. The dog was two houses away, watching and waiting for me to leave to collect its prize. I had trouble removing the gory images from my mind for the next few days.

I hadn't recognized the deceased man. He must have been living on the outskirts of town under our radar, because we saw no signs of him until…well, until it was too late. I found it a little disconcerting that we hadn't discovered his living presence at all. *Why hadn't he come to us to make his himself known?* I felt sorry for him, though; it was a shame he survived the virus, only to be killed by wild dogs. Now there was one more thing that we had to worry about during guard duty and when we were away from town: wild dogs.

We were seeing more and more dogs, and they were getting braver. One day, the kids were playing in the fenced playground behind the school and one of the dogs, a scraggly medium-sized dog, had found a way in. Hannah saw it run around the kids. It looked like it was going to play but then showed its teeth. Hannah put the kids in the gym and shot the dog. We all discussed what we should do about the wild dogs. Until then, we had mixed feelings on whether to let the wild dogs scavenge around the area. This incident with the kids combined with the dead man I found changed every-thing. We needed to thin out the population of dogs. Any feral dogs that we saw, we shot. It proved to be good practice for our snipers. If we weren't fully convinced of the dangers, there was one memorable event that solidified our decision.

Phil, Dad, Father Jay, and I all decided to go out hunting. It was open season for any animals we saw because there were likely no Oregon Fish and Wildlife agents around to question us. Still, we didn't abuse the privilege. We figured it would be good for the kids to learn to hunt, so each of us had a kid with us: Phil had six-year-old Elijah; Dad had Davey, who was only four years old; Isaiah, my oldest, went with Father Jay; and I had eight-year-old Abigail. We taught the kids how to be quiet and what tracks and signs to look for.

We got to a small wooded area across Highway 99. We found some signs of deer, along with a lot of dog tracks. We made a long, spread-out line within sight of each other in order to try to scare some game out as we entered into the forest.

As we began, I could instantly smell something dead. Abigail, who was at my side, made a face indicating she could smell it too. I heard a dog make a warning bark, so I called everyone in closer. A minute later, we came upon two dead deer carcasses. They were probably a couple days old. Soon after our discovery, we saw movement.

Ten dogs appeared out of the bushes and came within twenty feet of us and were growling, baring their teeth. Father Jay was trying to calm the dogs. He was saying softly, "It's okay. We don't mean you any harm." His soothing words were falling on deaf canine ears. They seemed to be trying to herd us. I was scared, and I could hear Father Jay's voice shaking as he tried to calm the dogs. We had our guns drawn. Phil and my dad helped the kids into a tree and told them to stay there. About ten more dogs came up behind us and then another ten or more on the sides. We were surrounded and way outnumbered. They wanted fresh meat, and we were on the menu.

In a low and calm voice, I told everyone to form a circle around the tree. In the same soft voice, I counted backward: "Three...two...one..." Suddenly, all hell broke loose. We started shooting and backing toward the tree and each other. Dogs were charging and retreating. We had our backs to the tree where we had put the kids. I chanced a glance up the tree. *Good, they're all there.*

Although my ears were ringing, I didn't let the smoke and commotion distract me. Everything seemed to happen so fast, and yet, paradoxically, time also seemed to slow down. The only thought in my mind was killing dogs and protecting my family.

The kids had climbed about ten feet up the tree and were safe for now. About ten of the dogs were already dead, but the others were still attacking. They were running around us in a circle, looking for a break in the line. A large, scraggly German shepherd sprinted through the rain of bullets and smoke. It grabbed Phil's left arm in his mouth and pulled him down. When the big dog chomped down, I thought I heard Phil's arm break. He yelled and dropped his rifle. The dog was shaking Phil's arm viciously.

I saw another large dog move in to go for the downed man. I shot it in the side, and it yelped and ran into the bushes. Meanwhile, with his good right hand, Phil pulled out his Browning .45 pistol and emptied its magazine into the German shepherd. The dog fell to the ground, dead. Realizing that Phil couldn't reload with one arm, my dad handed Phil his Beretta 9mm.

A good-size Doberman leaped at me, but Father Jay saw it coming out of the corner of his eye. With one fluid motion, he flipped the pump action shotgun around and clubbed the dog in the head with the butt of the gun. It yelped and was stunned, but before it could run away, I filled it with lead. Then I fired on the next dog I saw.

Once Father's shotgun was empty, he dropped it and took his Colt .45 long pistol out of its holster. It is called "The Judge." It could hold either a .45 long shell (more powder and power than a regular .45) or .410 shotgun rounds. He had .410s loaded. Animals that weren't killed ran wounded and yelping into the bushes. After he had emptied "The Judge," he retrieved the shotgun and was using it as a club.

A couple more dogs were looking to use me as a chew toy, but I had brought my .44 Magnum pistol, which was loaded with hollow-point bullets. They made huge holes in any dog trying attack. A large pit bull lunged at me, but I shot it in the chest. Somehow, one of its front legs blew off at the shot. The dog was instantly dead, but another dog ran off with its no-longer-attached leg. I dropped the empty .44 Mag and grabbed the .30-30 Winchester slung over my back and continued shooting.

Dad was like a machine. He had his semiautomatic Remington .22 rifle and was taking out dogs with one shot each. He was amazing. His face showed the controlled rage of a father protecting his family. The gun was steady in his hands, and he was quick to aim and shoot—a head shot here and heart shot there.

Isaiah was shooting from the tree above us. He had a Ruger 10/22 rifle and was shooting dogs right and left. He was raining shell casings on Father Jay from the tree above him. Father was startled at first and then took another step forward. Isaiah's gun soon went empty, but he must have popped in a new banana clip because he started firing again.

When the last living dogs finally retreated, we surveyed the carnage we had created and made sure everyone was okay. Thankfully, the kids were still safe up in the tree. Davie was holding his ears and crying, and Abigail was holding Davie ensuring that he didn't fall out of the tree. Isaiah wasn't crying but was very quiet with his eyes fixed on one of the dogs he had killed. The other kids were sobbing as well. Phil had his injured arm tucked into his coat. His right hand still held the Beretta, its barrel smoking.

Father Jay was breathing hard and looking right and left, peering into the bushes. He held the barrel of the shotgun like a baseball bat. There were three dead dogs at his feet.

Dad had his rifle pointed down but pressed against his shoulder. He was watching the few fleeing dogs scamper away. We stayed there quietly, waiting for our ears to stop ringing. Gun smoke filled the wooded area, and there were brass casings everywhere.

Phil said, "I don't think it is a good idea to move just yet, when we can barely see or hear."

Dad said, "What?"

We all laughed. We needed an outlet after the tense situation we had just experienced. Once the smoke had cleared and our ears were back to normal, we made a larger sweep of the area and counted the dead dogs. We had killed forty-three dogs, and who knows how many we wounded?

I think Dad and Isaiah killed most of them. Phil had the only human injury with a broken left arm in two places above his wrist, unless you count the slight burn on Father Jay's hand from holding the hot barrel of the shotgun like a club. We helped the kids down from the tree.

Isaiah was quiet with a look of turmoil in his soft blue eyes. He started to cry with his hands over his eyes in embarrassment. He said, "I've never killed anything before. They were going to hurt or kill you, guys. I saw the dog bite Grandpa, and I just started to shoot as many as I could."

We all started tearing up, and I side-hugged Isaiah as we walked. The other kids huddled around my dad and Father Jay. The whole area smelled of gunpowder, death, and not surprisingly, wet dog.

It was now very quiet, and we could hear some whimpering close by. We spread out again and soon found a litter of eight puppies. They were pretty close to where we were shooting. Perhaps the dogs were trying to protect their young. I couldn't fault them for that. The puppies looked like a mix between that of a Doberman and maybe a German shepherd. All the guys were thinking the same thing: Guard dogs!

I spoke up, finally, and said, "I really didn't think there would be that many dogs. We shouldn't have brought the kids."

Abigail whined, "I don't want to go hunting anymore."

Dad said, "Abigail, I don't blame you."

Phil's left arm was turning purple at the forearm. There were punctures in the skin and areas that had been torn from the dog's teeth. It really looked like it hurt, which Phil confirmed as he clenched his teeth while breathing through the throbbing pain. Dad took off his coat and T-shirt and gingerly wrapped the shirt around Phil's arm. He winced in pain with every wrap. Then Dad put his coat back on and zipped it up.

Phil said, "Thanks, Jay," with a tight smile.

Dad looked him over. "No problem. Are you good enough to walk back?"

"Yeah, I'll be fine," he grunted through clenched teeth.

We would need to keep an eye on his wound for infection and rabies. I wasn't sure what we would do if he ended up with rabies. I just prayed that wouldn't happen. Each of the kids picked up two puppies, and we walked out of the forest cautiously. We kept the kids in the middle of us. Thankfully, the puppies that the kids were holding took their minds off the horror show we had just survived.

On the way back to our cars, we saw a few more dogs in the distance. We took a couple of pot shots at them and actually hit two. Make that forty-five dogs dead. I said, "Well, that should have thinned them out a little."

Normally, we would have stopped to pick up all our brass shell casings to reload later. However, we decided to leave them and get Phil and the kids back to camp. When we got the puppies back to the gym, of course the rest of the kids swarmed them. The puppies ran around and licked the kids' faces. I wondered, *Is that safe? Can the kids catch something from the puppies?*

The next six months were mostly uneventful—well, not so much uneventful as blissfully calm compared to the incident with the dogs, and that was a good thing. Phil's arm was all healed and was usable. And the kids seemed to survive the licks from the puppies.

Thankfully, Phil didn't catch rabies, or we might have had to call him Cujo. He didn't need any serious medical attention, except for the makeshift cast we put on him and regular wound cleanings. Laura dispensed antibiotics to him that we had snagged from the pharmacy. After having mostly healed, he had some nasty scars that were evident when he rolled up his sleeve. Just for fun, he would often roll up his sleeves and chase the kids around, yelling, "This makes me want to bite your arms. Does my skin feel *ruff?*" Then he would chomp his teeth at the kids. His grandkids giggled and screamed with joy, running from him, but not quite so fast as not to get caught.

We had been training the puppies as watchdogs. The kids, being kids, had their own agenda and just wanted to play with the puppies. The dogs were learning, and we were learning to teach them. It is interesting what you can do when you need to. Before the plague, I could barely train our little dog, Daisy, to sit and stay. Our little dog died a few months before the virus spread. She had gotten out of our fence, and a garbage truck had run her over. *Stupid dog.* I guess that I can train dogs if it is really important to me. Besides, there were no garbage trucks to worry about anymore.

The dogs could hear and smell vastly better than we could, and their enhanced senses would end up making a big difference in our lives. The dogs went out at night with us for guard duty. Sometimes we would hear them bark. *Who knows what they actually heard and smelled?* More often than not, when we checked out the area, we would find some kind of footprints—mostly animal, but sometimes human. They seemed to be an effective deterrent, if nothing else.

Spring came and then faded into summer. We developed a regular rotation at our guard posts. At times, we saw a few strangers walking down the railroad tracks. The strangers would see or hear the dogs then make a wide berth around our town. We were not against people joining our group, but we couldn't just have people sneaking in.

As I looked up in the slowly darkening sky, I watched a couple of turkey vultures circling overhead. *It seems since the plague there are a lot more of them these days.* The vultures seemed to be an omen, as if they were waiting for death itself to arrive. I silently hoped that they would fly somewhere else.

13

They're Coming!

I don't hate those men… I hate the things that they do.
But I will kill them if they threaten my family.

—Eli McHale

We appreciated a long stretch of relatively uneventful months, but all things come to an end sooner or later. One night while I was on guard duty, I saw spotlights making big arcs in the sky, so I radioed it in. It seemed someone else had electricity too. The next morning, Seamus told everyone that the lights were a signal for another meeting. He seemed very excited. He and Connor loaded up the car to drive to the capitol. It was hard to watch them go, but we needed to know if there was any government left. We kept waiting and waiting for their return, but Seamus had warned us not to look for them unless they were gone more than two days.

I was on guard duty at the south entrance on the second evening of their absence. It was just after dusk, and it was quickly getting dark. It was a clear fall evening, and the temperature was about forty degrees. I was monitoring the radio as usual when I heard Connor's voice burst out over the speaker, yelling, "We're coming in fast. Move the west roadblock and stop the men chasing us." I looked up from behind my guard position. I saw headlights in the distance. Shadow, the guard dog I had with me, was going nuts, barking, and pulling at his leash. I supposed that he was sensing my tension. He was tied to the tree to my left. His coat of fur was darker than the other dogs, almost black with a brown patch at his chest. I whispered to him, as much as to myself, "Be ready, boy!" Shadow quieted and pulled against his leash like a coiled spring.

I radioed for the others to get into position. I could hear shots being fired in the distance. *Not good!*

Carter and his son CJ came running. Carter yelled, "Son, move that car off to the side and open the lane." CJ ran to the car and cleared a pathway into the town.

In the distance, I could hear an accelerating motor. I said, "Yeah, that looks like the headlights of Seamus and Connor's car, and they are coming in hot." Their lights flashed three times.

Carter said into the radio, "Don't worry! Everyone else is getting into positions."

Carter took the right side of the road, and I took the left. I was positioned in our makeshift bunker. *Oh, great! Just great! It's full of water!* I settled into a puddle. Carter was ready next to a tree. As the car got closer, I could see that it really was Connor and Seamus. They sped by yelling, "Don't let them through." They must have been going 70 miles per hour.

Carter yelled to his son, "Do not fire! Just hide for now! You'll know if I need you to or not." A second vehicle, which looked like a truck or an SUV in the dark, was quickly in pursuit about twenty seconds back.

I had a battery-powered spotlight with me in the bunker. Carter looked at his son and said, "I've got the right tire and you've got the left." Then he looked at me. "On the count of three shine the light into their windshield."

"Okay," I said.

As the vehicle got closer, it looked like a raised older pickup with large tires. I could hear its motor revved up, trying to catch up to the car. Carter counted to three quickly, and I pointed the spotlight directly into their windshield and flipped it on. A bright beam of light illuminated the truck. It must have been very disorienting for them. Carter and CJ shot out their big front tires.

My night vision was temporarily compromised by the muzzle flash and the headlights of the truck going into the ditch. There was the smell of dust, exhaust, and coolant. We could hear the ticking sound of a rapidly cooling engine. The front axle of the truck hit the ditch pretty hard, and the truck stopped almost instantly. Two dazed men nearly fell out of the truck with guns in their hands. They were holding their heads with their other hands; I guessed that they had not been wearing their seatbelts.

I kept the spotlight on them and yelled, "Those were your only warning shots! Drop your weapons or die tonight!"

They both immediately dropped their two assault rifles. I told Carter to cover me. CJ was ready in the ditch on the opposite side with his gun aimed at the men. They had no clue he was there. I left the spotlight shining on the two men from the bunker as I checked to see if there was anyone else in the truck, and then I checked the two men for any other weapons.

Shadow was snarling and pulling with all his might against the chain that secured him to the tree. He was aptly named; he seemed a vicious phantom with white teeth and glowing, bright amber eyes when the light hit them just right. He wanted a piece of them, and the two men knew it. I'm not sure if they were more scared of us or the thought of this growling menacing specter chained to the tree.

The man who was driving was perhaps six feet tall. He had his arms raised over his shaved and tattooed head. He was a white man with no facial hair, but a piercing under his lower lip. He was wearing camouflage, presumably from the National Guard. There was no name on the uniform. The second man was also an Anglo, and he stood around five and a half feet tall. He was also wearing the same style of uniform as his buddy. His head was also shaved except for a black Mohawk that ran down the middle. He had numerous piercings in his ears, nose, and eyebrows.

The man with the piercings looked at me and said, "The general is not going to be pleased. You're harboring criminals, and I bet his girls are here too!"

I said, "What criminals are you talking about?"

He squinted at me like I was dumb and said, as though he were talking to a child, "The two we were chasing. They were causing trouble, and the big one decked the general. And that offense is punishable by death!"

I knew he was talking about Connor, but I did my best to hold in my anger. Besides, I wanted to get some answers. Since he had already started flapping his gums, I'd get as much information as I could.

Then I asked, "What women are you looking for?" His mouth widened into an evil grin as he said, "His old lady and little plaything!" He cackled between some of his missing teeth. It was cross between a laugh and a hiss.

I really wanted to hurt this guy because I knew he was talking about Gina and Susan. I felt my blood pressure rise, and blood pumping through my ears. I didn't even notice the cold even though my body was soaking wet. I guess I get very protective of people that I care about.

I was trying to calm myself when I heard a ping behind me. The smaller man's eye's widened in terror. I started to turn my head and saw a black streak as Shadow launched himself at the smaller man. Shadow's teeth looked like they were glowing from the reflected light from the spotlight. The full force of the still growing seventy-pound dog hit the man in the chest and pinned him against the truck. I heard a high-pitched shriek escape the man's lips as Shadow slammed into him. Shadow would have had his throat if the man had not put his arm in the way. The tall one said, "Get the dog off him!"

The smaller man screamed in a high-pitched voice, "Get it off! Get it off!"

I must admit that I took my time pulling Shadow off him. Shadow scared me too, lunging out of the darkness. Shadow must have sensed my hostility toward Mr. Mohawk.

I looked at the two men and said in a calm tone, "Those two men you were talking about are part of my family. They're good men, and if they hit your general, then he had it coming. As for the other two, I haven't seen them." I figured, in this case, I might be forgiven that little white lie.

I held Shadow back from his new chew toy. Mr. Mohawk cradled his arm with his good one. I was sure that his forearm must have been broken. It was definitely bleeding, and I hoped that it hurt like hell. Baldy (the larger guy) was trying to back away without looking like he was backing away. Shadow was only a few feet from the men and was emitting a low growl and licking his teeth. The two men were completely fixated on him. We probably could have put our weapons away at that point. Shadow was enough of a threat to them.

The raised Ford pickup that they were driving looked to be in good enough shape even though the front was now dented up from the ditch. Its two front tires were flattened from the shots and the impact. I radioed to home base and told the others about our two "guests." Connor radioed back a minute later and told me to let them go. He said he would fill me in later.

I looked at the two guys. "I don't care what issues you have with my family...no one messes with my family. Get in your truck and get out of here! We won't stop at shooting the tires next time."

Shadow seemed to sense that it was time for them to leave, so he started barking and lunging toward the men. I could barely keep hold of the dog. Perhaps I pretended to have a little more trouble holding him back than I really did, but I didn't have to pretend much. I whispered to Shadow, "Good dog."

They both got in the truck. With a little effort they managed to back it out of the ditch. The front tires were completely flat and half off the rims. There were sparks flying from the front of the trucks rims as they slowly made their way back up the street. I kept the spotlight on them as they left. The passenger gave us the finger. Carter who had me covered the whole time shot the driver-side mirror. I heard a distant scream from the man and many cuss words as they drove off, now a little faster. Maybe it's my sick sense of humor, but I just started to laugh and said, "Heck of a shot, Carter! Now Mr. Mohawk has a broken left arm, and he should probably thank you because he doesn't have to look at his own ugly mug in the mirror."

Carter smiled and said, "Never mess with a sniper or a dog named Shadow." Then he reached down and scratched Shadow's ears. Shadow made a contented sound like something between a whine and an ecstatic groan.

I laughed and said, "I'll remember that. This fearless dog needs a special treat."

CJ brought Shadow back to the school and tossed him a piece of steak. Thankfully, the rest of the guard duty shift was uneventful. But we were more alert than ever before.

The next morning, we gathered the adults, and Seamus filled us all in on everything that had taken place the night before. He was obviously mad because his Irish brogue was thick. "The radio broadcast was right. It is obvious that a group of men had stormed the capitol and had forcefully taken over the meeting. The whole lot of them were scuttered and acting the maggot." His wife elbowed him to remind him to cut down on the slang. He looked over at her and gave her a mock scowl.

Judy translated, "They were drunk and causing mischief." Then she nodded for him to continue.

Mollified, Seamus continued, softening his brogue. "They had been demanding that all the people and communities in the area give them food and the 'use' of their women for what they called 'tribute.' Their group was larger this time and more organized." Seamus seemed to think that the other group in Keizer had joined up with the capitol group.

I could see that Seamus was having a little difficulty speaking through his bloodied lips and bruised face. Seamus was sixty years old, too old to be getting smacked around. I looked Connor over. I didn't see any real damage to his wide six-foot-four-inch frame. He seemed fine except for his messed up red hair and the scrapes on his fists, he seemed fine.

I smiled at Connor and asked, "I see the scrapes on your fists. Is that from hitting the guy who hurt your dad?"

He smiled back and said, "Yes, yes, it is."

Seamus smiled at him approvingly.

Then Connor said, "The problem was that the fistfight almost turned into a gun fight. His buddies pulled out their guns. I thought that we were dead. Fortunately for us, we heard a distant gunshot. Apparently, at just the right time for us, some others started fighting with the capitol group. We took the opportunity to make a mad dash to our car. Some of the guys saw us driving off and chased us. Now here we are."

I asked, "How many people were there who weren't part of the capitol group?"

He said, "About one hundred."

I rubbed my forehead. "How many men did capitol group have?"

Connor said, "I don't know maybe seventy-five men. It happened so fast. It could have been more."

I said, "Let's take a few minutes to get all the details down."

With wheels squeaking, Father Jay rolled in the chalkboard from the school so that we could take notes. I was amazed at how detailed the memories of Connor and Seamus were.

I asked, "What type of weapons did they have?"

Seamus said, "I'm not sure exactly. I just know they had automatic rifles."

Carter interrupted. "Well, they were probably just like these." He held up the two rifles that we had taken from the two men the night before. These are M16s."

Seamus confirmed. "Exactly right. And they had camo, handguns, grenades, and drove army Hummers. There were tents set up near the capitol building, and it is clear that they had taken it over." He drew a picture of the capitol building represented as a large block. He then drew little triangles to represent tents in front of it and on the sides in the grassy areas.

Connor said, "They have a lot of weapons at a large tent by the capitol building doors. It was marked with a spray-painted sign that read ARMORY. There were a lot of weapons just piled up there. I think they did that to intimidate all of us—and it worked!"

Carter said, "Well, let's assume they have full access to the National Guard Armory. We should probably double our guards."

I said, "We also gleaned some important information from the guys who chased you last night. I think that Gina's ex-husband is their leader. I think Ken and the general are the same person. Those guys, whom I shall lovingly refer from now on as Mr. Mohawk and Baldy, said that the general is looking for his *old lady* and *plaything*. His words, not mine." I looked around. "We need to teach all of you how to shoot. I know that some of you have been hesitant, but each of us should be comfortable with all the guns that we have gathered. We should know how to load, shoot, and maintain them all."

We spent the next few weeks doing our regular work—guard duty, cooking, and tending the fields and animals, and everything else, and we ensured that everyone except the very young kids was taught the basics of shooting. If they could safely hold and shoot a gun they were trained. We went over it until everyone knew how to shoot and load each different type of rifle and pistol. We were not experts by any means, but we could all hold a gun and defend ourselves.

We also made sure the dogs were nearby while we practiced our shooting. We wanted them to be accustomed to the sounds of gunfire. The dogs were good-sized by now, and we had them pretty well trained to be both guard dogs and hunting dogs. Shadow had already proven his usefulness.

Carter and Ray put their heads together and came up with some booby traps and trip signals that should warn us of a foot attack. They also trained the adults in the basics of making and disarming the traps.

One morning, we saw a trip flare go off, so we investigated the area. We could see signs that someone had come through there. We let two of the dogs go after the scent. They followed it to one of the many nearby abandoned houses. It was an old house, probably built in the 1940s. Before we could get there to stop them, the two dogs pushed their way into the house, and we heard several gun shots and yelps. The person in the house had killed the dogs. I yelled to the person to come out, but a cocky male voice replied that we should come in instead. The voice sounded familiar, but I couldn't place it at the time. I threatened that we would burn the house down if he did not come out. The man broke out the back door and ran through the field south toward Salem.

I had the man in my sights, and I could have easily shot him in the back, but I couldn't take a man's life in trade for the lives of two dogs. He got away, and we didn't give chase. We couldn't tell who he was. The dogs, Grizzly and Lady, had done their jobs well, and we buried them. Now we were down to six dogs. The little kids insisted on organizing a little memorial service for the fallen dogs.

My four-year-old son, Davey, used one of my shirts as his priestly outfit and set up a little table and celebrated a service that looked suspiciously like a mass using apple juice and cookies. I looked at Father Jay questioningly, wondering if this was *kosher*, or whatever the equivalent Catholic word is for *kosher*. I didn't want him to be excommunicated or something. Father Jay just smiled and nodded that it was okay.

Davey even gave a little homily in his "rhotacistic" speech pattern, seemingly channeling his best Elmer Fudd. "We ow hee-ew to say goodbye to Gwizwee and Wadie. May God bwess them. Amen!" Translation: *We are here to say goodbye to Grizzly and Lady. May God bless them. Amen!*

We all responded, "Amen!"

Then Elijah brought over some cookies and apple juice, which Davey awkwardly took from him and set up on the table. He extended his hands and read some lines out of one his children's books, and then he made something that resembled the sign of the cross with his left hand over the snacks. Then he handed cookies to everyone saying, "Da bawdy of Kw-eye-st." Translation: *The Body of Christ.*

We dutifully responded, "Amen."

Eden and Eve were giggling uncontrollably as they watched this awkward little minister amble around handing out cookies. I looked around. All the adults had smiles on their faces.

After Davey ate half his cookie, he set it down on the table, and then he took a swig of his apple juice, set it down, and he held up his chocolate smeared hands and chanted, "Wet us pway!" Translation: *Let us pray!*

Susan snorted, a laugh escaping her mouth. She quickly covered her mouth with her hand.

Not seeming to notice, Davey put his face really close to the children's book, quietly reading, or at least pretending to, and then he loudly chanted, "Amen!" And we dutifully responded, "Amen!"

He kissed the little table and walked around, the other side and said, "The Mass is ended!" Then he clapped his hands and said, "Yaaay!"

We all responded, "Thanks be to God!" and laughed and clapped loudly.

I couldn't think of a better way to send our dogs off to dog heaven, if there is such thing.

Unfortunately, Grizzly and Lady weren't the last dogs that we would lose. Two more dogs, Jade and Spike, got lured away, presumably by wild dogs. They either joined the wild dogs or were eaten by them. I've heard that wolves will do that too. They lure domestic dogs away from their home through play, or they draw them away because a female is in heat. Whatever method used, they turn against the domesticated dogs and eat them. We were now down to four dogs: Shadow, Butch, Georgia, and Fluffy. We had two males and two females, and each one had a corner of the camp to watch over. The name "Fluffy" was my daughter Eve's idea. Fluffy was nothing like her name. In fact, there was nothing fluffy about her; she had short stiff hair, a torn right ear, and scars all along her face. A better name for Fluffy would have been Nasty-Looking-Rottweiler.

Our dogs had become part of our large, patchwork family, or perhaps I should say, they had accepted us as part of their pack. We were glad that we had them to keep watch, even if some of their names were ironic. They were very protective of us and we of them. We missed the four we lost.

14

If You Plant It, Feed It, It Will Grow

Sometimes I wonder how I am going to deal with all this crap, but then I think, *Hey, I have all of these kids... I've changed thousands of diapers. I deal with crap all the time.*

—John Fide

We didn't know how the plague had started, but some of us thought it was terrorists. If it was, they likely terrorized themselves out of existence. But if it was terrorism, it didn't stop with them, it seems. There are kinds of big-time terrorists, and there are small ones. We were now dealing with the small-potatoes kind.

Every once in a while, a couple of men would get somewhat close to one of the roadblocks and would shoot harassment fire for a few minutes then leave. They never tried to communicate with us. We had already doubled our guards. We also saw some scout vehicles that seemed to be checking out different roads in the area. We figured they were testing us and our defenses. Obviously, they knew we were here, but they did not make any other moves. We were nervous, waiting for them to intensify their activities. We were as prepared as we thought we could be. It seemed that our defenses held; the harassment firing and road testing eventually stopped, for now, and as time went on, we saw fewer scout vehicles.

It was now moving toward the end of spring, and we had formed a nice little society. We were managing well. Everyone was working together, and although there were many challenges, we had made a life for ourselves. We improved at farming and raising animals. Over the last year, we had harvested corn, wheat, and berries in the larger fields. In the smaller gardens, we had planted other types of vegetables we needed. We also took advantage of the fruit trees at local farms and picked tons of produce in the late summer.

We were satisfied with our accomplishments, and we were happy to be eating something other than canned food. We had worked at getting more cows, sheep, goats, and chickens to sustain us and were getting fresh meat now. Eli slaughtered some of his cows, and we were able to eat wonderful steaks. In addition to the domesticated meat, our fields had the added benefit of attracting deer and elk, which gave us game to eat. Canadian geese flew over a couple of times a year and would land in the fields, so goose was on the menu too.

We had canned as much food as we could and returned to the stores in town to collect more often. We had our own swelling store of food now. We cleaned our little town out of canning supplies too, so it looked like we weren't going to starve to death any time soon.

There were still other challenges that we needed to overcome to improve our little community, but our ingenuity and hard work had served us well. We always needed to be vigilant about running into hostile groups at home and away.

When one of our generators broke down, Dad, Father Jay, and I decided to drive into Woodburn for supplies. We arrived at the outskirts of Woodburn and were thankful no one was in sight. We slowly and cautiously made it to our destination, the Woodburn Pet Clinic. We knew this clinic had a back-up generator for operating on animals. And if we happened across any medical items, we were going to take them because the pharmacies in the area had already been emptied or were in locations that were too dangerous to visit.

We carefully walked around the building to see if we could find easy entry. The building was made of concrete block and about the size of a convenience store. The building was white with black trim and a flat roof. It had large glass windows in the front and small ones on either of the sides. There was a double glass entry door at the front and solid steel doors at the back. The front windows were broken out, and the place obviously had been looted. We carefully made our way inside through the windowless front entrance. Father Jay took the right side of the building, and I took the left. Dad covered the entrance in case we needed to make a quick escape. It was all clear.

Father Jay yelled, "I found a ladder to the roof!" He climbed up and said, "The generator is still here, but it is going to take some work to bring it down."

About that time, Dad looked across the street and said, "Duh, they have portable generators on trailers over there! Why didn't we think of that before?"

I couldn't help but laugh. Maybe we weren't the brightest bulbs in the pack, but at least we showed a little illumination from time to time. That must count for something. We all had different strengths and weaknesses, but together, we were able to accomplish a lot using our individual gifts.

Father Jay climbed back down the ladder and began filling my Bronco with leftover veterinarian medical supplies. The rest of us crossed the street to the rental equipment yard. I found two rental pickups in the back. Dad and I wheeled two of the portable generators over to the trucks and hooked them to the trailer hitches. We hooked the third generator to the back of my Bronco after Father Jay drove it over to us. Then my dad and I went in to check out the rental store.

The store was big, probably a ten-thousand-square-foot structure. The glass doors were broken out and opened. We looked first for the keys for the trucks. *See, we are getting smarter!* We found a locked key box behind the counter. Since it was a rental business, it was a treasury of every kind of tool, and we quickly found bolt cutters and cut the lock off the key box. We grabbed the keys and brought them out to the trucks. Thankfully they both started with little cranking, and they had plenty of fuel. We went back into the store and grabbed all the tools and equipment we could carry. We may have overdone it, because the trucks were riding pretty low from all the tools, nails, screws, bits, and blades.

It was time to get back to camp, so we radioed home and told them we were on our way back and coming down Highway 99. Connor said he would open the barricade for our rigs. We arrived back at camp ten minutes later, encountering no opposition.

Dad, Phil, and I got to work hooking up the generators. We ran them mostly in the evenings for lighting. Thankfully, our solar power panels worked pretty well during the day. Now we had enough power to run our little town night or day.

On a Sunday, after morning mass, some of us wanted to drive to the Willamette River to go fishing. Dad, Eli, Connor, Jared, Father Jay, and I headed out; but since we could not leave the town unattended, everyone else stayed back to man the guard posts and get other things accomplished.

As we were coming back from our fishing trip, a glimmer caught our eyes. It was in the field near the school which had a good view of our town. It was near our trip wires and flares. We stopped the trucks and grabbed our rifles. Eli radioed to Carter back in town to let him know what was going on. We then circled around behind the spot. Meanwhile, Carter and CJ took up sniper positions on the church and school roofs, respectively. When we got to the spot, we found only an empty coffee thermos and a partially eaten can of sardines. I carefully opened the coffee thermos, and it was still warm. Someone had been watching us. The dirt was packed down the length of a body. Whoever it was had been watching us for a while.

"They may be watching us now," Jared said.

I said, "It's probably that same guy that killed Grizzly and Lady!"

Upon returning home, we told the others about our mysterious watcher.

I said, "And getting back to fishing, it took us all day, but we caught twenty trout and three salmon. Let the record show that Connor caught the biggest fish—this time." Grinning, Connor held up his large salmon. I gave him a mock glare.

Having caught the smallest fish, my *punishment* was to clean the fish. As I cleaned the fish, I reflected that we had been seeing military vehicles driving along the highway more frequently. I wondered if our *watcher* was alone or a member of the Prophets of Revelation cult. *The members of the cult were dangerous, organized, and they are expanding their territory.* We did not know why they were on the move, and we didn't care too much as long as they left us alone. But we knew the two men that chased Connor and Seamus were from the same capitol group, and they knew that we were here.

When we farmed with the tractors, we tried to stay out of sight of the highways. That was difficult because I-5 was off to the west of us and Highway 99 was to the east. We were careful not to plow next to either highway. The grass had grown tall there and was concealing our crops. In addition, we decided to plant trees there with the idea that they would eventually block the view, but this had disadvantages as well because we couldn't easily see if someone was coming.

Sometimes we found the crops nearest the highways partially harvested—that is, stolen. We just had to write off those crops because we couldn't patrol everywhere all the time. Another issue was that sometimes the tractors caused dust clouds while working the fields, which would announce our presence to anyone within miles, but there was little that we could about that. Besides, we figured that they already knew that we were here.

It was now close to two years since the virus had changed our world and our lives. This new life was so different and so much harder. The month of May was colder than usual, but our friendships with the newer members of our community grew warmer.

One cool morning, Seamus spotted a man spying on us in the field northwest of the school. The wind had caught the corner of the tarp the man was under, but otherwise, he was well hidden; he seemed to be just a slight mound in a field full of mounds.

We quickly grabbed our rifles and set out across the field after him. When he saw us coming toward him, he jumped up and sprinted away across the field. He appeared to be carrying a rifle of some kind. We chased him to a house that had been abandoned long before the plague had struck. It was located on land just south of Connor and Hannah's farm. We never used this house because it was in such poor condition. Its roof and the siding were rotten. It wasn't safe. A tree had fallen on it and was resting precariously on the roof, and it seemed that the house could come down at any moment. The peak of the roof was bowed inward dangerously, yet somehow the roof was supporting the weight of the tree.

We cautiously approached the house, unsure if the mysterious stranger inside could see us approaching from inside. We each took a corner of the house so that each of us could keep an eye on two sides of the house and have the possibility of catching our target in a crossfire, if it came to that.

Somehow this man had avoided us for months, and I was feeling on edge. Unfortunately, we didn't have any dogs with us to send in. And besides, that plan hadn't worked out very well last time.

I heard a muffled voice from inside, "John, is that you?"

I was startled; I didn't expect to hear my name. "Who's asking?" I yelled.

The muffled voice replied, "It's me! Sam from Heavy Transport Repair."

I had thought his voice had sounded familiar in our last encounter, and many memories of him returned to me. I worked with him years ago, and he was a pretty nice guy. He had a wife and three kids and seemed to be a good husband and dad, but I knew that the challenges of our new world could change people. *Why was he spying on us? Or is he spying on me? Why didn't he just come and talk with us?*

Well, I wasn't going to get any answers by asking myself questions, so I yelled, "What are you doing, Sam? Just come out! We're not going to hurt you. Come out and talk with us."

Sam's muffled voice came back: "No! If you want to talk, then come in here alone."

"Look, Sam, you're making me pretty nervous here. I'm not going in there unless you answer some of my questions."

His voice cracked as he said, "I thought I recognized you, and then I saw your family." He paused, and in a more melancholic tone, he said, "Your whole family survived...it survived...so I was trying to find out your secret. How did your whole family survive?"

My heart sank. *He must have lost his entire family to the virus.* I could only imagine how lost he must feel without his family. I replied, "Sam, we all got sick with the flu a few weeks before the virus, and we figured that made us immune somehow."

He lowered his voice and said, "Come in, and let's talk."

I turned to the others and told them that I wanted to try to talk to Sam in the house.

Carter said, "It's your call, John. You know the guy, but he makes me nervous. Just yell, and we'll come in blazing."

I grabbed my Glock and slid it back into the holster. I took a deep breath and passed my AR-15 to Carter. I went to the front door and yelled, "Sam, I'm coming in."

I heard a muffled, "Okay," so I entered.

The door creaked loudly as I pushed it inward. The smell of rot, mold, and candles immediately wafted out of the darkness. I put up my hands. I wished I had brought a flashlight.

My eyes were not adjusted to the dark. All I could see was the faint flicker of light from candles across room. The door slammed behind me, and before I could turn or speak, I sensed movement behind me and then felt a sharp blow to the back of my head.

I've heard people say that they saw stars when they were knocked out. I didn't see stars; I saw squares. Maybe it was because my face hit the hard tile floor, and then, darkness.

*****

My eyes opened. *Where am I? What is this tangy taste in my mouth? It's blood! Why is my head hurting?* I groaned. I reached up and felt my head. I felt something wet. *More blood!* Then I realized where I was. I wasn't sure how long that I had been out. My vision was clouded, and even sounds seemed muffled. I fumbled around a bit with my hands, feeling the tile floor underneath me. I pushed myself up onto my knees with something resembling a wobbly pushup.

My vision was blurry, and I saw something bright and flickering; it resolved into something that was not a pretty picture. Sam had a massive collage of pictures of his wife and kids on the wall with a row of candles along the wall burning below them. It looked as though he had taken every picture from his family albums and put them on the wall. Given the setting, it was a kind of morbid shrine dedicated to his lost family.

I could see the candlelight reflected off Sam's face, and more importantly, the rifle that he had slung over his arm.

He saw me looking at the photos of his family, and he said, "Look at them! How come your family survived, and I had to watch my wife and kids die? It's not fair. You don't have to live with it every day like I do."

As he continued talking, I couldn't help thinking, *He should have a photo of his mind nailed on the wall as well, because he had obviously lost it along with his family.* He paced back and forth as he talked, and his body and the rifle that he was holding were silhouetted in front of the shrine of burning candles.

I could feel a sharp pain starting to increase on my forehead. I could feel blood trickling down the gash on the back of my head. I cautiously looked around, and the house seemed to be empty besides the pictures and candles. I started to try to get to my feet.

Sam said, "Don't you even think about getting up! And don't look for your pistol, I've got it!"

I paused with my feet under me and was kind of crouched into a ball, and I said, "Man, I've got to pee, can I stand up?"

"No! No! Peeing is the last of your problems," he said. "Now your family has to suffer like I have to." He brought up the rifle and aimed it at my head. I was scared. I looked into his eyes, and there was nothing there that resembled compassion. I expected that my life would flash before my eyes, but instead, I thought to myself, *Great, I survive the virus, and now this wacko is going to take me out.*

Then I heard a large thump on the wall followed by an ominous creaking sound. Sam turned and pointed the rifle toward the thump. My friends outside must have heard what was going on. They couldn't see inside, but they were trying to find a way to enter safely into the house. Every couple of seconds, someone would hit the wall. Each time, it distracted Sam more and more. He looked from side to side nervously. I heard Carter yell to see if I was okay.

Sam tried to follow Carter's voice through the wall, and I knew that was my chance. In one swift motion, I stood while I swung my fist upward and drove a wicked uppercut under Sam's chin. I put the weight of my whole body behind it. I hit him as hard as I could, square under his jaw. Either bone or teeth gave way with the impact. Sam's head snapped back, and a muffled scream escaped from his lips. It turned out his rifle was a semiautomatic shotgun. As he fell back, the barrel of the gun rose. Shots rang out loudly, and I jumped to the side. The first shot hit wall beside me. The second shot blew a hole in the wall right above my head. As he fell back on the floor, his third and final shot destroyed the last remaining beam holding up the roof.

The repeated blasts from his shotgun had my ears ringing. Regrettably, my ears were still able to hear the creaking and splintering of wood as the house began to come down on top of us. *Great!* I jumped back toward the closed door in which I had entered. Unfortunately, I didn't make it out in time.

It was dark. I could taste and smell dust, and I could feel an immense amount of weight across my back, and my head was pinned in place. I was face-down, and I couldn't move. My right hand was free next to my ear. I was having trouble breathing. *This is probably what it would feel like to be wrapped up by an anaconda.* Each breath seemed to increase the weight. To make matters worse, after a little while, I could smell smoke. *Oh no, the candles.*

I could barely breathe. I could only make some wheezing sounds, so I started pounding upward with my fist on the wall that was pressed against my face. It wasn't a very loud knock because it was an upward thrust with my knuckles at a weird angle. Apparently, somebody heard it because Jared stepped on a beam that was already applying a lot of pressure on my head. Through clenched teeth, I yelled out at the extra pain, and I'm not afraid to admit that I could feel tears squeezing out of my eyes. It may be true that big girls don't cry, but apparently, this big boy does when his head is about to be squished like a grape. Thankfully, I was near the door, and it was basically off its hinges, so the three of them were able to lift the wall just enough for me to slither my way out. I'm thankful that I have a thick skull.

A few minutes later, we were able to clear some debris and see part of Sam's body, but he had obviously been crushed by the weight of the tree and the house, and one of the large broken off limbs had pushed through his chest. By that time, the fire had gotten out of control. Carter asked me if we should bury him. I said, "No, there is no way we could get his body out in time, besides the fire will take care of that."

As I limped home with the guys, I tried not to be mad at Sam. He had obviously snapped from helplessly watching his family die a horrible death in front of him. *Would the same thing have happened to me if I'd lost my family that way? No, I don't think so.*

Carter smiled and clapped me on the shoulder. "You need to find better friends!"

I returned the smile and said, "You're one."

I was thankful for my friends. Isolation did not work out well for Sam. Although living in community has its challenges, the alternative is far worse. Friendships are an essential part of what makes us human.

15

Reaching Out

A faithful friend is a sturdy shelter: he that has found one
has found a treasure. There is nothing so precious as a
faithful friend, and no scales can measure his excellence.

—The Book of Sirach 6:14–15

Some days later, late in the evening, one of my twins, Eden, lightly knocked on the door of the main bedroom and woke up Laura and me. She complained that she was scared and wanted to sleep with us. This wasn't unusual; often, one the kids would climb into bed with us. But she seemed especially frightened, so I put on my robe and took my Glock 9mm out of the nightstand drawer and checked around the house.

I checked each of the kids' rooms and listened for any unusual sounds. Nothing seemed out of the place. When I returned, Laura had gotten Eden calmed down, and she was snuggling in bed with her mom. I smiled to Laura, signaling that all was well. I turned off the light and climbed back into bed; I could hear Eden breathing lightly as she peacefully drifted back to sleep.

A short time later, after I had fallen asleep, my eyes popped open, the hairs on the back of my neck were standing on end. I had the overwhelming sensation that I was being watched. I expected to feel Eden lying between me and Laura, but she wasn't there. Concerned, I sat up and looked around the room. I could see Eden standing at the foot of the bed. She was illuminated by the moonlight. Her eyes were wide, unblinking. She was staring right at me. I had the strange sensation that she was staring through me. I said, "Eden, honey, what is the matter?"

She continued to stare for a moment, unblinking, and whispered, "Thunder and lightning...thunder and lightning! The sky is raining metal!"

I don't mind saying that I was a little creeped out. I got out of bed and knelt down next to Eden. Her unblinking eyes followed me. I put my arm around her. I said quietly, "It is time to go back to sleep." She didn't say anything, but her eyes became heavy, and I guided her back to bed, next to her mom. She lay down and immediately went to sleep. *She was sleepwalking. She must have inherited that from me*, I thought. My parents and my brother have told me stories of some of the strange things that I did and said as a kid when I was sleepwalking. *It is still kind of creepy, though.*

The following morning, over breakfast, Jared and Chloe returned from an overnight scouting expedition to see what kind of activities were happening in Woodburn. They reported that they had seen some members of the Woodburn group who were friendly, at least if the information from the radio broadcast was to be believed. They explained what they had found while we ate. They hadn't approached the people in Woodburn, but simply scouted out their location.

Father Jay said, "I think we should send out some scouting parties to find other survivors." This suggestion started a big discussion among us. As the we discussed these things, I walked over to Eve, my other twin, who was drawing a picture. At the top of the page, she had made a big dark cloud with orange and yellow fire in the middle. There were lightning bolts coming out of it. Down below there were stick figures that looked like they were running. She then drew little red and silver drops of rain coming down out of the cloud. The little stick figures appeared to be running from the rain.

I sat down next to her. "Eve, what are you drawing?"

She said, "It is a metal storm." She pointed to the cloud. "See there is fire in the cloud, and it makes metal rain. If the metal touches you, then you die." She continued drawing. I felt goosebumps along my arm. It was troubling how my twins were sometimes on the same wavelength over this—Eden last night speaking about the sky raining metal, and now, Eve drawing a metal storm.

Meanwhile, the discussion among the adults was wrapping up. It seemed we were in agreement that it was a good idea to seek out the other groups, but cautiously.

Phil said, "I think that we should talk to other camps that don't seem hostile and maybe unite with them in some way, or at least, find out if they are a threat."

After more discussion, we agreed on sending four people in two cars to the Woodburn group. But with Eden's sleepwalking and Eve's drawing, I had a feeling of foreboding. I wanted to say that it wasn't the right time, but I couldn't come up with any kind of rational argument to postpone, so I didn't say anything.

Phil, Connor, Jared, and Chloe volunteered to go. They left about noon that day and would stay in radio contact with us. But we knew that the radio had limited range, and as expected, reports stopped from them when they got out of range.

It was a tense time for those us who remained behind at the radio. Our cell phones no longer functioned for communication, and now they were little more than digital cameras and calculators. *How things have changed.*

It was always a tense time whenever someone ventured out beyond the boundaries of our little fortified town, but even more so now. It felt like we might be inviting trouble. I was glad that Carter and Gabriella decided to follow them for support. Carter had taken his AR-15 with an extended barrel and a 7mm Remington. Both rifles were capable of long-range shots. Knowing that a trained sniper was watching over them gave us great comfort.

I reflected on how Carter and his family had become such a wonderful addition to our group. He recently had begun teaching our group how to make the long shot. It quickly became obvious that he should be the man in charge of all our defensive and possibly offensive operations. He had also taught us how to conceal ourselves in our environment and how to stalk. We were not soldiers or real snipers by any means, but the more training and information we received from him, the better prepared we became.

I marveled at how God's divine providence seemed to provide the right people at the right time for our little group. My brother had begun teaching taekwondo to the children and a few of the adults. As I looked over to the little field in front of the school, I could see Father Jay facing a group of our children, wearing his white *dobok*, leading the children in a series of punches and blocks. He had become a first-degree black belt in this Korean martial art while he was in seminary at nearby Mt. Angel. He had never thought that there would be much use for it other than for keeping himself in shape. At first, the training just seemed a nice diversion for the kids, but the discipline seemed to have a positive effect on the kids as well. I even joined some of his sessions. It was a good workout.

Later that day, we heard over the two-way radio that our four scouts and their two backups were on their way home. I breathed a sigh of relief and said a prayer of thanks to God. They returned with good news and filled us in over dinner.

We ate Southern fried chicken with mashed potatoes and gravy that evening. Laura and my mom had cooked, and it was delicious. We all dined together on certain evenings, during the week, especially when there was important news or needed discussion. After Phil had wiped his face with a napkin, he hit his spoon against the side of his glass to get our attention. When everyone had quieted down, he began to tell us about the visit to the folks in Woodburn.

He stood up and took a sip of water. "As you know, we took a little excursion today to visit our neighbors to the north. We pulled our two cars up to the outlet mall where our scouts had located them earlier. As we pulled up, a man stepped out from behind a disabled car with a rifle and motioned for us to stop. He seemed to be in his forties." At this point, Phil looked over at Chloe for confirmation.

She nodded. "Yeah, forties."

Phil continued, "He was a white guy with black hair and a full beard. He was wearing these dirty blue jeans and a ripped black jacket, which seemed strange to me because he was at the mall after all. Anyway, he also wore an old Seattle Seahawk's ball cap. So we slowed down and showed him our hands to show that we meant him no harm."

Phil nodded toward Carter and continued, "Then I heard Carter say in my earpiece that he had the guy in his sights if anything went wrong. I don't mind saying that helped put me at ease. Then the man came up to my window and said, 'What do you want?' So I told him I was the leader of a group in Gervais and asked to talk to the leader of their group. Well, he radioed to somebody and waited for a response.

"After a short time, three more men came out: two Hispanic men in their thirties and a black guy, probably twenty years old. They weren't wearing any uniforms or anything, just regular clothes." He paused to take another sip of water. "But what was most obvious was that all three had shotguns on their shoulders. Then they told me, and only me, to get out of the car. The Hispanic man with the Mohawk searched me. He removed my radio and earpiece and set my pistol out on the hood of the car. Now this is where things got interesting."

Phil sat down and leaned back in his chair and paused a moment. Everyone was leaning forward, wanting to hear what happened. Phil took a moment to pick at his teeth. He looked down at his finger, inspecting what he had picked out of his teeth.

With mock exasperation, Karen said, "Just get on with it!"

Phil had a little smile on his face, and then he looked over at Connor as he continued his tale: "They grabbed my stuff off the hood and told me to come with them, and they said that Connor needed to stay in the car. So Connor says, 'Hell no! We don't know you guys from Adam!' Well, Connor had a point, but trust has to begin somewhere. So I looked at Connor and said, 'This is how we build trust.' I could tell that Jared and Chloe weren't too happy about this either." Phil laughed.

"Well, they told everyone else to stay in their cars. The white guy with the black hair drove me over to McLaren, you know, the juvenile detention center."

Phil ran his fingers through his hair, "I don't mind telling you that I was sweating. As we drove through the gates into the detention center, I saw it was clearly a well-fortified place. I noticed that they had some guys set up on the roof in sniper positions. It seemed like a good place for a base of operations. It had large fences to keep people in, which could also be used to keep people out. Besides, there are plenty of rooms in which to stay. I'm not sure how comfortable the rooms are, but there are plenty of them.

"When we reached the front of the building, a man in his mid-fifties wearing an Oregon State University sweatshirt walked out. He was clean-cut with short, cropped blond-and-gray hair. He had an aura of authority about him. I wondered if he had worked at the detention center. I got out of the car and stood up as I looked around. He said, 'Hello my name is Joe—and you are a big one, aren't you?' I smiled and said, 'Go, Beavers!' Well, Joe thought that was funny. At that point, they gave me my radio back and let me tell Connor that everything was okay."

Chloe flashed us her winning smile and said, "Yeah, he told us he would come back after an hour. Can you imagine? We were sitting there wondering whether he was really okay or not. We didn't know if they really had him tied up and were forcing him to lie."

Jared burst in. "Yeah, we should have thought up a code word so that we would know he was really fine—like, 'The eagle has landed,' or 'The toast is buttered!'"

Connor laughed. "Meanwhile, I was trying to figure out how to take out the three guys holding shotguns on us."

Jared said, "I tried to engage them in conversation, but they just kept saying, 'Don't worry. Just be patient.' Well, that just made me more worried and more impatient."

Phil shook his head and laughed. "I'm sorry about that, but you guys know how I like to talk. So anyway, I told Joe about what was going well for us here and about our setbacks. I told him about the farming and the animals. He was very interested in all that. All they have been eating is canned food and whatever they were able to hunt. I held a lot back because I decided it would not be prudent to give away too much information about us.

"They have had their ups and downs as well. He told me about the prison—how it has generators and lots of places to stay. They were down to fifteen people, six men and nine women. Thankfully, they hadn't had too much trouble from the marauding groups.

"Then we finally got around to talking about the possibility of combining our groups or at least trading our fresh produce and meat for things Joe's group has gathered. It was clear that they were set on staying there. He did invite us to join his group on a probationary basis. I told him that I didn't think that would happen, but I would bring the offer to the group. He was very interested in trade, however. I found out that they usually keep their radios on channel 18, and I told him that we keep ours on channel 7.

"Then Joe smiled and said, 'I think this is going to be a beautiful friendship.' I shook his hand and said, 'Me too.' Then I radioed our scouts and told them that I was coming back. Our new friends dropped me off at the mall and then we drove home without incident, and here we are."

Everyone was excited about the other group. I was too. And maybe I was starting to recover a little of my faith in humanity again.

Phil said, "We should probably try reaching out to some more of the groups in the area." He paused and said, "They were most excited about the animals we are raising, and fresh produce." Our farmers, Eli, Leah, Connor, Hannah, and Judy, all smiled. They were the brains behind our success in working the land and raising the animals.

For the next few months, we had fruitful exchanges with the Woodburn group. We were able to provide them with fresh water and food, and they regularly made trips to Portland and the other towns to scout for supplies for trade. We often traded our food for ammunition.

Phil became fast friends with their leader Joe, and Joe's wife had apparently been a nurse before the plague; she was of great use to us when any of us needed medical attention.

Time passed, and the days grew colder and shorter. It has been a relatively cold summer and fall, and the year was promising to be an even colder winter. It was now mid-November, almost two and a half years since the plague killed most of the world's population. It was becoming increasingly more difficult to find fuel that had not turned bad.

One evening, a Hummer stopped about a half-mile down the road and lobbed shots at us all night. We could hear bullets hitting the walls of the church and the school. We moved everyone to the back of the school. Then Carter and CJ crawled on their stomachs through the fields with their rifles to take out the threat.

Early next morning, Carter and his son returned covered in mud and gave us the all-clear. When we surveyed the damage, one of the stained-glass windows of the church had a hole in it where a bullet had gone through. In addition, there were numerous pockmarks in the sides of the buildings. Some of the cars were dinged up and had bullet holes in them.

We all sat down as a group and talked about it. Carter said that by the time they had gotten to where the shooters had been, they were gone. He showed us a handful of fired bullet shells along with some beer cans and wine bottles. *Alcohol and firearms—not a good combination.* We came to the conclusion that it was harassment fire, and judging from caliber of the shells and the lack of penetration from the bullets, it seemed they were using only pistols to harass us. Perhaps the shooters' motivation was simply to get under our skin and maybe keep us from sleeping. Well, it worked on both counts. We realized that we were truly in mortal danger.

As Carter explained the steps of how he and his son had checked the perimeter, I noticed the firm set of his mouth and the hardness in his eyes. I said, "Okay, Carter, what's on your mind?"

He briefly put his head down to collect his thoughts as though he was self-conscious about what he was going to say. Then he looked up at the group and said, "This was very dangerous last night, and I think that we need to respond to this threat in kind. We need to respond with lethal force. If any of us had been out in front of the school or the church, we could have been killed."

He looked around to let what he had said sink in. And it did; my heart sank. I had been trying to convince myself that if we just stayed under the radar, the bad factions out there would leave us alone.

I could see that not everyone was convinced. Even I wasn't convinced. Carter could see it in our faces.

"Listen," he said, "you have to understand what we are up against. I have come to understand through my military training that violence is a tool, and you have to know when to use it." He paused to allow us to comprehend what he was saying. "These men that we are up against may not be militarily trained, but they know how to use violence. They know how to win."

He scratched his head, trying to figure out the best way to explain. "You don't poke a bear with a stick. You either kill it, or you stay away."

I knew Carter was right. I looked around the room, and I could see that each face in the room reflected my own thoughts. I looked at my twin daughters, Eden and Eve, playing quietly in the corner. I remembered: *Thunder and lightning...raining metal...metal storm!* We took a quick vote and all agreed to respond, if necessary, with lethal force.

Then Father Jay stood up and said, "I think we should at least put up a warning sign or something."

Carter replied, "Okay, Father, but I don't think it will do any good."

We quickly got to work. Eli and Phil took guard duty on the east side of town while Chloe and Jared took guard duty on the west side of town. Carter and Ray loaded some heavier loads for the AR-15. Meanwhile, Father Jay painted some big signs that warned that any discharge of firearms in the area may be met with lethal force. My dad and I went to find some steel plates to better fortify against stray bullets.

We were as ready as we could be. Carter and his son were set up on the roof with their AR-15s as the sun began to set beyond the horizon. Those who weren't at the guard posts were huddled together in the library. Every light source in the town was extinguished. Carter was the first to radio in.

"We've got someone coming up the road," he said in a whisper. I decided to climb up to the roof to assist him. As I climbed the ladder to the roof, I heard shots in the distance. I could hear bullets hitting the building and the cars parked around the building. Suddenly it didn't seem like such a good idea to be on the roof. Nonetheless, I slithered to Carter's position.

"What have you got?" I whispered.

Carter was looking through the scope of his rifle as he said, "The idiots went to the same place they were before. I see muzzle flashes, but it's too dark to make out much more." He added, "I'm getting a good infrared spotting scope the next time I'm in town."

I could see headlights in the distance. I could hear loud laughing in the distance and the breaking of glass—probably beer bottles—in between the sounds of the guns they fired.

Carter said, "They ran over your brother's sign." He looked over at me. "It was a nice idea, but I knew it wouldn't deter them." He looked through his scope. "They had their chance."

Suddenly, I saw a flash of light in the distance, the trip flare had gone off; it was illuminating the men and their vehicle. Carter said, "Yeah, they are definitely shooting this way. I've got 'em now."

I jumped, startled from Carter's first shot, and then my ear was ringing; I guess I wasn't ready for Carter to shoot so quickly. Through the ringing, I heard, "Whoops, I missed. But I'm dialed in now."

Another loud report from his rifle. "Okay, one down…one to go. Dang! He got his radio out. All right, he's trying to hide, but he doesn't realize that he's on the wrong side of the truck. Okay, hold still…" and then another loud report, and it was done.

Carter was immediately on the radio. "Okay, we need to get to that Hummer and remove those bodies."

"Wait!" I heard a voice say come over the radio. "Someone else is coming!"

I thought to myself, *Crap!* By this time, I was looking through the scope of my own rifle; I could see in the light of the fading flare that a pickup had arrived. It seemed to be the same pickup which had chased Seamus and Connor home. Just as the light from the flare faded, a man got out of the passenger side to take the Hummer away. Carter tried to take a shot, but there just wasn't enough light.

Carter turned to look at me in the dim light. "John, I think that we've just started something." I could hear the uncertainty and pain in his voice.

I met his gaze. "We didn't start it, they did. But I think you're right. This isn't finished. I don't think they're going to be scared off."

16

Metal Storm!

I've often heard that there are two absolutes in life: death and taxes. I'm not doing taxes anymore, but there is a lot of death. When everything is taken away, it makes you appreciate the most important things. I'm so glad to be with my family.

—Victoria Fide

Gun shots! A lot of gun shots not very far away! We could hear Ray's voice crackling over the radio as we sat around a table in the gym. At first, we couldn't make out very much of what he was saying. Gun shots were heard over the radio. Then we heard in a loud whisper, "They're coming! They've got four military Hummers, and I would estimate about ten men with automatic rifles. They're firing their guns into the air... I guess it's a show of force."

Laura turned and yelled to the rest of us, "They're coming!"

I suppose that in the back of my mind, I knew they would come eventually. I had hoped that they wouldn't notice us or ignore us, but it wasn't meant to be.

I said over the radio, "Don't engage! Henry and Mabel, go and start the locomotive!"

Then Seamus's voice crackled over the radio, "Defensive plan E! Let's not start a fight. They were only firing into the air!"

Jared gave a tight-lipped smile, and Carter said, "Let's see if your crossfire idea works." We all split up. Each of us knew where to go and what to do. Jared, Carter, CJ, Laura, and Chloe climbed to the roof of the school and took up their sniper positions.

Leah, Mom, Hannah, Mario, and Father Jay were in the houses across the street. They were set up in their various firing positions. Connor, Seamus, Phil, Gina, and Susan were in the school and the gym, ready to defend.

I could see everything from the roof of the church. I could hear the sound of crunching metal in the distance as the invaders pushed one of the cars that was blocking the road out of the way. I saw the car roll over into the ditch as the Hummer pushed through.

Another Hummer drove past the school and blocked the north side of the street. Two of the Hummers drivers boldly parked conspicuously right in front of the school. The last Hummer had stopped at the street by the church, blocking the intersection. Now both ends of the street were blocked by the Hummers.

Hannah, Sally, and Karen had taken the ten kids to the school library for safety. Every member of our group was at or near the school with weapons in hand.

Ten men exited their Hummers and took cover behind their vehicles and their doors. They wore body armor and had fully automatic machine guns. The men were of different ages and races, and despite all the official-looking weapons and gear, they looked a little unorganized.

I could feel a low rumble reverberating up through the foundation of the church. It was the train rolling into position. Henry and Mabel had started the engine and had the train backing into town pushing several railroad cars. The surprised invaders turned around as the breaks squealed on the train and came to a full stop. The train had blocked both of the streets, effectively cutting the town in half, preventing any more invaders from coming that direction. The soldiers actually looked a little nervous. As they turned around, they couldn't help but notice that every adult and older kid had a weapon pointed at them.

I noticed one of the men was Jack Long, the young man Carter had elbowed and who we had kicked out. He was smiling with one tooth missing. His smug, toothless smile seemed to say, "I own you now."

I recognized two of the other guys as well. They were Baldy and Mr. Mohawk, Shadow's favorite chew toys. I figured these two who had chased Connor and Seamus would be here as well. They were both grinning.

After looking around for a minute, another man stepped forward and grabbed the microphone from a radio inside the Hummer. He held it up to his face as he looked around. He seemed to notice our preparations: the generators, solar panels, crops, animals, and fuel tankers. He was smart enough to realize that we were a larger and more organized group than he had anticipated.

He depressed the microphone button and a high-pitched whine from feedback came out of a speaker somewhere hidden on the Hummer. With his voice amplified, he said, "I am Sgt. Lawless. I'm second in command under the general, and I'm in charge of this area. Who is the leader of this group?"

Seamus spoke slowly over our own radio system, "He's one of the men from the group that took over at the capitol."

Phil whispered back, "You better let me talk to him since he has seen you before."

Phil stepped out of the doorway from the gym of the school and said, "I am. I'm in charge here."

Phil was wearing dark blue pants with a banded shirt. The shirt was light blue with an orange stripe across the middle. It in no way gave the appearance of a uniform or authority, not quite as intimidating apparel as our "visitors." But the .30-30 Winchester lever action rifle in his hands and the Colt .45 holstered on his right hip made him look a little more intimidating. The rifle for now was pointing at the ground slightly toward the sergeant.

The sergeant looked him up and down quickly and smiled. Then he looked over at Jack. Jack nodded and said, "Yeah, he's one of the leaders." Then Jack yelled loudly, "You kicked me out, and now it's payback time!"

The sergeant gave Jack a frown and said, "Jack, please...we don't want to wear out the hospitality of our hosts here."

Carter quietly spoke over the radio, "I can take out three before they know what hits them. They'll have to be head shots. They have body armor. I've got dibs on Jack's head shot. That leaves seven, what do you think, John?"

"Wait. Concentrate on the two middle cars and just hold off for now. Our families are in danger if it comes to a gun fight. I don't want to start anything," I whispered back on the radio. Then I added, "Dad and I will flank the north end Hummer. Ray, you and Eli flank the south Hummer."

I heard a "Roger" crackle over the radio confirming the plan.

Then I said, "We need to see if we can settle this peacefully or not. And I want to be in position in case we can't."

Henry said on the radio, "There aren't any more invaders in sight. Let me know if you want the train moved."

I said, "Henry, you and Mabel disable it and hide somewhere off the train!"

Phil looked at the sergeant and said, "Sgt. Lawless, what is it that you want with us?"

Lawless yelled, "The other day, a couple of our men were killed not too far from here. You wouldn't know anything about that, would you?"

Phil answered, "Yes, your men were shooting at us, so we shot back."

"That is most regrettable," the sergeant replied. "But our general can be forgiving. You see, he owns this area from Woodburn to Salem. If you want to stay on his land, then you have to pay me."

Phil replied, "His land? If it's money you want, we can march over to the bank in Woodburn and get you all you want."

"No, you misunderstand me. It isn't money we are looking for. Right now, I'm looking for two of our women. Their names are Gina and Susan." He paused to see Phil's reaction. Then he continued, "You see, they belong to us." Looking over at Jack, he continued, "I have it on good authority that they are here. Bring them to us, and we'll consider it a goodwill offering."

Then reaching into the vehicle, he flicked a switch and said, "The general has some words for you." Then he spoke into the handset, telling the general that he was on speaker.

There was some static for a couple seconds. Then a man's voice came from the speaker. "I'm known as the general. And good day to you, Susan and Gina. I told you that I would find you." His voice was low and elegant. He seemed to have a slight British accent.

"I've missed you," he continued. "You both need to leave with my men. Daddy misses you." I could hear the smile in his silky voice. He cleared his voice slightly. "You see, this little group of yours is in my area. And this area was given to me by my god. Perhaps you don't understand it now, but you will. I have been anointed to be king of this new creation. It is my destiny, and it is futile to resist destiny."

There was a pause to allow his words to sink in. "This is the way it will be: any resistance and you all will be killed. My women will be given back to me, and the rest of you will be allowed to serve me!

"You fired on two of my men, struck me, and stole my girls. You should know that I can be a forgiving master, so here is what we will do. I can forgive that you have fired on my men. I can even forgive that you have hidden my girls from me, but the man who hit me is going to die!

"Lawless, bring back my girls to me, and kill the man who hit me! I want his head. You can leave the body for them!" There was a pause and then he said, "I understand there is a church and a priest. We have no more use for priests now. I'm the chosen instrument of god now. Sergeant, kill the priest and burn the church." There was dead silence as the speaker clicked off. Lawless reached inside the Hummer and switched off the speaker. Lawless looked about and noticed some of the guns leveled in his direction. He briefly spoke on the radio to the general and seemed to be arguing.

I was trying to comprehend what had just been said. The general had just ordered the murder of my brother and Connor as though he were telling the sergeant to take out the laundry. This man was clearly a psychopath, surrounded by psychopaths.

Lawless and all of his men were grinning now. Lawless yelled, "You heard the general. Bring out his girls and the man who struck him! We will start there and then work our way to the church!"

Phil said, "This is a free county, Lawless, you can't just—"

Lawless cut him off and said, "No more discussion." Then he smiled a malevolent smile as if he were really enjoying himself. Then he added, "Bring out *all* the women." At this, some of the men in the Hummers began to spread out.

Seamus stepped out of the school, and perhaps because he was nervous, his brogue seemed especially think when he said, "We worked hard for this, and we're family here. You're not getting anything from us. We've got guns too, Sergeant. You're surrounded, outnumbered, and in our home. We'll kill you and your men if you don't leave right now!"

The tension was palpable, electric like a dark thunder cloud ready to release its angry arrows of destruction. *Metal storm!* I thought. The sergeant's smile vanished and said, "Well then, we'll start with punishing the man who hit the general."

Connor yelled out sarcastically, "Why, did the general lose a tooth like Jack there?"

A couple of Lawless's men laughed. It was obvious that they didn't think too highly of Jack either. Then I heard two quick shots. The sergeant had pulled out his pistol and shot Seamus twice in the chest. He was lightning fast and accurate.

Seamus with wide eyes put his hand to his chest. There was a look on his face as if he couldn't comprehend what had just happened. He looked down at his chest and his blood-soaked hands. Then he fell to his knees and then forward on to his face.

Phil had turned and with his arm stretched out toward Seamus, yelled, "No, no…you didn't have to do that!" Then he dived behind cover.

Then all hell broke loose. Everyone was firing a gun. Eli and Ray had already sneaked into firing positions near the end Hummer in the south intersection. Somehow, they had been able to keep Shadow quiet while getting there. That was our cue to do our part. My dad and I were running behind the cover of the church and the school. Eli had released Shadow off of his chain at the sound of the first shot. Shadow bolted past me and grabbed the throat of one of the men at the south end of the street where the Hummer was parked. I met up with my dad, and we began circling behind the north car. I had the AR-15 and my dad had a shotgun.

It was a massive gunfight. We weren't in position yet. My adrenaline was pumping, and I couldn't even hear myself running. My heart was pounding in my chest. Within seconds, the air was filled a smoky haze, the smell of gunpowder.

There were two guys in the end Hummer, and they were firing toward our group. Dad and I came up behind the two men at the truck. We shot the two men dead. It went against every instinct within me to actually line up my sights on a human being and to pull the trigger, but it had to be done. Fortunately for us, they were too busy firing on the rest of our group to see us coming from behind. We took them with headshots. They both just crumpled to the ground.

Dad upgraded from his shotgun to one of their machine guns and got into a firing position over the hood of the Hummer. I grabbed the other machine gun along with two full magazines.

I could only hope that Ray and Eli had succeeded in taking out the men at the other end of the street. I could see that Shadow had clamped his jaws down on the arm of one of the men and was shaking vigorously. The man was screaming and trying to slice the dog with his knife, so my dad shot him. Shadow ran off to chew on another bad guy.

Now that we had taken care of the end vehicles, it was time to concentrate on the two remaining. Eli saw my dad and me. He signaled toward the center two Hummers. Bullets hit next to him, so he jumped behind the Hummer.

There was a terrible firefight around two vehicles in front of the school. All the guys in the Hummers had machine guns and were pinning down our snipers on the roof. Our people on the ground floor were getting showered with glass. Those in the houses were also pinned down. The soldiers may have been outnumbered, but we were outgunned. I couldn't tell if we had killed any of the guys in the two middle Hummers. And because of their machine guns, they were setting the pace of the firefight.

Suddenly, one of the men threw a grenade at the school. It seemed to fly in slow motion, and I was powerless to stop it. I saw it fly toward the window, but thankfully, it hit the frame of the window and bounced back and landed at the exterior of the building. It fell to the ground, and I ducked behind the Hummer. In fact, the firefight stopped for a moment while people on both sides found cover. It exploded and glass chunks and bricks blew inside. I knew that if one those grenades made it inside the building, it could kill a lot of my family.

I could see Seamus's body on the ground in front of the school. Blood was pooling down the sidewalk toward the street. The front of the school was pockmarked with bullet holes. The whole front of it had little explosions of bullets hitting concrete and making craters.

All the glass that I could see was shattered from the massive gunfire. The Hummers in the middle had bullet dings all over them, but they seemed to be better cover than what we had. The men were using every inch of the armored vehicles for cover. The armored doors were all open providing enough cover for them.

The grenade turned out to be just the distraction I needed. I ran around to the Hummer and pulled the driver's side door open. I got in and started the vehicle. I must admit that I was not really thinking clearly. I was reacting. Dad opened the other door and said, "What are you doing?"

I shrugged my shoulders and said, "I've got to do something." Dad got in the passenger side and leaned out the window for a firing position. I said, "They need help, and we're it." The Hummer was set at an angle, so I spun the Hummer around, hitting a curb and brushed a parked car. Dad had to bring his body in the window when I hit the car. He gave me a dirty look and then leaned back out the window again. I straightened it out and floored it. The engine roared, and the rear tires chirped. I drove straight for the two vehicles in the center of the firefight. Dad was firing full auto out the side window. Bullets started coming through our windshield. I was hoping the windshield would stop them, but I guess our Hummer was not armor-plated. Dad ducked back inside. I was already ducked down, and we hit heads. I just tried to hold the steering wheel straight since I couldn't see. Glass from the windshield was raining down on us.

We had no way of knowing if we were also coming under friendly fire from members of our group up on the roof. We were in the soldiers' Hummer after all. The bullets coming in the windshield were too intense for us to fire back anymore, and I was smart enough not to take a look. Dad was crouched down to the floor looking at me.

Dad yelled at me, "I shouldn't have gotten in. You are nuts!" Little glass chips were raining down on us as he held his head, waiting for the impact or death. I would have gotten lower too if I wasn't driving blind. It seemed like miles, even though it was only a block or so.

I did my best to gauge our course by framing the tops of the buildings with the Hummer's window opening, but because of the large number of rounds flying over our heads, it was impossible for me to look up. When I saw the corner of the gym roof, I said, "This is going to hur—" Then my Hummer found its mark, and everything went black.

17

Tipping Point

Sometimes, in the midst of all of this, it seems like there is little to live for, but then I look at my kids, and find strength to go on.

—Laura Fide

I'm floating in this blackness. "John, wake up! They're all dead!" I heard distantly in the darkness.

My own inner voice cried out in despair, "Oh no, they're all dead. Dead. Dead. Oh no, my family, my friends, they are all dead!"

Then I heard a familiar voice reach into the darkness: "You stupid, stupid man."

Suddenly, it was like popping my head out of the water. Sounds of commotion filled my ears, and my eyes opened. Laura was holding me tight and yelling at me. Things, images, sounds were coming into focus. I pushed free and grabbed my gun. "Where are they?" I asked in a panic.

"They are all dead. All the bad men are dead." I stopped and put down my gun. I could not have done much anyway; I was still wedged under the steering wheel. I worked my way out of the wrecked Hummer. I could feel shattered glass digging into my skin as I wriggled free. There was steam hissing out of the front of the now mangled Hummer. I could smell the radiator fluid spilling out and spraying on the hot engine.

"Is Seamus okay?" I asked. "I saw him on the ground. Is Dad okay?" I saw my dad, and he waved to me while shaking his head. *I guess he still thinks that I am nuts.* He was near the gym with a bandage on his forehead. I said, in a panicked voice, "I'm sorry, I wasn't thinking. I just saw them shooting at the people I love. Did I cause more people to get hurt?"

"No, oh no," Laura said. "That's what gave us the edge. After your mental breakdown and crash, our guys on the roof picked them off after you smashed into them. Besides you ran over two of them when you crashed." She paused and said in an uneasy tone, "The sergeant jerk was coming for you in the Hummer after the crash. You were unconscious and a sitting duck. He was crouched down making his way toward you." She stopped and started to cry. I held her for a moment, and then she pulled away enough to look at me again. Then she said, "I shot him from the roof. I was the only one with a shot." She was crying but continued, "John, I was far away and on the other side of the Hummer. I just prayed, 'Jesus, let this bullet find its mark.' Then I shot. It hit him right in the head." Laura hugged me and said, "Don't you ever make me do that again!"

Laura turned away from me and said, "I'm going to be sick." She threw up copiously next to the Hummer. All I could do was put my hand on her shoulder.

I said, "You did what you had to do. You saved my life. I'm sorry you had to do it, but I'm glad you did." We held each other for a few moments.

I was starting to feel pain in my head and face. It must have shown on my face. She said, "You smacked your head, and I see some glass stuck in your right cheek and nose." She reached toward me and pulled a piece of glass out of my cheek.

"Ouch! What's wrong with you, woman! Can we do this later with tweezers or something sterile? Besides, you smell like vomit!"

She punched me in the arm. I could see on her face that she was somewhere between crying and laughing, and she said, "I'm sorry, I couldn't help myself." She smiled.

I said, "I'm okay. Let's just help the others and check on the kids."

The kids! Those words suddenly impressed upon my mind the magnitude of what had just happened. I suppose Laura could see the instant worry on my face, so she assured me that the kids were fine. I could hear crying and wailing behind me. Laura was saying something, but I didn't hear it. I found myself shaking and looking around. There was death everywhere; death that I had helped cause. Yes, the soldiers were dead, but at a heavy cost.

My hands were shaking. I could hear one of our dogs whining in pain. Her whines seemed to echo the feelings in my own heart as I looked around at the carnage. Lawless and all his men were dead. Seamus was dead. Two bullet holes in the chest from Lawless. Among our dead were Ray, Mario, Seamus, and Sally.

I could see Sally on the ground, unmoving. Her nephew, Andrew was crouched next to her, crying and shaking while he petted her head, trying to get her to wake up.

Laura explained as I stared at poor Sally. "I don't know how Andrew got away from the rest of the kids, but Andrew saw his grandfather die, and he ran toward the doors of the school. Sally saw him and grabbed him and put her body in the line of fire to save him."

"A heroic death," I whispered to no one in particular. "But still, she is dead." *What terrible psychological scars will these children have? What scars will we all have?*

Laura physically turned my head toward her. "But Andrew is alive," she reminded me.

Mario had gotten hit in the throat, a wound that severed his spine. *At least he died quickly*, I thought. But Ray hadn't gotten off so easily. He had been shot in the leg and stomach, and then, he slowly bled to death in extreme pain. I was told later that his last words were of gratitude: "Thank you for letting me be part of your family."

All our fallen heroes had been by the front of the school where the enemy's fire was most concentrated. I could see Father Jay praying over the dead. He had on his purple stole. He had his right hand stretched out as he bent over Sally. I couldn't make out the words, but I knew he was praying for her eternal repose. The rest of us were making sure no one else was missing or hurt.

We found Jared holding a blood-soaked towel to the side of his head. He had been grazed in the left temple. He pulled the towel off long enough for Chloe to put a bandage on it. Jared looked at me and said, "Look who woke from his nap," and smiled at me. I didn't much feel like smiling, but I smiled back and immediately regretted it as I winced in pain. Jared really thought that was funny.

I said, "That's funny coming from a guy with a maxi pad on his head." I started to smile again, and the pain hit again.

Connor and Hannah had gotten small cuts and abrasions when the windows near them were blown out, either from bullets or the exploded grenade. There was blood coming out of Connor's ear, perhaps a ruptured eardrum from the grenade. They were now in front of the gym, standing near the bodies of Seamus and Sally.

As Leah, Eli, and Hannah made their way to the gym, I looked them over for injuries. It seemed like there wasn't anything physically wrong with them, but who knew what kind of emotional scars would be left? They were now crying over their father and sister.

I turned to see Carter and CJ pulling the dead men of the former sergeant's group and setting them in a line for Father to pray over them. I immediately felt a red, intense rage rise to the surface, and I said, "No, not them!" I pointed my shaking finger at the bodies there, and I could feel hot tears streaming down my cheeks. "They don't deserve your prayers, Father Jay!" I knew that I shouldn't have said it even as the words escaped my mouth.

He came over to me and put his arms around me, and I cried into his shoulder. He whispered in my ear, "John, that's not for me or you to decide."

I felt raw and at the breaking point. Suddenly, I heard a scream and shouting that seemed to perfectly capture what was going on inside me. "No, no! This is all my fault!" I looked up, and I could see Gina and Susan. Gina was hysterical, the perfect picture of anguish on her face. Susan just curled up with her hands over her ears with her eyes tightly closed. "Don't you see?" Gina continued. "Wherever we go, death follows us. It is all our fault!"

Phil walked up to her and said, "We knew they would come. They would have come sooner or later anyway, with or without you here."

"No, you don't understand," she whispered to herself. She shook her head, and then she looked up and spoke loud enough for everyone to hear: "The general, or whatever he calls himself now, is my ex-husband. I told you before that he went to prison for molesting Susan and for other terrible crimes. Now he wants to let his men rape me while he molests Susan again. And he will kill all of you—everyone!"

Karen walked up to Gina and Susan and said, in clear and distinct words, "That's not going to happen!"

Phil looked around at each of our faces, and then he looked at Susan and said, "Susan?" When she looked up, he added softly, "If we had to do it all over again, we would still defend you." I believed him.

18

Aftermath

Even though I walk through the valley of the
shadow of death, I fear no evil; for thou art with
me; thy rod and thy staff, they comfort me.

—Psalm 23:4

What a devastating, disturbing day! Lives were lost, and people were hurt. We won a battle but lost loved ones and perhaps what was left of our innocence. Death had been with us since the beginning of this adventure, but up to this point, we hadn't done much to contribute to it. Death, it seemed, was not satisfied with just the ravages of its plague. It was a bloodthirsty, vicious animal still thirsting for more.

"What to do with the dead?" was the question of the day. Some of us gave serious thought to just dumping the sergeant and the bodies of his men into a mass grave and leaving them for the vultures and wild dogs, but Father talked us into doing the right thing. We decided to burn them. However, we buried the dead from our own group in their own graves. Father Jay celebrated a funeral mass for all the dead. During the homily, he spoke of the bravery and self-sacrifice of our family and friends who had died, and how that self-sacrifice in some way mirrored that of Christ's sacrifice on the cross. He also spoke of the importance of praying for the eternal repose of their souls and added that we need to continue to hold on to our humanity and forgive our enemies.

I found those last words difficult to swallow, but I reflected that before all of this I never really had enemies. All the slights and difficulties that I had received in my past life were easily pardonable in light of what I had experienced recently. This, I knew, was where faith would be put to the test.

We had built a large fire for the bodies of Sgt. Lawless and his men and watched as they burned. In hindsight, we should have burned the bodies farther away from the town or buried them. The smell was something like burning pork. I'll probably never be able to eat pork again.

We kept up our guard duties as we took care of the dead, but everything else that was not essential came to a stop. We took time to salvage what we could from the attack. We salvaged two of the four Hummers for our use and stored away the automatic rifles. We took their military fatigues for possible future use. Understandably, everyone's spirits were down. A dark cloud hung over our little town.

The following day, Father Jay spoke up and said, "If you guys want to leave this place, it's okay with me. I will go where my flock is. I just need to bring some things with us."

Phil said, "Thank you, Father, it's good to know, but for now, we are staying." He looked around, but Carter stood up.

Carter said, "Look, I'd like to stay here for the rest of my life, but I am not sure that it is safe. I don't think that the Salem group is going to let this go." Many others murmured similar thoughts.

Laura asked her father, "Dad, when you were in Woodburn did Joe say anything about the other groups he knew of?"

Phil said, "Sorry, I did not ask him. The meeting that I had with him went so well, and there was so much to discuss." Then he said, "I'll call him on the radio and ask him some more questions, if he's up for sharing. He should know what we just went through too."

Carter spoke up. "You do that. I think that John and I should make a trip to Salem to check things out first." I gave Carter a dirty look for volunteering me. He just grinned.

I said, "I agree, we should check on the Salem group." My dad wanted to go too, but one of the generators was having issues, and he had already started troubleshooting it. Besides, we needed some sharpshooters around to help protect the camp."

Carter said, "I'd like to see if I can infiltrate their group. I've got some mean-looking tattoos, which might help me fit in. Hopefully, John can be in a nearby house monitoring the CB stations. We'll probably need a couple of days."

I wasn't too keen on his plan, especially because it meant I'd be away from my family for a while. But it made sense. We needed information on their plans.

We gathered weapons, ammo, and other supplies for the trip. We grabbed the AR-15s, two shotguns, my Glock, and Carter's .44

Magnum Desert Eagle semiauto pistol. We could have taken the fully automatic machine guns that we had "inherited" from the attackers, but we thought they would be of better use back at camp. We took my Ford Bronco because it was small, agile, and had four-wheel drive.

We said goodbye to our families, and Father Jay gave me last rites in case I didn't make it back, like a soldier going into battle. He also gave Carter a blessing, since he wasn't Catholic. I had mixed feelings about receiving this sacrament because I wasn't planning on dying.

Carter and I got into the Bronco and made our way south. We made sure to stop and inspect before passing through intersections or any place that seemed ripe for an ambush. It was very slow going, but we wanted to make it home alive.

Along the way, we noticed a couple of smaller groups, one was in Keizer along River Road. They didn't seem hostile and appeared preoccupied with the old folk's home they were attending to. I noted on our map that they may be friendly, but with a question mark. We didn't make contact because we had more important business facing us.

We saw signs of another group along Lancaster Road, probably gathered there because of the mall with its many stores. I put them on the map, and we kept moving.

As we approached the capitol, we could see vultures hovering over the historic spire of the Methodist church west of the capitol. We decided to see what was going on. We came in from the south following the road called Church St. The Salem group had turned the area into a dump. All around the church and its office, we could see cans and bottles stacked up along with piles of garbage. Between the two buildings, there was a huge pile of human corpses that had been stacked up to get them out of the way. Most of them appeared to have been killed by the virus, judging by the state of decay. More alarmingly, we saw fresher bodies among the dead. The stench of this mixture of decomposing flesh and garbage was beyond description. The smell attracted great numbers of turkey vultures and crows along with stray dogs, feral cats, and ugly rats.

Garbage lined the streets as we went. It was clear that the members of the Salem group didn't want to be bothered by carrying their trash all the way to their designated dumping site. We decided that we wanted to approach the capitol building from another angle, so made our way a little west and then south down Thirteenth Street, which turned into a little alley. When we reached Ferry Street, it was beginning to get dark, so we went east until we found an abandoned house to stay in. We tried to radio back to home, but unfortunately, we were out of range. We were definitely on our own now.

We ditched the truck at the abandoned house, which was only a few blocks from the capitol. I pulled the distributor cap to make sure it stayed there. We walked from building to building slowly for cover as we drew closer to the capitol.

The closer we came, the more garbage we found strewn along the ground. It was clear that this group was surviving off the canned food they would find at local stores and warehouses. They didn't seem to have any long-term plans for survival. They just took what they could find as the need arose.

Once we arrived near the capitol, we entered into the Oregon Supreme Court building, which was directly across the street from Wilson Park on the east side of the capitol. We needed a vantage point where we could see enough of the landscape to make a sketch of their layout. The top floor of the Justice building gave us a good view of the park and the capitol building adjacent to it. We could see army tents in the grass surrounding the capitol. Chain link construction fencing had been set up as a barrier to keep people out. *Or perhaps to keep people in?* There were several fires burning in barrels, and the main streets were blocked by trucks and cars to stop anyone from driving too close and, of course, garbage lined the street.

We watched the group there for a couple of hours, trying to discern their numbers as well as their strengths and weaknesses. We saw people of all ages and races making their way in and out. I didn't see any women wandering around freely. We noticed one of the tents had a large sign that read, "New Recruits."

"Well," Carter said, "I think that is my way in. I was thinking that I'd just put on these fatigues that we brought with us and try to blend in, but I could just go in there as a new recruit." He paused and looked at me. "You, on the other hand, need to stay here and monitor your radio. Take my radio too. That way you can monitor two channels at once. Also, I am going to leave my weapons here—everything except my knife. I'll see if they will let me take this little tape recorder too."

I watched him as he unstrapped his pistol and lay down his rifle, and I said, "This doesn't feel like a good idea." I was getting a sinking feeling in my stomach.

Carter grinned. "Of course, this doesn't feel like it is a good idea. It is a terrible idea. Who would be stupid enough to sign up as a new recruit? That is why it will work!"

I shook my head. "Well, with logic like that, how can we go wrong?"

Carter squatted down and looked me in the eye. "Seriously, John, I don't see any better options for getting information. I will try to sneak back here this evening to fill you in on anything I find out. Be patient! If you don't see me in two days, then you leave and assume that I am gone or dead."

What could I say? "All right. I don't like it, but all right." I watched as Carter put some nice rips in his shirt and rubbed dirt all over himself. By this time, he hadn't shaved for three days and was looking pretty scruffy. He tore the arms off of his long-sleeved shirt to make sure his tattoos were showing. I looked him up and down said, "You'll fit right in." Then I watched for him out the window until he appeared at the "New Recruits" tent. I watched through the scope of the AR-15 as he was frisked. Not surprisingly, they took his knife and seemed to appraise it admiringly. One of the men gave him a welcoming pat on the shoulder. It seemed that he was in. Then they disappeared around the other side of the tent.

It was now time for me to do my part. I turned on the radios and slowly cycled through the forty channels, hoping to catch some chatter. I was able to catch talk from some distant groups speaking about various mundane activities. It was a while before I picked up something on channel 37. It seemed to be an hourly checkpoint check. It went something like this:

"This is crow's nest for checkpoint verification—checkpoint one?"

"Checkpoint one—check."

"Checkpoint two?"

"Checkpoint two—check."

"Checkpoint three?" There was a long pause. "Checkpoint three, are you there? Dammit, Crocker, are you going to respond or what?" There was another long pause. "Crocker? Checkpoint three?"

"Yeah, I'm here. I mean, checkpoint three—check."

"You stupid, good-for-nothing piece of—"

"Hey, man, this is grunt work and boring as hell."

"Okay, okay, Crocker. Get off the radio…checkpoint four?"

"Ha, ha, yeah, checkpoint four—check and bored out my mind."

I was encouraged at this point that there wasn't a lot of military discipline. Channel 37 seemed to be a valuable channel to keep tabs on. I continued searching the other channels with the other radio.

After a few hours of searching, it seemed that the two main radio channels that this group used were 36 and 37. It seemed that the checkpoints were verified roughly every hour on channel 37. I had heard orders being issued on channel 36. One order was for everyone to gather for a conference. Later on, another order sent all the new recruits to some place called the testing center. I prayed that Carter was doing okay.

It was boring work listening to a radio for hours on end. It was getting pretty late. My eyes were feeling heavy, and I was just going to find some place to lie down when I heard a horn sound in the distance coming from the direction of the capitol. *What the heck is that? Is it some kind of alarm? Have we been found out?* I waited, listening, wondering, *Had something happened to Carter?* Then I heard a noise downstairs. I turned off the radios and aimed my pistol at the door to the room. I could hear the unmistakable sound of footstep echoing up the stairway and then down the hallway. Then I heard a voice in a loud whisper on the other side of the door. "John! Don't shoot! It's me, Carter!"

My endocrine system responded immediately by pumping my bloodstream full of adrenaline—my heart was pounding fast and hard in my chest. I responded shakily, "It's safe, come in. But I have to tell you that I will now probably not get any sleep this evening whatsoever."

Carter came in. "Neither of us is getting any sleep tonight. We need to go."

19

Decisions

Is this the end of the world? Has time run
its course? Or are we starting over?

—Karen McHale

We left the abandoned house and had to walk stealthily to our vehicle, which was parked several blocks away. I realized as we walked that if ever I needed a good workout, I could try walking with stealth for a long distance. As we carefully drove back home, Carter filled me in on what he had discovered. When we were close enough, we radioed ahead to our very relieved loved ones. We also radioed to Joe's group.

We finally arrived home about three hours after we began our sneaking away from the capitol. Joe showed up about the same time we did. We woke everyone up to fill them in on what we had discovered. Time was of the essence. I let Carter fill everyone in on what he had discovered.

Carter said, "We are dealing with a madman, and he has a cult following." He rubbed his face and looked over at me, explaining. "John stayed in a house nearby while he monitored the radio frequencies. I entered pretending to be a new recruit. They showed me around along with about fifteen other new recruits. They showed me much of their base of operations, which surrounds the state capitol building. The place has become an absolute pigsty, and pretty much anything goes. Men are camped out in tents or whatever they can put together. There are barbecue grills, firepits, propane heaters, lawn chairs, and garbage everywhere.

"The only thing that seemed to be produced in the community is moonshine from a still. It looked like they lived exclusively off canned food, dried foodstuffs, water bottles, soda, and a full assortment of alcohol. There was a moving truck filled with all these items, with its back door rolled up, and it seemed that anyone had access to its contents. Presumably, they filled the truck from time to time from a local warehouse or store."

He paused, trying to collect his thoughts. "Also, they have a tent set up that seemed dedicated to giving out marijuana. There were piles of leaves and buds for the men to take. Nearby, there was a kind of hookah bar or station set up on a table where people could come by and grab a tube and take a puff of the weed that was being burned in the pipe. And there was a very forceful expectation that everyone smoked."

He looked up at everybody and shrugged his shoulders. "So I was a bit of a rebel in my youth, and I could tell there was an expectation, so I preempted needing encouragement. I pretended to be into it. I was the first to get a drink. I was the first to *appear* to take a hit from the hookah. I pretended to drink a lot more than I actually did. I also took a rolled-up joint and tucked it between the top of ear and my temple. Oh, I looked the part."

Carter's eyebrows pinched together as though he were recalling a bad memory. "They have a lot of supplies and weapons and vehicles. They had their weapons sitting out in neat stacks, probably for the shock value. The entire perimeter was well-guarded with four main checkpoints. I'd say that our initial assumptions were correct. They did get into the National Guard armory."

At this point, I pulled out my map and taped it to the rolling chalkboard in the gym so everyone could see it.

Carter said, "Thanks, John." Then he pointed out where the base was set up on the map. He filled us in on the fortifications and the position of everything he could remember, which was a lot. Carter straightened up and looked around the group. "We are out-manned and outgunned. We do not have enough cover or experience to fight that many men. Even if we join Joe's group at the prison, eventually, they will beat us." He paused and shook his head; his eyebrows went up and the corners of his mouth went down, and in a serious tone, he said, "We need to run, while we can." It must have been hard for him to say that.

Many of us, including Joe, were hesitant to agree. This was our home, but Carter was insistent. "I need to give you all an idea of what we are up against." He pulled out the recorder that he had brought with him. He waved it around saying, "Luckily, while I was there, they had a kind of conference with the general in a large room in the capitol. He stood on a raised platform and spoke into a microphone."

Phil asked, "So they had restored power to the building somehow?"

"Yeah," Carter replied, "I think they had some large generators running—probably from the armory. So anyway, there were about two hundred men gathered around in this room, including us fifteen new recruits. I want you to listen to this to get an idea of what we are dealing with." Carter set the recorder on the table and pushed the play button.

The tape recorder began spitting out what sounded like static until I recognized that it was people clapping and cheering, which soon died down. Then we heard the general's voice: "Yes, indeed, we are gathered here for a common cause, the cause of humanity. For you see, we, you and I, have been chosen for a special purpose. We are the few who have survived the apocalyptic plague. Why were you chosen? Why was I chosen?"

Carter said during the break in the general's speech, "It wasn't a problem for me to have the recorder out. I just had to pretend that I was hanging on his every word."

The recording continued, "We were chosen…" The general's voice reached a fevered pitch. "To dominate this new world. The world is ripe for the picking. We can create a new Eden, free from the pathetic impotence of the government. This is not a world where weak, soft-hearted bureaucrats dressed in business suits rule the people. It is the strong that rule."

There was roar of assent from the crowd.

"We have proven this! History has proven this! We were strong enough to withstand the plague!"

There was another roar of approval from the crowd, along with shrill whistles.

The general's voice was softer now, "I predicted the plague. Did you know that? Yes, it was revealed to me in a dream. One of my most trusted advisors can confirm that for you." Here the general paused, and his voice took on a touch of sadness. "Ah, but sadly, he has died. He was murdered. You all knew him, Sgt. Lawless. You see, he even changed his name for our cause. He recognized that the law, which had tried to squash him, and all of us, under its thumb, was no longer relevant. Being the visionary that he was, he changed his name to Lawless. He was an Obedient. Don't you see? For him, that name meant freedom." The volume and intensity in his voice increased. "Freedom from oppression! Freedom from some outdated moral codes meant to castrate a man from his full potential!"

Phil said over the shouts coming from the tape, "He is turning Lawless into a martyr for his cause!"

Father Jay slowly shook his head sideways and added, "And listen to the roaring of the crowd!"

Carter confirmed it. "If you guys had been standing there, you could have felt the power, almost hypnotic, that he had over this crowd."

In a much lower voice, the general continued, "It has fallen on me, my brothers, to lead you to this new vision. This vision has been imparted to me by a higher power—and I do mean power. This is a new age in history in which might makes right. It is the age of man subjugating all else under his boot: rocks, plants, animals, women— everything. Everything is ripe to be plucked, and pluck it we shall." At this, the crowd began to roar.

"An Angel of God appeared to me. The Angel of the Great Unicity! He told me, 'Now is the time for mankind to receive the True Revelation in its fullness, untainted by man. You,' he told me, 'shall be his chosen instrument!'

"You know me as the general, and rightly so, but to the Great Unicity, I am known as the Obedient Servant. In his mercy, the Unicity has given me an uncorrupted revelation that I reveal to you through the message of his angel. Don't you see? The concepts of good and evil are corruptions of the pure revelations that were revealed at the appointed time by unfaithful and disobedient men. There is only the Will of the Unicity, and we are called to be obedient to His Will!"

I could hear Carter in the recording with a roar in the background, "Yeah, do you hear this guy? Yeah, this guy is something else! Wooohoo!" He was playing his role well.

I looked over at Carter. He had his head down, which was slowly shaking side to side. He turned off the recorder. "There is more of the same. He skillfully worked the crowd into a fevered pitch. It sounded to me like he was priming the crowd toward revenge for Lawless. I was able to confirm that later as I overheard someone talking about organizing an attack for payback."

Carter continued, "Near as I can tell there are two tiers of followers. There are the Initiates and the Obedient. The Obedient ones are the real fanatics."

I said to Carter, "You have to tell them the rest."

Carter nodded his head, looking melancholy. "Later on, they had a special meeting for the new recruits. It was in the capitol building, the only place that wasn't covered in garbage. They called it the testing center for Initiates. I knew it wouldn't be good when we approached the door and the sign was written in blood: 'Initiate Testing Center.'"

Carter closed his eyes and slowly shook his head as he continued, "As we stood at the door, the guy leading us took some strips of cloth out of a bag he was carrying and handed one to each of us. I noticed that he had a similar strip of cloth tied loosely around his own neck. One the guys in our group hesitated and said, 'What is this for?'

"The guy handing out the strips smiled and said, 'Just take it! You'll need it later.'"

Carter pointed to the white cloth tied around his neck. "So I took it and tied it around my neck."

Carter's voice was shaking. "The fifteen of us entered the room past the guard at the door, and I could hear whimpering in the center of the room. There was a woman gagged and strapped down to a table. Behind the table was a tattooed and scruffy-looking white guy with a Mohawk holding a very large knife. The man told us to come in.

"As we came in, another man with a fully automatic rifle blocked the door. This looked like trouble. Thankfully, I was at the back of the group. The woman strapped to the table had obviously been beaten up and was stripped of her clothes. I had a feeling that I knew what was coming next.

"The man behind the table said, 'Rape her!' He looked at the first guy in our group and said more forcefully, 'Rape her!' The guy standing at the front of us 'Initiates' looked at the guy with the knife and then back at the group. He shrugged his shoulders pulled down his pants and did as he was instructed."

I saw tears form in Carter's eyes as he continued, "I wanted to stop him, but I couldn't. I wanted to save her, but I couldn't." Carter breathed deeply to get control of his emotions.

He clenched his fists. "Rage built up inside of me. I was planning in my head how I might disarm the guy with the gun and kill him. I was thinking about how I'd take out the guy with the knife and then fight off the new recruits if I had to, but then a strange thing happened." He wiped his mouth with the back of his hand. "I got violently sick. Almost without warning, I put my hand over my mouth and vomited. This was not merely some little gagging reflex. It was major projectile vomiting. I turned and vomited on the wall. I fell down on my hands and knees, and then more came out." Carter was holding his stomach as though he were reliving it. "This obviously drew a lot of attention. The guy with the knife says, 'Steve, get that sissy outta here!' So the guy with the gun drags me out by collar to the hallway. He is cursing me and cussing me out. He is making remarks, putting down my masculinity in a way that I will not repeat in polite company. The whole time I am retching. I was still dry-heaving in the hallway when the guy with the gun gives me a final curse before he goes back in the room to continue watching what is going on."

Carter paused and looked up thoughtful. "Well, there was another guy who had been standing guard on the other side who was suitably disgusted at me emptying the contents of my stomach on the floor. He looks down at me and says, 'You sick pig! I'm going to get one of the women to clean this up.' He walked off, cursing me under his breath."

A weak smile came over Carter's lips. "So there I was, left all alone surrounded by puddles of my own puke. Then, all at once, I was fine. I had no more need to vomit."

He shook his head with a look that was mixture of confusion and awe. "I stood up, looked around, and then I just walked through the hallways as if I belonged."

Carter looked around at the group. "The more I think about it, the more convinced I am that if I had not gotten sick at that moment, I would be dead right now."

He looked at Father Jay. "Do you think God did that? I honestly cannot think of any other way that I could have gotten out of that room alive. I would have either been killed trying to fight those men, or I would have lost my soul by being forced to participate in what they were doing on the other side of that door."

Father Jay shrugged his shoulders and said, "I don't know. God has been known to work in unexpected ways."

Carter continued, "Well, anyway, I decided to look around. I did one reckless thing, but thankfully it paid off. There was a room marked, 'Only the Obedient May Enter Here.' I had a sense that it might be important. I listened at the door and heard no movement, so I opened the door slightly and took a peek. Inside, there was a glass case with some pages in it. I lifted the case and stuffed the pages into my shirt, and I walked out like I owned the place. Then the strangest thing happened. I heard some kind of horn blow. It was about 9:00 PM, and suddenly everything went quiet. It was eerie. I walked around, and anyone I saw seemed to be face-down on the ground with a blindfold on. I made it past the checkpoint, sneaked back to where John was, and we came back here."

I looked around and everyone's face was in shock. Carter looked as though he was trying to hold back tears.

Father Jay finally said, "This general is using guilt and shame to bind members to his group." His eyebrows were knitted together, and there was anger written all over his face. "He's forcing them to participate in a deeply sinful and evil act to shame them into staying and into submission. He is lowering their inhibitions with drugs and alcohol and breaking down their moral defenses." He looked over at Carter. "I'm sorry you had to experience that. It isn't your fault. There is nothing that you could have done without getting yourself killed." He paused. "Let me look at the pages you took!"

Carter absentmindedly handed the pages that he had taken to Father Jay, and he turned toward Joe and said, "Look, Joe! They are after our group. You guys might be safe for the time being, but I think it is only a matter of time before they come after you."

As Carter was talking to Joe, I briefly glanced at Father Jay with the pages; it looked like some of them were written in blood. Father Jay was studying them intently. He looked up at me and mumbled, "I'll figure out what this is all about." He got up and seemed to be muttering, "This isn't good…"

"Listen, you guys," Carter said, "the whole atmosphere is like a party there. There isn't a lot of discipline in the Initiates. They are drinking and having a good time. They are grubby and unwashed. But the Obedients are different. They are a smaller group that has more discipline. These other guys have bought wholeheartedly into what the general is selling. They are the ones who are keeping order through fear and force."

I added, "Also, we need to take into consideration that they don't seem to have any plans for the future. The place there looks like a garbage dump. They are living day by day, and very soon, they are going to run out of the food and alcohol that they have been looting in the Salem area. They will start looking in a wider area. Eventually, they will want to take what we have created here."

"Listen, you guys," Carter said, "the only way that we could possibly stay here is if we did a preemptive strike—if we went in there and took them by surprise—if we had no qualms about killing those men, recognizing that eventually they would come after us. We've already got enough provocation from Sgt. Lawless. With the element of surprise, we could pull it off with minimal casualties to ourselves."

My stomach was turning sour even considering the idea. I could see my own feelings mirrored in the faces of the rest of the group.

But then Carter added, "But that is not our way, and I'm not sure that I could live with myself if we did it."

I turned and looked at Joe's ashen face; he seemed to be in shock, but he managed to say, "I hate to run from a fight, but better to fight another day than die today." Then he said, "Let me get back to my people and discuss it with them. I'll keep in touch on the radio. I'll leave it switched to your channel. This sucks, but thank God we had a warning." Then he and the others he had with him left in a hurry.

Phil looked at everyone and said, "Well, I guess we've got to go." Then he picked up Abigail and gave her a hug. Everyone nodded in silence.

It was my mom who asked the important question. "Where are we going?"

Phil looked around. "I figure that we could head south to the free zone in California. Obviously, we can't just take the freeway down there, so we will need to head east to hopefully get around the roadblocks."

Eli took a step forward. "Well, for the time being, let's meet at my farm. We can hide there for a day or two while we decide the best course of action. It is clear, however, that we need to get out of here fast."

I knew in my heart that this was what we had to do. The general was clearly a psychopath, a very charismatic psychopath with an ego the size of Texas, who was surrounded by brutal men with lots of guns.

I looked out the window, and I could see that it was just starting to get light as the sun threatened to rise in the east. *It is going to be another long and sleepless day.* Dad got my attention. "John and I will back up the semis to the school so that we can load them quickly."

Everyone started loading the trailers. CJ and Isaiah filled the fuel tanks of the big rigs from our tankers. Dad and I filled the tanks of the cars and trucks that we were bringing along. It took us three hours to load the provisions we wanted to take. We had loaded as much produce and water containers as we could. We took the refrigerated trailer with the frozen meat from our slaughtered cows and sheep. At some point, some of the family members just started tossing the canned foods in the trailer. They rolled the jars of food in on carts, hoping they would not break along the way. We did not have the luxury of time to stack and pack. Everyone grabbed piles of clothing and loaded their vehicles.

Phil was in constant communication with the group in Woodburn. They were going to join us, and they were almost ready.

We were all paying close attention to the clock. When you are in a hurry, it seems like there is never enough time. Conversely, when there is nothing to do, there is an overabundance of time. Well, we were in a hurry, and time was fleeting even as we hustled.

Eli said, "I've got an idea." He drove the empty truck and trailer to the nearby farm and brought some cows and sheep. He put the livestock in the gym and the school. Then he cracked open the propane valve on the tanks inside and shut the doors. Carter was able to set up matchbook strikers on the doors. He also set up trip flares.

Meanwhile, the Woodburn group had arrived and refueled. Unfortunately, we were not able to take both of the fuel tankers, so we figured we would make a big bomb out of them. Dad and I drove the tankers around the properties with the valves open and spilled fuel everywhere.

Father Jay protested the deadly booby traps we were leaving behind, but Eli told him, "This may be the only thing that allows us to leave safely. They are invading us. They are bringing violence to us. They are bringing this upon themselves."

Father Jay said in a tone of resignation, "It just feels like there ought to be another way."

Although we wanted to stay together, Henry and Mabel decided that they were going to strike out on their own and take the locomotive as far south as they could go. They stocked it with supplies that they would need. Henry said that without pulling cars, the engine had enough fuel to get to Guatemala. Mabel said with a fake smile, "See you in California." We said our goodbyes to them, and they got into the train and prepared to leave. Before they left, they once again backed the long line of train cars to block Gervais from the east. They uncoupled the cars from the locomotive and headed south.

Most everyone had driven their vehicles out near the Sacred Heart Cemetery on the east end of town. We had left parked cars along the school to make it look like we were still there. The cows and goats were moving around inside the buildings, attempting to look out the windows. I hoped that it would look like we were still there. I smiled and said, "This might actually work." I was just hooking a portable generator to the trailer hitch of my car when a warning burst on the radio.

"They're coming! Get out of there now!" It was the Woodburn group giving us the warning. The capitol group must have taken the Woodburn exit.

Dad and I drove off east toward Mt. Angel and Silverton to meet up with the rest of our group. Then Dad and I stopped the car and watched from a distance. We were afraid that our moving vehicles might catch their eyes, and they might follow us. I could see that the group had come up and around from the north, so they were still able to reach the school and church without being blocked by the train cars. *They must have guessed about the train.* Thankfully, the train cars were between us and them and would keep them from us for a while. I silently prayed that Henry and Mabel had made it out.

I could make out several vehicles circling the town to surround it. Suddenly, I could hear a lot of gunfire. It was continuous and seemed to last for an eternity.

Most of the members of our group were on some smaller roads heading toward Silverton. I wondered if they could hear the large BOOM! A huge fire ball lit up the sky and several smaller booms followed. Dad and I could actually feel each blast. I said to my dad, "Did you remember the marshmallows?"

We figured with all of the chaos from the explosions, it was now safe for us to catch up with the rest of the group. Then we heard Joe yelling on the radio, "Are you okay? Talk to me!"

Dad responded, "Yes, we just left a going-away present for them."

I heard Phil ask, "Joe, are you out yet?"

Joe's response: "Yes, we'll meet you at the locations you gave us."

Dad added, "Okay, it is radio silence from here."

Twenty minutes later, we were all in the town of Silverton at Eli and Leah's farm. We parked our cars behind the house, some in the barn, and some in the neighbors' barn. The semis and trailers were parked alongside the barns. Eli and Leah had a farm with ten acres of pastureland for their animals. Of course, the animals had already been moved to the Gervais camp. The animals left behind were probably extra crispy by now; hopefully our attackers were as well.

We could not all fit in Eli's house, so we took two of his neighbors' houses. By some miracle, there were no bodies in either of the houses.

By combining the Woodburn group and the Gervais groups, we now amounted to forty-two people. After we settled in, Carter and I went outside with eight others to set up our defenses.

As we huddled together, I said, "I don't think that they can track us. The local roads are not that overgrown yet. I don't think that we left much in the way of tire tracks."

Carter said, "We still need some protection to give us a chance at fighting or running."

"Okay," I said, "what do you want us to do?"

He bent down and started drawing on the ground. "It's starting to get dark. Let's make a 360-degree perimeter but concentrate on the one road coming in. We should be able to hear any vehicles by road or if they come through any of the fields. Let's try to use only natural barriers. We don't want to announce that we're here. A small element of surprise may be all we need.

"John, see if you and your dad can use the four-by-four truck and winch to pull a tree down over the road. If you can avoid chopping or cutting, all the better!"

Carter oversaw the rest of the defenses and people placement as we left to pull down a tree. Dad and I drove down the road a few hundred yards before we saw a suitable fir tree. We pulled over to the side of the road and inspected the tree. Dad pulled out a cigarette and lit it up while he looked over the tree.

I said, "I thought you quit?"

He shrugged. "I've been sneaking them for the last couple of months. I didn't think Victoria would approve." He looked over at me. "I kind of need it to stay calm these days."

I nodded. "I think I understand." I bent down and rubbed the bark at the base of the tree. "I can tell that this tree is not going to be pulled over by the truck, so what do you think? Chainsaw?"

He took a puff of the cigarette. "Yeah, I think we are far enough away that sound won't carry, but then again, there isn't any noise of traffic or anything to cover the noise."

"Ax?" I said.

He dropped the cigarette on the ground and rubbed it into the dirt. "Nah, I think quick and easy is better. I'll go back to the house to get the chainsaw."

Neither one of us were lumberjacks, but we have cut down our fair share of trees before. Dad cut a nice notch in the tree that was directed toward the road. The tree was leaning a little bit to the south, but we thought it would work out all right. Then with the chainsaw slicing through the wood on the other side, we heard the unmistakable sound of cracking wood. We both stepped back as the tree slowly began to topple. It made a huge thump that shook the ground. It fell at more of an angle across the road than we had aimed for, but it served as a fine roadblock. And there were deep ditches along either side of the road to prevent someone from merely going around it.

With Carter's guidance, we decided to take four-hour guard duty shifts because everyone was worn out from the stress of the day. Carter and I were the first to get some sleep since we had been up scouting the enemy camp the night before. Inside the house, Phil and Joe were discussing with the rest of the group where to go next. It was then that Father Jay interrupted.

"Listen, everybody! I've been reading through these pages, and this is not good. We all got a sense of the danger on Carter's recording. But we are not dealing with just some group of criminals here. We are dealing with a kind of religious cult, a very zealous religious cult.

"These pages are called 'The Manifesto of the True Revelation.' They say the general is the Obedient Servant to whom God has given a revelation through an Angel of Light."

As Father Jay was speaking, I could feel the hairs on the back of my neck come to attention.

He continued, "Listen to this! This is what the angel said to him:

"'At the appointed time, the people of the Old Testament, whether the Christian Scriptures or the Torah, were given the true revelation by the Unicity. At the appointed time, the people of the New Testament of the Christian Scriptures were given true revelation by the Unicity. At the appointed time, the people of the Koran were given true revelation by the Unicity. At the appointed time, so many others were given true revelation by the Unicity, but all of them have corrupted the true teaching.'

"You see," Father Jay said, "it is ingenious. He validates the other religions by saying that they were valid for an appointed time, but then invalidates them by saying they are corrupted, and that he has the True Revelation. He makes himself out to be, or at least his teachings out to be, the only reliable revelation." Father Jay looks at us in order to let it sink in.

Phil says, "So what? There are all kinds of religions that people believe in. What makes this so special?"

Father Jay nods. "Okay, okay, I'm not making myself clear." He flipped through a couple of pages. "I mean what we have here is diabolical genius. At one point, the Obedient Servant questions the angel, and the angel says, 'How dare you question a messenger of the Great Unicity! You are nothing, and you are not worthy to know my name or the true name of the Great Unicity! For doing this you shall be mute until the task is fulfilled!' Then it goes on to say that the Obedient Servant was made mute until he had faithfully written all that was commanded." Father Jay looks up. "You see, in this line, he takes away reason. You are not allowed to ask questions. You are not allowed to disagree. You are to be obedient."

Father Jay then turned a page and says, "And that reminds me. Carter, you were right, there are two groups. There are the Initiates and the Obedient. And there are special tattoos that indicate an Initiate and an Obedient. The Initiate gets one version of these written Revelations, a redacted version. The Obedient get another version, and the other longer version has parts that are written in blood…in their own blood." He looks around the room, and his gaze stops on me.

I nodded for him to continue. Although it wasn't clear to me, this seemed important. The hairs on the back of my neck were really standing up now. Sometimes in my life I have noticed that when I am in the presence of evil or something supernatural, I get goosebumps and the hairs on my neck and arms will stand up. It was happening now, not because I was in the presence of evil, but because I could sense the impending damage that the ideas and supposed revelations could cause—how they could lead others astray.

Father Jay looked at Carter. "I'm glad you managed to grab the full version written in blood." He looked down at the pages. "So the Initiates are given a prayer regimen. They are to pray at certain times of the day. It involves reading these words every day." He shook the pages for emphasis. "It involves wearing a blindfold and placing your head on the dirt because, and I quote, 'so that you remember you are little more than dirt to the Unicity,' and they are to meditate on nothing, 'for the ways of the Great Unicity are beyond human understanding.' They meditate on nothing! Who knows what they are opening themselves up to?"

Father Jay looked over at Carter. "That is why you saw them wearing those white cloths around their necks. They are blindfolds. The horn must have been some kind of signal for prayer"—he looked around at the rest of the group—"and if they miss a prayer time, they are to make atonement to the Unicity in blood, cutting themselves. There are promises of paradise to those who are Obedient and spread the True Revelation. There is no concept of human dignity. There is only obedience. There is a promise of paradise for those who die while attempting to punish the disobedient. There are those who are destined for paradise and those who are destined to be blotted from existence. All is according to the Will of the Great Unicity!"

I could feel the tension in the room, and I wanted to get clarification. "So are you saying that we might be dealing with a bunch of religious zealots who are willing to kill and maybe even be willing to die to serve this Great Unity?"

"Unicity," Father Jay corrected. "And yes, that is exactly what I am saying."

After our meeting, I looked outside, and it was beginning to snow. Thankfully, we had just finished our defenses. Normally, when it snows in our part of the world, we might get a light sprinkling, and then it would melt the next day. But it seems that nothing has been normal since the virus. It snowed for two days straight, and we had over twelve inches of snow. We had to risk burning wood in the woodstoves of the houses, hoping that no one who might be looking for us would see the smoke.

"Since not all our vehicles are four-wheel drive, we're stuck until this snow melts. I'm guessing the county won't have its snowplows out anytime soon to come and clear the roads for us," Phil said.

Many of us didn't have the proper clothing for the snow and cold, so our shifts of guard duty tended to be pretty miserable. The kids, however, had a blast. It had been a long time since I'd heard them play like that. They made snowmen and snow angels in the back pastures, and of course, there was the occasional snowball fight. Some of the adults joined in too. I think everyone needed a little time to play.

Thankfully, one of the neighbors' houses had a propane tank and furnace, and we were able to keep the wood burning to a minimum. We were going through food pretty fast. Some of us were starting to smell a little ripe since we didn't have access to regular water supply. However, we were able to boil snow for bath water and to refresh our water supply. The weather immediately warmed a bit after the snow, but the snow remained for two more days before it melted enough for us use the roads. After the roads were clear, we figured that it was safe enough to leave. There were no signs of the group from the capitol.

We did have one scare before we left, however. Chloe called in on the radio, "Everyone hide! Someone is driving up the road."

We all huddled in the house, waiting for the all-clear to be sounded. I prayed that our fallen tree would be enough of a deterrent. After about ten minutes, we heard the all-clear over the radio.

My dad went to relieve Chloe, and she came back and filled us in. She smiled as she walked in the door, clearly enjoying being the center of attention. "Hi everybody. It is good to see you all." She smiled, knowing that we all wanted to hear what she had to say.

Jared, finally feigning frustration, stated, "Come on, don't keep us in suspense! What happened?"

Chloe explained, "I heard the car coming, so I gave the warning over the radio, and I watched through the scope. It was a Hummer. It drove up to the fallen tree in the road and two men got out. They were wearing military fatigues and carrying rifles. They looked at the tree, got in the Hummer, turned around and left." She paused. "I think they are searching for us. But the tree seemed to deter them from looking further."

Needless to say, we were relieved; however, that close encounter made it clear that we needed to move. From monitoring the airwaves, we knew there were several possible safe areas: one was in Los Angeles; another in Dallas, Texas; and another in Salt Lake, Utah. These were the ones closest to us. There were others in the central part of the country as well as on the East Coast. Lastly, there were two more in Florida.

Joe and his group wanted to go to Utah. Our group wanted to go to California or maybe Texas as a backup. We figured that since we had a choice, we would choose nicer weather. Unfortunately, that meant that we were going to have to divide our group.

20

Sickness

Dad? I don't understand why those men are trying to hurt us. Why can't they just share or go away? We're not bothering them—why are they bothering us?

—Isaiah Fide

"Mommy, I don't feel good," Eve said to her mother, Laura. Several of my other kids were also getting sick. Isaiah threw up and had a 102-degree fever. Eve had a fever and was nauseous. The younger ones were lethargic and were on their way to being sick. *Was it just the flu, or is this the end?* They all had terrible wet coughs and were spitting up little bits of red foam. I felt helpless, and I didn't know what to do. Thankfully, none of the other kids in our group were getting sick, just mine.

Everybody left my immediate family alone. The others were scared, and for good reason. Most of the world's population was now dead because of a virus. We quarantined ourselves from the rest of the group, but we could communicate through the closed windows or by radio. Outside, several people were arguing on whether or not to leave without us or stay and see what happens. Joe and his group decided to leave and head toward Utah.

I pleaded with the rest of the group just to leave, and we would catch up later if we were able. I told them that they should go while the Salem group is still recovering and regrouping.

Father Jay said, "Not before I pray over you." He stood at the door with his mouth covered by a surgical face mask and hands in latex gloves from our medical kit. He gave us each the sacrament of the anointing of the sick.

Then Phil and Karen knocked on the window. Phil stood at the window expectantly. "John," he said, "I've spoken with Karen, and we want to wait until your family either gets better or…" His words trailed off, leaving the morbid alternative unsaid.

I couldn't think of a way to get them to go. It was too dangerous for them to stay, so I hardened my face and my voice and said, "Look, Phil! I've put up with you sticking your big foot in the middle of my marriage too long. You always have to make decisions for everybody else, don't you? You always have to stick your nose into other people's business. I think it's better if we just separate. You go your way, and I'll go mine."

I watched Phil's eyes harden and his face turned red. "Fine!" he said. "You don't want us around, we'll oblige!" He turned around stiffly and said out of the side of his mouth to Karen, "Let's go." Karen followed, turning her shocked face away.

I sensed Laura behind me. She moved toward the window to try get their attention and bring them back. I grabbed her shoulders, turned her toward me, and looked into her worried eyes. "Let them go!" I pleaded. "It will be safer for them. I had to do something to get them to go."

She looked me in the eyes. I saw a flash of anger, but then her face softened, and she looked down and nodded in resignation. I felt a stab of guilt as she walked out of the room. I acted badly but felt that I did it out of love. I didn't want them to be here when the Salem group caught up with us, or we died from our sickness.

I had strained my relationship with Laura, and for the next hour, figuratively speaking, it was cold enough to hang beef in the house. Laura wouldn't talk to me and wouldn't even look me in the eye. The only thing good about having sick kids was that they took my mind off the rupture that I had caused in my relationship with the McHales.

There was a knock at the window. Phil and Karen were at the window again. I hesitantly came to the window. Laura followed me in. I looked back, and she gave me a hard look that that said, *You better not try to make me stay away from the window*. I made room for her.

Phil said, "I know what you are doing, John. You are trying to make the decision easy for us by driving us away." He put his head down and rubbed his forehead. "I must admit, you almost had me fooled." He looked up and smiled.

Laura punched me in the arm. I looked over at her rubbing my arm. "Ouch!"

I heard Laura's mom laugh. "You deserved that! You jerk!" Karen looked over at her husband, smiling. "But I guess that he is a loveable jerk," she said.

I felt embarrassment wash over me. My face must have been a nice bright red by now.

Phil broke in. "Look, John, I know that you are right. We need to go."

Phil went over his intended route with me through the window and gave me an alternative route if something happened. They would leave a sign if they went that way. He showed me a sign that read "House for Sale" and said that it would be pointed in the direction they would be going if they used the alternate route. The plan was that Phil's caravan was going to circle around Salem using secondary roads to the east and then head to Los Angeles after they got well past Salem. Then they would rejoin I-5 and continue heading south. They also had a coastal route mapped out just in case.

We all said our tearful goodbyes. We waved goodbye from inside the house, at least those of us that were well enough to, as they drove out of sight. By now I was feeling kind of weak. I could tell that my temperature was elevated, and I felt chilled.

Everyone had left grudgingly, except my mom and dad. They refused to leave. I tried everything that I could think of to get them to go, even stupidly trying to the same trick I used on Phil and Karen; my parents merely laughed at my mock anger. They wouldn't go. If I was honest with myself, deep down, I really didn't want them to leave anyway. They camped out in the house next door and took turns checking on us. It was terrifying not knowing if we were going to live through this sickness or not.

The most difficult decision, I think, was that of my brother. I knew that he really wanted to stay with us. He didn't want to break up the family, especially since my parents were staying. But I convinced him to go. I reasoned with him, "Look, Jay! If it's just a passing flu, then we will catch up with you. If not, then you are better off with those who need you most."

It was a long week after the group left. That same evening, Laura and I got really sick. We still needed someone to keep watch, so with a temperature of 102 degrees, I made my way to the lookout post. I vomited and couldn't stop coughing. I was coughing up little bits of red foam and spitting them out on the ground. I could hear a gurgling sound deep in my lungs every time I coughed. It did not sound good. Thankfully, no one came down the road, or I probably would have given away our position by my constant coughing. My dad relieved me, but he gave me plenty of space and set himself up some distance from where I had positioned myself.

Two days later, Eve was fine. Thankfully, it was just a bad case of flu or a mild case of the plague. *Maybe we got it from someone in Joe's group.* I prayed they were all okay. A week later, my whole family was feeling better. We were finally able to break quarantine, and we all went outside. The snow had melted, and it was a cold morning. It was now the beginning of December.

Dad and Mom ran over and gave each of us kisses and hugs. Dad said, "I guess we're off to California!" Laura laughed and said, "Let's go as soon as possible. I've spent the last week trapped in that house surrounded by puke and diarrhea."

The vehicles we had remaining were our big, silver Ford passenger van, the red WinCo semitruck and its fifty-three-foot refrigerated trailer, and a black Ford F-450 pickup. Laura drove the van. My dad took the semitruck, and I drove the F-450 pickup. We unhitched the reefer trailer and left it behind. We loaded the food and equipment into the back of the pickup truck and strapped other various items to the rear deck plate of the semi. We estimated that we had enough supplies to get to Los Angeles with some to spare—if we had clear roads and a quick trip. We siphoned the diesel from the reefer tank on the trailer and put it in the pickup.

As we started our trek, I radioed to Dad in the semi who was leading. I said, "Let me find a motorcycle so I can speed ahead and scout for trouble." We searched a few houses until I found a Yamaha 250-CC dirt bike. It was a few years old, but it started right up. It was also a four-stroke, so it was relatively quiet. My mom took over driving the pickup. Then we worked our way down the side roads, trying to get past Salem with the intent of eventually getting back to I-5. It was painstakingly slow, and we burned up the whole day, but eventually, we did get around to the south side of Salem and wound up stopping just north of Stayton.

We had not seen any For Sale signs directing us away from the original route Phil discussed with us. That night we found a house off the main road where we could hide our vehicles for the night.

Unfortunately, the house did not have working propane heat. The kids were shivering and the rest of us were cold too, but we could not light a fire because the house didn't have a woodstove or fireplace. And even if it did, the visual of the smoke would have been too risky. We couldn't leave a car running either because we needed to conserve our fuel. So we just huddled together around candles and our portable propane heater, with sleeping bags wrapped around our shoulders.

To get our minds of the cold, we talked about what the free zone was going to be like. It was important to have hope and some kind of goal to achieve. The kids imagined the free zone as something like the Promised Land; they also thought that Disneyland somehow would be involved. I almost told them that it was unlikely that Disneyland would be open and running, but I didn't have the heart to ruin that dream.

In the morning, we got up and made breakfast on a portable propane cooking stove. After breakfast, we divided up duties to prepare for the day. Eve and Eden helped Isaiah syphon fuel out of a tractor for the diesel pickup and the semi. Other than Isaiah getting a mouthful of diesel, they did well. As I supervised their work, I reflected on how fast my kids had adapted to this crazy life. The rest of the group searched the house and surrounding houses for useful supplies and water.

We gathered up all the gear up, and we were ready to go. I scouted ahead on the dirt bike. Dad and Isaiah took the rear with the semi. We were getting close to I-5 now, and I think we were all feeling a little jumpy. As I drove ahead, I could see a little bit of smoke rising into the crisp blue sky. Around a nearby corner, I stopped the engine of the motorcycle and coasted to a stop. I held up my fist signaling for the group behind me to stop. I got off the bike and made my way to the tree line, clutching my pistol.

I crept around the corner and saw a semitruck and trailer on the side of the road. *That was our truck!* It was in the ditch along the right side of the road. The trailer was still attached and partially blocking the road.

I couldn't see anything past the trailer. It was blocking my view. My heart was beating loudly in my chest. I radioed back to my dad and Laura and told them what I was seeing.

They had pulled to the side of the road a good way back and had shut off the engines. Dad got out of the truck and took up a position behind our vehicles to watch our backs. Isaiah joined his mom and the other kids in the pickup truck. Laura backed up her vehicle to another cross street for an easy escape if needed. I assumed that she had Isaiah, Eve, Eden, and Abigail in the back of the truck with their rifles at the ready, as we had practiced. *This is not ideal to have my kids fight, but desperate times call for desperate measures.*

I sat there in the brush and studied the area. It was a blind corner, perfect for an ambush. There was plenty of cover with brush and natural barriers such as a ditch on one side and a steep roadway cut on the other. There was no movement ahead. I crept along the bushes and trees, and as I did, I noticed that I was stepping over a lot of shell casings. There was definitely a firefight here, a big one.

The leaves were crunching loudly under my feet. I winced with every step. A little farther along, I spotted a small walking trail next to the road. *That will make less noise.* The trail brought me close enough to see inside the trailer. Although empty, it was riddled with bullet holes. There were three bodies on the other side of the trailer. I couldn't make out whom the bodies belonged to through my scope. I felt a knot form in my stomach.

As I moved forward, I spotted a familiar-looking motor home that had been blown apart into large pieces. It was Phil and Karen's motor home, at least what was left of it. It was smoldering and partially burned. *Oh no! This was definitely our people!*

There were four more bodies about thirty feet beyond the carnage and near a small SUV that was turned on its side in the drainage ditch. It was Connor and Hannah's. *Please, God, let my family be okay,* I prayed. I wanted to run forward to check the bodies, but I didn't know if it was safe. There was still no sign of the enemy.

As I made my way to the cab of the semi, I could see that there were holes in the windshield and side windows and shell casings everywhere. I sneaked past the semitruck and the pieces of the RV. As

I looked into the ditch and the SUV wedged in it, I could see there were unmoving bloody bodies in the car.

I waited, watched, and checked the perimeter for another fifteen minutes and saw no signs of danger or the enemy. Then I checked on the casualties. Connor and Hannah were dead in the SUV. The front of the car and windshield were riddled with bullets. They were probably the first to get hit in the ambush. I leaned over the car and forced myself to look in the back seat for their children. I was shaking and crying. The two car seats were empty. I was thankful for that. I didn't think that I could handle seeing the bodies of my nieces or nephews.

I radioed to my family members around the corner to stay where they were.

I walked back to the smoldering RV and looked inside of it. Phil and Karen's partially burned and bullet-riddled bodies were in the front seats. I had trouble seeing anything through my tears. *My family members were dying all around me!* I immediately felt a pang of guilt. *They left because I made them go. This is my fault.* I went down on my knees, trying to catch my breath. The guilt and the shame were overwhelming. I took a few deep breaths trying to climb out of the pit of despair that had just dropped into. I told myself, *You can't think about that right now. Keep moving! You don't have time for this. Worry about the living!*

I got up; and then I moved to the semi, carefully opened the door, and saw blood on the driver's seat. I expected to see Carter's body because he was most likely driving at the time. As I looked into the sleeper of the truck, I saw that Carter's daughter Cassie was dead. There were dozens of bullet casings scattered all over the floor of the truck. Carter is a fighter. I knew that he would give it his all. Perhaps he was alongside the trailer with the other two bodies. I got out and slowly walked back to the three bodies. The bodies belonged to Judy and two men that I didn't recognize. The two men were probably the attackers; their corpses were dressed in camo gear. There was no sign of any of the other cars from our group.

Where was the rest our group? I checked the other four bodies. There were four more men I didn't recognize. They were stripped down to their underwear. It appears that someone had taken their gear and clothing. All the bodies showed signs of having been there several days.

I radioed to Dad and Laura and asked them to come a little closer. I warned them that some of our family members were dead. They pulled the vehicles near the back of the bullet-riddled semi-trailer. We took the time needed to bury only the people from our group.

Laura bent over and fell to her knees, and she shook with great sobs and copious tears. I knelt down next to her and put my arm around her as she shook, grieving the loss of her parents and possibly her siblings. I could feel myself trying to slip back into the pit of despair. I steadied myself. The kids all gather around us in a giant group hug as they tried to comfort their mother. We all cried and cried until we couldn't anymore. Then a kind of peace descended upon us, and we picked ourselves up off the ground. The children said their final goodbye to their grandparents.

As we were walking back to our vehicles, I noticed a medium-sized crucifix on the ground near the SUV. I reached down and picked it up; it belonged to Father Jay. I looked in the back of the car, and I could see his mass kit. I reached through the broken window and grabbed it. *These*, I thought grimly, *might be the only things that I have to remember my brother.* I held the crucifix to my chest. Sadness and tears threatened to overtake me, but I kept walking.

We drove on slowly, keeping an eye out for signs of trouble and a place to stop. Soon we found a house and hid our vehicles. The truck went into the garage. Laura parked the van behind the house. The semi was too large to place in the garage of course, but we parked it behind the house in a cluster of large fir trees. In the house, we taped aluminum foil over the inside of the windows so that light wouldn't show outside. We quietly unloaded some supplies into the house, including the portable propane heaters and tanks.

Since the weather was so cold, it was difficult to determine how long the bodies had been there at the attack site. *Had the survivors escaped or been captured?* The repulsive thought of those men having their way with our family members and friends was unbearable.

My dad had just returned with a propane tank from the truck, and we were just settling in for the evening, when we heard a knock at the door. My heart leaped. *We've been found!* We turned out the lanterns and kept quiet. Dad had the shotgun in his hand. I gripped my Glock 9mm. There was another knock, and then a woman's voice that said, "Let me in! It's Gabriella."

We all breathed a sigh of relief, and Laura opened the door. Gabriella and CJ were outside. They were cold and frightened. We placed blankets over them and hugged them tightly.

Once they sat down, and we got some hot soup into them, I asked the pressing question. "What happened—and how did you find us? Are we that obvious?"

CJ shook his head. "No, we were sneaking along the other side of the street, and we just happened to catch sight of Jay carrying the propane tank. No, you guys are good. It was just pure luck that we saw you."

Dad smiled and said, "Well, I didn't see the two of you. Good job concealing yourselves!"

Gabriella warmed her hands, rubbing them together in front of the propane heater. Then she spoke in a low, solemn voice as she stared at the glowing orange burner. "They caught us completely off guard."

"Yeah, it was an ambush," added CJ.

Gabriella nodded for CJ to continue.

"I remember that I was just looking back at a wild turkey running between a couple of houses, when I heard the gunfire start. I looked around at Connor and Hannah's car getting riddled with bullets. The car went sideways into the ditch. Then they concentrated their gunfire on the RV."

Laura breathed in sharply. "Mom and Dad..." She shook her head back and forth.

I put my arm around her as CJ continued. "Well, the propane tank or something must have been hit because the side of the RV blew out. They were getting shredded." He sheepishly looked over at Laura and continued. "They got hit hard with bullets. We felt the shock of it in the semi. I think Judy was blown out the side. The other cars in the group quickly veered to the side.

"My dad slammed on the brakes so hard that I smacked my head on the windshield of the semi. He kicked us out of the side of the cab, and we landed in the drainage ditch—I mean, literally. He shoved me out with his boot. I got the wind knocked out of me. I think that I landed on Gabriella, and she was unconscious. It was just after that that they opened fire on the semi." CJ shuddered. "I heard Dad yell, 'Cassie!' I saw the truck speed up as he pulled out his gun and began firing rounds through the windshield at our attackers. I lifted Gabriella and dragged her into the trees."

Gabriella rubbed her legs. "I was wondering where I got all these scratches." She gave CJ a weak smile.

CJ rubbed his head. "I just had to lie there in the bushes and watch. The semi ended up in the ditch further up, blocking part of the road. By this time, the men had stopped firing and ordered everyone out of the vehicles. One of the men reached into the Connor's car and pulled his kids out. By some miracle, the kids were still alive. They were screaming and crying. One of the men slapped the littlest one and put his pistol to the kid's head. Then he yelled, 'Surrender, or the kid gets it!'"

I interrupted. "Are your dad and the others still alive?"

CJ barely able to speak said, "They had too many men, like twenty, all ready for us. We didn't have a chance. I wanted to save them…but…but I couldn't. They dragged my dad out of the cab. He was bleeding down his side. They beat him badly—I think maybe because he took out a couple of their men when he was returning fire." He put his head down. "I really wanted to save them. I really did. But I couldn't. All that I had was my pistol." He pulled his hat down over his eyes so that we wouldn't see him crying.

As calmly as I could, I said, "Were they alive when you last saw them? Do they know that you two are alive?"

He nodded his head and breathed deeply. "Yes, I think that those who survived the initial ambush are alive. And no, it all happened like two days ago. I don't think they knew we were even there. They would have come back by now."

Laura leaned forward. "Wait! You left a week ago, you should have made it to the free zone by now."

Gabriella shook her head and held out her hand. "No, we had spotted some vehicles and thought it was too risky. We decided to wait to learn their patrol patterns. We thought we had it down, but they knew we were coming somehow."

I said, "They were probably monitoring the airwaves. They probably picked up our radio signals."

My mom broke in. "But we were using the radios today!"

I soothed her. "Yes, but we we've been using a different channel."

CJ said, "I don't know. The other day, one of our heaters sparked a fire on one of the mattresses or blankets. My dad dragged the burning mattress outside, and it caught some dried grass. We were all scrambling to stomp out the flames. Someone could have seen the smoke. I don't know. But all the commotion didn't seem to draw any attention because we were watching for it."

Mom interrupted. "What about Jamie, uh, Father Jay?"

"Yes, we did see him," Gabriella added. "He was in the back with the kids in Connor's car. He looked okay."

My son Elijah, my six-year-old, said, "If they are captured, then you have to rescue them, Daddy."

A tear formed in my eyes; and I grabbed Elijah, sat him on my lap, and said, "I'm not sure that I can." My dad reached over, and I felt him squeeze my neck. Then, I looked at CJ and said, "How would you feel about trying to get our people back?"

He looked up and smiled. "My dad said you were his friend."

I looked at CJ and then at the rest of my family gathered around the propane heater. "Your dad is part of my family. No one messes with my family. I don't know how we're going to do it, but if it's God's will, then we will rescue them." Then I nodded toward the heater. "And let's keep the mattresses and blankets away from that thing."

We burned the midnight oil—well, the midnight propane—late into the night coming up with our plan.

21

Behind Enemy Lines

I don't know why God has allowed all of these things to happen to the world. There is disease and violence and pain, but I guess that points us to the power of the incarnation. Jesus, Emanuel, is walking with us in the midst of it all. God is bigger than all of this.

—Father Jay Fide

The next morning, as we were eating breakfast together, we reviewed the plan. It was simple to remember, but we knew that it would be difficult to execute. It consisted of three main parts: infiltration, rescue, and escape. We spent the entire day setting it up, one of the most crucial elements to our success.

The following morning, we carefully made our way back north to the south of Salem to set up our escape route.

There were three of us who were going to infiltrate the enemy compound. It was a crazy plan, but just crazy enough that it would be unexpected. The only advantage we held was the Salem group didn't know we were coming, and they were not even aware that there were any of us left—or so we hoped. It was a small comfort because we were outgunned and outnumbered. They had our family, and we wanted them back.

Although my older kids could shoot well and could be a lot of help, I wouldn't intentionally put them in harm's way. They were willing and wanted to help, but I made them stay with their mom, grandma, and Gabriella. If there were any problems—and chances were good there would be lots of them—then the women and the children could make a break for the free zone. We already knew how women were treated at the compound, so it was only the men who would execute the rescue mission.

Everything inside me said, *Stay and protect your wife and kids!* But we wouldn't just leave our captured family and friends behind. God only knew what kind of hell they were going through, and we had already spent a day setting things up. I sent out a silent prayer to our captured companions: *I hope you guys can forgive us for allowing you endure another day of hell.*

It was an emotionally charged moment as we were preparing to leave. With a tear-stained face and quivering lips, Laura said, "Bring them back."

My mom added, "And remember, you're no Rambos."

I said, "Yeah, but I always liked Arnold better anyway." That earned me a punch in the arm from my wife.

Gabriella hugged CJ tight and said, "Be safe! Remember everything your dad taught you!"

As we began to take off on the quads that we had obtained the night before, out of the corner of my eye, I caught my two oldest boys, Isaiah and Elijah, following along behind us on a motorcycle. We stopped, and I called to the boys. Reluctantly, Isaiah pulled the motorcycle to where we stopped.

They both had tears running down their faces. Isaiah looked a little ashamed and said, "We can shoot! We can help, Dad! I want to kill the men who killed Grandma and Grandpa!" I saw tear-soaked rage in Isaiah's face. Elijah just nodded emphatically. I got off the quad and knelt down. I hugged both the boys. They cried into my shoulders for a minute or two.

There were tears in my eyes, and my heart ached. "Look, boys. We are *not* doing this for revenge. We are going to save our family members. Yes, we might need to hurt some of the bad men—not because we want to but because we have no choice." I looked them in the eye and rubbed their heads. "I need you two *men* to help protect your mother and sisters. I wasn't sure you were up for the task, but now I know that you are. This is a very important job. My family means the world to me. Will you protect our family for us?"

They both straightened and said, "Yes, Dad!"

I smiled and said, "Good job, I'm proud of you. Now go and set up a perimeter." They both flashed proud smiles and rode the motorcycle back toward the little house. As they rode away, I looked over at my dad and said, "I'm impressed that they managed to make their plan to follow us, find that little motorcycle, fuel it up, and get it running—without any of us knowing about it." My dad smiled approvingly.

With a wave goodbye, we took the quads the long way around Salem, staying to the east following Howell Prairie Road. As we headed south, I reflected how all the surrounding fields had once been meticulously maintained, but now they were overgrown and wild. When we reached the small town of Shaw, we turned west down Highway 214. After taking various secondary streets, we crossed under the I-5 freeway at Turner Road and slowly made our way toward the capitol from the southeast.

These four-wheel drive, all-terrain vehicles were an afterthought by my dad, but they turned out to be a great idea. They allowed more room to carry our gear, and they were four-stroke engines, which made them quieter than the dirt bikes that we originally had planned to use. We reasoned that if we were spotted by the enemy on the way to the capitol, we could more easily escape through fields, up embankments, or any other place that typical automobiles cannot follow.

As we entered the city limits, we were careful to refrain from revving the engines and tried to idle along until we got within half a mile of the capitol.

Dad pointed to a small, yellow house with white trim. CJ and I followed him toward the garage. Dad quietly forced open a small window. CJ was just barely able to get through as we lifted him to the sill. He unlocked the garage door and raised it up just enough to get the quads in. We hid the quads and ourselves inside. The house and garage smelled like death and rot. There was a badly decomposed dog huddled in the corner.

We slowly worked our way on foot toward the capitol pausing at each house along the way. When we thought that there was the possibility of being spotted, we covered each other as best we could until everyone made it to the next advancing position.

As we got closer, we could see the gleaming golden statue of the Oregon Pioneer perched prominently and permanently on top of the capitol building. We were near the Salem group's headquarters. This building was constructed by the citizens of Oregon to create and uphold the laws of the state and preserve its democracy. That was a stark contrast to the anarchy it now possessed. If we hadn't been able to see the statue, the increasing amount of garbage accumulated along the sidewalks and roads would have told us we were getting close.

We could see the army tents that were set up all around the building, including the open-sided tent set up as their armory. There seemed to be a lot of activity going on at the moment. Men were cheering and shouting, but we couldn't make out what it was all about.

On the other side of the road, on what used to be immaculately cared for lawns, were what can only be described as large dog kennels surrounded by tall grass. These cages weren't holding dogs but people. There seemed to be only two guards watching the kennels.

I needed to get a better view of the area. I signaled for Dad and CJ to remain where they were, while I edged closer for a better look. I entered the same Justice building that I had been in with Carter. I climbed the stairs to the top floor, found the westward facing window, and surveyed the area with my rifle scope.

I was able to recognize a couple of our people caged in the kennels. Beyond the kennels, there was an open amphitheater with stone benches. A lot of noise was coming from the amphitheater. Most, if not all, the men or soldiers were in two large circles, yelling and cheering at some commotion that was going on in the center. As spaces opened between the excited men, I could just glimpse what the commotion was all about. The men in the circles were gang-raping two women simultaneously.

The two guards were smacking the chain-link kennels with their black batons and taunting the occupants. I could only imagine what was being said.

Fuming with anger, I came down from my second-story perch and joined my two comrades; they informed me that they recognized Eli and Jared's voice coming from the kennel. And I filled them in on what the commotion was all about. I was shaking with rage. I whispered in a gravelly voice, "We need to kill those guards and get our people.

When I started to stand up, my dad grabbed my arm. "Think, John!"

"I can't right now. You think for me," I said as I wiped the tears off my hot face. Then I added, "We need a vehicle big enough for all of us. I can't tell how many people are in those kennels."

Dad put his arm on my shoulder. "Give me ten minutes." Before I could stop him, he was off. Ten minutes were almost up when he came back and said, "There's an armored troop transport a block from here. Look through those trees there." He pointed out the top of the transport between two fir trees about one hundred yards away. It seemed a viable option if we could be stealthy enough or lucky enough. Dad held a set of keys in his hands. "I guess they thought that no one would be crazy enough to attack them and steal their truck."

CJ smiled and said, "They thought wrong."

Dad looked through his scope toward the kennels. "Yeah, just as I thought, the chain link mesh on those kennels is fastened with aluminum wire ties. With some pliers, you could get them out the back with minimal noise."

The three of us carefully backed out from our positions and searched a few of the abandoned houses in the area. We came up with eleven pairs of pliers. Then we worked our way back to the kennels. Fortunately, the guards were now distracted by the commotion in the amphitheater.

I held out my hands. "Give me all the pliers. There are about ten cages there. If I can get the prisoners to help me free them, then it will be quick."

We got CJ set up with my AR-15 in a large fir tree with a perfect perch about twenty feet up so that he could provide cover fire for the escape.

Before I boosted him up to the first limb, I said, "Don't stay too long. I can't face your dad if I get you killed."

He said, "I won't, and I've got your back."

It was now or never. As I handed my dad his compound bow, I said, "Aim for the throat, even if it doesn't kill them, hopefully, they won't be able to scream. Use the broad tipped arrows for maximum damage. And we are going to need some help from heaven." I looked up, hoping that God had heard my indirect prayer.

My dad leaned his head side to side and rotated his shoulders and took a deep breath. "I know that the compound bows are the best option, but man, if we miss—that's it! We are done for!" I made the sign of the cross and whispered a more intentional prayer for God's assistance. My dad did the same, and then we split up.

Dad and I got near each of the guards. Lucky for us, they were still focused on the commotion in the amphitheater. We nodded to each other and counted to five as we planned. I pulled back my bow and said another little prayer, and knew my dad was doing the same. Both arrows somehow hit their mark and the guards both collapsed in a heap and died instantly. The guards fell hard next to the kennel. I heard a little yelp from one of the women in the cages. I felt a little vomit rise up in the back of my throat. I had never shot anyone with an arrow before.

I swallowed hard, and then we both approached the kennels. I handed the pliers to the grateful captives and instructed them to untwist the aluminum fence ties. Dad and I went to the other side of the kennels, and we each quickly grabbed one of the bodies and dragged them back behind the kennel. We hurried to disrobe the bodies and put on their fatigues.

I took the guard's automatic weapon and slung it over my shoulder and pulled his hat low on my forehead. Now was the tricky part, which was going to take nerves of steel, but right now, my nerves felt like tinfoil. I silently prayed for strength as I began to nonchalantly walk over to the armory. I had to keep telling myself, *Look like you belong! Don't walk too fast! Nice and easy!*

I made it to the armory. There was a huge array of weapons before me. Fortunately, there were also two duffle bags. *How nice of them to leave those for me too!* As I watched the commotion of the crowd, I cautiously filled the bags with fragmentation grenades and a couple of automatic rifles. It was heavier than I thought, but with a bag hanging from each hand, I managed to calmly walk back to the kennels trying to look as inconspicuous as possible. As I got back, my dad whispered, "You're nuts, but I love you."

By this time, everybody was just out of the kennel and standing behind it. My surviving family members were all there, plus nineteen more. Thankfully all the children were quiet. I didn't realize how many people were crammed into those cages. I looked around and asked. "Where is my brother? Where is Father Jay?"

Chloe said, "He's not here. They took him into the building."

Oh, good and gracious God! Must I leave my brother behind? I closed my eyes for a moment. I handed out the grenades to the men and said, "If things go south, pull the pin and chuck it into that crowd." Jared said, "But Gina and another woman are over there— and what about your brother?"

I shook my head. I hated to say it, but I did. "I wish we could save the poor women in middle of all that commotion, but we can't. As for my brother…" I paused to try to hold back my tears, afraid to speak. I couldn't look Jared in the eye. I could feel my lips quivering; I took a shuddering breath. "He'd want us to get these people to safety."

I held an open bag toward my dad. "Take some! You might need them to help keep our ride. These are fragmentation grenades." Two of the men I didn't recognize, who had been imprisoned in the kennels, grabbed automatic rifles out of the bag in order to cover the rest of group fleeing toward the transport.

Then a horn blared from the capitol building, a long, loud horn. We froze. *No! No! No! They've spotted us!* I turned to prepare for a firefight. But it didn't come.

As I looked around, everyone went down on their knees and put on blindfolds and prostrated themselves. I could see poor Gina and some other woman tied and slumped on the ground in the middle of the men who had gone to the ground to pray or meditate on nothing. I looked at my watch. It was six o'clock in the evening. *Apparently, it was prayer time.* I held my hand up to my lips in a gesture for everyone to be quiet, and they all began tiptoeing their way to the truck. I knew that I'd never have another chance like this. I turned and mouthed, "Wait for me!" Then, I walked toward the capitol building.

It was very strange walking past all the blindfolded men prostrate on the ground. I looked over toward the two women slumped on the ground. One of the men that had been caged with the members of our group was tiptoeing through the group of blindfolded men, trying to save the women. I hoped that he would be quiet. I reached the doors at the main entrance of the building. I was stunned to see Father Jay lying on the Oregon state seal in the center of the capitol rotunda. He was tied in a cruciform shape to a piece of lumber under his back. His legs were tied together around one of the stanchions normally used to hold decorative rope to keep people away from the seal. He was beaten badly. It looked as though he was being used as a kicking or punching bag by anyone who walked by. Perhaps, his suffering was meant to show how obsolete Christianity was compared to the religion started by the general.

I looked around to see if there were any guards posted to watch over him. There weren't. I ran over to him. "Jay!" I whispered. He opened the one eye that wasn't swollen shut. His breathing was ragged.

"John!" He rasped. "How did you...?"

I shushed him and began cutting him free of his bonds. The ropes had cut pretty deeply into his wrists. As I cut his feet free, I asked, "Can you walk?"

He coughed roughly, and I pulled him up. He put an arm around me and limped along beside me. I whispered, "I don't know how much time we have. They are meditating or something."

He nodded and limped beside me as I walked him passed blindfolded men prostrate on the ground. I could hear him rasping and mumbling something as he walked. *I hope these men don't hear it.* Amazingly, we made it past the cages.

I looked back and could see the man helping Gina and the other woman navigate their way through the blindfolded men. They had just about reached the tent where the weapons were stored. Some of the freed men came to help me with Father Jay. Suddenly, I heard a shot. CJ had taken someone out. *Oh no! We have been spotted!*

At this point, all hell broke loose. I looked back and could see that we were drawing a lot of attention. The general's believers were pulling blindfolds down from their eyes and standing up.

Gina screamed as she grabbed a grenade, pulled the pin, and ran headlong into the group of men who had violated her. The other woman that had been with Gina took up one of the rifles stacked in the armory tent and began firing. There was a loud explosion as Gina and any men near her were thrown into the air and then to the ground.

Some of our people pulled pins and threw grenades. I yelled to our group, "Run to that truck and get inside." Three seconds later, the grenades started exploding. There was screaming and gunfire. Fortunately for us, most of the Salem group's weapons were still in the armory. CJ, who was still in the tree, was firing his rifle and had killed the two other armory guards. Dad was laying down cover fire from the transport at the advancing capitol group.

Now there was a mad rush for their armory tent. One of our group had thrown a fragmentation grenade near the armory tent. Sadly, this wasn't the movies. Even though the grenade went off, it didn't blow up the rest of the armory with it.

Most of our newly freed prisoners were already in the transport, but four men had scrambled toward the armory yelling something about "Payback!" They reached the armory about the same time as the panicking Salem group. There was massive gunfire but not much in our direction. Most of the explosions and fighting were by the armory. I could hear CJ picking off soldiers as fast as he could pull the trigger. As I passed by the tree where he was perched, I yelled, "Go, go, go!" He got down from the tree and headed for the carrier.

Eli was at the carrier shooting and throwing grenades as fast as he could. By the time we reached the carrier, it was already moving with the back hydraulic door lowered. We all piled in the unit and raised the door. By now, there were bullets pinging all over the carrier. Two men that had helped carry Father Jay had been the last to get inside.

My dad's face was the perfect image of rage when he saw his eldest son. Father Jay's face was beaten badly. One of his eyes was completely swollen shut; the other was black. His nose was broken, and his lips were bloody. There was blood all over his clerical shirt. Some of the blood was dried, and some was more recent. Both of his hands seemed black and blue. My dad said as he got up, "Take the wheel!" One of the men quickly sat down in the driver's seat.

My dad grabbed his rifle and started to go to the backdoor controls. I was certain that he would have killed anyone in his sights until he himself was dead. I'd had the same feeling, but now, we needed to go and get these people to safety. I yelled, "Dad, we came here to save these people and they're not yet safe. Jay's still alive. Let's keep it that way! Get your head in the game! We need you!" Most everyone was aboard, and it was crowded, but there were a few of the men who we had freed from the cages running alongside the vehicle providing cover fire. I saw one of the men take a bullet and go down.

Dad reluctantly pushed his way back to the driver's seat. He drove down the side road that we had talked about and then down toward the freeway. On the carrier's radio, I could hear the general yelling for his men to stop our carrier. I could see through the windshield that there was a formidable roadblock. Two cars were bumper to bumper, blocking the way, but now we had an armored truck.

Dad yelled, "Hold on everyone!" The blockade would have been enough to stop any normal car or pickup. But it was not going to come close to stopping this six-by-six carrier with a powerful diesel motor. We broke right through the roadblock of cement and cars. Everyone hit their heads on the roof and was trying to hold on to something or someone. I could hear bullets pinging off our vehicle, left and right. I said, "Good choice on the vehicle, Dad." He kind of smiled but was focused on the road ahead. I changed the radio frequency and radioed Laura, Mom, and Gabriella telling them to go to the freeway. They radioed back and said they were a mile past the roadblock. Dad said, "I hope they found a big enough vehicle for all of them."

We rounded the corner about a mile after the roadblock and stopped. I said, "Get out, cross the freeway, and go south along the other edge of the highway. There will be rides up ahead." The hydraulic door whined and lowered. We watched our family members, and some people that I didn't recognize at all, quickly get out.

I realized that I'd left out an important bit of information. I radioed ahead to the women. "Mom, we rescued more people than we planned. We might need more vehicles."

Her voice came back over the radio. "Okay, okay, we'll be ready."

I set down the handset of the radio. I watched as two men helped carry Father Jay. Two other men were helping Carter out. I was so focused on everything else that was going on that I hadn't seen him until now. The enemy had beaten him pretty bad too. His wounds looked a lot like Father Jay's, but he also had a bandage on his left shoulder where he had apparently been shot. We watched them lift him over the highway divider.

Everyone had escaped except me and Dad. I said, "What are we doing?"

Dad said, "Improvising. Let's draw some fire, and God help us." *There was that look of determined rage again.* As I looked out the window, I could see that the others had run to the awaiting cars, and Laura radioed in, saying, "They're in, they're in!" Dad put our vehicle into gear, turned it around, and rounded the corner driving directly toward the enemy. Then he wedged a rifle against the gas pedal. We were picking up speed. I could see another armored vehicle bearing toward us. I lashed the steering wheel with a handy bungee cord to keep us moving straight ahead, and then ran to the back, joining my dad at the already lowered hatch. It was causing a lot of sparks as it dragged along the ground behind the carrier. I smiled a nervous smile and said, "You're nuts!"

He said, "I learned from the best."

Then, we jumped out the back of the moving armored truck.

In my head, I pictured us rolling a couple times then getting up and dusting ourselves off. However, it was nothing like the movies. We got scraped and bumped all over our bodies, but at least we had the sense to protect our heads. After we stopped rolling, we watched the carrier as it smashed into the other armored vehicle that was coming our way. The sound was deafening. It was like hearing two train cars slam together. We ran very stiffly to the familiar Ford pickup, which Gabriella had backed up to us. I could feel my elbows and knees stinging from the road rash. Thankfully, as we looked back, we could see that the two smashed armored vehicles were effectively blocking the roadway.

22

Make It or Break It

The cords of death encompassed me, the torrents of
perdition assailed me; the cords of Sheol entangled
me, the snares of death confronted me.

—Psalm 18:4–5

Now it was time to escape. A mile or so down the freeway, Gabriella slowed down and pulled us through a gap of cars that were blocking the highway, the fruits of our earlier preparations. Once all of our vehicles were through the barrier, then Mom pulled a car in front of the gap and did her best to wedge it in. She opened the hood, took out the distributor cap, and shot out the tires. We repeated this process three more times, keeping any eye out for the enemy.

Our red, bobtail WinCo semi and an old Greyhound bus were waiting for us on the other side of our roadblocks. Most everyone decided they wanted to be together in the bus, so we left most of the vehicles behind. We drove south as fast as we could. We now had just four vehicles: the semi which carried our fuel, the Greyhound bus, a Jeep, and a Ford pickup. My dad and I remained in the back of the Ford pickup to cover the rear. Gabriella was driving. We got into prone positions facing the tailgate. We placed some of the heavier canned foods and camping stuff between us and the tailgate for ballistic protection. A couple cans fell over the edge and bounced along the freeway behind us. I yelled to Gabriella at the wheel, "We need to be the last rig back." The pickup was faster than the other three vehicles and more maneuverable.

CJ and his injured dad were in the semi leading the way. My mom was driving the bus behind them. Gabriella yelled back to me, "We're going south toward Junction City and then out to the coast." I noticed for the first time that Jared was in the passenger seat.

"Great," I yelled back over the wind whipping by the truck. After about fifteen minutes, we didn't see anyone giving chase, so Dad and I settled into the rear-facing van seat that was loosely butted up against the cab of the truck. It was a little after six o'clock, and it felt good to be escaping.

After about forty minutes of driving, a very dark storm over-shadowed us. The wind began to blow, and it began to hail. We got wet. I began to shiver in the back of the truck, and we were thinking about pulling in somewhere to rest, but Dad saw some lights in the distance trailing us. He yelled, "We've got company!" Three motor-cycles were rapidly approaching. I could tell because each vehicle had only one headlight. They were now coming into view. We sat down on the floor of the truck again with our rifles ready. I looked through my scope and thought I could see gun barrels across the handlebars. The ambient light was dim, so I couldn't see much. Dad radioed the other two vehicles. We hoped that our makeshift barrier of camping gear and canned food would stop or at least slow down their bullets.

Jared stuck his head out of the window and asked if he could help. He had blackened eyes and split lips. I handed him a rifle. I guess that I hadn't had the chance to look at the wounds of my family members. They must have gone through a lot. There was too much going on to worry about that right now.

We had several rifles in the bed of the truck. The women and children had done a great job for their part of our great escape plan. Dad grabbed the first rifle that he could and made sure it was loaded. Jared had one of the fully automatic rifles. Dad grabbed a camping spotlight. He aimed it at the bikers but did not yet turn it on. I said to him, "I'll see if I can get them at a distance."

As we drove, hail was pelting down. Lightning flashed across the sky, illuminating the road behind us. I could feel the hail tapping the back of my head as I peered out of the back of the truck over the tailgate. The little pellets of ice stung as they bounced off my head; it was especially irritating when they struck the exposed areas of road rash from jumping out of the transport. I hoped it would be worse for the forward-facing drivers of the motorcycles.

The riders drew closer, so my dad flipped on the floodlight; and then I aimed, shot, and missed. I muttered to myself. Then I shot again and saw the lead driver go into a death wobble and wipe out. There were sparks and pieces of the bike scattered all over the freeway. Dad yelled, "Nice shot."

"I was aiming for his head, but if he crashes instead, that works for me. Have Gabriella drive straight until they start shooting." I heard him yell the command. Another bike whipped forward, and I shot. I missed again, but this time, they fired back. They were quite a bit closer now, but it couldn't be easy shooting from a moving motorcycle while taking hail to the face. I heard a bullet hit below, maybe the tailgate. There were two other shots, but I couldn't tell where they went. This time, we all shot at him. His helmet exploded, and his body fell off the back of the motorcycle. The other rider had to slow down in a hurry, dodging the body that had tumbled off the bike in front of him. The dead man's bike coasted riderless for a long time unmanned before it too wiped out.

I looked at Dad and yelled over the wind, "That's a good shot! I'm not sure who got the shot, but it was a beauty."

A few minutes later, several cars were speeding toward us. Dad looked at me and said, "I would rather shoot at motorcycles."

By now, the road and surrounding landscape were covered in a thin layer of hail. I realized that the road must be slick. Thankfully, Gabriella was doing a good job of keeping us straight.

Gabriella radioed to the others in the group and told them about the cars. I could not see the drivers, and their headlights were off. Lightning flashed, and I thought that I could see five vehicles, and the rigs were gaining on us. *Not good!* Our semi and bus each probably had a top speed of 70 mph.

I said, "It is time to slow them down a bit." I knocked on the window of the cab. "Jared, hand me those buckets!" He managed to muscle the five-gallon bucket out of the sliding rear window to hand it to me. I stood up and grabbed it by the handle and gave it to my dad. Then I grabbed the second one he passed through the window. "Thank goodness for hardware stores," I said as I looked down at the bucket filled with a variety of nails and screws. Gabriella maneuvered us to the center of the freeway, and Dad and I did our best to cover the freeway behind us with the hardware we had obtained. There was a satisfying sound of tinkling metal as we emptied the buckets.

Up ahead, we heard shots. We saw people on the overpass we were approaching who were firing at cars that passed beneath them.

Dad dropped his bucket, grabbed his gun, twisted, and fired—killing one and making the others duck for cover. The people on the overpass also fired at the enemy rigs following us. *Well, that is something at least!* They threw large chunks of concrete and crippled one of the five rigs. A large chunk of concrete went through the windshield near the driver. The vehicle went off the freeway into the bushes.

The four remaining rigs crossed the freeway using the grass median and were trying to come parallel with us. I yelled, "Concentrate your fire on the lead vehicle. Aim for the engine, front tires, and cab." We peppered the rig in front. The bullets caused spiderweb fractures in the windshield, and the hood flipped open, blocking the windshield. The vehicle hit a guard rail and then was rear-ended by the rig behind it.

"We're down to two," I yelled. One was still on the other side of the freeway, but the other had crossed back to our side and was coming up fast behind us. I could see sparks from the many nails and screws that the tires had picked up. Its thick off-road tires weren't yet flat. It came up beside us. Then bullets started coming our way from both sides. A large hole was ripped into the bed of the truck just behind us. The man with the shotgun kneeling in the bed of the truck grunted and fell from the truck. His body hit the ground and rolled behind us on the freeway. Jared yelled and held his cheek. He was grazed and bleeding. He ducked into the right side of the cab.

The right front tire of the pursuing truck to our left finally did go flat and the truck veered to its left; the right front tire seemed to fold under the truck as it flipped. It skidded on its side in a shower of sparks. We saw coolant and steam spraying out from the other enemy's car, but it sped up trying to get ahead of us. I yelled, "Don't let them get to the bus!" The freeway started to split wider between the north and south lanes. We could see them shooting at the bus, but there was little that we could do.

Gabriella sped up and passed the bus and semi on the opposite side. I could feel our truck fishtail a little bit on the slippery highway. Thankfully, she knew not to hit the brakes, and she skillfully turned toward the slide. Consequently, it took us a little longer to pull out ahead of the bus. The opposing lanes of the freeway had come together again, and the bus was taking heavy fire. I heard a terrible crash, and I could see that the Jeep that had been covering the front of our caravan had been taken out. It had slammed into a car that had been blocking one of the lanes of the freeway.

We passed the two fused vehicles at about 90 mph. We came out in front of the of the bus, but the enemy rig was ahead. We shot as much lead into their vehicle as we could. Their vehicle fishtailed left and then right and spun sideways, which caused it to swerve toward the median, hitting the center divider. It was flung into the air and rolled end over end toward us like a spinning cartwheel of death. It was a gruesome sight.

Two people were thrown from the car. One was thrown into our lane. Gabriella swerved to miss the body and the rig. The semi hit the body, however, and with a sound of screeching rubber, narrowly missed the vehicle; however, the bus did not. Their rig had landed upside-down and had slid into the left-front quarter panel of the bus. There was a sickening sound of crunching glass, metal, and plastic. The front tire of the bus lurched upward and drove over the rear of the overturned vehicle, which spun it around so that the front end of the rig smacked into the side of the bus.

Many side windows on that side of the bus shattered, peppering safety glass along the highway. It must have been terrible for any of our group in the back of the bus. The bus took a lot of damage, and it slowed down but dared not stop. I could only imagine how shook up the passengers in the bus were, both physically and emotionally. We resumed our place in the rear our little convoy. Thankfully, we could see no more vehicles following us. The bus was smoking badly. We had missed our exit for Junction City, so we pushed on toward Eugene. I could smell coolant, burning oil, and rubber. Minutes later, we took the first exit off the freeway toward Coburg.

The bus's engine sounded terrible. Steam and smoke were pouring out. As we parked behind the bus, I could see bullet holes through the rear engine compartment and all along the side. There was no fixing this one. We needed more vehicles. We forced the bus to keep going a little further until we found a nearby farmhouse. Unfortunately, a trail of coolant and oil marked our exit from the freeway. When we finally stopped, I discovered that two people in the bus had been killed from enemy gunfire; two more were injured. Father prayed over their bodies, extending his bruised and beaten hands. We could not bury them. We had no time. The hornets' nest we just kicked open would be swarming after us.

We managed to scrounge up a few vehicles, but it took precious time to do so. We had decided to get back on to the freeway and push south a few more exits before making our way west, since we had left a visible trail of fluids. As we passed by our abandoned Greyhound to get back on the freeway, we saw a fire had started in the engine compartment and was spreading to the front of the bus. I thought grimly, *Well, the bodies will be cremated after all.*

Finally, a few exits further south, we turned west toward Eugene, and it wasn't long before we found a large steel garage for tractors and farm equipment off the main road. It was easily big enough to hide all our vehicles.

The storm clouds lifted to reveal clear skies. It was growing dark, and the stars were visible in the night sky. It would have been a beautiful sight if we hadn't just emerged from such horror and terror.

Once we had all the vehicles in the large garage, I turned on the minivan's headlights for light. Some of the people got out and some stayed in their vehicles. I could hear weeping all around. Our remaining family members found each other. Chloe had been caring for Connor and Hannah's kids, Andrew and Margie, who were now orphans.

Some of those we had rescued came over to thank us. Others were so traumatized that they just huddled together.

Laura began putting ointment on my arms where skin had scraped away and wrapped the scrapes in gauze. One tall man came and asked if I needed anything. His name was Matt; he told me that he was a doctor. I was happy to hear that.

I told him, "I'm being well taken care of here. My wounds are mostly just skin-deep. I know there are others who need your help more than me."

Matt stood awkwardly for a moment, wanting to say more. I nodded. He said, "Look, what you and those others did was crazy—I mean in an awesome way. Just, well…thank you." I stood up and shook his hand. He pointed back over his shoulder. "That is my wife, Patty, and my two kids. We are grateful."

A couple of other people walked over as well. A man who looked to be in his thirties had his hand out as he walked up to me. "Please, sir," he said, "let me shake your hand." He grasped my hand with both of his, with tears in his eyes. He looked like a bodybuilder and was almost shaking with emotion. "What you did back there was incredible. If you need me to do anything, just ask!" He paused. "Oh, yeah, my name is Ben—Ben Longfellow. Thank you!"

I could see another couple behind him waiting to say something as well. I was feeling self-conscious about the attention.

After Ben walked away, the couple stepped forward. They looked young, probably in their early twenties. The woman grabbed my hand. Her husband had his arm around her shoulder. They both had tears in their eyes. "Thank you," she said. Her husband nodded his head vigorously. "We are the Bartles. I'm Sandy, and this is my husband, Tony." She wiped her eye while her husband, Tony, continued speaking on their behalf. "We just want to say how much we appreciate all you have done. Let us know if we can help out in any way."

I didn't know what to say, so I just nodded and smiled. I couldn't say anything in the moment because I was starting to get emotional. It was all that I could do to keep from getting choked up.

Dr. Matt walked over, looked at Jared's wound, and put a maxi pad on it. Jared looked at me and said, "Don't even say it." I just hugged him and said, "It's good to see you. You did good."

He returned the hug and said, "It was really good to see you tonight." He looked around. "I'm glad you guys are all right. When we left, you guys behind at the house, I didn't know if we'd ever see you again."

"It all worked out," I said. I asked in a whisper, "Did they… well, uh, you know, do anything to Chloe or Leah?"

He said, "No, but they were going to. They left them alone because they were the only ones who could keep the kids quiet. Some of the other ladies here were not so lucky. Gina and another woman named Heather were in the middle of the soldiers when you freed us. They had been there for quite a while, so—"

I interrupted. "I don't know if you were able to see it," I said, "but I think they saved us." I looked down at the floor, and my voice caught in my throat trying hold back tears. "Gina…she ran with a grenade right into the middle of them. And the other woman, Heather, stood in the breach with a rifle."

Jared stood wide-eyed. "Really? Wow!"

I looked up, realizing that I hadn't seen Susan. "What about Susan?"

Jared shook his head. "The general had her, but I don't know where. I don't know if she is even alive."

I said some silent prayers for her and her mom. For some reason, this news hit me hard. *Poor Susan. She has had such a terrible life, and all at the hands of her own father.* All the events of what we had been through began playing through my mind: sickness, shoot-outs, car chases, and death.

Eli put his big hand on my shoulder and said, "Are you all right?"

Startled, I look up at him. "Yeah, I just can't believe we actually lived through all that."

Then I realized that I had said something really dumb. Eli had just lost his mother, father, and sister and brother in-law. I looked up, and he was already crying. I said, "Eli, I'm sorry, I just meant just getting you guys free."

I hugged his wide, six-foot-four frame. It seemed bizarre to have this large man crying on my shoulder. Actually, no, it should not have been strange. He's my brother in-law, and he's my family. We both cried for several minutes, and then he wiped his eyes with the back of his hand and looked away sheepishly. He said, "I need to check on my wife and kid." Then he stopped, turned slightly, and added, "John, thanks for coming for us." I was raw, weeping and could not respond with anything but wiping my nose. Eli walked over to Leah, his wife, and held her and his son for a long time.

23

Licking Our Wounds

Why did God choose us? Is this a blessing?
Or is it a test? Or is it both?

—Jay Fide Sr.

Dad, Carter, and I were the mechanics in our community. Carter was injured and attending to his family, so my dad and I looked at the vehicles. The semi had two flat tires. Both the left side outside rear tires had bullets holes in them. One of the treads had already ripped free somewhere on freeway. The left side fuel tank also had a couple holes in it, as did the radiator. Fluids were leaking onto the floor. I grabbed several pans from along the wall of the garage to catch the dripping diesel.

I said, "The semi is done. We will need better vehicles."

I called two of my boys, Isaiah and Elijah, over and told them to dump the catch pans into the Ford pickup when they got full. The Ford pickup took some hits in the left side body and tail gate but nothing major. We were going to need to find some other rides.

As I was mulling over what kind of vehicles we should try to get, Laura walked up to me and said, "We're going to need blankets, more food, and water for the extra people."

"Okay, thank you, dear," I whispered. I kissed her on the cheek. "I'm just trying to figure out what is most important." I turned and looked into her eyes. She looked tired and weary. I realized what a strain all of this had been on her. Over her shoulder, I could see my children huddled together. Their eyes were wide, almost unblinking, perhaps looking inward or replaying events in their heads. *What am I doing to my family?* I thought. I felt a sense of dread well up from within.

Laura seemed to read my mind or my face, seeing me look over her shoulder. "You are protecting them," she said in whisper but firmly. "You are doing right by them. You are doing right by me. You are taking more on yourself than anyone should have to."

I looked down into those beautiful eyes. I said, "I want to keep moving. I want to get as far away from those madmen as we can. I think distance from danger is more important than food or shelter."

"Well," she said, looking thoughtful, "let's take it to the group." She turned and headed for the bed of the truck. I followed her and stiffly climbed up into the bed of the truck, feeling a dull pain from the scrapes and bruises as I pulled myself up. I spoke up to get the attention of everyone, "Hello, everybody. Can I have your attention over here?" I paused, waiting until I could see that most everyone was looking in my direction. "I know that you have all been through a lot. However, we need to make some important decisions right now." I looked down at Laura; she nodded encouragingly. I continued, "I know that some of you would like to stay here and rest for a while, but I think that we should keep moving, getting as much distance as we can between that cult and ourselves."

A teenage boy from one of the families that we had saved stood up said, "Who made you the boss?"

A woman, who I presume was his mother, grabbed his hand and shushed him; she looked mortified.

I involuntarily showed a half-smile and then tried to give her a reassuring look. I said, "That brings up a good point, thank you. Who wants to be the leader?" No one raised their hand.

Dr. Matt spoke up and said, "You're doing just fine." No one else said anything.

Suddenly, I felt the heavy weight of responsibility on my shoulders. I closed my eyes to collect myself. Up until now, our family had a nice system of shared leadership. I missed the deep baritone voice of Phil. I longed to be able to turn to Seamus and bounce ideas off of him. I wanted to be able to see the reassuring smile of Connor. I could think of so many others who were more qualified to lead, but somehow, everyone was looking to me. Carter was injured and recuperating. My dad never much cared for speaking to groups of people. My brother, Fr. Jay, was injured too, and I am sure that he would rather put himself in a supporting role, attending to the spiritual needs of the group. In subtle ways, Jared showed that he was deferring to my leadership. The women in our family are very capable to lead, and they would do a fine job of it, but they prefer to be in supporting roles to their husbands in a kind of collaborative leadership.

As I stood there with my eyes closed, all of these thoughts and considerations flooded my mind in an instant, and I almost froze… I almost physically bent under the weight of it all. *Who was I to lead? What if I lead all of these people to their death?* But at that moment, I turned the eyes and ears of my heart toward God. I prayed silently in my heart, *Lord, give me the grace I need.* And in an instant, a kind of peace settled over me. I squared my shoulders and looked up.

"Okay," I said, "as I see it, we have a couple of options. We can stay together, or we can split up. I want to say to those of you who are newcomers to our group, I am so happy that you are with us and that we were able to help you escape. I want you to know that you don't owe us anything." I looked around to let the words sink in. I continued, "I don't expect anything of you. You are free to go if you like. That being said, we need to be prudent in our choices. I don't think that these men who are pursuing us are just going to give up."

One of the newcomers spoke up and said, "I think we lost them, and we need rest. We're tired."

I looked over at him. "I know that you are tired, and I hope you are right. I pray that you are right." I looked upward toward the heavens and then looked back down. Then I softened my voice. "But you see, there is a missing variable." I paused for effect. "We don't know. We just don't know. So as a matter of prudence, we have to take the safer course. We have to make the assumption that we are being pursued. We have to make the assumption that these wolves in men's clothing will not give up so easily." I looked the man in the eyes. "It would be irresponsible to presume otherwise." I turned to look around at the rest of the group and shrugged my shoulders. "I could be wrong. Maybe they did give up. But I'd much rather be wrong and lose a few days of sleep running and find out later that we ran for no good reason." I slowly shook my head side to side. "The alternative is a much worse choice. If we assume that we are safe here, and we are not, then we are giving our enemies the time they need to regroup and hunt us down. I'd rather assume the worst and flee to safety." Everyone seemed convinced.

When I was done speaking, I smiled to try to reassure them; it felt like a hollow smile. Sometimes we have to mask our own inner turmoil as an act of charity to others. Some of the group smiled and nodded their heads in understanding, mainly my family.

The next couple of hours were spent scavenging for supplies in the dark, through the surrounding houses and businesses. Dr. Matt and a few adults stayed behind with the injured and the children. Thankfully, we found a nearby car lot with many large SUVs. The car lot had its own gas pump; I smelled the gas, hoping that it hadn't gone bad. It seemed a little stale but okay. Perhaps the owners had added some kind of fuel stabilizer to it for storage. The tank was an aboveground, which allowed us to fill the fuel tanks of the SUVs using gravity. In the end, we returned to the group with seven large SUVs loaded with supplies. We converted one of the SUVs into a kind of ambulance. We took out the back seats and laid a mattress with clean sheets in the back along with any medical supplies we could find.

We decided to wait until morning before we left, which meant that we would need people for guard duty. I said, "Ben, CJ, Eli, and I will guard tonight until 4:00 AM. Leah, Tony, Dad, and Sandy, you'll relieve us for the morning shift. Everyone agreed to do their part, and they found spots in the vehicles to sleep. We turned out the headlights. The four of us each took a corner outside of the building. An hour later, we saw one car speed through town. The same car came back through an hour later. I quietly went over to where Eli was for guard duty. I asked him, "Did that car look familiar? Do you recognize it from when you were captured?"

Eli said, "No, sorry, John. They had a lot of cars to choose from, and besides, it is too dark. I can't even tell what kind of car that is." He shrugged his shoulders. "But did you notice how it was slowing down at the different driveways?"

I nodded and said, "They're scouting. They're looking for us." I was about to say something else when I heard a horn sound long and loud from one of the vehicles in the building. Eli and I looked at each other and ran toward the entrance of the building. We entered through the door cautiously. People had their flashlight on, and I could hear children whimpering in the dark. Someone was talking loudly, "Sorry, I'm so sorry, my foot hit the horn. Sorry, false alarm. Everything is fine."

I had a little debate with myself as to whether to tell everyone about the car that we saw scouting the area. I decided that it could wait until morning. People were going to have a difficult enough time sleeping as it was. I knew that the horn was an accident and that it wouldn't happen again, so I decided not to chastise the one who made the mistake.

The morning watch relieved us as planned, and we got a few hours of sleep. No one slept very well. We were all uncomfortable, cold, and scared.

We all had a cold breakfast for fear that if we cooked something, the smell might lead our enemy toward us.

I took the opportunity to check up on the injured members of our group. Dr. Matt was looking after Carter's left arm where he had been shot. Carter winced as the doctor prodded his wound. He didn't look good. His eyes were sunken, he looked pale, and it didn't look like he slept well. Irritated, he said to Dr. Matt. "Hey, Doc, go prod and poke someone else. Leave me alone! Just let me die!" The doctor nodded curtly and quickly wrapped up his arm and started to walk past me. He paused and said quietly, "The bullet passed through his bicep and out his tricep. Fortunately for him, it only grazed his bone. Barring an infection, he will heal up in about month or so. His other wounds are, for the most part, superficial." He walked off.

I looked at Carter and put a little anger in my voice. "I didn't take you for a quitter!" He muttered something under his breath. I decided to push a little harder. "Fine! Just lie down and die! I'm sure that your wife and son will do just fine on their own!" He started to get up, but his wife held him back. I think he might have hit me, but I got the response I wanted. What I said might have seemed cruel, but I could see that Carter was spiraling into despair. I knew that anger can be a good motivator, and I needed to help him climb out of the psychological pit he was descending into.

"Why are you angry at me?" I asked.

He looked at me with daggers in his eyes; after a moment, his eyes softened. "I'm not," he said. "I'm angry with me," he croaked. He put his hands over his face, and I saw his shoulders shake as he started to cry. "I couldn't save her! I couldn't save her."

I said as lovingly as I could, "No, you couldn't. It was a blind corner—the perfect place for an ambush. They had enough men and fire power to wipe all of you out in seconds. You guys killed seven of theirs to our seven. They made you surrender by threatening Andrew and Abigail. They threatened children! You went down fighting Carter. You did your best, and it wasn't your fault."

"My best," he said sarcastically under his breath.

"She has to be in a better place now. Where she is has to be better than where we are." I could feel a hot tear stream down my cheek. "I couldn't save some of my family either, but we have to keep going. We have to get our families to a safer place. Can you help me do that?"

Carter nodded. As I began to walk away, he said, "Thanks for the sissy boy pep talk." He smiled weakly.

I said, "Don't mention it. I need you to be healthy ASAP, so just rest for now—sissy boy!" I gave him a wry smile. I started to turn around, and then as an afterthought, I looked at him and asked, "Are you willing to talk with Father Jay? I think that may help a little."

He nodded almost imperceptibly.

I made my way over to my brother to ask him if he'd talk with Carter. I saw him hobbling around. I was startled at how beat up he was. I saw him gingerly bending the fingers of his right hand. Both his hands were black and blue, but he was able to bend them, if painfully. I was glad to see that he could use them, because a priest's hands are sacred. I remembered being present in the congregation when the bishop had anointed his hands with the sacred chrism oil during his ordination. *That was a happy day.* He looked up and saw me with his remaining good eye; the other was swollen shut. He gave me a crooked smile, which obviously hurt because he winced in pain. I laughed at his discomfort, which earned me a much more discerning smile.

"Father Jay," I said as walked toward him. "How are you feeling?"

"Well," he said tentatively, "that is what I am trying to figure out." He flexed his hand a couple of more times. He tried to stand up straight and winced in pain. "At this point, I hurt practically everywhere, and everything is stiff." He looked at me more seriously. "I'm just grateful to be able to feel anything at all." He nodded and said, "Thanks for everything back there."

"Well," I said lightly, "you can make it up to me by going to talk with Carter. He is taking things pretty hard."

Father Jay looked down. "Oh," he said, "I'd almost forgotten that Cassie had been killed." I could see him reproaching himself in his mind. "I was focusing so much on the losses of our own family…" He trailed off.

I wanted to put my arm around him, but I wasn't sure if that would cause him pain or not, so I just stood awkwardly.

"John," he said, "when they had me tied down and were beating me, I thought I was going to die." He gently prodded his swollen eye. He looked down as if considering something. He put his hand on my shoulder and looked me in the eye. "I've never seen such evil." He seemed to shudder. "That leader, the general, took great delight in mocking me and putting down our Catholic faith, saying how it is impotent and useless."

I felt the hairs on the back of my neck standing on end.

He continued, "I could feel an evil presence that surrounded him." He lifted his hand as if grasping for the right word. "No, it inhabited him. When I looked into his eyes, I could feel that there was something else looking back at me that wasn't him." He held up his finger. "And it knew—it knew that I recognized it, and it laughed at me, so I said to him—to it, 'In the name of Jesus, Satan be gone!'"

Father Jay shook his head and quietly chuckled. "Well, he didn't like that at all. He let out an inhuman shriek and then kicked me in the face."

He paused and looked up at me. "He wasn't the only one. So many of his followers are the same. I could see their rage directed toward me—well, not to me, but who I represent." He held my gaze for a moment and said, "This is more than mental illness or madness. He is possessed! So many of them are possessed! This religion of the great Unicity is opening them up to dark spiritual forces. This is more than just a physical battle—it is a spiritual battle." He leaned in conspiratorially. "When you picked me up off the floor of the capitol building, I was praying what I could remember of the exorcism prayer."

"Okay, Jay," I said, "you've got me sufficiently freaked out now." I could feel my scalp crawling with goosebumps.

He looked up and said, "Oh, don't worry! That is just the devil." He smiled tightly. "We've got the Lord on our side." He clapped me on the shoulder. "I thought you should know." He looked down at my pistol strapped to my side. Then he reached into his pocket and pulled out his rosary. "Don't forget your most important weapon!" He tried to wink with the eye that wasn't swollen shut and failed miserably. "I'll stop by to see Carter." I watched as he hobbled off in Carter's direction. I couldn't help but think that his bruised body was a good metaphor for the current state of the Church and the world. I wondered, *Are there any other priests left? How are we going to fight this evil?*

In a very short time, we were about ready to leave. I looked at our little caravan, which now consisted of seven SUVs and a beat-up pickup truck, and I racked my brain trying to determine if we had everything. I was just ready to tell everyone to get in the vehicles when my dad caught my attention. He pointed to some steel plates along the wall and said, "Give me thirty minutes, and it'll be worth it."

He did a quick measurement at the back of the SUV and used the cutting torch to cut a piece of the steel plate. He and Eli lifted it and slid it behind the rear window of the first SUV. It made a nice shield.

I wondered if this would make too much noise or if the smell of burning metal would lead them too us. But I could hear the rain falling on the metal roof of the building we were in. *No,* I thought, *the rain will cover for us.*

I turned to my dad. "Why didn't we do this before?" I said in mock exasperation. "I think this is worth the delay. Keep cutting, and we will bring more metal!"

He made quick rough cuts, and we dragged the freshly cut pieces outside in the rain to cool them before we set them into the SUVs. It took forty-five minutes, but each vehicle now had a shield in back with a hole large enough for the barrel of a gun to poke through if it became necessary. I hoped and prayed that we wouldn't need them.

24

On the Boardwalk

And in the last days it shall be, God declares, that I will
pour out my Spirit upon all flesh, and your sons and
your daughters shall prophesy, and your young men shall
see visions, and your old men shall dream dreams.

—Book of the Acts of the Apostles 2:17

We were finally ready to go. I had wanted to leave sooner, but considering that we had families with small children, we were doing okay. One of the men had been busy installing CB radios taken from some big rig trucks at a nearby truck stop into our new vehicles. Regardless, we had decided not to use the radios unless absolutely necessary.

I got into the lead SUV with Jared and Carter. Although we had done our best to scout the immediate area to be sure all was clear, when we pulled onto the road, we saw a man on a motorcycle passing a cross street. There was no way that he could miss seeing our caravan. I prayed he was not part of the Salem group out looking for us. We just kept going and hoped for the best.

When we got about a mile into the forested area, Eli cried, "Stop!" He grabbed the chainsaw from the back of the SUV and jogged back to the end of our caravan. He cut down a few trees across the road behind us to make it impassable. I nodded in satisfaction. It was, however, a calculated risk; I prayed that we wouldn't encounter anything ahead of us that would force a retreat down the same highway. If so, we had effectively trapped ourselves. I could hear Laura and the kids singing songs in the SUV behind us. I was glad that Laura and my mom were able to keep the kids' minds off the danger we were in. After Eli put the chainsaw in the back of our SUV, I could see a grin on his face. "That should slow them down," he said.

Our lead vehicle had a good quarter mile lead for scouting ahead. The small curving highway made for slow progress. There seemed to be so many places ripe for ambush. I wondered if it would not have been better to just plow forward as fast as we could. At the rate we travelled, the usual hour to the ocean became four hours, but Eli and my dad took advantage of the slow progress by cutting down more trees behind us. Thankfully, we made it without a hitch.

We were now heading south down Highway 101. We made progress much more quickly along 101. Along the way, there were few signs of life. We pushed on until we reached Florence, Oregon.

In Florence, we paused for a more substantial meal. We had found a rambling old diner looking onto the Siuslaw river inlet, and thankfully, it had gas ovens that still worked and some cans of chowder, only recently expired, in the back. We ate steaming bowls of clam chowder. We were glad to see that the diner had a large stash of bottled water. The water that we didn't drink, we stowed away in the vehicles.

After lunch, we stopped at the local gas station. Without electricity, the pumps at the station were useless, but thankfully we had a couple of 12-volt liquid pumps with which we could snake the suction hose down the fill port of the underground tanks to suck up some fuel. We discovered that any of the fuel with ethanol in it had gone bad, but the regular unleaded fuel still seemed to be usable. It took a while, but we were able to fill up all the vehicles. Then we continued heading south toward California. At this point, we risked using the radios. I heard Dr. Matt on the radio. He said, "We need to stop," knowing enough not to say more on the radio. We pulled over in the parking area of an old motel. The weather-beaten sign said "The Sunny Seas Motel."

I saw the doctor get out of the vehicle and jog over to where we were. He said, "One of our patients isn't doing so well."

I frowned. "I'd really like to keep moving."

He nodded knowingly. "I know, but he has an infection, and the antibiotics that I gave him are causing a bad case of diarrhea, and he's nauseous. I can give him something that will help if we can find a pharmacy nearby, but it will take a little time for it to kick in."

"Well," I said, "we do happen to be at a motel. Besides, my back is killing me. Could you pick up something for that too?"

The doctor smiled and nodded his head.

"The Sunny Seas Motel" had enough rooms for all of us. We broke into the office and found keys for all the rooms. It was only the front office, doubling as a residence, that had the familiar smell of death. The rest of the rooms were clear. We parked the vehicles in back to ensure that it wouldn't be easy for a passing car to spot us.

For the first part of the evening, Jared and I stood watch. Highway 101 was a two-lane highway, so I chose north, and Jared headed south. We each found a spot about a half mile up and down the highway from the motel for our lookout points. Thankfully, it was an uneventful and boring night with not a soul to be seen. The only advantage of staying up all night was that the sunset was the most beautiful I had ever witnessed. The thin, wispy clouds feathering out from the setting sun seemed to reflect every color of the rainbow, even long after the sun seemed to dip into the ocean. Then the clouds dissipated or passed over head and opened up to a clear evening; the stars shone brightly in the night sky. It gave me an opportunity to pray and to meditate on all of God's good creation. I needed the reminder because I had been feeling that everything was against us.

At about 2:00 AM, after finishing my third Rosary, Leah and Tony took over for us at our guard posts. I was glad to have the opportunity for sleep. My eyes had grown heavy, and I was shivering from cold.

When I arrived back at the motel, I found there was hot food ready for us. I ate and got a couple of hours sleep before packing up and forging further south.

Highway 101 is a narrow, two-lane highway winding up and down along the coastline. As we traveled, I heard Carter behind me: "If we are attacked, the lead vehicle is a sitting duck."

My dad chimed in. "If we can find another metal shop, I can make front and side shields for the lead vehicle." We began looking for repair shops along the way.

We found several, but it wasn't until we checked the fourth shop that we found what we needed. We broke into Buck's Truck Repair in Port Orford and found a service truck with a gas-powered welder and plenty of steel in the garage.

Dad was grinning ear to ear. He figured Buck wouldn't mind if we helped ourselves.

He said, "Pull the lead car up." It took us two hours to get the front shield fabricated and installed. We welded brackets to the top of the car and hood. The shield covered the windshield except for two small rectangular holes to see out of. We extended the shield away from the windshield about three inches so that we could still use the wipers. On the four side doors, we cut plates that extended from the top of the vehicle to the bottom of it. We cut slots out to see and shoot from. In the end, the vehicle was significantly heavier, but its armor would stop a wide range of bullets. Since it was the lead vehicle, we made a tube steel bumper and grille for the front. It looked like something out of a *Mad Max* movie. Altogether it took us about five hours to retrofit the lead car.

We decided not to waste any more time, so we stacked some roughly cut sheets of metal to line the insides of the other vehicles for protection. After all the modifications, we drove another hour before deciding to stay in another hotel.

We were close to the California border now and everyone was excited, terrified, and nervous. Unfortunately, on this morning of the second day, we woke up to two inches of snow. Our night watch came back almost frozen to the bone. They didn't see signs of anyone pursuing us.

We were not making the kind of progress I had hoped for. I decided to call a meeting. The hotel had a nice dining area where we all gathered. I said, "I don't like this snow. I'd really like to keep moving, but I'm afraid that we will leave tracks behind that are easy to follow." I looked around at the people huddled together in the room.

Eli spoke up. I could see his breath as he said, "Look, we already have left tracks in front of this hotel. Assuming that this snow is not just in our location, it will make it hard for anyone who is pursing us to follow as well. I say we keep going." There were a few grunts of assent from the group.

No one was very talkative, so I just made the decision. "All right, let's eat, pack up, and be on the road in an hour." There was some murmuring, but everyone began to pack up. An hour later, we were back on the highway going south. The snow grew worse. Our lead vehicle with the makeshift armor plating was a disaster in the snow. The snow piled up on the metal over the windshield making it difficult to see anything. The vehicle was so heavy, it became unstable on the highway. To make matters worse, about fifteen miles south, the highway was washed out. A small hill side had turned to mud and slid onto the road, making it impassable. We found an alternative route—a small road leading into a state park going into the Rogue River-Siskiyou National Forest. It snaked around in a more or less southernly direction parallel to the highway. We had to cut the lock off of a swinging gate at the end of the road, but thankfully, we were able to get back on the highway.

Once we had covered another ten miles, we encountered another wash out. I said, "Looks like this highway is not going to work." We decided to head toward I-5 by way of State Line Road, which eventually turned into State Line Lane. It was slow going. There were trees that had fallen onto the road because no one was maintaining them. We had to use the chainsaws to cut them into pieces before we could make any progress. We managed another twenty miles but decided to find shelter and rest. The slow going had made for a hard and depressing day. We would need more gas for the convoy. The further east we drove, the larger the trees became. We were entering into the Redwood forests. We spotted a diner called Shelly's Home Cookin'.

The small restaurant was a log cabin, and it looked to be untouched since the virus. All the windows were intact. It was a homey little place with red plaid curtains. Eli broke in one of the back doors, walked in, and opened the front doors for the rest of us. In the center of the dining room was a fireplace open on two sides. You could walk on either side of it to enjoy the warmth. A large pair of elk antlers hung above over the fireplace. Shivering from cold and finding a supply of split, well-seasoned firewood stacked in the back, we lit a roaring fire.

As we warmed ourselves, I took in the surroundings. It was a beautiful and rustic place. Heavy wooden chairs were stacked on the dark wooden tables. Scattered around the room were stuffed elk, bear, and deer. High on the walls were head mounts of various game. An expert taxidermist had been employed to mounted them. The animals' glassy eyes seemed to be looking around for unseen danger. Other animal heads and mounts crowded the walls and shelves—a bird here, a squirrel there. Their eyes looked alive in the reflected firelight. The children were fascinated, especially by the large grizzly bear on its hind legs with a frozen roar permanently fixed on its face.

The electricity had gone out a long time ago, and when we opened the freezer, we were sorry we had. The stench of rotted meat filled the kitchen. We found canned food to serve up as a meal. In addition, we had Top Ramen and crackers. We managed to heat up all the food in the fireplace. The adults enjoyed bottles of beer and wine that we had scavenged in a storeroom.

I asked Eli to help me ensure that everyone drank in moderation. It would be easy for someone to be tempted to drown their sorrows in alcohol. We needed to be ready for anything.

Eli and Carter found some five-gallon propane tanks and smiled at me. I nodded. "Great! We have enough for the camp stoves."

Carter smiled wickedly. "Nope. This is different." He and Eli took some of Shelly's silverware and duct-taped the forks, spoons, and knives around the tanks along with a fragmentation grenade for each. We put the tanks in the back of the pickup for possible use later.

Then Eli happily showed me at least seven cases of vodka, whiskey, and other assorted liquors. I looked at him with a mock concern on my face and said, "Eli, you have a problem."

He smiled. "You're darn right I have a problem. I don't have enough Molotov cocktails." He loaded the bottles along with some rags in the back of the truck with the customized propane tanks. These would make crude but handy incendiary devices.

While some of our group worked on improvised weapons, Father Jay insisted that we utilize our spiritual weapons; he celebrated a mass for us since it was the Solemnity of the Immaculate Conception, December 8. After Father Jay led us in the Rosary, I prayed that Our Blessed Mother would cover us all in her mantle of protection. Then we all slept on the floor and tables around the fire. The fire crackled warmly; I could almost imagine that we were on a campout. I woke in the middle of the night to stoke the fire. The coals gave a gentle glow around the room. I could hear gentle breathing and snoring around the fireplace. The group spread out on the floor looked like a giant patchwork quilt.

As I eased back into my sleeping bag, I could hear Eve whimpering. I leaned over to place a calming hand on her shoulder. She was whimpering in her sleep. I could see her eyes moving back and forth under her eyelids. She was having a nightmare. I was tempted to wake her, but then I could hear her whisper, "The cross! The cross! It shines! *In hoeck seen yew veen chez.*" I couldn't understand the last thing she said.

She said it again: "*In hoeck seen yew veen chez.*" She smiled in her sleep.

I wondered what her dreaming gibberish might mean, but I thought to myself, *Good! Her nightmare is over.* I could see she still had her Rosary beads clutched in her hand. I laid down again. I was glad her faith had comforted her. I closed my eyes and went back to sleep.

The next day during breakfast, it became clear that most of the group wanted to stay here longer. I couldn't blame them; we had food, shelter, and a warm fire. The snowfall had probably covered any tracks that we left along the way. There didn't seem to be any signs of scouts looking for us; I wondered if they had given up, but after my conversation with Father Jay, I doubted it. They seemed to be literally hell-bent on finding us.

The incident with Eve in the middle of night was on my mind, so I sat down with Father Jay and asked him what he thought. I said, "Last night, Eve was talking in her sleep. I didn't understand everything that she said, but I think it could be important."

Father Jay looked at me for a moment and asked, "How so?"

"Well," I said, "do you remember the firefight we had in Gervais with Sgt. Lawless?"

"How could I forget?"

"A night or two before that terrible day, Eden was scared and slept with me and Laura. In the middle of the night, I woke up, and Eden was standing at the foot of the bed. She said, 'Thunder and lightning…thunder and lightning.' And she talked about metal raining from the sky. Then, the following morning, Eve was drawing a picture of a metal storm."

Father Jay looked down at the table, thinking. He looked up and said, "I have heard of such things before—premonitions, prophetic dreams."

"Yeah," I said, "and it's more interesting because the twins were on the same wavelength."

Father Jay nodded. "So did something else happen?"

Feeling a little self-conscious, I continued, "Well, it might be nothing, but Eve was talking in her sleep. She said, 'The cross, it shines!' And then she spoke some kind of gibberish. It went something like this: '*In hoeck seen you veen cheeze.*'"

Father Jay's eyebrow went up. He asked, "Have you been teaching your kids any Latin?"

I shook my head.

He continued, "Have you been teaching them Church history or something related to it?"

"No," I said. "At least not anything recently."

Father Jay nodded his head and mused to himself. "Interesting." He looked me in the eye. "If what you remember is correct, I think she said, '*In hoc signo vinces.*'"

I nodded my head, "Yes, that is right. That is exactly what she said."

He smiled slightly. "That is a Latin phrase that means, 'In this sign you will conquer.' And are you sure she said, 'The cross, it shines?'"

"Yes," I replied.

Father Jay smiled. "Let me tell you the story of Constantine." He leaned back in his chair. "Constantine was a Roman emperor during the early Christian Church. He was in a battle of power against... oh, I think his name was, Maxentius. Anyway, the night before an important battle, Constantine had a dream. He heard the words: '*In hoc signo vinces*' or 'In this sign you will conquer.' And he saw a large cross in the sky. When he awoke, he had his soldiers paint that sign, the cross, on his shields and armor. They had an overwhelming victory at the Battle at the Milvian Bridge."

I breathed in sharply. "What do you think it means? Should we paint crosses on our vehicles? Are we supposed to paint a cross on the door of this diner?"

Father shook his head. "I don't know, but I think that it's a message to help us. We'll know when the time is right." He stood up. "In any case, thanks for sharing that with me. It gives me hope, something that I have been struggling to hold onto lately." He smiled and walked into the next room.

I turned to look out the window. Thankfully, the weather was better, and the temperature was a little warmer. Carter, Father Jay, and the others seemed to be healing well. Dr. Matt was glad that people had the opportunity to rest a little. We enjoyed an uneventful couple of days.

On the third night, however, an elderly member of our group died in her sleep. She had been injured during the escape, and perhaps it was all just too much for her. Her husband, Jerry, was shaken, but he said that he was happy that she died free. We buried Joan next to the diner. It was a shallow grave because the ground was very hard. Her husband made a wooden cross out of a couple of fir tree branches and pounded it into the ground to mark the grave. *There was the cross again. Was this what Eve had dreamed about?* Father Jay led the small funeral. It set a very somber tone for the rest of the day.

Jerry was quiet. Everyone found excuses to get out and away from the diner. Carter and a couple others searched the nearby small town and found a gun store and a small gas station. We were able to load up on ammunition and refuel the vehicles.

I took a couple of the oldest kids with me hunting; Isaiah shot his first deer. With the freshly fallen snow, it was easy to track the buck. Isaiah took aim and shot him behind the front right leg and into the animal's heart. I was amazed at how calm and still he was. Thankfully, the deer died near the road. We gutted and quartered it and carried it back to the truck. Isaiah was able to enjoy bragging rights when we got back to home base. We hung the meat in the cold outside to let it age for a couple of days. Water was running low, so we melted and boiled snow. Everyone was content, until someone asked, "Where is Jerry?"

We spent the next couple of hours in a fruitless search for Jerry. The next morning, a small search party found his tracks and followed them to a river that was swollen from melting snow. The tracks simply ended there at the riverbank. Apparently, he felt that he couldn't live without his beloved Joan. Grief can make people do crazy things. I entrusted his soul into God's hands.

25

They're Back!

Be sober, be watchful. Your adversary the devil prowls around like a roaring lion, seeking someone to devour.

—The First Letter of St. Peter 5:8

Later that morning, Chloe drove quickly into the diner's parking lot, locking up the brakes and spraying gravel as her vehicle came to a quick stop. She was returning from a morning scouting trip to check for any signs of trouble behind us on the road back to the coast. She was out of breath. She said, "We have to go now! I saw a Hummer heading south down Highway 101. It is only a matter of time before they reach the washed-out area and come back this way. They will probably be looking for some way to get back to I-5 like we were."

Several of our group just stood and stared at her, wondering what this meant.

"Listen to me," she said. "It is only a matter of time before they come up this road and find us and our little diner. We have to go now!"

There was a mad rush to load up the vehicles and leave. We didn't dare cut down any trees over the road for fear that someone would hear the chainsaw.

We headed east, trying to make our way to I-5. Eli and Father Jay were in the lead vehicle with a head start to make sure it was safe for the rest of us who were following. Every once in a while, Father Jay would make a couple of clicking sounds on the radio to let us know it was clear. We didn't want to say anything over the radio to give away our position. Carter and CJ were in the trailing vehicle with Gabriella at the wheel to protect us against any threats from the rear.

We couldn't know for sure that the Hummer Chloe had seen on the highway was from the Salem group, but deep down, *we knew* it was them. We also knew that they would surely see signs that we had stayed at the diner. I kicked myself for allowing us to stay so long there. *We should not have gotten so comfortable.*

We were now traveling over the Siskiyou Mountains toward I-5. We were twenty miles east of the diner when the first Hummer caught up to our trailing vehicle, our tail-gunner. Gabriella radioed to warn us.

I said, "Are you sure it is them?"

She responded, "Who else is it going to be?"

Then I could hear the not-so-distant sound of gunfire. I heard Gabriella yell over the radio, "They are turning us into Swiss cheese here!" Branches were falling on to our vehicles as stray bullets knocked them out of the trees. I could hear bullets ricocheting along the pavement on either side of our vehicles.

I heard Gabriella say over the radio. "They've got armor plating. Our guns aren't doing much, but they are going to have a hell of time seeing out of that windshield."

I hated not being able to see what was happening. After a brief pause, the gunfire continued. There was a flash, and I heard a large explosion. I yelled over the radio, "What the hell was that?"

I could hear yelling over the radio and Gabriella cried out, "That was one of Carter's custom propane bombs. That Hummer is toast!"

"Gabriella, drive up to where we are," I said over the radio. "Let us take the rear." As they passed, I could see the back of the vehicle was riddled with bullet holes. The steel plate seemed to have served its purpose. But I could also see that both back tires were flat. I told them, "Pull over! You are not going to get very far in that thing. Get in our rig!"

Then I radioed to Eli and Father who were in the lead vehicle. "Father! I need you guys to slow down. We are way behind you."

"Okay, okay," I heard Father Jay say over the radio. "We are scouting ahead." Almost immediately after, I heard him say, "Hey, guys! We've got a problem." The radio went silent, and I could hear distant gunfire ahead of us, and a lot of it! Then I heard the radio again. Father Jay yelled, "Ambush ahead! There are about three or four vehicles blocking our way." I could hear the sound of bullets ringing off the metal plates as he spoke into the CB. *They had been pushing us into a trap!*

I called back on the radio, "Everybody listen! Take the logging road up to the right!" I didn't know where this road went, but it was our only chance.

"Okay," I heard on the radio, "we are headed your direction."

We came to the narrow logging road. It was overgrown. I watched as the first two vehicles started up the road. I could see our armored scout vehicle come around the corner of the road we were on. There was steam coming out of the hood. It lurched and bucked as it came down the road indicating there was something seriously wrong with the motor. I could see the front of it was peppered with marks where hundreds of bullets had hit the armor plating. Both its front tires were flat.

The vehicle lurched to a stop. Father Jay climbed out carrying his mass kit and rifle. He half hobbled and half ran as he made his way to our parents' vehicle. Eli was beside him trying to make him go a little faster. He grabbed Father's mass kit and pushed it through the window of the vehicle, and then he sprinted to the vehicle behind and climbed in.

Mom radioed and said, "We've got them." Then I saw my parents' SUV get on to the logging road. It seemed painfully slow as each vehicle entered the logging road, single file. We were the last vehicle and just as we were pulling on to the road, I could see a Hummer coming around the corner toward us. Thankfully, Eli had parked the broken vehicle right in the middle of the road, which slowed them down a bit.

The driver of the Hummer tried to push it out of the way and inadvertently hooked his Hummer's bumper on the bumper of the downed SUV. After we got a little way up the road, I grabbed my rifle and said to my wife, "Take the kids up the road as far as you can, I'll catch up."

She quickly looked at me as if she wanted to object. Then she said, "I know you will protect our family. I love you." She slid over to the driver's seat and started piloting the SUV up the road.

I saw Carter and CJ get out of the vehicle as well. They each had a propane bomb in their hands. They came over to me and said, almost in unison, "We'll leave a little surprise for them." They both flashed their teeth in a wicked grin. *They are definitely father and son,* I thought.

"Okay," I said, "I'll cover you." I moved down to get a view of the main road. One of the soldiers had emerged from the Hummer to free it up. He was trying to shake the bumper loose by rocking the SUV back and forth "Wrong choice," I whispered to myself. I lined up my shot and fired. He went down. His body crumped to the ground, leaving the passenger door open. I couldn't see inside the Hummer, but I shot as many bullets in there as I could. The Hummer burned its tires, trying to free itself from the bumper of our now dead SUV. With the metallic sound of something snapping loose, the Hummer was free, and it backed into a tree.

I looked back. Carter was just tying a piece of twine from the pull pin of one the grenades that was taped to the propane tank to the makeshift bomb on the other side of the road. He had made a trip wire, which would blow a grenade-propane tank combo on either side of the logging road. "Time to go," he said.

We hoofed it up the side of the embankment. The lead vehicle of our convoy was just making its way around a tight switchback on the steep hillside. We continued climbing. Out of breath, we converged on the rear vehicle. Gabriella was driving the rear vehicle. We got in. I looked at her questioningly. "I put your family in the vehicle just ahead," she said. "I figured that we'd take up the rear." Carter kissed her hard on the mouth.

He looked at me. "You see, this is why I married her." He smiled wryly.

We made it up a couple more switchbacks when I heard a loud boom. When I looked back, I could see a fairly large tree fall in the distance. Carter said, "Looks like they found my present." He smiled. "But that won't hold them for long. They've got winches on those rigs."

I looked around. We were in the middle of the forest, but there were signs this place had been an active logging area not long before the virus. After we came up over a rise in the road, we found ourselves in a clear cut. It was about a half of a mile long and wide, mostly open except for a few trees and log slash piles. *This is not good news. We don't have many trees providing cover.* The last thing we wanted was an open field for a fire fight. And now I could hear chainsaws revving in the distance below us. *That tree is not going to keep the enemy back for long!*

Thankfully, at the far edge of the clear cut, there was a huge, steep hill facing us. The road to the top crisscrossed its face, but it was muddy. The first vehicle in our convoy was just nearing the top, but it was having trouble. The road switched back and forth tightly up the hill. I could see that there was a log skid trail on either side of the switch back road. I knew that the loggers had used those skid trails to winch logs down to the clear cut for decking and loading on to log trucks.

We crossed the clear cut and came to the steep zigzagging road and started to climb it. The road formed two reversed letter Zs carved into the hillside. The corners were so tight we had to make a three- or four-point turn to navigate each corner. To make matters worse, after each vehicle went through the muddy slush filled ruts, the road became only more difficult to traverse.

We were two corners from the top when bullets began pummeling the side of our SUV and the hillside around us. Gabriella panicked and drove too far backward. With a loud thump, the rear wheels came off the side of the road, and the undercarriage of the SUV settled on the ground. The front tires merely spun. Bullets were pinging the metal shields and the windows shattered with one barrage of bullets. Carter yelled, "Get out and run for the hill!"

Thankfully, those who had already made it to the top had set up their guns and gave us cover fire as we climbed to the top of the hill. They let loose with a barrage of return fire, and we made it safely to the top. I lay on my back panting from the exertion.

Staying low, Father Jay came over to me and said, "Those corners sucked, didn't they?"

I said, "Well, when you are being chased, yes, they suck bad."

He smiled and said, "We could see you coming all the way up."

This seemed a strange conversation to be having right now. I was a little frustrated. "Okay, so were you going somewhere with this?"

He held his smile and said, "Well, if it was hard for us…"

"Right," I said, finally understanding. "They will have a hell of time coming up this hill. We'll make our stand here." The firing stopped. I rolled over. Moving quickly in a crouch, I made my way to the vehicles. I reached in and took out the walkie-talkies. I handed the other two-way radios out to the men and women gathered around. I instructed CJ to make sure that those currently guarding the top of the hill each got one as well.

It was a sad sight to see the children gathered around their mothers looking so scared. I said, "We are going to make a stand here."

I pointed toward an old logging road going further back. "Chloe," I said, "can you see where that road goes? See if there is a way out of here!"

She nodded, got into one of the SUVs, and headed down the road.

I looked around at the women and children gathered around. I said, "You all stay behind these SUVs. These are your shields against any stray bullets." I looked around at the kids. I got down on one knee to be more level with them. I continued, "I know that it is very tempting to want to look around the corner to see what is happening, but just stay here behind these vehicles, okay?" I saw all the kids nod their heads in unison.

Some of the men muscled a few of the metal plates that had been installed in the SUVs and propped them against the sides of the vehicles for extra protection.

Just as they were finishing, Chloe came driving back out from the old logging road she had scouted. She brought the vehicle close to us and got out. She was shaking her head as she said, "The road only goes in about one hundred yards in, and then it just stops. The forest back there is just too thick with trees for a vehicle."

I nodded. "I was afraid of that." I rubbed my forehead as I tried to think. I walked over to Laura. "Okay," I said as I put my hands on Laura's shoulders; I looked her in the eyes and rested my forehead against hers. "Laura," I said, "if it looks like we're not going to make it, and you have nowhere else to go, then head east on foot through the forest. They will have a hard time catching all of you in this dense forest." I could feel her nod against my forehead. I pulled back, and I could see her eyes were swollen and red with tears. My heart almost broke in that moment.

I tried to compose my face into a more neutral expression. Then I looked around and said to everyone, "Monitor the radio!" I said as I held up a walkie-talkie. "If it looks like we're done for, then head into the forest, we are right on the edge of the wilderness to the south, but there will be homes and farms to the east. They are going to be pretty far away but eventually you will run into something."

I turned around to survey our chosen battlefield. *What can we use to our advantage? We have the high ground, but how much help is that in modern warfare?* We were trapped; unless we wanted to abandon all of our vehicles and make our way through forest. There was no way back down this hill except through the enemy now gathering at the bottom of the hill.

I turned to face the families assembled behind me. "By the way," I said, "I don't plan on losing, but I want you to be ready in case I'm wrong."

I said to the remaining men, "Do you remember the Swiss Family Robinson?" Most of them nodded. "Do you think we can use gravity to our advantage?"

My dad clapped me on the shoulder. He said, "Let me see if I can get that old log skidder running." I looked dubiously over at the old rusted Caterpillar tractor partially covered by a tattered, old tarp.

"Okay," I said, "but don't spend too much time at it. We're probably going to need your sharpshooting skills."

He nodded and made his way to the old skidder.

Carter said, "I don't have any coconut bombs, but we do have our Molotov cocktails." He smiled wickedly.

I looked around at the men gathered around me. I said, "Not one of those men gets up that hill! Do we all understand that? If they make it up here, we are all dead. We need to do whatever it takes to keep them off the top of the hill. We'll sacrifice cars if needed. We've got the high ground and a good vantage point. Let's wait for all the Hummers to start up the hill. If we can disable the one in the front and the one in the rear, we can trap the ones in the middle."

I held up the walkie-talkie. "Okay, everyone, we'll use channel 16. Got it? Stay in communication!" I turned to Chloe. "Which reminds me—Chloe, can you monitor the other channels to see if we can pick up our enemies' communications?"

She nodded and flashed a bright smile. She turned and sat herself down in the SUV to monitor for any communication.

We all headed to the edge of the hill. I made my way over to where Ben was keeping an eye on the enemy. It was quiet. There were two Hummers at the bottom of hill. Obviously, they were assessing the situation. I could see a couple of others waiting at the tree line on the far side of the clear cut. One of the vehicles nearer to us remained in place, but the other one turned around and headed back toward the tree line where the other enemy soldiers were waiting. In the silence, we could easily hear the gravel crunching under its tires and the low growl of the engine.

The sky was overcast, and unfortunately, a cold wind picked up. There was still a light skiff of snow around us. The snow covered the ground and gave the impression that a giant had sprinkled powdered sugar over the trees. We were all feeling the effects of the cold. To make things even less comfortable, the wet ground was soaking into our clothes as we lay on the ground surveying our battlefield.

I radioed Laura. "Laura, the enemy knows we are up here. We are not hiding. Why don't you have the kids build a fire so that you all can stay warm."

"Roger that...honey," I heard over the radio. I smiled. I was sure that the others of our group found it amusing as well.

We all heard a scraping sound of metal coming from the direction of our abandoned vehicle along the switchback. Our stuck SUV had begun to slide backward, and the front tires lifted off the ground. The SUV angled down the skid and slid sideways down the steep bank, picking up speed. Catching the edge of a fallen tree, it did several sideways somersaults. We could hear the sound of crunching metal with each flip. Any gear that had been stored inside was flung out of the vehicle with great velocity. With one final crunch, it landed on its side on the other side of road at the bottom of the hill and slid to a stop.

At my right elbow, Father said, "Well, we've all seen what this hill can do. Now let's just do that to the Hummers."

I glanced over at him. "You make it sound so easy."

Then I heard a low rumble. The Hummers were coming out from the tree line. They seemed to be emboldened by the sight of our destroyed vehicle. Five Hummers drove in a single file, making for the toe of the hill where we had chosen to make our last stand.

Then I heard a loud sputtering rumble behind me as if some ancient beast was coming to life. My dad had the old skidder working. I looked back. Black smoke was coming out of it as it snorted and hiccupped. My dad looked small sitting in the old metal beast. Dad throttled it up a couple times, and it seemed to roar in protest. More black smoke poured out of it, but it kept running. Then it idled in a deep, throaty rumble.

I ran back to my dad. I yelled to him over the idling engine. "They are coming. Let's wait until they get about halfway up the hill and start pushing stuff down on them."

In a loud voice, he said, "It doesn't have much fuel." He looked out at our vehicles. "It's too bad that none of these other vehicles run on diesel." He hopped down from the skidder. "But I'll do what I can."

When I made my way back to the brow of the hill, five Hummers had joined the one at the bottom. One by one, all six vehicles crowded onto the switch backs. Fortunately for us, they had to stop, back up, and go forward a couple of times just like we did at each turn. The turn radius of the Hummers was even worse than our SUVs, but they had better traction. Still, their progress was slow. By this time, we had begun firing at them, but the vehicles were well-armored. The enemy were content to remain in their vehicles.

While the vehicles made their slow progress up the hill, I spotted a large boulder resting at the edge of the hill. Four of us, Ben, Tony, CJ, and I, set our feet into the ground and pushed with our legs to budge it to its tipping point. By now, the Hummers had made it about halfway up the hill going back and forth up the switchbacks. We waited for the right moment, and with one last shove, we pushed the boulder over the side. The boulder bounced toward the lead Hummer, which we were aiming at, hit a stump, changing its trajectory, and bounced over the lead Hummer. We all yelled, "Noooooo!" But by some miracle, it landed on the rear Hummer on the switchback just below it, and it crushed the top in. The Hummer in front of it, seeing what had happened, tried to go straight down the side of hill to avoid any more flying boulders. It pointed its front end down the hill, gained speed, and slammed into a tree. It was stuck—and it must have been quite a jarring impact for the men inside. Men started clamoring out of the vehicle, looking for cover.

I heard the skidder's engine working hard. I turned to see my dad using the powerful machine to push another very large boulder toward the brow of the hill. It was an oblong shape and didn't roll very well. The skidder was laboring to push it across the ground so that the boulder heaved forward slowly. The tires of the large skidder spun, struggling to gain traction, but the boulder kept sliding along the ground toward the edge. The engine on the old skidder was throttled up to the max. Black smoke billowed out of the exhaust. Finally, the boulder reached the edge and slid down the hill. At first, it just slid on its bottom, but then, it flipped and gained speed, and my dad's aim was true. This erratic spinning projectile of death slammed into the lead Hummer and smashed it against a tree.

Then the skidder's engine just stopped. My dad tried in vain to get it started. More gunfire erupted from the enemy, and we all ran for cover. There were fifteen men slowly climbing the road up to us.

Jared asked, "Is the skidder in neutral?" My dad nodded. Jared said, "I've got an idea. He ran back to the SUV that his wife was in and asked her to step out. He started the vehicle and pulled up behind the skidder. As I watched, Chloe came up beside me. She said, "Hey, John, I heard the general over the radio. He is here. He is in one of those Hummers."

"Good," I said, "maybe we can end this thing once and for all."

With the SUV spinning its tires, Jared nudged the old skidder over the edge. It sounded like a freight train as it bounded down the hill. The men climbing the hill darted frantically out of the way. Unfortunately, the skidder sailed between two of the Hummers and continued down to the bottom of the hill until, with a rumble and thud of groaning metal, it settled itself into the clear cut below.

We fired our guns down the slope of the hill while the enemy was distracted by the large metal projectile that Jared had sent down the hill. We took out maybe eight of them.

Then a very strange thing happened. I could see a white flag tied to a stick come up behind one of the Hummers. It waved back and forth. I held up my hand for everyone to stop shooting. A man in military fatigues came out from behind the vehicle with his hands up in front of him holding the white flag. He began making the slow ascent to our position. It was painfully slow.

My dad and Father Jay crawled to my position. I looked at them and whispered, "This is so weird. If they wanted to stop fighting, they could just leave." Then I remembered how we have their vehicles trapped between two smashed Hummers. "Maybe," I said hopefully, "we can end this without any more bloodshed."

Dad said, "I don't like it."

I looked over at our people scattered on the hill. I shook my head slightly and said, "But I'm not sure what to do. I don't want to go down to meet him because it is too exposed along that hillside. I think we'll just let him come up here, but we'll keep a gun or two pointed at him."

The man with the white flag made slow progress climbing up the hill. The enemy vehicles had only made it about halfway up the switch backs. They had only three functioning vehicles now, and they were effectively trapped between the two crushed Hummers. Strangely, none of the enemy seemed to make any movements; they just stayed where they were. We scanned the area, looking for any deception.

Finally, after what seemed an eternity, the man made it to the top. He was breathing hard and holding his white flag almost like a crutch to hold himself up. He kept his back to the hillside and stood at the edge facing us. He kept his hands raised. He went down on one knee as if trying to catch his breath. He seemed to lean heavily on the makeshift flag that he carried.

I cautiously stood up but stayed back from the edge of the hill. Father Jay stood up with me.

The man asked between ragged breaths, "Could I get a glass of water or something?" I looked dubiously at Father Jay. This man was in no position to ask for anything.

I said, "What do you want? What is this all about?"

He looked up, and with what seemed genuine worry in his eyes, he whispered, "Take me with you! You don't know what it is like. The general—he's a madman. He sent me up here to make terms—to come to some kind of agreement." He said all of this while still trying to catch his breath."

He lowered his head, and his shoulders began to shake, and I could hear him sobbing. In between sobs, he said, "You don't know... what...it's...like."

My mom by this time had gotten a water bottle and had gingerly approached him; she had her hand extended out, holding the water bottle toward him doing her best to stay out of his reach.

His sobs quickly turned to laughter, and with a quick motion that caught us all off guard, he dropped the flag, grabbed my mom's wrist, and pulled her to himself. She was facing us, and he was using her as a shield. He had his right arm around her neck, and he held her hair in his left hand.

I yelled, "Stop! What are you doing?" I pointed my gun in his direction, but I was afraid of pointing it at my mom.

The man smiled malevolently and pulled up on my mom's hair sharply. Her breath sucked in involuntarily. I could see a tear stream down the side of her nose.

I could see my dad slowly rise up out of the corner of my eye. I didn't have to see his face to know the rage that was building inside him. I said through clenched teeth, "Let her go!" I paused. "What do you want?"

He reached back behind himself with his right hand, pulled out something with a black handle, and held it up for us to see. A blade appeared. *A switchblade!* I could see Ben start slowly making his way from the side toward this man who was threatening my mother with a knife.

The man said, "I am one of the Obedient." He paused. "And the general has sent me up here to tell you that..." He lifted hard on my mother's hair with his left hand and then stabbed her in the back with the knife he held in his right. Then he punctuated each word with a stab in my mother's back: "There...are...no...terms!"

My mom arched her back and grimaced in pain and slumped down. She would have crumpled to the ground except that this monster held her up by her hair. I wanted to shoot. I wanted to do something, but he held her up like a shield. I looked at my mother's sweet face. Her eyes fluttered open. Discomfort was written on her face. She looked up at me. She looked right into my eyes. Her eyes softened, and with a hint of a smile, she mouthed, "It's okay." Her breathing was ragged.

Ben, who was now standing next to Father Jay, suddenly lurched backward but not on his own power. He looked down. There was a hole in his chest. We heard a distant boom echo through the forest. *A sniper!* Ben fell forward on his face, dead.

Then everyone was in motion. I felt like I was moving through molasses. The man holding my mother flung her down the side of the hill. I saw her disappear over the brow of the hill. My dad yelled, "Victoria!" He dove for her over the side of the hill. This wolf in sheep's clothing who had carried the white flag reached behind himself again and produced a grenade. He pulled the pin.

26

In Hoc Signo Vinces

For many, of whom I have often told you and now tell you
even with tears, live as enemies of the cross of Christ.

—The Letter of St. Paul to the Philippians 3:18

I was in shock. This man—this monster had just stabbed my mother in the back and thrown her over the side of the hill like she was a piece of trash. I was so stunned by what I had just seen, I almost forgot that I had a rifle in my hand. I was still registering that he had reached behind his back and produced a grenade. He had pulled the pin. I was just lifting the rifle in my hand when I saw a swift movement to my left. My brother quickly moved forward, spun, and kicked the man hard in the chest. At the force of the kick, the man flew backward off the hill. His eyes were wide in shock, as head over heels, he sailed backward over the side of the hill, taking the grenade with him.

Gunfire erupted, and I dove for cover. Father Jay had scrambled back to safety behind one of the vehicles.

We heard a large boom down the side of the hill when the grenade exploded.

Sandy, Ben's wife, dropped her rifle, grabbed for Ben's leg, and struggled to drag him to cover when the left side of her head exploded. Then, a split second later, I heard the loud report from the gun that fired the bullet.

It was all a ruse so that we would let our guard down, and it had worked. We were so focused on the man carrying the white flag, none of us had noticed that a sniper was setting up.

I heard Carter's voice over the radio. "Listen, you guys!" His voice was hard and commanding. "Get behind cover! Now listen! The sniper was able to scope us out back behind the brow of the hill. He has to be up in a tree. Keep an eye out in the trees behind the enemy!"

My heart was beating fast. I was breathing hard. I was crouching down behind a log. Hopefully, it would be thick enough to stop a sniper bullet. But my parents were somewhere over the brow of the hill exposed, vulnerable. I held the walkie-talkie up to my mouth. "Does anyone have a visual on my parents?"

It was Dr. Matt who spoke. "I can see them. They are on the road just under the brow of the hill. Your dad has his back to a tree. He is holding your mom. It looks like he's got a wound in the stomach."

I heard a voice over the radio. "Hey, Tony, see if you can draw the sniper's fire."

Tony replied, "Okay, will do." I watched in horror as Tony got up and ran from the cover of a large log toward one of the vehicles. His knee buckled under him with the force of the impact of a bullet. There was the report of a distant gunshot echoing through the forest. Tony lay bleeding and screaming in pain out in the open.

I heard over the radio, in a voice that sounded very much like mine, "Hey, Eli, can you go get Tony to safety?"

Frantically, I pressed the send button of the walkie-talkie and said, "Eli, stop! That is not me, someone has our channel!"

Then, to my horror, I heard what sounded like my voice say, "Hey, Laura, we are surrendering. Bring the kids out from behind cover with your hands up."

Frantic, I pressed the send button, "Do not listen to that! Someone has our channel and is trying to confuse us."

I heard the voice over the radio say, "Don't worry, honey, it will be fine. Everything is okay. Just come out."

I yelled into the walkie-talkie, "Who is this? What kind of monster would want to harm women and children?"

I heard laughing over the radio. The voice resolved into the general's voice. It once again took on the prim and proper tenor that I had heard before. It was laced with a slight British accent. He said, "You harbored my wife and little princess. It seemed only fair. You killed my men in your crappy little town. Then you attacked my home at the capitol. No one tangles with the brotherhood and lives."

As if to emphasize his point, Tony was thrown to the ground. A gunshot could be heard in the distance. He lay twitching on the ground.

The general continued his monologue: "I killed insignificant detritus like you in prison. You are already dead. You just don't know it yet." Over the radio, I could hear a faint, "Daddy, no, they are my friends!"

It is Susan! She is still alive! The general, still holding the send button on his radio said, "Oh, my dear girl, did you want to say something?"

She said, "I hate you! Let me go to my friends!" Then her voice went up in pitch, and I heard her say, "No, no, Daddy!" A gunshot was heard over the radio and then silence. After a moment, the general spoke, his voice was thick with rage; it sounded almost demonic. "Do you see what you made me do? You turned her against me! You did this! You did this!" He screeched an inhuman scream, and the radio was silent.

I sat stunned behind my log. *Poor Susan! She didn't deserve that—and for trying to protect us! All her life, she lived in fear of her father. All her life, she had that dark shadow hanging over her.*

Then I heard Carter yell, "The sniper is over there!" I looked to where he was pointing; there was a little movement in a tree opposite the hill. We all lifted the sights of our rifles and fired. The old fir tree seemed to shake and fall apart as though it had decided to finally shed it needles as the bullets shredded it. The sniper fell out of the tree.

Jared and I took the opportunity to run forward and gain more ground. I could see three guys advancing along the road, trying to flank us on the right. We drew their fire, and Carter and CJ took them out.

The general spoke over the radio, "We're not done yet! Reload that .50 caliber and kill their snipers!"

Then I heard the .50-caliber machine gun firing. The log in front of me began to disintegrate. The rounds strafed along the brow of the hill. I looked to my right and left. Everyone with me on the hilltop was ducking down in fear of the rounds. Then the gun stopped. I could hear the loud reports of the gun echoing through the hills. I peeked over the log. I could see the soldier with the .50-caliber gun mounted on the Hummer trying to reload the monstrous weapon.

I heard Father Jay over the radio, "Yes, we are done!" I looked over, and he came around the side of the SUV. He had the walkie-talkie up to his mouth, and he held the crucifix in front of him. He spoke, "In the name of Jesus, Satan be silent!" In response, I heard a growl over radio.

My brother looked over at me and said, "I'm counting on you, John." He walked along the road toward where our parents lay wounded and bleeding. His purple stole was draped over his neck and flapped in the wind behind him.

As he walked, he repeated over and over again into the radio, "For the sake of His sorrowful passion, have mercy on us and on the whole world."

I could see that he had his sacramental kit slung over his back. He walked purposefully toward where our parents lay dying. At that moment, it seemed that sun had parted the clouds, and I could see the sun reflected off the cross that he held in his hand. It shimmered like gold. *What is he doing?* I thought. *He is going to give them last rites in the middle of a firefight! He is going to get himself killed!*

He was exposed. He had no barriers to protect him, but he walked on, purposefully, holding the cross in front of him like a shield. I looked back at our attackers, and they literally seemed to be gnashing their teeth at the sight of it.

"For the sake of His sorrowful passion, have mercy on us and on the whole world! Jesus, I trust in you!" he said over the walkie-talkie.

All of the enemy seemed to come out from behind their protective barriers to take aim at him. Every one of them smiled a hateful smile as if relishing the thought of being the one to kill the priest, and they fired.

As Father Jay walked, there were bullets hitting all around him. Dirt, snow, and rocks were being thrown up around his feet. One bullet even seemed to hit the purple stole that was flapping behind him as he walked; another bullet shattered the walkie-talkie he had been holding in his hand. He ignored the bullets all around him. And yet, the crucifix shone in the sun. *It shines! In hoc signo vinces.*

I realized, suddenly, that Eve had predicted this moment in her dream. *The cross, it shines! In hoc signo vinces! In this sign you will con-*

quer! I thought, *What am I supposed to do?* I looked down. I could see one of Eli's Molotov cocktails propped up against the side of the log I was hiding behind. Its label read, "Constantine Whiskey, 100 proof." *Constantine! In hoc signo vinces! The cross, it shines!*

I knew what I had to do. I slung my rifle over my shoulder. I grabbed the bottle of whiskey; I took the lighter out of my pocket, and I lit the piece of cloth sticking out of the one-hundred-proof whiskey. Ducking down, I ran parallel to the brow of the hill. I passed by Carter a little way back from the edge. His wife had his head on her lap and was trying pull debris out of his eyes.

I looked over the brow of the hill as I ran. I could see Father Jay boldly walking. My people at the top of hill were firing back at the enemy, trying to take them out before they shot my brother.

I knew that, somehow, I had to take out that .50 caliber machine gun before he got it reloaded. I ran toward the edge of the skid trail.

The radio on my belt sounded. The general's voice, seething with anger and hate, said, "Priest! How dare you use that name! He has no place here, priest!" The radio went silent. The door of the of the second to last Hummer was kicked open, and the general fired a barrage of bullets up and down the hill. Then he fired the attached grenade launcher. His shot went long and blew up one hundred feet behind me, too close to the women and children hiding behind the SUVs.

I slid behind a stump near the edge of the skid trail. I looked down the steep slope. It almost looked like a muddy cliff. Then an idea stuck me. *Two can play at the game of confusing the enemy.* I pulled the walkie-talkie off my belt and pressed the send button. In my best British accent, I spoke, trying to imitate the general's voice. I said, "This is the Obedient Servant." I paused, trying to remember what I knew about the strange cult that was attacking us. I said, "The Great Unicity has said, 'Cease your fire!'"

I could hear that some of the enemy stopped firing. *Good! They are confused!* I looked over the stump that was concealing me. I could see many of the soldiers were looking questioningly over at the general. I knew that their confusion wouldn't last long.

As I looked out from behind my protective barrier, I could see that Father Jay had made it to our parents, but he was still exposed. He knelt down at our parents' side and began to give them their last rites. Under my breath, I said, "Thank you, God."

Then the general fired another grenade from the launcher. We all ducked for cover. There was a large explosion just beneath the brow of the hill. When the dust settled, I looked over the edge. The embankment above Father and my parents had come down. Dirt and rocks slid down in an avalanche, covering my family.

I looked at the flaming wick of my Molotov cocktail. *It is now or never*, I thought. I stood at the edge of the skid trail, said a little prayer quietly under my breath, and jumped over the brow of the hill onto the skid trail, feet first. I slid down the skid. It was nothing like going down a slide in a playground. The ground was rough with little rocks and roots and sticks that roughly slid across my underside. My teeth rattled as I slid, but thankfully, it was slick, and I was quickly gaining speed. *I need to protect this bottle from breaking!* I noticed I was now drawing some of the gunfire toward myself. Most notably, the general had his rifle pointed in my direction. I could see flashes of light flaming out of the barrel as he tried to take me out. I hoped that I would be a difficult target to hit.

I slid quickly down the skid trail, and I waited for the right moment. I could see the Hummer with the .50-caliber gun to my left; awkwardly, using my right hand, I threw the flaming Molotov cocktail at the Hummer as I slid past.

I watched as the flaming projectile arced in the air. My aim was true. I rolled on to my side and craned my neck as I slid by to watch. The bottle hit the shield of the .50-caliber gun and shattered. The flammable liquid splashed all over the soldier behind the gun and splattered on the general. Both men caught on fire.

Then I hit the bottom of the skid—hard! I rolled and slid into a log that was at the bottom. Pain erupted in my left side. I quickly climbed over the log for cover. The impact had knocked the wind out of me. I struggled to inhale, but after a moment my spasming, diaphragm relaxed, and I was able to catch a breath. I pulled the rifle off my shoulder. After I took a couple of breaths, I popped up, aimed my rifle, and I pulled the trigger as fast as I could at the enemy still on my side of the Hummers, trees, and stumps that they were using for cover.

Some of the enemy had tried to go around to the other side of the vehicles and tree stumps for cover. Everyone in our group with a gun took aim and fired, and it seemed that every bullet found its mark. In an instant, the enemy fell to the ground dead or wounded. I shot the general with a couple of rounds as he was trying to put out the flames that had engulfed him.

I could see Jared and Eli sliding down the brow of the hill to finish off any of the enemy still left. As I climbed back up the hill to the enemy's position, Jared and Eli carefully checked for enemy survivors in the vehicles.

I climbed up to where the general was lying. He had propped himself up against the tire of the nearest Hummer. He was breathing heavily. He was still smoldering from the flames that had engulfed him. His hair was all burned off on the right side of his head. There were gunshot wounds in his leg and in stomach. He held his hand over his stomach, but he couldn't slow the flow of blood. Blood oozed out between his fingers. I kept my pistol aimed at him. As added insurance, I kicked his rifle out of his reach.

He looked up at me with a confused expression on his face. Between ragged breaths he said, "This wasn't the way it was supposed to be. I'm the Obedient Servant." He looked at me questioningly. "Why?"

I had my pistol aimed at his head. I wanted to end him. This monster who had haunted my dreams and my life now looked pathetic. His face and jacket were blackened and burned from the flames. He seemed confused. I looked up to where my parents and brother had been buried under the dirt and stones of the small avalanche the general had caused with his grenade launcher. I could see some of our group trying to dig away the rubble.

I felt an immense hatred for this man lying here before me. I looked into his pathetic eyes. I wanted to see evil in those eyes. If only I could see or feel that evil presence, I would feel justified in killing him. But he just looked confused and pathetic.

He said in an almost childlike tone, "Are you going to kill me?"

I said through clenched teeth, "I want to!" My tone softened. "But no, I'm not going to kill you." I looked down at the blood pooling around his leg and oozing between his fingers. "And I can't save you. You rejected the One that could save you!" I looked up toward the mound of rubble that entombed my family, and I added, "I have others to look after." Then I turned my back on him and started to climb up the switchback to help dig out the bodies of my parents and brother.

I heard the general mumble, "No, it can't end this way! This isn't how it is supposed to be!"

I ignored him but heard a click behind me—the unmistakable sound of the hammer of a revolver cocking. I put my hands up, afraid to turn around and afraid not to turn around. The revolver fired!

27

Mourning

Blessed are those who mourn, for they shall be comforted.

—The Gospel of St. Matthew 5:4

At the sound of the revolver firing, I flinched and rolled to the ground. I came up with my own pistol pointed at the general. I did a mental check trying to be aware of the various parts of my body, mentally searching for the pain of a gunshot wound. *Had he missed? Am I in shock?*

As I aimed my own gun at the general, I realized that I had not been the target. I could hear a hissing sound. Air was escaping out of the tire where the bullet had punctured it; that is to say, after the bullet had gone through the roof of the general's mouth and out the back of his head. I could see the revolver still in the general's hand resting on his chest. His eyes were bulging behind his eyelids.

As I got up off the ground, I realized that there could be more of the enemy around the area, so I climbed into the general's Hummer and grabbed the microphone-handset of the CB and pressed the talk button. "Listen up! Any of you who have been following the general, know this—he is dead. The team that came with him is dead. You need to leave now and go back to Salem, or the same fate awaits you!" I looked down at the LED indicator. It read channel 16. I asked, "Chloe, what was the channel that you originally heard the general on?"

After a moment she replied, "It was channel 22."

I switched to channel 22 and repeated my message to any enemy that were left. Then for good measure, I repeated the message thirty-eight more times on each of the remaining channels. I hoped this would deter any other followers of the general who might be left in the area.

I looked in the back of the Hummer, and the terrible truth was confirmed. The general had killed Susan—*his own daughter!* I had hoped that it was only another deception, but no, he'd really done it. Perhaps, his own suicide was a sign of his remorse.

I got out of the Hummer and began my ascent up the hill. By now, the group had been able to dig out the bodies of my family members. At the sign of the lifeless bodies of my parents, I fell to my knees, and tears streamed from eyes. *This is too much! Too much death!* Someone put a hand on my shoulder. I didn't check to see who it was. I'm not sure how long I knelt there weeping, but eventually, my tears stopped flowing.

I wiped my eyes on my sleeve. Looking around for my brother's body, I got up with Jared's help. It was then I realized that he had been the one with his hand on my shoulder. It was good of him to stay with me as I mourned my parents. I looked at him and asked, "Jared, where is my brother's body?"

Jared pointed up to the top of the hill. He said, "Your brother's body is up at the top of the hill, and it is still alive and kicking."

I ran up the switchback to the top of the hill. Huffing and puffing, I came around the SUV. Father Jay was sitting in a folding lawn chair, leaning forward as Dr. Matt was stitching up his arm. The kids were gathered around, watching with great interest.

Father Jay was covered in dark mud, except where his arm had been washed for the stitches. He turned to me, and I could see his white teeth forming a smile in stark contrast to his muddy face.

My children and wife were gathered around my brother. *They were okay! They were okay!* Then from somewhere, more tears came—from where, I don't know. Perhaps, tears of joy are stored in a separate duct than tears of sorrow. This time, when I went down on my knees, it was to receive the hugs and kisses of my children gathered around me.

The next few hours, we involved ourselves in grim work. We moved the bodies of the dead enemy soldiers to the bottom of the hill. We made a large pyre with available wood and stacked the bodies on top. As for the six members of our own group who had been killed, we decided to bury them on the top of the hill.

Fortunately, at the top of the hill there was a large pit that had been dug sometime before the plague. Next to it stood a pile of the removed dirt. The pit's original purpose was a mystery to me, but it had a noble purpose now. We lovingly placed the bodies of my parents along with Tony, Ben, Sandy, and little Susan in the pit and carefully covered them with dirt.

Jared and Chloe volunteered to keep watch in case any enemy were left, while the rest of us gathered for a funeral led by Father Jay.

I looked around at all those gathered, friends and family. When I thought about what we were up against and what could have happened, it nearly made me sick. I was amazed we had survived. The numbers in our group were reduced significantly since the beginning of the plague. Laura leaned against me holding our youngest. Our other six kids were gathered around us. Father Jay was offering prayers for our dead. I was too tired to pay much attention. I looked over toward the brow of the hill. I could see Jared and Chloe embracing their two newly adopted kids Andrew and Margie as they kept watch. A couple of new members to our group from the rescue in Salem were sitting next to each other on a log. I couldn't remember their names. Dr. Matt and his wife stood with their two kids. Carter, with a patch on his eye, had his arm around his wife, Gabriella, and CJ stood next to them. I could see Eli and Leah standing at the end of the line of people; Eli had his arms around Leah and rested his chin on top of her head as they listened, with Conrad at their feet. Now we were down to twenty-six people, and about half of those were children.

Perhaps it was the wrong thing to think, but I was glad that none of our attackers survived. Quite frankly, I wouldn't have known what to do with the captured enemy.

As if he had been reading my mind, Father Jay said it was only right that we say a few prayers for the dead soldiers piled up on the pyre at the bottom of the hill before we burned them.

Using the winches on the Hummers, we were able to clear a path down the side of the hill that had been the site of our final battle. It didn't take us long after that to pack up and get moving again. We were down to four SUVs, so we commandeered one of the Hummers of the enemy. Laura, the kids, and I were all crammed into one SUV. Justin, Rachel, Dr. Matt, and his family rode in another.

Eli, Leah, Jared, Chloe, and their kids rode together in a third. Father Jay rode with Carter, Gabriella, and CJ. The rest of our ragtag group followed in the Hummer.

We solemnly drove past the abandoned Hummers and the burning bodies. It was a large fire indeed. None of us wanted to stick around until it was done burning. We figured that we had already given these soldiers' bodies more than they deserved. The weather had been wet enough and the fire was far enough from surrounding trees that it would be okay to leave it unattended.

It was starting to get dark when we finally got off of the old logging road and back onto the two-lane highway. Laura drove so that I could quickly get out of the passenger-side door of the SUV in order to assist if we needed to cut up a tree blocking the road. We decided to continue heading east, trying to make it back to the I-5 freeway. After following the winding road for over an hour, we connected with Highway 96. After another two hours of driving, we found the I-5 freeway in the town of Yreka. We briefly stopped in the small town, taking the opportunity to fuel the vehicles, stretch our legs, and switch drivers. I took over at the wheel, relieving Laura, and we headed south. The night driving was quiet, and it allowed me time to calm down, but I couldn't suppress the persistent and terrible memories forcing their way into my consciousness—images of what we had endured. They resurfaced whenever my guard was down.

The night was overcast, and it began sprinkling. The repetitive beat of the windshield wipers tried to lull me to sleep. I realized how deeply tired and weary I was. The children were all asleep in the back. Laura also had fallen asleep in the passenger seat. *It is good that they are resting*, I thought. *This has been just as hard on them as it has on me.* Our little caravan had to go slower than the posted speed limit on the freeway because, of course, there were no streetlights illuminating our way. The wet weather and the dark night cut down visibility significantly, and we had to remember to watch for the occasional obstacle or car parked in the middle of the freeway.

Jared was driving the lead car, and he and I talked over the CBs to ensure that we stayed awake during the trip. As we drove, neither of us talked about the carnage that we had left behind. Instead, we spoke about mundane things—unimportant things—on second thought, perhaps those everyday things are more important than we think. Those things are what ground us. The weather, for instance, is something that we experience every day and is universal to human existence. The emotionally charged and terrible things are but little marks on the map of one's life. They are mere speedbumps. Perhaps, it was our curse and blessing to be able to compartmentalize feelings and emotions. It might have been a much different conversation if our wives were driving and speaking to each other.

We were all eager to get as much distance between us and the place of our final battle with the general and his men, so we kept driving. We drove through Redding, Sacramento, Stockton, and Modesto until we could barely keep our eyes open.

Around 3:00 AM, we took a detour off I-5 driving toward Madera. We came upon a motel called the Knights Inn, and each family found an abandoned room for the night. Yet since there was no longer any infrastructure throughout the country, there was no electricity, and no water came out of the faucets. I would have given anything for a warm shower. I considered washing in the swimming pool in the courtyard, but any chlorine that had been in the water had long ago lost its effectiveness. Consequently, the water had that sickening sour smell of water that had remained undisturbed for too long; it was stagnant. It was still gently raining, so I resigned myself to removing the downspout of the gutter, and I stood under the trickle of water that came out. I used the little complementary bar of soap and bottle of shampoo that I had found in the room to remove the grime that I had accumulated. It was cold but refreshing. Soon, hastily found buckets were put under the downspouts of the surrounding buildings, and we collected enough water to wash our entire group.

We all felt better after getting cleaned up. Also, our mood was vastly improved after having put some distance between us and the place of our battle. I wanted to stay up and keep watch for the rest of the night, but I couldn't keep my eyes open. The women offered to keep an eye out for trouble; I could hear their voices chatting away in the courtyard. As I managed to squeeze my way between two of my kids already sprawled out on the bed, I overheard Laura say to her sister, "Do you realize that our battle took place on the feast of Our Lady of Guadalupe?" I didn't hear Chloe's response because I immediately fell into a deep sleep.

When I woke up the next morning, I couldn't figure out where I was. My little Davey was curled up in my arms. My back was up against something hard. It felt like someone had shoved me into a box. I tried to lift my head but hit it on wood. *What in the world?* To my left, I was blocked by a wall. I felt along the wall, and I was able to make out the shape of an electrical outlet with an electrical cord plugged into it. I could feel the rough texture of the carpet on the floor, and to my right, I could see that I was sitting near the opening of a box. Out of that opening, I could see the wheels of the bed frame with the mattress and box spring stacked on top of it. Over the bed, I could see sunlight bleeding around the edges of the dark curtains that covering the window. I realized that during the night, I had climbed underneath the desk. Perhaps, I had huddled here in fear, looking for someplace safe from a remembered or imagined enemy.

It shouldn't have been much trouble to extract myself from under the desk, but I had a sleeping child curled in my arms. I guess he decided he wanted to sleep with his daddy, even if his daddy decided for some inexplicable reason to climb under a desk to hide. With effort, I was able to lay Davey on the floor and climb out and over him. I laid him back on the bed and tried to work the kinks out of my neck.

I made my way to the door carefully, stepping over children, sprawled out everywhere. It was like a child explosion. There were now two on the bed, and three others spread out on the floor; another was halfway on the carpet in the main room and halfway onto the linoleum in the bathroom. I assumed that Laura had the youngest with her. I could hear Laura and Chloe still talking outside in the courtyard over the rhythmic breathing of the sleeping children. I quietly opened the door to see how the night watch had gone.

Chloe had her arm around Laura and was hugging her consolingly. They obviously had been discussing all that we had been going through. Our youngest was sleeping contentedly on Laura's lap. Laura looked up for a moment and then blew her nose. She gave me a smile. "Hi, honey," she said. "Did you sleep well?"

"I wouldn't go so far as to say 'well,' but I slept." I rubbed my stiff neck. "What about you? How did the night watch go?"

Chloe looked over at Laura and smiled. She said, "I think it was productive." Laura nodded her head.

I smiled. "Normally, night watch isn't something that is very productive."

Chloe smiled and gave me a mock scolding, "There, you see, you've been doing your guard duty all wrong."

I shook my head and smiled. "Well, I just woke up, and it is too early for me to give you a witty comeback, so just pretend I said something clever."

They both just smiled. Laura said, "Nice one, honey!"

I chuckled. "Okay, okay, mock me all you want—but who will have the last laugh when I come back with some breakfast for everybody?" With that parting comment, I turned around and walked toward the entrance of the courtyard to survey what abandoned businesses in the area might provide for our needs. *Ah, this was nice. Joking around was good. It provides some semblance of normalcy.*

As I stood out in the parking lot, I listened for any signs of human life. There were none. I could hear the chortling of little birds and the faint breeze, but none of the sounds we associate with humanity: no cars, no planes, no machines whatsoever. In front of the inn, I could see a Perko's Café. To the left, I could see a gas station, and to my right, I could see some kind of tractor dealership. Across the main street, I noticed a Grocery Outlet. *Perfect! We have everything we need!*

Even from the inn, I could see that the windows of the store had been smashed in. At some point, someone had helped themselves to items inside. There were no cars in the parking lot. I went back into the room and put on my shoes. I strapped on my Glock 9mm and made my way toward the abandoned store.

Since the beginning of the plague, my senses have been heightened. I listened, I looked, I felt, I smelled, I used my intuition. When I reached the entrance of the store, I looked around at the surrounding buildings. On the other side of the tractor dealership, I could see a large Walmart discount store. *That could be useful*, I thought. I turned and peered into the Grocery Outlet store. There was no sign of danger. I could hear the sounds of birds and perhaps rodents that had taken up residence in the store. I could smell the malodor of long since rotted produce and old decay. I hoped that there would be some useable canned food inside. Quietly, I made my way in. When I was satisfied that there was no danger, I grabbed a shopping cart and went looking. There were still supplies to be found. I filled the cart with still edible dried foods, bottled water, and canned foods. I noted that there were still plenty of other items that would be useful to us: batteries, matches, charcoal, paper, toys, and various odds and ends.

After breakfast, we raided the Grocery Outlet store and the Walmart across the street for anything that we thought useful, and we loaded the vehicles with the supplies. Providentially, there was wine that was suitable for Father Jay's mass supply, so Father Jay celebrated Mass for us. Since we hadn't had time or supplies for a funeral mass after our final battle, Father Jay offered the mass for the eternal repose of the souls of all our fallen family members and friends. Then, fed physically and spiritually, we were ready to go.

We fueled the vehicles and headed out, hoping that today would be the day to reach the free zone. For that matter, we hoped that the free zone was a real place and not just some wild goose chase.

28

The Free Zone

For freedom Christ has set us free; stand fast therefore,
and do not submit again to a yoke of slavery.

—The Letter of St. Paul to the Galatians 5:1

It took another few hours of driving through wide open spaces and past long-abandoned vineyards before we arrived at the northern edge of Bakersfield. All along the way, there were no visible signs of human life. But we had learned to be wary of other people anyway.

Thankfully, we were able to go much more quickly in the daylight. We had to make a couple of stops for food, fuel, potty breaks, and to remove the occasional obstacle blocking the freeway. It makes for a longer trip when you have to manually pump gas, sucking it up from the gas station's underground tanks, and you have children with bladders the size of thimbles.

With the view of Bakersfield growing smaller in the rearview mirror, the flat landscape was replaced by small brown hills covered sparsely with vegetation. As we rounded a bend, I heard a strange sound. There was a kind of high-pitched whine along with a repetitive beat, like someone was beating a drum really fast. *It was a helicopter!* A split second later, we heard rapid fire gunshots and a cloud of concrete dust splintered the road in front of us in a line. Our vehicles screeched to a halt.

I yelled to my family, "Get down!" After a moment, all the adults rolled down the windows of our driver and passenger side windows, and we stepped out of the vehicles using the doors as shields, holding our rifles aimed through the opened door windows. A helicopter descended facing us and hovered above the road in front of us. It had wicked-looking guns mounted on each side of the fuselage. We kept our rifles trained on the helicopter. Thankfully, there was no more gunfire. The chopper merely hovered in place, blocking our way forward.

Not far past the chopper, I could see a large barricade blocking the highway. It was a large concrete wall. There were five soldiers aiming rifles at us: three on top of the barricade, and two on the ground behind large concrete blocks. I could hear another helicopter flying behind us. Father Jay said over the radio, "Just relax! And do not move or do anything quickly! And definitely do not shoot!"

Over a loudspeaker from the front chopper, a man's voice boomed. "I'm Sgt. Reynolds from the US Army and the LA free zone! Put down your weapons and get out of the vehicles now!"

It was abundantly clear that we were outmanned and out-gunned. I lay my gun down on the ground and put my hands up. I slowly reached for the handset of the CB and said into the micro-phone, "Do what they say." We all spilled out of the vehicles.

I heard over the loudspeaker: "Step away from the vehicles!"

We did as we were told. I could be mistaken, but when the soldiers were able to see the children, they visibly relaxed. We had to shield our eyes because even from this distance, the chopper was blowing wind and dust into our faces. The chopper set down for a moment, and a man quickly got out of the chopper. The chopper immediately lifted back off the ground and flew high in the air to cover us with its guns.

Two soldiers came out from behind barriers and joined the man who had been on the speaker. They all walked toward us. I presumed that the man in the center was Sgt. Reynolds. The soldiers on either side had their rifles pointed away from us, but they were obviously ready to use them in a moment's notice. The man in the middle looked us over. He looked down at the children who looked back with wide fearful eyes. Looking up, he said, "What do you want?"

I glanced at his uniform. The name "Reynolds" was sewn on the front of it.

I said, "Well, Sgt. Reynolds, this is the free zone, isn't it?"

He said, "For some, but that depends on your definition of free." He said, "Where are you from?"

I said, "From Gervais." I paused. "It is a little farming town near Salem in Oregon."

He just grinned and said, "Yeah, I know."

I added, "Well, what's left of it." Then I stopped. "Wait! How do you know?"

He grinned. "Come in! I'll tell you all about it inside." He turned around and started walking. He looked over his shoulder and said, "Welcome to the free zone!"

One of the soldiers said, "Sirs and madams, please remain where you are. We must make a search of your vehicles and remove any weapons. Do you understand?"

We all nodded. The large gates set in front of the wall rolled open toward either side of the freeway. A Jeep came out of the opening and drove to where the sergeant was. Three more soldiers climbed out of the Jeep, and the sergeant got in. The soldier behind the steering wheel drove the sergeant back through the gates. The five soldiers searched us and the vehicles, removing all of our weapons and stacking them along the side of the freeway. One soldier warily pulled a five-gallon propane tank wrapped in duct tape and copious amounts of cutlery and silverware out of Carter's vehicle and set it next to the pile of firearms. I heard one soldier remark, "I didn't expect to find that many guns!" The other soldier just laughed.

Meanwhile, another Jeep had come out of the compound. The soldier that had spoken to us before said, "Sirs and madams, would you please get into your vehicles and follow us."

Abigail asked, "What's a madam?"

I saw the soldier try to hide a smile. He turned, and then he and two of the other soldiers got into the Jeep. The other two soldiers ran back to their posts in front of the immense barrier blocking the freeway.

We got into our vehicles and zigzagged through the barriers. After passing through, a tank rolled in, blocking the way we had come in from the compound. I looked back at my kids and tears welled up in my eyes. I said, "We made it to the free zone, kids."

Laura looked at me with a hint of worry on her face. "I hope it's a good thing," she whispered.

One of the soldiers directed us with hand signals to where we should park our vehicles. We got out and stretched. Everyone looked around in awe. There were Jeeps, tanks, Hummers, choppers, jets, and several unmanned flying drones. Beyond them I saw two F-15s. I supposed that a freeway without traffic makes a perfect landing strip. The compound had buildings and small fields surrounded by twenty-foot walls with men and women watching all sides. There were ramps up to the walkway near the tops of the wall. A person could walk along the top and spot any approaching dangers from a long way off. The walkway followed the wall but stopped at the freeway gates. As the gates were closing, I heard a loud dull metal clunk, locking them into place. I wasn't sure if it was a reassuring or an ominous sound.

Sgt. Reynolds came up, shook my hand, and said, "Welcome to LA free zone, soldier."

I looked him in the eye and said, "We're not soldiers. We're survivors."

29

Revelations

The truth does not change according to our ability to stomach it.

—Flannery O'Connor

"We're not soldiers. We're survivors," I had told the sergeant.

He laughed at that and said, "I beg to differ."

I said "Sergeant, I feel like we are both speaking English but not speaking the same language."

"I like that…I like that," he said as he walked ahead of us.

"Sgt. Reynolds!" I said, trying to get his attention. "You said that this is the LA free zone—and this isn't LA. I'm a little confused."

He turned his head toward me and said over his shoulder, "If we had called it the Lebec free zone, no one would have had any idea where we were located." He continued walking at a brisk pace. We all struggled to keep up.

One of the soldiers blurted out, "We've been watching you since the first talks at the capitol. We watched you kick some serious butt."

Sgt. Reynolds looked at him sternly, and the soldier realized that he had spoken out of turn. Duly chastised, he fell in behind us. We stopped at a building with a soldier guarding the door. The soldier saluted the sergeant and opened the door for him. The sergeant saluted back. I realized that they had power, water, food, equipment, and weapons. We all shuffled into building.

The sergeant pointed to a series of screens that were illuminated by various topographical maps overlaid with coordinates. "By satellite and unmanned drones," he said, answering the unasked question. "That is at least partly how we followed you. Yes, they still work. A lot of people all over the country have been watching your group. Unfortunately, you guys live in Oregon where you often have heavy cloud cover." He looked at me disapprovingly, as though I had some control over clouds. He continued, "So we sent a soldier to keep an eye on you guys, to see whether you were friend or foe. But your damn guard dogs made it impossible to get good intel on you."

I was startled at that revelation. I said, "Then why didn't you help us?"

He said, "We've had our hands full here and everywhere else in the world."

The eager soldier behind us said, "You guys whipped their..." He looked down at the kids and amended what he was going to say, "You whipped their behinds." He seemed proud that he stopped himself from swearing in front of the kids.

Annoyance and frustration rose within me. I snapped at the soldier. "Did you see all the people in my group fall down dead?"

He said, "Yes, sir, I did."

"Those were all family members and close friends that died. They weren't expendable. It wasn't a video game. I killed other human beings—not for pleasure, but because I had to—because I had no other choice. Try to remember that!" I felt Laura grab my arm, signaling me to calm down.

"Sorry, sir, I was just excited to meet you." He was sincere, and now I felt like a jerk.

"Look, Mr. Fide, don't take it personally," said the sergeant. "You have to understand, most of these men and women are young and have never seen any real combat. They have been following the exploits of your family since your group was trying to organize things in Salem. We have had reports on you from our asset on the ground in Oregon, and we have images from satellite and drones."

He nodded his head and continued, "We cheered your victories, and we mourned your losses." I thought that I could see a tear form in his eye. "We felt powerless when all we could do was watch from above." He slapped the table. "But by God, you survived! You survived!"

I turned toward the sergeant. "This is all a lot to take in. I have so many questions. How did you keep in communication with your soldier in Gervais? There is no power. Walkie-talkies have too short a range. There are no phones."

The sergeant pointed to the corner, and I heard Isaiah say, "It's a ham radio."

The sergeant looked down at him and said, "Yes, very good little man!" Then he looked up at me. "And besides that, we have satellite phones that still work."

Eli chimed in. "Excuse me, Sergeant, and don't take this the wrong way, but..." He paused, trying to choose his words carefully. "But you seem to be the guy in charge here. Uh, what about the higher-ranking officers?"

"No, no, that is not a bad question at all." He smiled grimly. "I'm it. As far as I know, I am the highest-ranking soldier we have left in this part of these United States."

His words felt like a kick in the gut. I had hoped the plague's devastation was somehow less severe in other parts of the country. I imagined that we would encounter many civilians protected by a strong military presence in the unaffected free zone.

He took off his hat and looked at it. "Oh, I could probably artificially increase my rank, call myself captain or general, alter my uniform—but I refuse to do that."

He put his hat back on. "No," he said, "I will not do that because, you see, we did this to the world."

I stepped back, reeling from what he was saying. "But what..."

I could see him reproaching himself for his simplistic statement. "No, no, not me personally." He gestured around to the men and women in the building. "Not them." He looked me in the eye. "I mean, 'we' the government. I mean, 'we' the politicians. I mean, 'we' the scientists."

It was Chloe who broke the silence. "You mean the plague?"

"Yes, yes, the plague." Sgt. Reynolds was turning red just thinking about it. "We've been putting the puzzle together piece by piece." He paused. "Look, I wasn't going to tell you about this yet. I was going to let you get settled." He sighed. He looked at the kids. "It is your kids. I look into their faces." He looked at the adults. "You know, I haven't seen a child since the start of the virus. Not one child! Do you know how much hope they give me? How beautiful they are?"

I looked down. I saw my children smiling at the compliment. I looked around at the soldiers gathered in the building. They seemed uncomfortable on the sergeant's behalf for his uncharacteristic expression of emotion. The sergeant straightened himself up and cleared his throat. "Please, follow me."

He walked us through a corridor into a room where we could all sit down. It reminded me of a classroom. There was a whiteboard at the front of the room. We all sat down.

"I'm sorry," he said. "Where are my manners?" He gestured with his hand. "Around the corner is the latrine. There is one for women and another for men."

Abigail asked, "What's a latrine?"

Isaiah said, "It is a bathroom, silly!"

The twins laughed, and I couldn't help but smile.

The sergeant smiled and added, "And there is water along the wall, a water bottle dispenser."

As everyone went off to use the facilities, I could overhear the sergeant speaking with Father Jay. He said, "Hey, Padre, we would all be very appreciative if you could hold a religious service for us. We don't have a chaplain, and it would really boost our morale." Father Jay nodded.

I was distracted by one of my kids crying, and I realized that we were making a lot of noise. Feeling self-conscious, I looked out the window of the conference room toward several soldiers in the office area. They didn't seem to mind the chaos; in fact, they seemed to rather enjoy it.

Once we were all gathered together again, Sgt. Reynolds explained his earlier comments. "You all know that over two years ago, a plague devastated the world." He shook his head in a self-reproach. "Well, of course, you know," he said almost to himself. "We have come to discover that the original strain originated in a bioresearch lab in China. There had been rumors that the Chinese were developing a new biological weapon. We, the United States and Great Britain, had obtained a sample of this virus. It is a type of coronavirus—a modified flu virus—that is able to quickly infect and kill its human host."

The sergeant leaned on the table in front of him with both hands. "Our governments were worried about this virus—so worried, in fact, that they began working on a vaccine immediately, which, of course, means that they were creating more of the virus in order to make a weaker strain. They didn't believe there would be time to go through the regular testing and trials. Such things take years."

Father Jay interrupted, "So they began testing it on prisoners."

Sgt. Reynolds looked at Father Jay with a look of complete and utter stupefaction. He blinked a couple of times and said, "How did you know? How…?"

Father waved dismissively. "Don't worry. I wasn't privy to any top-secret information or anything. It's the only thing that makes sense. I made a visit to a prisoner at the jail, got sick, and passed on the virus to my family members."

The sergeant regained his composure; he nodded. "Well, that makes sense, and by some miracle, you visited the jail at precisely the right moment, because there was only one strain of the vaccine that was contagious. It was shortly after that they decided to test the real virus on the inoculated prisoners. In each location, there was one test group that had received the vaccine, while another had been given a placebo. Of course, the group that had received the placebo died very quickly and very painfully. What our scientists hadn't counted on was how absolutely contagious the virus was, and its ability to jump species." The sergeant took off his hat and ran his fingers through his hair. He gestured vaguely outside. "Flies were infected, mosquitos were infected, birds were infected, dogs and cats were infected. In fact, right now you can probably test any animal in God's good creation, and you will find some remnant marker of the virus. It doesn't kill the animals. It just kills humans."

The sergeant held up his finger, twirled it around, and pointed to himself. "Then the flies and the mosquitos and all those other animals infected us—the human race."

"And so, thinking that we were above the moral law, above being ethical, we thought we could use those that we considered to be expendable." He laughed ruefully. "We ended up inoculating the worst members of society and killing off everyone else."

Laura asked, "What about the soldiers? You survived."

The sergeant put his hat back on and said, "Well, it appears that some of us were test subjects too." Then, almost as an afterthought, he added sarcastically, "And here's the ironic part: China never even released the virus. We did this to ourselves and the rest of the world."

This was a huge and terrible revelation, but I was hesitant to swallow the story hook, line, and sinker just yet. Apparently, Eli was skeptical as well. He said, "Look, Sergeant, what you are saying sounds quite plausible, but this sounds like some real top-secret stuff, and quite frankly, above your rank."

"Yes, yes, you are right, of course." He nodded. "And I appreciate that you want some proof or confirmation. The main proof I can offer is the uninhabited world that surrounds us. I can point to the fact that there is a disproportionate number of prisoners who have survived this plague." He gestured vaguely with his finger.

"You see, I was good friends with a general in the Pentagon. Her name doesn't matter. She's dead now." He shook his head slowly. "It was quite literally her last living act to grant me top-secret privileges—access to top-level documents—as the virus ravaged the world, while she herself was drowning in the red foam filling her lungs. She deeply regretted what she and her colleagues had unleashed upon the world." The sergeant was hunched over the table as though the weight of all that he shared with us was piled upon his shoulders.

I said, "But, Sergeant, it wasn't your fault."

The sergeant said stiffly, "Yeah, I know."

Then, Father Jay said, "No, really, it wasn't your fault."

The sergeant looked up at him.

Then each person in that room said to the sergeant individually, "It wasn't your fault."

As the litany of affirmations came at him, I could see the sergeant's jaw clench, and I could tell he was fighting back tears. His façade was beginning to crumble. It wasn't until little Davey joined in and said, "It wawant you fawt," that the sergeant broke down into tears. He went down on his knees, put his hands over his face, and rested his head and elbows on the desk—and he sobbed. As I watched his shoulder shake, I could only imagine the hardships that he had endured, the losses that he had experienced.

I think we all broke into tears in that moment. It is amazing how most of humanity is innately empathetic. All of us needed some kind of catharsis, and this strong, tough sergeant breaking down before us was all we needed. I briefly wondered what the other soldiers in the office thought about all of this. I decided that I didn't care. We are human beings with emotions and hopes and dreams. We are not unfeeling robots.

After we had pulled ourselves together, the sergeant checked his reflection in the window and straightened his jacket. Then he showed us around the base and the free zone area. He said, "This base is on one hundred acres, and we have another three hundred acres off-site for farming and other purposes. We have a mess hall, and we have shower huts. You'll each get two minutes of hot water every other day. And we have bunkhouses for you to stay in."

He turned to face us. "You have seen the command post. We have a community latrine. Over here is a small hospital." He looked at Dr. Matt. "We could sure use your help there, Doc." Then he continued pointing out the different elements of the compound. "Our supply warehouse is over here, and this is the repair garage." He looked at me. "I understand you are handy with a wrench."

He walked us to the barracks and continued speaking: "I have twenty-three soldiers under my command. We have three Apache helicopters, ten Hummers, three tanks, a water purification truck, three large generators, two Harrier jets, the F-15s you saw, and ten drones. Oh yeah, and enough fuel at our nearby tank farm to fill an ocean-going tanker."

He held out his arm, gesturing to the barracks. "You may stay here for the night, but if you decide to stay with us longer, all of you will need to pitch in and do your part. If that is a problem, you may gather your things and leave anytime you like, understood?"

We all said, "Yes."

I heard Isaiah say loudly, "Yes, sir!"

The sergeant looked down at him and smiled. "I like this one."

"Sergeant," I said, "if we stay, we will do our part, but remember, we're not soldiers."

He nodded. Then he started turning to walk off toward the command post but stopped himself. "Hey, Padre," he said, "can I talk to you?"

Father Jay walked over to him. As Sgt. Reynolds walked off with my brother, I could overhear him say, "Padre, I happen to know that there is a bishop in Nevada who survived the virus. We may have to arrange a visit to increase your rank." I turned and watched as the sergeant and my brother walked toward the command post. *I suppose that has a nice ring to it, Bishop James Fide.* I smiled at the thought of it.

Laura leaned into me and said, "I think the sergeant looks a little lighter on his feet than when we first met."

I nodded. "Yeah, I think we have brought each other hope."

We walked into the barracks and found simple cots set out in rows. There was a stack of sleeping bags and pillows on the wall by the door. All the bedding was vacuum-wrapped in plastic. We each grabbed one and picked our beds. I ripped opened the plastic, and the sleeping bag expanded with a whoosh of air. Once my wife and kids were in bed, I knelt next to my cot. I thanked God for getting us here safely. I blessed each of my children, and then I stoked the fire in the two potbellied stoves. I slid my cot over to my wife's cot and laid down to go to sleep. I put my arm over my beautiful wife and wondered, *What will tomorrow bring?* I decided, *Tomorrow will bring the joys and sorrows of another day, and God will be with us through it all.* Then I closed my eyes and drifted off to sleep.

The End

Afterword

My brother and I began writing this book about eleven years ago. We started writing this long before there was any threat of the coronavirus. With the advent of this pandemic, it spurred me on to finish what we had started. We both have busy lives, so the story had to wait to come to fruition. My brother Bob had the idea of writing a story surrounding a family; he imagined what it would be like to survive if a deadly virus had ravaged the world. How would a regular family survive? How would they hold on to their humanity?

This work is set in a Judeo-Christian framework. A key theme running through it is the recognition of the human capacity for evil. This boils down to the concept of Original Sin; that is to say, we are all born with concupiscence—an inclination to sin. Consequently, we see an interplay between evil and grace. We see the battle between light and darkness. It is a battle that happens on a universal scale, and on a small scale within each of our hearts. We see true society contrasted with a false society. We recognize that we cannot walk the path alone. We need the grace of God to accomplish anything of value, and we need each other.

We have purposely left out reference to a specific year. The idea is that it could be set in any year in our modern times. However, the story takes place over a time period of about two and a half years. Hopefully in whatever year that you are reading this it will speak to you in your current time.

The work has gone through many revisions and has been paired down to its current form, and we are excited to be able to share it with you. It isn't perfect, but we believe that it is a compelling story that speaks to the heart.

Ronald Nelson

Acknowledgements

I would like to make some acknowledgements on behalf of my brother and myself *because that is a lot easier than trying to write as two people.*

Robert would like to thank his wife and his children in supporting the hair-brained idea of writing a book. He would also like to thank his friend Dan Reid for his help in brainstorming and kicking around ideas and scenarios for the book.

I would like to give special acknowledgement to Barbara Breaden and Doug Keeler for their invaluable support by going through the manuscript with a fine-toothed comb, looking for errors in grammar, spelling, and continuity.

I would like to thank Robert for the freedom he gave me to significantly change the plot and storyline.

We would like to give thanks our parents for life, for nurturing us, for our strange sense of humor, and for their love and support; *and since they conceived and birthed us into existence, if this whole endeavor fails, it is all their fault!*

Robert and I would like to thank each other for our support; *hopefully, that doesn't sound too weird and self-serving.*

Above all, we give thanks to God for his love, strength, and care for us and our families.

Ronald Nelson

Family Tree

Parents   Children   Grandchildren

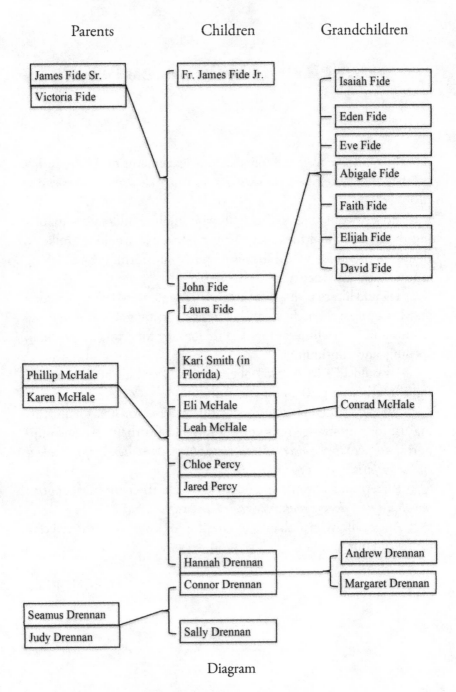

Diagram

About the Author

Robert and Ronald Nelson are brothers who are up and coming in the literary world as coauthors in a truly unique collaboration. These brothers were born and raised in Oregon, a place known for its natural beauty and a place where its inhabitants are known for their rugged individualism. Robert, a lover of action films, brings his life experience as a husband and father of twelve children to his writing, and Ronald brings unique insight into the human condition through his vocation as a Catholic priest. There is something magical that happens when you combine Robert's action-packed imaginative visual descriptions that drive the plot forward and Ronald's psychological and spiritual insights into a character's mind and heart. Both are men of faith whose lives have taken drastically different directions. Robert thrives in the lively (sometimes messy) atmosphere of family life, and Ronald, in between his many duties in ministry, enjoys dabbling in musical composition, writing, or just spending some quiet time alone (with a steaming hot cup of coffee).